D0794088

Beneath the Seams

Center Point
Large Print

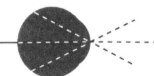

**This Large Print Book carries the
Seal of Approval of N.A.V.H.**

Beneath the Seams

A Social Impact Novel

Peyton H. Roberts

CENTER POINT LARGE PRINT
THORNDIKE, MAINE

To Nick, Sadie and Nate

Grateful I'm forever stitched to you.

*"You can't buy happiness,
but you can buy fabric,
and that's pretty close."*
—Unknown

Chapter 1

August 2012

Shelby's insides twisted into a knot as the photographer stepped behind the tripod. Warm studio lights beamed down from the rafters, illuminating everything she wanted seen and absolutely nothing she didn't.

"Are you ready?" the photographer asked.

"Ready when you are." Shelby tamed a few strands of her blown-out, highlighted hair and smoothed the skirt of her holiday dress over her shapewear. After months perfecting every pore and curve of her exterior, she couldn't believe this long-awaited day was finally here. The next few minutes would launch her face, as well as her handmade brand, into the glossy pages of *Buzz Now Magazine*, a springboard from which anything felt possible.

The trouble was, Shelby wasn't the only one posing for the photos. Her young daughter Paisley, the unknown variable of the day, stood beside Shelby, wearing an identical crimson and white dress. Despite how frustrating they'd been to sew, their Christmas outfits turned out precisely how Shelby sketched them to—a nod to Mrs. Claus but without looking like a costume.

As the photographer fine-tuned the lighting,

Shelby used the remaining seconds to finesse Paisley's appearance. She ran her fingers through her daughter's golden ringlets then straightened a stray fold in the dress's ruffled skirt. The hem was last to adjust, but Paisley batted away her mom's hand.

"Stop, Mama."

"Stopping." Shelby didn't want to risk annoying her child, but the pressure to master every detail was intensifying by the minute.

The photographer, a polished local artist named Felipe, looked up from behind the tripod. Shelby's heartbeat accelerated. She leaned over to plant reminders into Paisley's ear. "Time to smile, Little P. Just like we talked about, remember?"

But Paisley didn't reply. Her eyes shifted left and right, examining the room full of backdrops, lamp reflectors, and stage lighting.

For weeks Shelby had coached Paisley to smile on command, bribing her with lollipops and extra screen time. Despite the trainings, the question remained whether a fickle four-year-old would feel like cooperating in the spotlight. More than any other trial since becoming a parent, this photo op was the one Shelby needed to conquer. Absolutely everyone would see the outcome of the next thirty minutes.

"Okay, it's go time," Felipe said. "Mom, I want you to kneel behind Paisley so I can capture your faces side by side. Now look right here and give me your best Christmas smiles."

Kneeling into position, Shelby glanced at her daughter for the promised smile. But Paisley's mouth was busy exploring a thick layer of pearly lip gloss.

"Little P, it's time to smile," Shelby said.

Suddenly shy, Paisley looked at the floor and stuffed her fists into the pockets of her dress.

"Let's get started," Felipe said. "Hopefully we'll see some smiles once we're warmed up."

Shelby slid her shoulder blades down her back and tilted her chin up, just slightly. Focusing her gaze straight into the camera, she smiled like it was the most important day of her life.

Felipe clicked away on his monstrous camera. Moments later, Paisley pulled one hand from her pocket and pointed at two large lamp reflectors. The camera clicks stopped.

"Mama, what are those umbrellas for?"

"Those aren't umbrellas, sweetie. They're Mr. Felipe's helpers. They create special magic with the lights to make our pictures look even more beautiful in the magazine." Shelby repositioned Paisley's arm at her side.

"Is it real magic? How's it work?"

"I bet Mr. Felipe can answer that." Shelby raised her eyebrows, happy to punt the question.

"The light bounces off the reflectors and softens across your faces," he said.

"Wait, light can bounce? Like a ball?" Paisley asked.

"Yes, exactly. But it can only bounce off a pretty smile."

Paisley blushed. A bashful grin crept onto her face.

"Now we're getting somewhere," Felipe said, and the clicks resumed.

After another minute of posing, Paisley twirled around to peek at the set. At their backs stood a faux Douglas fir, styled with twinkling lights, red velvet ribbon, and glitter-spangled gold ornaments. A colorful pile of foil-wrapped presents spilled out below the tree. Frosted windowpanes suggested a snowy winter morning. No one would have guessed it was easily a hundred degrees outside.

"Mama, can I have one of those?" Paisley pointed to a shimmery gold ball dangling from the Christmas tree. "They're so sparkly!"

Felipe stepped in. "Sweetheart, as soon as you let me have all your beautiful smiles, you can pick out any ornament you want."

Paisley's eyes widened. Her lips slid into a generous smile.

"Excellent. That's great, ladies." *Click. Click. Click.* "Exactly what I want to see." He checked the screen on the back of the camera. "These are looking great."

The first hint of positive feedback brought

Shelby a glimpse of relief. Hopefully all her efforts—the eyelash extensions, the months in the gym, her first-ever forearm waxing—would pay off.

Felipe continued. "Okay, Mom, let's have you stand. I want these matching dresses to get the attention they deserve."

As Shelby stood, Paisley inspected the tree again. "Mama, can I have one of those sparkly balls now?"

"Just need a few more really big smiles." Shelby placed her fingertips on Paisley's shoulders, pivoting her small frame to face the camera.

"Paisley, you don't like Christmas, do you?" Felipe asked.

"Yes, I do." Paisley giggled. *Click. Click.*

"You don't like presents, do you?"

"I looove presents." *Click click click.* An even wider smile grew across the girl's face.

"You really don't like Santa Claus, do you?"

"I love Santa Claus!" Paisley's shoulders and hands shook with excitement.

"Excellent. Hold those smiles," Felipe said. This guy knew his stuff. Shelby suspected he must be a father, or maybe someone's favorite uncle.

"Mama, is Santa really coming?"

"Well . . ." Shelby paused, formulating her reply. It was only August. But sure, Santa would come eventually. No use jeopardizing Paisley's mood with a technicality. "Yes, Santa is coming," she said definitively.

Paisley's hazel eyes opened wide as walnuts. The biggest smile of the day exploded across her face, plumping up her buttery cheeks. As it did, the forced smile Shelby had manufactured melted away, becoming something real.

"Got it! That's the shot," Felipe said. "Almost done, ladies."

The thought of the photoshoot coming to an end, smiles in the bag, made the tension in Shelby's jaw release. She folded the moment away into the sweet layers of victory.

Her thoughts immediately transitioned to the afternoon ahead. Like it or not, the most significant decision of her career was due tonight and waiting in her inbox. Beyond that, an ocean of tasks promised to consume every waking hour between now and Christmas Eve as thousands of her dresses arrived in stores across the country.

Shooing her to-do list out of her mind, Shelby squeezed Paisley's little palm into hers.

"That's a wrap," Felipe said. He scrolled through the raw images on the camera's screen. "These look fantastic. Nice work."

Praise for all her efforts sent a rush of excitement that warmed Shelby's skin. She kissed Paisley on her blush-swept cheek. The girl skipped off to the decorated tree to select an ornament. Shelby followed, amused.

Like Paisley, she wished with all her heart they could skip ahead to Christmas Day. But for entirely different reasons.

The magnolia tree stood as still as the brick mailbox when Shelby drove her Lexus into their driveway on Oak Blossom Lane. Considering the blowout hair appointments and makeup sessions, plus the traffic-filled drive to West U and back, it felt like a week had passed since they left the neighborhood that morning.

"Mama, can I get the mail?" Paisley asked.

"Sure. Just look out for cars." The clicks and jingles of car seat buckles filled every crevice of the SUV's interior as Paisley tumbled out of the backseat onto the driveway. Bobbing from her wrist, the large gold ornament accompanied her on the endless hunt for new things.

As Shelby turned off the car's ignition, her ovulation tracking app pinged with a green light notification. Of all days. Hopefully Bryan would be home early.

Shelby began collecting the shopping, makeup, and garment bags from the car. Paisley meandered up the driveway sandwiching a messy stack of papers between her hands.

"Anything good today?" Shelby asked.

"It's all junk," Paisley said, mimicking how she heard adults describe most mail.

Thank goodness. Shelby didn't need anything

else slowing her down. In addition to hauling every bag in from the car and putting it all away, she still needed to call her mom, upload teasers to Instagram, and conjure up dinner. Most of all, she needed to email Dennis the final designs for *Surface Trend Market* to carry in stores. This single decision could secure her dream job on their impressive design team.

"'Cept for this one, maybe." In one hand, Paisley jumbled together carpet cleaning ads and fast-food coupons. In the other, she raised a business-sized white envelope. "Who's it from?" she asked, handing the envelope to Shelby.

"Let me see. It's from . . ." Shelby eyed the return address label. "Oh! It's from the Caring Hope Organization."

"What's that?"

"It's the people who picked out a sponsor child for us."

"What's that?" Paisley asked.

"Kind of like a new friend."

"Like a playdate friend?" Paisley twirled a crispy ringlet around her pinky.

"No, we won't be able to play with this friend. This friend lives very far away."

"But if he lives very far away, then how is he our friend?"

Shelby collected her thoughts before offering a concise explanation. "There are some children all over the world who don't have nearly as much as we do. We are going to share some of what we have with one of these children."

"Is he four like me?"

"I don't know. And we don't know if it's a boy or a girl. We won't know any of that until we open it up and read what it says."

"Can we open it?" Paisley asked.

Shelby's hands were as loaded down with bags as her mind was with obligations. She simply didn't have the capacity to add one more thing to this afternoon, especially knowing how many hundreds of questions Paisley's curious little mind would ask.

"Let's wait until Daddy gets home," she said. "We can all find out together."

That night at dinner, Paisley nearly fell out of her booster seat at the kitchen table, recapping every detail of the photoshoot to her dad. "I got to wear makeup, and they made my hair curly. It was the bestest day ever!"

"That's great, Little P. So everything went okay?" Bryan asked Shelby.

"As far as I can tell. The photographer sounded really happy. I took that as a good sign."

"Did you smile nice and pretty?" Bryan asked Paisley.

"Uh-huh," Paisley replied, her mouth full of dinner.

"Tell Daddy what you got to pick out for

smiling so nicely," Shelby said, cutting a nibble of chicken with the side of her fork.

"An ornament from the Christmas tree." Paisley loaded her fork with a stack of elbow pasta.

"Good. I can't think of anything we need more in August than a new Christmas ornament. Which one did you pick?"

"The biggest, sparkliest one. I'm gonna sleep with it." Unlike other children, Paisley didn't have a favorite blanket or doll. Her signature move was attaching herself to the newest item in her life, whatever that happened to be.

"Oh, perfect. You needed one more thing in your bed," Bryan said.

Shelby wondered at what point Paisley would be old enough to detect sarcasm. Thankfully, comments like this still went straight over her head.

"Daddy, I have ninety hundred macaronies on my fork. I bet you can't fit that many."

"Please don't play with your food," Shelby said.

Paisley shoved the cheesy pasta in her mouth, took a long slurp of milk, then slammed her magenta cup on the table. "The envelope! Mama, can we open the envelope? You said when Daddy got home we could open it."

"Sure, we can open it. Soon as we finish dinner." Shelby investigated Paisley's plate. "Eat your peas, please."

"What's in the envelope?" Bryan asked.

"We get a new friend, Daddy. 'Cept we don't know if it's a boy friend or a girl friend."

"Sure hope it's not a boyfriend." Bryan turned to Shelby, brows raised. "What's in the envelope?"

"Our new kid," Shelby said.

Bryan stopped chewing, his forest-green eyes brimming with questions beneath his dark, wavy hair.

"It's from the charity Maye told us about, the Caring Hope Organization."

His blank stare continued.

"We're sponsoring a child."

"Oh, right." Bryan resumed chewing. "How much does this cost again?"

"Not much. It's like $39 a month. Tax-deductible. We can cancel it whenever." Shelby was awkwardly aware she sounded like a sales-person.

Bryan nodded. "Okay, Little P. I bet I can fit more peas on my fork than you can."

"No way," Paisley said.

After all the macaroni and cheese, most of the chicken fingers, and enough of the peas disappeared from their plates, Shelby piled the dishes on the kitchen counter and returned to the table with the white envelope.

"Mama, can I please open it?" Paisley asked.

"Let me get it started. You can do the rest."

Shelby tore a corner of the envelope back.

Paisley ripped it open. A bundle of folded white pages flopped out onto the table. A 3″ x 5″ photograph fell onto the floor by Bryan's chair. Paisley hopped down to pick it up. Holding the picture in her hand, she stared into the face of a thin child in a muted blue dress, a smile lingering behind her eyes.

"She's a girl!" Paisley held onto the photo but handed the wordy pages to Bryan. "Who is she? What does it say?"

"Let's find out," Bryan said.

Instead of returning to her seat, Paisley stepped toward her mom's. Shelby wrapped her hands around Paisley's narrow waist and lifted the child into her lap.

Remembering their hair and makeup were still done, Shelby retrieved her phone from beneath the placemat. She stretched her arm out far as it would go and snuck a selfie to share with her growing list of Instagram followers.

Bryan cleared his throat and read aloud.

"Dear Mr. and Mrs. Lawrence, We are sending you the introductory letter and latest photo of your newly sponsored child RUNA BINU ZAMAN, age 11, who resides near Dhaka, Bangladesh. With your commitment, your sponsored child may continue her studies, make a difference in her community, and fulfill her life's dreams. With overwhelming gratitude, Cedric Flores,

Sponsorship Director, Caring Hope Organization."

An unexpected silence punctuated the room. Bryan's eyes scanned the page. Paisley's remained fixated on the picture.

"What do you think?" Shelby asked.

"That's interesting," Bryan said. "Did we pick the place?"

"We could have, but Paisley wanted to be surprised," Shelby said. "Any idea where Bangladesh is?"

"I feel like I should know this. It's in Asia." Bryan pulled out his phone. "Next to India. To the right."

"I'm completely unfamiliar with that part of the world," Shelby said.

"Same here. Remind me, how did we connect with Caring Hope?"

"Maye said they're in desperate need of more sponsors. I thought it would be fun to learn about a different culture and to broaden Paisley's perspective of the world. And maybe ours too, for that matter."

"What else does it say, Daddy?" Paisley snuggled down further into the soft welcome of Shelby's lap as Bryan continued reading.

"Runa is an only child who lives with her mother in a crowded community near Dhaka, the capital city of Bangladesh. Her mother works full-time but struggles to meet their family's needs on her own. Runa attends school and loves to read. Her favorite subject is Bengali, the national language. She enjoys playing with dolls and helping at home.

"Her health is satisfactory. The typical diet of the region is fish, rice, and vegetables, though fresh food is often difficult to afford. Homes in her neighborhood are typically constructed of corrugated iron sheet walls, a tin roof, and a dirt floor. By supporting this family, you are easing their struggles and helping them embark on a promising future."

Paisley sat still, silent in her mom's lap, her eyes tethered to the photograph of Runa.

"What are you thinking about, Little P?" Shelby asked.

"Why is the floor made of dirt?"

"They don't have a lot of money, Little P," Bryan replied. "They can't afford to live in a big, finished house like the ones in our neighborhood."

"Don't her feet get dirty?"

"Maybe," Shelby said. "Or maybe she wears shoes inside her house? I don't know how that works."

"Can we ask her?" Paisley said.

Bryan scanned the paperwork. "Probably not."

"She lives very far away and doesn't speak English. The letter says she speaks Bengali," Shelby explained.

"Can we try?" Paisley persisted.

Shelby shrugged at Bryan. "I mean, I guess I could email the man at the bottom of the letter. No idea if he'll write back."

"Can you email him now?" Paisley asked.

"Not now. I have a lot to do tonight. But I can tomorrow." Shelby opened her task app and added the item to tomorrow's growing to-do list.

Paisley stared again into the picture. "Her dress looks old, Mama. Why is it old?" she asked, the Ferris wheel of whys still turning.

"They probably don't have extra money to buy new clothes," Shelby explained. "She might even wear clothes other children have outgrown. They're called hand-me-downs." Strange she hadn't used this term since becoming a parent. Shelby grew up wearing nothing but her cousin's pilling, stretched-out old clothes.

"Why can't they just get more money?" Paisley asked.

"Because that's not how money works," Bryan said. "You have to earn it in order to get it. They might not have many ways to earn it."

"I wish Runa could come play at our house," Paisley said.

"That's a nice thought," Shelby said. "Why don't we put her picture on the fridge?"

Paisley wriggled off Shelby's lap and skipped to the refrigerator. Relocating a squiggly stick figure drawing, she cleared a spot and pinned

Runa's picture to the fridge with a butterfly magnet.

The microwave clock reminded Shelby of the time. Bedtime.

"Bry, can you get Paisley to bed so I can finish this deadline?"

"Not tonight. I'm meeting up with Jared."

Shelby stared into him with the eyes of a wife who required further explanation.

"We have a bunch of details to tweak on the Nashville job."

"Now?"

"Keith scheduled us in nonstop meetings all week. We just haven't had enough time."

"I could really use some help here." Shelby picked at the cuticle on her thumbnail where her French manicure already started chipping. A screenshot scrolled through her mind of the mountain range of shopping bags and clothes piled across their bed. "I have a ton of stuff from this morning to put away, all these dishes, and I still have to email Dennis with the final decision."

"I thought you told him already?"

"No. I keep going back and forth. I needed to get through this morning, so I could focus."

"How about this—you put Paisley to bed. I'll meet up with Jared now and clean the kitchen when I get back. Floors and all."

It wasn't a bad offer. Even without doing

the dishes, Shelby would be pushing it to get everything done by midnight. But she didn't want to spark an argument that would mess up their chances to try for a baby.

"Okay, that works," Shelby said. "Thanks."

"Goodnight, Little P. Be good for Mama." Bryan kissed Paisley on the forehead.

"Goodnight, Daddy." Paisley curled her hand into a small fist and rubbed an eye.

He grabbed his wallet and keys and exited to the garage.

The door shut.

Shelby glared at it, whether with envy or anger she didn't quite know. Bryan had arrived home minutes before dinner. Food had only just disappeared off dishes, and he was already headed back to work.

Thirty more minutes of teeth brushing and book reading and blanket tucking. Then she'd proceed with the daunting task of choosing which of her dresses would make or break her future with *Surface Trend*.

"You ready to go up, Little P?"

"Go fish." Paisley giggled.

Shelby blinked a heavy blink. Her eyes scanned the room, the dirty dishes on the dining table, soiled pans crowding the countertops. "It's been a long day. Up we go."

"Okay, but first I'm gonna say goodnight to Runa." Paisley leaned toward the fridge and pressed a gentle kiss against the picture. "Goodnight, Runa. I hope I get to play with you one day."

By the time Shelby got Paisley to bed and unpacked everything from the photoshoot, Bryan had texted he was on his way home. With the most pressing task still to tackle, Shelby sat down at the desk in the office and opened her laptop. A lump in her throat reminded her she was about to make the biggest decision of her life.

Of course, it wasn't. Not really. Surely deciding who to marry or when to start a family were far more significant crossroads. But defining as they were, those variables had been relatively easy to solve for. They hadn't stirred up such an intense inner struggle.

Bryan came from the dream of a stable, loving family. Throughout their college years, he proved himself hardworking, reliable, loyal—everything Shelby's father was not. The easy friendship between Shelby and Bryan stair-stepped its way to a delicious first kiss on the front steps of her dorm building at North Texas.

Three years later when he proposed under a sprawling live oak on a Hill Country hike, saying yes wasn't a tough decision. It felt like the next right step toward creating her own loving family. Leaving the workforce after having Paisley was the next right step. When Shelby took the human resources job at an oil company's headquarters, she looked forward to training employees and resolving conflict.

Instead, she spent her workweek compiling detailed paperwork and tedious reports. But her income and benefits covered them while Bryan finished up his expensive architecture degree at Rice University. The move to Houston was well worth it so he could attend a top program in his hometown. But after Paisley was born, Shelby's drive to file reports and meet someone else's deadlines completely fizzled.

As she opened her email, her focus shifted from those earlier life decisions to the daunting choice awaiting her now. Which dresses would be the steppingstones to capitalize on winning the grand prize of *Buzz Now Magazine*'s design contest?

Loading the file from Dennis, Shelby felt the cumulative weight of all her toil to reach this milestone. All the times in the early months of motherhood she put Paisley down for a nap, lowering the sweet baby gently into the crib, wrapped tight like a spring roll in soft organic muslin. All those naptimes tiptoeing out of the cool, dark nursery, pressing the door to the frame without making a sound.

Then speed-racing to the dining table to sew for the world's shortest 45 minutes until Paisley awoke, wailing to be held. Somehow the sleeping baby timer ticked away faster than any other clock.

Tonight's decision was the culmination of all that early work—all the hours spent hunched over the sewing machine, all the Friday afternoons hurrying to the post office, juggling stacks of boxes atop the stroller. She hoped by now a decisive gut feeling would lead her to select the perfect dress styles, as if the winning combination lay before her on a lottery ticket needing to be scratched off just right.

Her feet swiveled the office chair side to side. Staring at the PDF, a dozen of her matching dress styles stared back at her, having been tweaked and formalized by *Surface Trend*'s design team.

How to choose which two? Fit? Pattern? Trendiness? Gut feeling?

She considered the many learned lessons from owning a virtual dress shop the last few years. Which styles sold the best? And, just as important, on which styles could she confidently stake her brand's reputation?

Up to this point, her least expensive dresses amassed the highest sales, even though Shelby knew they weren't the most fashionable or complimented. But opting for nicer fabrics and more complex designs raised costs considerably. The more expensive the dress, the greater the risk of not selling enough units and not being invited to join *Surface Trend*'s design team.

With that notion guiding her, she went against her instincts and chose the two dresses that cost the least to make. They were still plenty cute. Hopefully cute enough to lock in her dream job.

Clicking reply, she relayed her final choices to *Surface Trend*'s design team and *Buzz Now*'s editorial board. If nothing else, low prices meant the dresses were more likely to sell out.

As she sent the email, the garage door rumbled, interrupting the silence. Bryan was home. Shelby ran her fingernails through her done-up hair and moistened her lips with her tongue.

With this massive decision finally behind her, it was time to switch gears and seek progress on an entirely different dream.

Chapter 2

Thanks to a long overdue trip to the post office, Shelby was running late for coffee group the next morning. Finally parked at TexEspresso, she checked her phone one more time even though the ringer volume was on high. Still nothing.

Dennis, who worked at *Buzz Now*'s headquarters in L.A., was meeting with the editorial team to review her design choices and decide how in-depth a story to include in *Buzz Now Magazine*'s holiday issue. Every minute that passed without hearing from him fueled her growing apprehension about whether or not she chose the right dress designs.

She set the ringer on silent and headed inside the cafe to find her friends.

"Hey, y'all! So sorry I'm late." Shelby whooshed around the table in a flowery wrap dress. She sat down in the empty bistro chair, hung her indigo leather handbag on the curvy metal armrest, and slid her tortoiseshell sunglasses to the top of her head.

"Oh, don't be silly. We're just glad you're here." Blakeley said, tossing her shiny auburn hair over her shoulder.

Years ago, the first week Shelby moved to Houston, she met Blakeley at a networking event. The two friends had remained close ever since. Together they navigated the journey from corporate grind to part-time professional, full-time mom.

"The post office was a nightmare. Is it Tax Day or something?" Shelby joked.

"For heaven's sake, don't worry about it," Elise assured her. "We just got our coffees."

"I love that dress," Whitney said. With her long, wavy natural-blonde hair and soft Southern accent, Whitney was the unsuspecting drama queen of the group. She was known to stir the pot but remained fiercely loyal to the women at this table. "Did you make it?"

Shelby's insides did a little flip. "I did, thanks. And I've missed y'all so much. How is everyone?"

"Look around," Elise said, sweeping her hands mystically over the tabletop like a fortuneteller. "Zero children. I'd say we're pretty fabulous."

As mom of a two-year-old boy and a three-year-old girl just 16 months apart, Elise had every reason to bask in the glorious calm of a preschool day. She hadn't wanted to leave her job as a nurse, but the logistics of caring for two babies so close together combined with her husband's unpredictable schedule monitoring offshore rigs left her with crummy childcare options.

"What is this? Some kind of fairyland?" Shelby said.

"Better than that. It's back to school." Whitney flashed a mischievous grin.

"I honestly didn't know if I was going to make it through the summer." Elise's parents lived in the Philippines, and her husband's lived in Georgia. She had the double whammy of babies close together and no local family.

"I know that feeling," Shelby said.

"Love all your updates on Instagram, Shel. I get exhausted just thinking about how you do it all. Especially the sewing part," Blakeley said.

"I basically haven't slept. In fact, I really need a coffee." Shelby waved to the server across the room.

"You came to the right place. They make everything Texas sized." Whitney lifted her kettlebell of a mug off the table. "Takes two hands to pick this thing up."

"I need one of those. Stat." The server approached, and Shelby ordered a latte just like Whitney's. "Y'all, is it me, or is it freezing in here?"

"I think I had fewer goosebumps on our ski trip," Whitney said, warming her hands on her mug.

"Which doesn't make any sense," Blakeley said. "It's hot enough out there to pop popcorn on the hood of the car, and it's barely ten o'clock."

"Everywhere is over-airconditioned right now. I had to buy an actual sweater." Elise rubbed the sleeves of her satin-lined yellow cardigan.

"That's super cute. Where's it from?" Shelby asked.

"I found it on clearance at *Surface Trend*. It was like $7.99, if you can believe that. I bought the orange one too. Wouldn't usually go for such bright colors, but just couldn't help it."

"Geez, at that price, you might as well," Shelby said.

"Well, I wasn't about to drag the winter clothes down from the attic. It's a thousand degrees up there," Elise said.

"So, how have y'all been? I feel like I haven't seen anyone in ages," Shelby said.

"We've been absolutely crazy, that's how," Elise said. "Prepping for back to school about did me in. And the kids have been quite the little handfuls. Completely bored with summer. They were so happy to be back in school."

"We did all our shopping online this year. Saved me so much headache tracking down all the supplies," Blakeley said.

"We did too," Shelby said. "Between school supplies and her birthday, Paisley is officially addicted to the mail."

"So, Shel, we all really want to hear about yesterday." Whitney leaned toward Shelby, as if expecting to hear a juicy secret.

"Your hair looked amazing in the teaser. How did it go?" Blakeley asked.

"Thanks. The style team was over the top. Hair and makeup were a blast. We had a bumpy start with Paisley not smiling, but in the end, I think it went well."

A server delivered Shelby's massive latte to the table. A five-point star reminiscent of the Texas flag floated in the froth, courtesy of the barista. Shelby pulled her phone out of her purse to capture the steamy spectacle resting before her. Artistic espresso could collect a heap of likes on a hump-day morning.

"Any idea how the pictures turned out?" Whitney asked.

"The ones the photographer showed me looked great. Plus, they're going to airbrush the tar out of them. I left feeling pretty relieved. Haven't slept through the night in weeks I've been so nervous."

"Well girl, you shouldn't be. You look absolutely stunning," Whitney said. "Did you get lashes?"

"Oh, thanks," Shelby blushed. "Yeah, and not just that. Short of Botox, I think I've had everything done you can possibly do. I haven't looked this polished since our wedding day." She smiled and fluttered her eyelash extensions, still getting used to the ethereal way they brushed against her cheeks when she blinked. "I think I dropped close to a mortgage payment on all this, not to mention my trainer and all the accessories.

Let's hope I can recoup some of it in dress sales."

"Your hair looks so natural. Did you go to Veronica?" Whitney asked.

"I did. She's every bit as quirky as you said she'd be." Shelby combed her fingers through her effortless-looking waves, strung along from yesterday's styling session with the help of her miracle-working dry shampoo.

"She's also every bit as expensive," Blakeley said.

"It was crazy expensive. Biggest hair bill of my life," Shelby said. "But I'm okay with that because when I have highlights, I don't have to wash my hair every day. That's three less morning showers a week. Huge time saver."

"So eventually, it pays for itself." Elise shrugged.

"That's what I explained to Bryan," Shelby said. "Apparently he doesn't do math the same way we do."

"None of them do," Whitney said.

"So, what's the latest with y'all? How is Wylie doing two weeks into Kindergarten?" Shelby drew in a long, frothy sip of latte.

"So far, so good," Blakeley said. "We're really glad he did the bridge year. Y'all know, the whole summer birthday debate. He can focus so much better than this time last year. And by that, I mean focus on something other than baseball."

"Nice. And now for the real question," Shelby

said. "How are *you* enjoying Kindergarten?"

"Oh, I'm loving it. My life is so much calmer. The bus picks him up and drops him off. It's five days a week and, best of all, we're not paying an extra cent. So I pocket all the money from the consulting calls."

"That's amazing, Blake. That sounds like my dream right now," Shelby said. "We're paying a fortune for Paisley's Pre-K, and it's only three days a week. I could really use those extra two days, but who can afford that if you're not working full-time?"

"I just wrote the September tuition check for Scarlett and Jeremy," Elise said. "I'm pretty sure a semester of college costs less."

"Ouch!" Shelby said. "I know what I'm paying. Can't imagine that times two."

"Jason wants me to pull them out," Elise said. "I told him I'd happily do that when he quits his job and *I* go back to work."

"We know how that one ends," Whitney smirked.

"Exactly," Elise said. "Which is why we will continue to fork it over to St. Sebastian's."

"Double the tuition, double the fun," Whitney said. "I cannot believe you're already trying again."

"You're trying?" Shelby's shapely eyebrows arched up toward her starry highlights. She knew Elise and Jason wanted more kids . . . eventually.

But it felt like only weeks ago, baby Jeremy was starting solids and pulling up for the first time. A few blinks later, he was tinkering away with manipulatives in the two-year-old class. "That's so exciting!" Shelby managed to say.

"We're very excited. And a little terrified thinking about going through the newborn stage again. But we've always known we wanted three kids, and Jason and I are ready to get the brutal sleepless part over with."

"So, Shel, when does the magazine come out?" Blakeley jumped in.

Shelby welcomed the change of subject even if it twisted the spotlight back to her. "Well, it's the holiday issue, so it should be out in November. And get this. Carrie Underwood is slated for the cover."

"Are you kidding me?" Blakeley nearly dropped her mug on the table.

"I love her," Whitney said. "Too bad you don't get to meet her."

"I know. That would make this whole thing even more unbelievable," Shelby said.

"*Buzz Now* gets the best celebrities." Elise took an enormous bite of a chocolate muffin.

"Shel, this is all so exciting! How are you feeling about all of it?" Blakeley asked.

"Umm . . . a little nervous, not gonna lie," Shelby replied. "I've known about it all since February, so part of me is like, okay, it's finally happening. But when I think about walking into the grocery store and seeing the actual issue of the magazine, I want to go hide in my car."

"Well, it's gonna be awesome. Everything comes so easily for you," Whitney said.

"Thanks." Shelby took in a mouthful of latte, its foamy star dissolving. She had poured so many hours into every dress, in addition to the massive undertakings of creating a brand and generating a following, all while running a business from home with a child who was always there and a husband who never was. Nothing had come easily. The compliment, though surely well intended, made Shelby feel somehow . . . discounted. "It's been a long road."

"So, what will the dresses look like?" Whitney asked.

As the server swept in to remove crumb-filled plates, Shelby held up her phone and revealed screenshots of the chosen designs.

The group erupted in a chorus of oohs and aahs.

"Oh my goodness! I want them both," Elise said. "Scarlett would look so cute in the mini one."

"Thanks. That's such a relief. I just submitted these last night, so I'm still waiting to hear back from the design team."

Blakeley scrolled back and forth between the two dress images. "Girl, they're gonna love these."

"I really hope so," Shelby said.

Everything, it felt, was riding on that.

Shelby's phone finally rang as she stepped out of the coffee shop into the steamy bake of the day. Her fingers trembled as she retrieved the device from her purse pocket and lifted it to her ear. Maybe there *was* such a thing as too much coffee.

"Dennis, great timing!" The shake in her voice gave her away. Too excited, too eager. "Great to finally talk to you. Busy couple of days around here."

"Tell me about it," Dennis said. "Do you have a few minutes?"

"Yes, now is great." Shelby sat down on a wooden bench not far from her parking spot. Ever since she won the contest, her calls with Dennis were a bright spot, offering industry insights and clarity. She knew from a few video calls that Dennis was a stylish Asian man in his late forties whose signature look was a black blazer over a white T-shirt. Even having never met him in person, Shelby was certain she could pick him out of a crowd.

"I talked to Felipe. He loved your dresses, and he adores Paisley. He said she was charming and delightful and gorgeous. Just like her mama."

"Aww, thank you, Dennis." Shelby blushed even though no one was looking. "He's such a wonderful photographer. So talented. And so patient with us."

"He said your pictures are, and I quote, 'mesmerizing.' And that's coming from a self-proclaimed perfectionist."

"Ha! I don't know about that. Maybe after the editors erase a few fine lines."

"The thumbnails look great. He's sending over some images this afternoon. And Gwen has already turned in the copy from your interview. We'll have you review the feature before it goes to print."

"Feature?"

"Yes. We're doing three full-page spreads."

"Six pages? That's . . . amazing!" Shelby nearly fell off the bench. Collecting herself, she added, "I can't believe a story that's not coming out until November is already written in August."

"Many of our stories are time sensitive and can't be touched until closer to print. We were able to push this one along sooner."

"Well, I guess that's one thing to feel ahead on. I've felt so far behind during this whole process. You got my email last night, right?" Shelby tugged at the tips of her hair, pinching the crunch of yesterday's hairspray.

"I checked with *Surface Trend*'s design team this morning. Everyone is on board with the cost-reduction strategy."

"I'm so glad to hear that. I went back and forth

for days but felt like those styles made the most sense for this first run. That is, *first* and hopefully not only run."

"The potential for higher margins will make the execs at *Surface Trend* happy. Can't go wrong with that."

Over the last few months working with Dennis, Shelby caught on that *Buzz Now* had an intricate partnership with *Surface Trend*. They were separate entities, but their devotion to fashion and celebrity news commingled. More than that, it seemed like Dennis and his team were just plain good friends with the creatives at *Surface Trend*.

Shelby let out a long exhale as she considered her progress along this chaotic but exciting journey. The photoshoot went well. The magazine coverage would be a full-length feature. The design slate for her first run of dresses was approved. Soon all her late nights and early mornings spent piecing together dresses for faraway customers would yield something more significant than a side hustle to cover their family's growing expenses.

"So, how many dresses will there be?"

"We don't have the exact numbers yet, but we're ordering around 30,000 of each piece."

"Okay, wow. That's a lot. When will they arrive in stores?"

"There's typically about a six-week turnaround from when our counterparts in Guangzhou get the order to when the designs are shipped to distributors in L.A."

Guangzhou was yet another place Shelby couldn't locate on a map. Based on past conversations, she presumed it was in China.

"We're looking at the middle of November," Dennis said.

"Same as when the holiday issue comes out?"

"Yep. That's not a coincidence."

Shelby let out a reserved laugh. Her conversations with Dennis always made her feel like such an amateur. "That's great. Can I just say again how lucky I feel to have this opportunity? I would be so lost without y'all."

"It's great for us too. You're like our own American Idol."

"Well, that's a fun way to think about it." Shelby couldn't help but smile. She deserved to let the glory of this victory sink in. Winning *Buzz Now*'s By Design contest may have expedited all this exposure, but no one could argue with how hard she'd worked to earn the opportunity.

"So, what should I be doing next?"

"*Surface Trend* will have the samples sent to you. After we have your final approval, production begins," he said. Shelby admired his certainty, the kind of knowing that came from decades of experience.

"Sounds good. I can't wait to see them. Anything else for me?" Shelby asked.

"Keep up the push on socials. Retweet us every chance you get, and we'll do the same. Goal should be for *Treasured Pockets* to gain about a thousand followers a month, however you can get them. The more followers you have when the issue hits, the bigger the bump you'll get from all the promotions."

"Got it. Okay, last thing. Our family is sponsoring a child through the Caring Hope Organization. The info just came yesterday. She's a darling little girl. Can we plug Caring Hope in the social media push somehow? They need more sponsors, and I thought our followers might be interested."

"Sure, whatever you think will get people's attention. You're launching a mommy-and-me line, so that sounds pretty genuine."

"Okay, great. I've got my homework cut out for me. Sounds like you do too?"

"It never ends."

As soon as the call clicked off, Shelby glanced at the time. Only 45 minutes until preschool pick-up. She reviewed her to-do list.

The most pressing item was sewing the next pair of dresses for her backlogged online orders. But she needed several consecutive, uninterrupted hours for that.

Instead, she started chipping away at social media posts, sharing the foamy star latte pic to Instagram and Facebook and prepping the Caring

Hope announcement. She added "Take a picture of Runa's photo" to the list. Everything would be ready to upload Friday afternoon, the prime time of the social media week when her posts collected the most comments and shares.

The only other task she could complete from a bench at a strip mall was to contact the sponsorship director at Caring Hope. She whipped up a couple lines of Paisley's questions and emailed them to the contact on the letter, then crossed it off her list.

With a few remaining minutes before preschool pickup, the sale posters across the parking lot at *Surface Trend* caught her eye. It wouldn't hurt to peruse the aisles and start to visualize where her dresses would go. And peek at the fall boots.

Only a matter of weeks remained until her dream—and all that came with it—became a reality.

Chapter 3

Before the sun rose the next morning, Paisley's little feet clunked onto the floor, traipsing the well-worn path from her twin bed down the hallway to her parents' room. And just like that, another day began before 6 a.m.

Thankfully, the early morning brought an easy bedtime. Paisley was too sleepy for her usual chorus of more stories, more songs, more sips of water. Shelby said goodnight and closed her door before Bryan even left the office.

P is zzz

Shelby texted Bryan. No reason for him to rush home from late meetings hoping to catch Paisley awake.

Pattern piece in hand, Shelby lowered down to the floor, pressing her knees into the soft white carpet of the front room by the foyer. The long table in the dining room had been her first choice for a sewing space. But when a large section of $14/yard satin blend soaked up unforeseen grease splotches from Tex Mex takeout, she couldn't again risk mixing food and fabric. The front room, where the cushion of carpet met the flat hardwood floors, became the next best place.

Smoothing the pattern piece across pink and white dotted fabric, Shelby double checked its position, ensuring her first cut was precise and efficient. For all the equipment and notions needed to sew a dress, the pattern was the single most important factor that determined how the dress would look finished.

Style, trendiness, and fit were all a byproduct of pattern choice. Every single piece, whether large or small, played a significant role. Alter the pattern in any way, and the entire outcome would change.

Shelby cut into the cross grain, guiding her sewing scissors along the fabric's edge. Her grandmother Dear, who taught her to sew, gave her this exact pair for her twelfth birthday. Back then, Shelby's sewing repertoire included unique pajama pants and sundresses none of her friends were wearing. Showing up in her own creations drew in heaps of praise from friends and teachers, making her life feel stable—even when it wasn't.

Shelby's left hand secured the slippery rayon fabric while her right hand squeezed together the shears' silver handles. She sliced pieces of the soon-to-be dress into existence. Scraps fell away into the rejection pile. All scissors made noise when they cut, but these sounded like a sword, slashing through the future dress with precision and might.

A text rolled in from Blakeley.

Are you coming?

They were at Zia's, the Greek place, for the neighborhood moms' night out. Shelby had originally RSVP'd, but later canceled, realizing the outing fell smack in the middle of the baby-trying window.

In addition, Shelby was desperate for the extra sewing time. The online exposure from winning the contest in February created an explosion of orders overnight. Shelby went from sewing six dresses a month to a surge of 58 new orders in the queue within 48 hours of *Buzz Now*'s announcement.

Part of the seemingly insurmountable challenge of fulfilling so many orders was due to the hook of her business model. She wasn't just making women's dresses, competing with the zillions of retailers who could make dresses better, cheaper, faster. *Treasured Pockets* created matching dresses for mothers and daughters to wear together. The classic premise with up-to-date designs set her shop apart.

Can't tonight. Bryan's not home yet.
Hate to miss!

Shelby replied to Blakeley. Baba ghanoush and baklava couldn't compete with the lure of slaying this dragon.

Shelby laid the opaque tissue-paper pattern on the bias of the dotted material, preparing to cut the next piece of dress. The child-sized dresses took about four hours from first cut to final hem. She could sew them faster without pockets. But for her clientele, those were a key selling feature. In fact, they had inspired the name of her label.

Pockets, after all, created options, alternatives. A child could decide whether to leave found treasure behind or take it with her, safe in a pocket. Shelby knew firsthand how helpful it was when a little girl could haul away those treasures herself instead of loading down mommy's purse with fascinating rocks and twigs.

The mommy dresses took closer to seven hours because of the invisible zipper, added lines, and extra darts and seams to ensure a flattering fit. No pockets on this dress, though. There wasn't a mother out there who would want extra material bunching up around her midsection.

Shelby methodically pinned the front middle to front side pieces of the A-line dress, preparing to sew the princess seams. She'd sewn this exact dress so many times, she knew the steps by heart.

In the months after winning the contest, she'd

considered hiring another seamstress to help her fill the backlogged orders. Adding another person complicated everything about owning a business. Hiring a friend sounded simple enough, but she didn't know anyone who could sew with her speed and skill. Dear would have been the perfect person to help, but she passed away all too soon, not long before Shelby launched her shop.

Having no sewing help and only so many workable hours in the day, Shelby had to shut down her online store to sew the existing orders. She was finally on track to mail out the last orders this week.

With the fabric pieces pinned in place, Shelby sat down at her sewing table in front of the top-of-the-line overlock machine she inherited from Dear. A surge of energy ran through her as she prepared to tackle her favorite part of sewing: stitching the seams. Securing one remnant of fabric to another transformed unshapely scraps into a thing of order and beauty, a metamorphosis of pure magic.

Her favorite seam of all was sewing her paisley-flourished label, *Treasured Pockets*, into the neck of the dress. Winning *Buzz Now*'s design contest had created an unbelievable opportunity for her designs to be worn by so many women and girls, season after season, bringing moms and children together. As a mother, she could think of no better compliment than for her daughter to want to look and be just like her, from the pattern of her dress to the very fabric of her soul.

Another text rolled in, this one from Bryan.

Getting an oil change then picking up BBQ. Want anything?

No thanks. See you soon.

To prevent any more interruptions, Shelby turned her phone face down on the sewing table. She ran the first pinned edges of material under the energetic feed dog of the serger. The ball of her foot edged the pedal toward the floor, causing the machine to whirr into action.

An intricate quartet of needles stabbed each stitch of thread into place, securing one swatch of dress firmly to another. The buzzing noise from the machine was oddly soothing, reminding her of all the long, hot summers at Dear's sewing sundresses for the schoolyear to come.

Amid the hum of progress, Shelby could sense the prize peeking out from behind the mountain of work. For the better part of the year, she spent all her free time sewing dresses for customers. Finally, there would be help—*so much help*—scaling up production. No more emergency trips to the fabric store to select missing notions. No more Friday afternoons waiting in line at the post office.

Standing at the ironing board pressing open the completed seam, her thoughts turned to the months ahead. Blakeley's comments about elementary school planted a vision of the future that didn't feel so far away. Only one more year lay between them and full-time Kindergarten, when suddenly, miraculously, so much of Shelby's time would be hers again.

Unless, perhaps, a new little one emerged to need her.

Another baby would blanket a layer of challenges over every aspect of their lives. Having grown up as an only child, she welcomed any extra load a new life would bring.

This part of the baby-making month always left her feeling jittery, so excited to become pregnant again, but also dreading the disappointment if things didn't unfold as she hoped. For too long, that had been the unfortunate trend.

Even so, she couldn't wait to start testing.

As she paired together two elbow-shaped pieces of fabric and interfacing, right sides together, excitement brewed inside thinking about the weeks ahead. For an exhausting sprint to finish up at her sewing station. And a sweet little marathon to be, hopefully, underway deep within her.

The next day was as hot as the one before. Paisley spent the lazy afternoon on the sofa behind her iPad. Shelby spent the screen time hours finishing the next dress, completing everything except the final hem.

"Time to go, Little P," Shelby said.

"But my show's not over," Paisley said.

"Doesn't matter. Miss Maye is home now. We need to go tell her about Runa." It was Maye who informed Shelby of the dire need for sponsor families at Caring Hope. Considering she lived across the street, it was only right to introduce their sponsor child in person before Shelby plastered the announcement all over social media tomorrow.

At the mention of Runa's name, Paisley popped up from the sofa without any fuss. They walked to the foyer, where a pile of shoes rested like an anthill on the floor. How many times had she asked Paisley to put them away?

Ignoring the mess, Shelby nudged her daughter outside onto the sunbaked front walk. Before shutting the door, she clicked through her mental checklist.

Iron off. *Check.*

Phone in purse. *Check.*

Sponsorship envelope. *Check.*

Oh right. The picture.

"Be right back." She dashed inside and pulled Runa's photo off the fridge.

The cicadas hummed ceremoniously from the treetops as Shelby and Paisley started across Oak

Blossom Lane in matching chevron sundresses.

Paisley rang the doorbell. Moments later, Maye opened the door, her blue eyes shining under a curtain of short, sandy brown hair. "Why, hello to my favorite mother-daughter models! Those dresses make me want to grab my camera. Y'all come in, come in."

Shelby and Paisley followed Maye inside. In the kitchen, she offered iced tea and lemonade. A plate of warm chocolate chip cookies rested on the rustic farm table. Paisley scurried over to a bowl full of chocolate candies. She popped a red one into her mouth and two blue ones into her pocket.

Their catch-up about the photoshoot puddled together as predictable chit-chat until Paisley snatched the white envelope from her mom's purse.

"Miss Maye, look at this," Paisley interrupted.

"What is it?" Maye leaned forward and rested her hands on her knees.

"We got a new friend."

"Did you make a new friend at the photo-shoot?" Maye asked.

"No, we got a new friend in the mailbox." Paisley took the picture from Shelby's hand and passed it to Maye. "Look, see? Her name is Runa. She lives on the other side of the ocean."

"Runa. What a lovely name," Maye said, furrowing her brow. As Paisley darted off toward the living room, Maye drew the picture close and pulled down her reading glasses from atop her head. "Wait, Runa Binu?"

"Umm, yes . . . I think so." Shelby took the papers out of the white envelope and double-checked the name on the student profile. "But—how on earth did you know that?"

Maye's eyes wandered up from the photograph to meet Shelby's. "Because I've met her."

"Wait, what?" Goosebumps formed on Shelby's arms as the questions tumbled out. "How on earth would you have met Runa?"

"I met her in Bangladesh."

"But when?" Shelby asked, feeling a sudden need to collect proof.

"On our last trip there . . . nine, ten years ago. Gosh, I can't believe it's been that long. She was really little then, maybe two. And so tiny. Somethin' like 15 pounds. But I remember her. She had these huge, bottlecap eyes." Maye peered into the photo as if looking for lost treasure. "Still does."

"Seriously?" Shelby found this hard to believe. Caring Hope had randomly selected a sponsor child for their family from over 30 supported countries. *Small world* seemed too much an understatement to even say. "What were you doing in . . . in Bangladesh?"

"Roger and I went on a medical service trip. For part of it, we did physicals at an orphanage just outside of Dhaka. We gave the kids vitamins, vaccinations, checked their vision and hearing. That sort of basic care," Maye explained. "That's how I connected with Caring Hope. Their donors subsidized the orphanage and supported the staff."

Shelby glanced at the paperwork again. She didn't want to sound skeptical, but it seemed farfetched that this could be the exact same girl Maye met at the orphanage, especially considering their sponsor child wasn't an orphan.

"The student profile says Runa lives with her mother," Shelby said.

"Yep, I met her too. Can't remember her name. Just that she was a single mom working full-time. That's why Runa went to the orphanage during the day. It was a children's home, really." Maye tucked a tidy strand of sandy hair behind her ear. "I believe her dad had walked out on them right after Runa was born. Just disappeared from their lives."

Hearing the words, Shelby felt a familiar ache deep inside. When she was five, her own father had done the same disappearing act. Except she'd been old enough to remember watching him leave. He was home one day, then never again, completely evading the duties of having a family to start a new life without one. "That's . . . that's terrible," Shelby said.

"Yes, it is. The children's home had a daycare, and certain families would qualify if they couldn't make it on their own. Runa's mom qualified for childcare and some extra medical resources. They have a sister school across the street that goes all the way up to Grade 10. It's a really wonderful program for the orphans and street children. Caring Hope has supported them for a long time. That's probably how Runa was picked to be a sponsor child."

"Probably so," Shelby said, absorbing the new information. "I just hate to hear that about her father."

"It is really sad. Though not completely uncommon," Maye said.

Shelby agreed but stayed silent. In the four years since she moved in across the street, she never told Maye about her father. It never came up. And even if it did, Shelby was ill equipped to bring up painful wounds from the past.

In the confusing weeks and months after her father left, she was bombarded by all the grown-ups in her life asking how she was doing. She quickly learned to tell them what they wanted to hear. She was fine. She was great. She was happy.

Using her imagination to pretend everything was okay was the only way to stop all the painful questions. Besides, disclosing how she really felt would do nothing to change the outcome.

"Does it say if Runa has any siblings? I can't remember," Maye said.

"The student profile says she's an only child." Shelby stood silent. Paisley pulled a wooden puzzle from a shelf of toys and dumped out the pieces onto the coffee table.

Shelby skimmed the paperwork one more time. "This is a really crazy coincidence."

"It would be. Except, my dear, I don't believe in coincidences." Maye half-winked at Shelby, then kneeled on the carpet next to Paisley, who was almost done connecting the frame. "Paisley, did you know that I've met your new friend?"

"You know Runa?" Paisley stopped assembling the puzzle and looked up. Her eyes widened and her lips curled into a smile. "*My* Runa?"

"Met her when she was very little. Even littler than you." Maye poked a tickly finger toward Paisley's tummy.

Paisley giggled and swatted half-heartedly at Maye's hand. "Mama said I couldn't have her over 'cause she lives too far away."

"She does live far away. But I have an idea." As she spoke, Maye's eyes sparkled like Paisley's ornament.

"What's that?" Paisley looked at Maye, focused and eager.

"Maybe you two could be pen pals."

"What's a pim pal?"

"Good question. A *pen* pal is someone who lives far away, and you talk to them by writing letters back and forth. You can ask them questions

55

and find out more about what it's like where they live."

"But I can't write. Or read."

"I bet your mama can write to Runa if you politely ask her to."

Hearing the brilliant idea, Paisley's eyebrows rose. Her ears perked. "I want to be a pim pal! Mama, can I be a pim pal with Runa?"

"That's a fun thought. And it's pe*nnn* pal. *Nuh-nuh-nuh.*" She turned to Maye. "But we can't send her anything. I emailed Caring Hope last week, and they said it was too difficult to get specific items to individual children."

"Well, Miss Maye might know a sneaky way around that." She tucked her lips together, suppressing a smile. "Wait here. I have something to show you."

While Shelby and Paisley worked on the puzzle, Maye disappeared upstairs. She returned minutes later, her hands gripping an oversized green album.

When she returned to the kitchen table, they each pushed back lemonade and tea glasses to clear a spot. Maye opened the book wide, revealing images of leafy forests, tin-roofed buildings, flooded rice fields. She turned page after page until she found what she was looking for.

"Here she is." Maye's finger landed in the bottom corner of a group picture containing what must have been around 40 people. Most were young children.

"That's Runa?" Paisley asked.

"Yes, that's Runa."

"But she's a baby."

"She *was* a baby, a toddler actually, when I met her. Looks like she's grown quite a bit. She's bigger than you are."

"Did you get to play with her?" Paisley asked.

"I did, some. She liked to collect rocks."

"Hey, I collect rocks too." Paisley reached into her pockets and procured three rocks, a leafy twig, and the blue chocolate candies. "I found these magic crystals in the driveway."

"Are these all the kids at the children's home?" Shelby asked, still engrossed in the album.

"Yes. And their caregivers. We took the picture so we could remember all their faces. I was just getting into photography at the time. Had no idea I would be pulling these out for something like this."

"I wanna meet her too. Mama, can we go see her?"

"Oh goodness, no, sweetie. It's way too far away."

"But we can go in an airplane. Like we did to Florida. And we can color and watch movies and eat snacks 'til we get there."

"Sweetie, we can't go see Runa. It's too

far and too expensive." Not to mention she probably couldn't even locate Bangladesh on a map.

"But what you *can* do," Maye said, "is email my friend Ravi." She turned a few pages in the photo album. Her finger guided their eyes to a picture of Roger standing next to a much shorter man with dark brown hair, vibrant eyes, and a smile that leaped off the page. "He's the rep from Caring Hope who took us around and organized our stay. He works very closely with the children's home."

"Really? Are you still in touch with him?" Shelby asked.

"Sure am. He emails out a newsletter every month. Always sends inspirational updates about the work he's doing. Sometimes I write back, but I haven't in a while. I bet he'd be happy to ask Runa your questions. He might even help if you want to send her a little gift or something."

"Mama, can we do that? Can we mail Runa a present?"

"Yes. That is something we most certainly can do." Shelby was enjoying Paisley's fascination with their sponsored child more than she realized she would.

Maye walked across the kitchen to retrieve her phone from its charger on the countertop. "I'm going to forward you his latest email. He's a wonderful writer. So sincere and really dedicated to his work. You can reply straight to him. Tell him you know me. He's very good about writing back within a day. Sometimes in minutes."

"And he'll give me an address to mail something to Runa?" Shelby asked.

"I'm sure he will."

"I'm curious, though. How will we know if she gets it?" Shelby felt like Paisley, flooding her friend's ears with so many questions.

"Knowing Ravi," Maye said, "he'll probably give you the address of his office, and he'll deliver it himself."

"That would work," Shelby said, still hesitant at how seamlessly this was coming together. And how close she suddenly felt to this faraway child after learning what they had in common, growing up as the only child of a single mother.

"Mama, can you email him now?" Paisley asked.

Shelby considered the request. She was happy to email Ravi but saw an opportunity for cooperation. "Yes, I will email him. Soon as your shoes are all picked up and put away."

"Ugh," Paisley groaned. "Fine."

To: shelby@treasuredpockets.com
From: ravinder.amon@caringhope.org
Date: September 10, 2012
Subject: Re: Mail for Runa Zaman

Dear Shelby,

It is wonderful to hear from a friend of Maye! Thank you for sponsoring our sweet angel Runa. I would be happy to share your daughter's notes and packages with her. My address is below. Runa attends Eternal Promise School for Girls, which is not far from my office. It would be very easy to drop off mail to her and would bring me great joy to do so.

We are really grateful you are supporting a family in so much need. Thank you again for your continued generosity. May the Lord bless you with the peace, happiness, and love you truly deserve.

Sincerely,
Ravi

Ravinder Amon
Dhaka Community Programs Manager
Caring Hope Organization

Chapter 4

The stick was pink. Euphoric pink.

Day after day, the stick revealed the faintest pink stripe that grew a tiny shade pinker with each day. Pink was the color of hope. The color of dreams. Day after day after day, the lines revealed pink, heavenly pink.

Shelby's thoughts drifted to some sacred other world. She was more than ready to live out this other dream that nestled its roots so snuggly inside her. Tiny fingers, wiggly toes, storybook names danced across her stream of consciousness. A door had opened for her, for Bryan, for all of them. A spark was lit. Finally, her daughter would have a sibling, a forever friend to walk with through life. The friend Shelby never had.

Then right on time, everything turned red.

The dancing stopped.

The door shut.

The flame went dark.

A chemical pregnancy, the fertility sites called it. Her body produced the hormones of being pregnant, started on the path of carrying new life, enough to trick the prophetic stick into proclaiming *yes, yes you are*. But the reality was *no, no you aren't*.

This vicious tease of a pregnancy had happened

twice before, early last year and again in the spring. There was no textbook evidence stating that the darkness of the pink line on the test determined how pregnant a woman actually was. Technically, the HCG pregnancy hormone was either present, or it wasn't.

But Shelby had only seen the testing strip become dark, solid pink when she was pregnant—sticky pregnant—with Paisley. Otherwise, the pink display was only faintly there, an apparition of wonder. But there, existing, nonetheless.

Faint or not, the trauma to her soul couldn't be undone. There was something unspeakably permanent about a mother anticipating a baby who would never once fall asleep in her arms.

When Shelby came out of the bathroom, the light of dawn was not yet visible beneath the Roman shades in their bedroom. Paisley was already awake, propped up against a stack of pillows on her mom's side of the king bed. Wedged in the crook of her elbow rested a stuffed teddy bear wearing a satin ballet ensemble. Paisley's eager hands clenched Shelby's phone, poking at the locked screen.

Bryan was in Nashville working on their firm's prized build, a 26-story mixed-use commercial high rise. So many chances to try for a baby had been thwarted by his unfavorable travel schedule. She wrestled with, then rehearsed in her mind, how she would share the morning's disappointing news with him when they talked later.

The house felt still.

Empty.

Shelby blotted her tear-streaked face with the sleeve of her bathrobe, a habit she always fussed at Paisley to stop doing. *Use a tissue,* she heard her mom voice insist.

None of that mattered now. It was one of those illogical moments when she needed her child more than her child needed her. One of those grief-filled, crampy mornings when the only right thing to do was to crawl back in bed.

"Good morning." Shelby scooped up Paisley's yarn ball of a body into her lap. The two burrowed into the cozy cloud of the white down comforter.

"Mama, can I look at pictures on your phone?" Paisley asked.

Without speaking, Shelby entered the code to unlock it. She generally didn't allow Paisley to use her phone in the house. Such a treat was reserved for waiting rooms and post offices, occasions around town when she needed to complete some urgent errand without being interrupted. But in this early morning hour of loss, Shelby wanted—needed—to be close with her child. How fitting that the quiet relief of skin-to-skin therapy was accessible thanks to a touch screen.

Paisley swiped through sunny photographs of

recent family outings. Roasting marshmallows at their first family campout. Waving an oversized foam hand at the Astros game. That first victorious day riding a bicycle stripped of its training wheels.

While family highlights swooped past one after the next, Shelby's thoughts floated elsewhere, imagining through a veil of loss what the baby would have looked like snuggled up in her arms.

So close. And yet, not to be.

Shelby blinked a tear down her cheek. Somehow her mind needed to catch up to her body in restarting the four-week routine of making a baby. All the reckless hope required lay ahead of them again. Obsessing over Bryan's trip schedule to make sure dates lined up. Monitoring scant changes for signs of readiness. The urgent sense of intimacy that erupted amid the fertile window. The two weeks of waiting that consumed her, forcing her to negotiate the fine line between staying hopeful and being realistic. All the fragile nuances of making a baby that would-be fathers appeared to skip.

The sing-songy melody of Paisley's morning voice interrupted the flood of Shelby's thoughts. "Mama, what's Runa doin' today?"

Shelby looked down to see Runa's sweet eyes staring back at them from the phone screen. The Instagram story and picture had garnered so much love and attention. Two of her followers committed to becoming Caring Hope sponsors too. Amid the waiting game until her dresses were ready, it made her feel like *Treasured Pockets* was doing something good, beyond just making dresses.

"I'm pretty sure Runa's day is over, sweetheart. It's nighttime there. She's probably going to sleep soon."

"How is it nighttime?"

"Because they're on the other side of the world from us. When the sun is up here, it's down over there. Tomorrow morning, she'll eat breakfast and go to school, just like you."

Paisley enlarged the picture, zooming in on Runa's face. "Mama, did Mr. Ravi ever write back?"

"Yes. He did, actually." Shelby hadn't meant to hide this news. So preoccupied by the positive tests, she forgot to mention it. "He said he'd be happy to drop off letters and any small gifts for Runa."

"Really? So we can mail things to her?"

"Yes. A few small, simple things." No reason for the gift-giving to get out of hand.

Paisley looked down, then burst out with an idea. "Can we send her Ballet Bear?"

"That's a really sweet thought." On a day with such a sad start, Shelby welcomed the opportunity to smile. She marveled at how the little person she and Bryan created could be so kind. She ran the backside of her fingers down Paisley's upper arm. The girl's little frame of a body rose and fell with each breath, undulating with life, and life, and life.

"I'm going to the post office tomorrow. We can send it then. Maybe we can write a note and ask her a few of your questions."

"On my unicorn stationery?"

"Sure. I bet you can write the letters of her name."

"Can I paint some hearts on the envelope?"

"Of course." Shelby kissed the back of her daughter's head, detecting the flowery scent of detangling spray.

She wondered whether Paisley would still feel like letting go of her beloved stuffy when the time came to tape up the box and walk away from it on the post office counter.

It was, after all, so impossibly hard to part with a baby.

Dear Runa,

My name is Paisley. I live in Texas in the United States. I am four years old. I am excited you are my friend. I like to play ponies and do gymnastics. Do you wear shoes in your house? What's your school like? I hope you like Ballet Bear. I want you to have her and these princess stickers. Rapunzel is my favorite. Who's yours? I love you!

Love,
Paisley

P.S. Please write back.

The after-lunch slump was already upon them when Shelby stood at the kitchen sink, prying squiggles of hardened cheese off last night's pizza dishes. As with most grievances, not dealing with the mess in a timely fashion multiplied the effort to fix it. She scraped the metal spatula back and forth against the food residue, begrudging every fussy second spent on the chore.

A preschool music channel played phonics and counting songs through a speaker by the sink where Shelby scrubbed. Paisley sat at her activity table beside the kitchen window, coloring a picture to accompany Runa's letter. Maneuvering each chunky marker in her little hand, she drew a rainbow and, beneath it, two stick figures in dresses holding hands.

Next, Paisley grabbed a pair of scissors and trimmed the corners of the drawing.

Shelby poured a half-full cup of warm milk down the drain. "What are you doing with the scissors?" she asked.

"I'm cuttin' these corners," Paisley explained.

"Why are you doing that?"

"Because they're too pointy. I don't like them."

She watched as the pointed clippings drifted to the floor below Paisley's chair. Shelby could think of a few corners she would cut if given the chance.

Wiping countertops, for example. *Snip snip.* Weren't breadcrumbs, onionskins, and dried-up beads of ground beef all destined to find their way to the floor?

Or hemming a dress by hand. *Chop chop.* Could she please just serge the bottom edge and call it finished like the ready-to-wear places did?

Then there was the biggest corner of all—becoming pregnant. Could they somehow skip ahead 28 days to know if the stick would show bright pink this month?

Shelby dried her hands and checked her phone. Bryan was supposed to call any minute on his lunch break. She pulled a bag of pretzels from the pantry and poured Paisley a snack.

The phone rang. She slipped away into the guest room. "Hi, Bry. How are you?"

"Okay. Things are a little . . . busy."

"Everything okay?"

"They will be. Crews are installing restaurant equipment, and it's not all fitting as planned."

"Sounds fun."

"We'll sort it out. That's what we're here for. How are you?"

Somehow the simplest question stirred up the

most complicated emotions. Teardrops staged themselves in the corners of Shelby's eyes.

"I have some bad news, actually," Shelby said. "No baby this month. We were really close."

A silence fell over the call. Which was just as well. In the face of fresh grief, words always proved insufficient.

"I'm sorry, Shel. It'll happen. We'll just keep trying."

"I hope so. I just never thought it would take this long," Shelby said.

"Me neither."

Shelby hated that they were having this conversation over the phone. This was the kind of news that should be shared in person. "I wish you were here, Bry."

"I do too. The good thing is we're wrapping up. Only a few months left out here."

"That's good. Any more talk about what's next?"

"Yes, actually. There's another commercial office building we've just been asked to put in a proposal for. And since I have some experience, they're eyeing me to take the lead."

"Where would that be?" Shelby hoped so badly it was somewhere near Houston. Or at least in Texas.

"It's in San Francisco."

"I see." A lump formed in Shelby's throat. This seemed like yet another conversation they should be having in person, not rushed over the phone on Bryan's lunch break. She could only imagine how much more time away that would require.

"Might be a five-year job. It would put me on track for partner."

Hearing that should have made Shelby so pleased. She knew how hard Bryan had worked to land this opportunity. He survived the fierce competition of architecture school then graduated right as the economy tanked. He took a less desirable job in the industry and stayed there for years longer than planned, waiting for a position to open up at a big firm. All his long hours were finally paying off, right when she needed him home more than ever.

She didn't know what to say, so she said the simplest words on her heart. "I miss you, Bryan."

Another silence fell between them before he spoke.

"I miss you too. Give Paisley a hug for me."

The doorbell rang unexpectedly, but also oddly on time at two o'clock, the hour the mail carrier seemed to arrive every day. Paisley dropped the scissors on the table and sprinted to the front door. "Is it for me?" she yelled.

The letter carrier gave a friendly wave from the open door of her truck then pulled forward to the next house. A brown box the size of a silverware drawer waited on the doorstep. Shelby had no idea what it was, but given the disappointing morning, she was just as eager as Paisley to see what was inside.

Paisley managed to haul the box inside on her own. "It says S-H-E-L-B-Y. It's for you, Mama. What is it?"

"Good reading, Little P. Let's find out." The label read RMG Couture with a Los Angeles return address. She was ticking through the mental list of recent online shopping ventures that might be arriving today when the answer struck.

"No way!" Shelby blurted out. It seemed like just a few days ago she was confirming their dress sizes with Dennis. How in the world could the dresses have been patterned, sewn, and shipped from who knows where to her doorstep already?

Inside the box was a stack of dresses neatly wrapped in crispy, untouched tissue paper. "The samples are here!"

"Samples? Like at Costco?" Paisley asked.

"Our dresses. *My* dresses." Shelby unwrapped the tissue paper and flung it to the floor. Her hands gripped the soft stretch velour of a slate blue baby doll dress, which featured a scoop neck and rising empire waist. The hem length just above the knee looked ideal. It could easily pass for a cocktail dress or could be thrown over leggings and worn as a tunic with boots.

Pinching the shoulder seams, she draped the dress over the back of the recliner and took a long look. She ran her fingers across every seam, inspecting the dress from top to bottom. The color was pretty, though the construction looked . . . hurried. The back of the dress featured a hook-and-eye closure instead of a zipper. It went on overhead instead of being stepped into, which didn't create as focused of a fit. The fabric, a blend of polyester and spandex, would make up for that, offering both stretch and forgiveness as it flowed over the hips.

The scoop neckline, where Shelby often struggled to force the interfacing to lay flat, was simply turned under like a hem, completely skipping that arduous step. The seams were tightly serged with an overlocking machine. A few stray threads hadn't been snipped.

These shortcuts were easily overlooked once her eyes landed on the best part of the dress: the label. *Her label.* Her brand name, *Treasured Pockets*, swirled across the tag in its signature curly font beside a pink and green paisley flourish.

It was a strange feeling. She'd never seen this garment before. And yet, the dress looked remarkably like one of her own.

"What else is there?" Paisley asked.

"Here, open this." Shelby handed Paisley the next package. The same stunning slate blue velvet peeked through the tissue wrapping.

Paisley held up the smaller, but otherwise identical, version of the velvety baby doll dress. "It's so pretty. Did you make this, Mama?"

"I didn't make it. I *designed* it." The word tasted heavenly as it drifted off her tongue.

"Who made it then?"

"Well, I suppose a seamstress at a big, big sewing company made it. Mr. Dennis sent us these to make sure they're exactly right before they make thousands more to sell in the store."

"What else is in here?" Paisley asked, inspecting the box.

"Should be the pink one."

"Ooooo. You made a pink one?"

"Technically, it's sparkleberry. But yes, we can call it pink." Shelby unwrapped the next folded package.

The tissue paper floated to the floor, revealing a sleeveless, A-line dress with a boatneck and a trendy hi-lo hem that just hit runways that summer. The fabric was a poly blend with a bit of sheen that featured a playful but subtle looping pattern, adding the appearance of texture without the expense of a lace overlay. The smaller version matched perfectly, but with pockets sewn into the skirt. Shelby draped the dresses side by side over the back of the sofa and took a step back.

"They're so pretty, Mama!"

"They are, aren't they?" Shelby tiptoed over

each word, as if too much praise would cause the dresses to vanish as quickly as they appeared. "Shall we try them on?"

"Yeah!" Paisley picked up the sparkleberry dress. "I wanna try this one first." In one fluid motion, she whipped her striped sundress onto the floor, her wiry little arms flying this way and that. She pulled the elegant dress over her head and requested help with the closure in the back.

"Look, Mama. It fits me," she said, twirling the skirt from side to side. "And it has pockets!"

Shelby tore off her neon green workout tank and put the matching dress on over her sports bra. She smoothed the sides around her yoga pants then reached behind her neck to close the hook and eye.

Leaping over piles of Legos and doll accessories, they scurried across the living room to the downstairs guest bedroom. Once there, they peered into a full-length mirror on the back of the closet doors.

"We're twins." Paisley whirled around, watching the skirt of the dress puff out around her like a blowfish's belly.

As Paisley spun dizzy circles, Shelby began to giggle.

"What's so funny?" Paisley stopped spinning.

"Nothing, I suppose." Shelby swished the skirt back and forth. "It's just kind of ridiculous how adorable we look."

"Yeah, we should be on stage." Paisley curtsied.

"Or in the pages of a magazine." Shelby couldn't stop herself from smiling at the thought.

"Spin, Mama!"

Shelby indulged the request, spinning in place, returning her gaze to the mirror as quickly as possible to watch the silky blend of the material glide across the tops of her knees. The fabric cinched in tight across her rib cage, then skirted out into classic A-lines creating an eye-pleasing curve at her hip. Shelby stopped spinning and stared in awe at her reflection. Despite the dress's shortcomings, she felt amazing matching her darling daughter.

"Let's go show Miss Maye!"

"I have a better idea. Let's invite Miss Maye over here. Then we can show her both dresses."

Shelby picked up her phone. "Hi Maye, how are you?" Pause. "We're great, thanks. We have something exciting we'd like to show you."

Pause.

"Your camera? Sure, why not?"

For all the dedicated hours Shelby poured into growing her business, she owed Maye credit for all the photographs that spurred her windfall. The unexpected partnership with Maye began one fall Sunday morning shortly after Paisley started walking.

Ready for church, the Lawrence ladies were out

front wearing the first pair of matching dresses Shelby had ever sewn. The pink and blue plaid sundresses took a full week's worth of naptimes and bedtimes to finish, all while Bryan was out of town for work.

That morning, as they strolled back and forth across the brick walk in the shade of the magnolia tree, Maye came out of her house, also dressed for church.

"Oh, my word. Y'all look like you stepped right out of a catalog," she hollered from across the street. She went inside and returned moments later, her SLR camera with its bulging lens hanging from her neck. "Can I please take a picture of you two pretty ladies?"

They spent the next few minutes posing and smiling and chatting.

By the time Paisley woke up from her nap that afternoon, Maye had emailed Shelby four edited images, all of them breathtaking in clarity and composition. One of the pictures was especially captivating, the kind of photo that stunned your eyes for a split-second. The focus was pristine. The depth of field, flawless.

In it, Shelby held baby Paisley's little hands as she toddled along, the lavish arms of the magnolia tree swooping down behind them. Shelby's carefree gaze was directed toward baby Paisley, who was smiling with her whole buttery face and staring dead center into the eye of the camera.

Shelby still remembered that exact moment the photo was taken. After unsuccessfully trying to get Paisley to look at the camera, Maye chanted "Abracadabra." Paisley's belly spilled over with unremitting baby giggles hearing the silly spell for the very first time.

That same chance afternoon, Shelby posted the photo on Facebook. The response that followed was overwhelming. Likes and comments rolled in for weeks, making it easily the most popular photo she'd ever posted. Even more than the number of likes, it was the palatability of the comments, soaking with surprise and dripping with approval, that made Shelby suspect she was on to something.

"When did you and Paisley start modeling?" asked Kara Martin, her college roommate.

"You should have an Etsy shop," suggested Linda Cho, their high school Valedictorian who was halfway through a Stanford MBA.

"Can I place an order for my sister and her two chickadees?" asked the Scottish lady she kept up with ever since their honeymoon to the British Virgin Islands.

"I can't believe you made those," shone through as the general reaction, a simple amazement at the notion of an otherwise busy person making the time to construct her own clothing. As her Pinterest following would attest, the online world was overflowing with undue admiration for something handmade and truly original.

The Sunday photo sessions continued over the next few months. Every time Shelby and Paisley wore homemade, matching creations, Maye met them in front of the magnolia tree, ready with her camera, faithful to return impressive images later that day for Shelby to use however she wanted.

As their helpful neighbor strolled up the same brick walk where Shelby's dress business began, Paisley raced to the door, opening it before Maye had a chance to knock.

"Look at me!" She curtsied, fanning out the skirt of the sparkleberry dress. "And look at my Mama. Don't we look cute?"

"Oh, my heavens. Y'all look adorable!" Maye followed Paisley to the mirrors in the guest room. "Congratulations, Shelby! How do you like them?"

"They're great. I mean, they're here. They're done. And I didn't do any of the sewing."

"So, you're happy with them?"

"I think so." Shelby bit the side of her lip.

"Uh-oh. What's wrong?" Maye asked.

"Nothing at all! They're really cute."

"But what?"

"It's just . . . they seem a little thrown together. But it's all fine, really."

Maye ran her fingers slowly along the hem, as if buying herself time to choose the right words. "It looks to me exactly like a dress you would buy at a store." The breathiness in Maye's voice seemed to make her words float through the air, never landing too hard.

"It does. I don't know what I was expecting. I guess I thought they would look more . . . more like how I make them." Shelby couldn't put her finger on what was bothering her about the dresses' construction. The silhouette and the fabric were exactly what she submitted to Dennis. They felt somehow . . . thinner, flimsier than she envisioned.

"How would you have made them?"

Shelby stood still as a mannequin, contemplating what looked off. "For starters, my dresses are fully lined. It uses twice the amount of material, but it ensures the skirt floats away from the body and isn't see-through. And I always match up the pattern on the sides. It takes more time and fabric, but it completely hides the seam lines."

"I see," Maye said.

"And I use an invisible zipper, so the fit looks more tailored."

"I'm just curious. How much are they selling these for?"

"Girl's will sell for $19.99. Women's will sell for $29.99, if you can believe that."

"Wow. Amazing prices. And they still make money?"

"They make plenty. Dennis said that's why they

make so many dresses. They don't make as much per dress, but they sell a hundred thousand pieces from one order. All the little margins add up to a big profit."

"And what would you sell them for if you made them your way?"

"My customers pay around $120, and Paisley's would cost more like $60. Of course, it depends on the costs of material and notions."

Maye's silence prompted further explanation.

"I have to charge at least that much to cover my costs *and* make any money." Shelby stared into the mirror. Shortcuts and all, the dress was growing on her, if for no other reason than she hadn't spent a second of her own time constructing it. She was certain her customers would think the dress looked just fine.

But something continued to bother her. How could there be such an enormous price difference? She made a mental note to clarify this with Dennis, even if the question further highlighted her vast inexperience.

"Well, I think it's wonderful that so many mothers and daughters will be able to wear your lovely dresses. You're so talented, Shelby. What a joy to share your special gift with the world."

"Thank you, Maye." Shelby blinked quickly to suppress the unexpected stirring of emotions. She never used to get teary-eyed from a compliment. Growing up, she lassoed in every opportunity for praise, relishing every prized word.

But ever since becoming a mom, with so much self-doubt swirling through her mind all the time, compliments didn't have the luxury of bouncing off the surface anymore. They burrowed into the childlike part of her soul that, even as a mom, still needed nurturing.

"Mama?" Paisley was standing on top of the guest bed, jumping up and flopping down on the mattress. "Did this dress cost nineteen thousand and ninety-nine dollars?"

"No, sweetie. It costs nineteen *dollars* and ninety-nine *cents*. That's about twenty dollars."

"I have twenty dollars in my piggy bank. Can I buy one for Runa? Then she can match with us too."

"Now that's a really thoughtful way of spending your money," Maye said, half-winking at Shelby. "What a generous little girl you are, Paisley."

An honest, hopeful smile reached across Shelby's face. It made her feel like she was doing something right as a parent whenever Paisley brought Runa into the conversation.

"Can we, Mama?" Paisley asked.

"Maybe. Do you think Ravi would tell me what size to send?" Shelby asked Maye.

"Oh, I'm sure he would," Maye said.

"Here's an idea, Little P. The dresses should be here in November. What if we send Runa's mommy one too?"

Paisley squealed. "Then we can all be twins. That's the bestest idea ever!"

"Well, that's the loveliest idea I've heard in a long time," Maye said with smiling eyes. "Now how about we take some pictures?"

As the page in the calendar turned, even the muggy Bayou City started to take on the likeness of fall. Daytime highs dipped out of the nineties, making the steam of a pumpkin spice latte tolerable. Pansies replaced tropical varieties in landscaping zones, in case winter temperatures dipped below freezing for a night or two in the cooler months to come.

Weeks from voting day, triumphs and hiccups from the election dominated the news. Everyone wanted to know if the first African American president of the United States could hold on against the Mormon business mogul turned governor.

As election news intensified and Hurricane Sandy pummeled the East Coast, a lightness descended over Shelby. An inner peace she hadn't experienced in some time blanketed her life. Shipping the last of her homemade dresses meant no longer living in the shadows of unfulfilled orders.

In the weeks that followed, Shelby planned ahead for the holidays, including purchasing the highly coveted Diggity Doll for Santa Claus to surprise Paisley with on Christmas morning. She shopped the sales for shoes, jewelry, and hair accessories to embellish her sample dresses in anticipation of media coverage. In between his trips to Nashville, Shelby and Bryan went on a long-overdue date to try the farm-to-table Tex Mex place in the Heights everyone was talking about.

As Shelby relished free time for herself, she remained not just aware, but grateful, that tens of thousands of her dresses were being sewn in the background of her life. Part of the reward for winning the contest meant *Buzz Now Magazine* and *Surface Trend Market* were footing the bill for the order and, therefore, absorbing the risk of lost revenue if dress sales didn't meet their projected targets.

One slower afternoon, while Shelby was cutting out the pattern for Paisley's Rapunzel costume, Dennis called with updates about the launch.

"Hi, Shelby. You got a minute?"

"Of course. What's the latest?" Shelby set down her scissors and reached for the notepad on the sewing table.

"Your dresses shipped. Ended up with 31,000 missy and 36,000 girls dresses for each of the two styles."

Shelby jotted down and quickly summed the numbers. "Wow. That's a lot of dresses."

"*Surface Trend* has over a thousand locations.

This should fill a rack or two at the front of every store."

"Well, that's exciting. And what about the magazine?"

"The issue is at the printer, set to land in mailboxes around the second week of November. Same time the dresses arrive in stores."

"Any updates on publicity?" *Buzz Now*'s PR team was handling media outreach across the country. The prospect of being interviewed by national publications made Shelby both nervous and excited.

"Team's on it. I'm hearing some decent early interest so far, but we'll have a better idea after we send the press release."

"Okay, great. Anything else I should be doing?"

"Leave your schedule wide open the rest of the year. We want to be able to accommodate as many interview requests as possible."

"Will do. And what about the next order? How will I know if I've done enough to get another chance?" Shelby listened closely for the response.

"*Surface Trend* will base that completely on sales," Dennis said. "Media attention is great, but it's more important that the dresses sell."

When the call was finished, Shelby set down the notebook and picked up the scissors. Only a few weeks of normal life remained until this chance opportunity might blossom into a lasting dream job. Anticipation needled at her—in more ways than one.

The next morning, as first chirps rang out from nearby trees, Shelby came out of the bathroom holding the missing piece of another dream.

She climbed back in bed and rubbed Bryan's shoulder until his green eyes slid open. She held up the stick so he could see.

"Are you ready for this?" she beamed.

The stick was pink. Exquisite, eye-stunning, life-altering pink.

Bryan's face awoke with a jolt. He sprang up and threw his arms around her. "Such great news!"

"I almost can't believe it." Shelby wiped a tear from her cheek.

"Do you think this one is for real?"

She considered their previous close calls. Of course, there was always a chance of loss. But the vibrance of this pink line resembling her test results with Paisley gave her every reason to think that yes, this baby would make it.

"I have a really good feeling. I think it's baby time." A smile rose up straight from her heart as the little plastic stick stirred their lives with hope.

Chapter 5

Laying on the bamboo floor of the yoga studio, Shelby felt like she could have rested there until nightfall. But the gym members attending the mid-morning Pilates class were already invading the room, forcing her to vacate her cozy spot.

A look into the expansive wall of mirrors revealed her ponytail had fallen loose during one of the morning's inversions. She straightened her hair, noticing dark roots starting to show. Time to schedule a touch-up with Veronica before the launch.

She snuck an inconspicuous peek at her profile. The fold-over waist of her yoga pants fit comfortably over her tummy. At five weeks, it was far too early to notice a bump. But it was never too early to start imagining one.

Not a hint of morning sickness had struck yet, though she was bracing for it. When pregnant with Paisley, she'd been sick almost every day during the first trimester. The daily battle eased up but didn't fully stop until after the 20-week ultrasound when her bump finally started to show. For now, she was just extra tired.

Shelby rolled up her mat, took a sip from her water bottle, then picked up her phone.

Exciting news! Call back ASAP.

The text from Dennis was accompanied by two missed calls and a voicemail, all of which caught Shelby off guard. He rarely called unannounced. Or used exclamation marks. And he certainly never bothered to leave a voicemail.

In any case, Shelby thought *she* was the one with news. She skipped the locker room where she might get tied up in small talk and headed straight to her car.

The first noticeable cold front of autumn swept through last night, welcoming a crisp breeze to the mid-morning air. Shelby slid into the cozy leather driver's seat, letting it hug her sleepy skin like a sun-warmed blanket. Having no idea what to expect, she called back. Dennis answered immediately.

"Shelby, what's going on?" His voice revealed an urgency that furthered her curiosity.

"Hi, Dennis. You've got me all nervous about your text. I called soon as I could."

"Are you sitting down?" he asked.

"Yep. Why, what's up?"

"Bad news, good news. The bad news is we need to push Carrie's cover story to February."

"Oh no! I'm sorry to hear that. Is everything okay?" Shelby felt disappointment barrel into her.

"Just a schedule conflict."

"So what does that mean for the cover?" Shelby froze, awaiting the news of who would be on the cover of her issue. What if some sullied celebrity were chosen, and her dresses were forever associated with that image, that reputation? Would she be able to overcome such a setback right out of the gate?

"What that means is very good news for you."

"How is that?" Shelby braced.

"Because it's you and Paisley." His words landed deadpan, like a dry punchline.

"Wait, what?"

"You and Paisley are going to be on the cover of the 2012 holiday issue of *Buzz Now Magazine*."

"No way! Are you serious?"

"Dead serious."

"But—what does this mean?"

"It means your dresses are going to have a whole lot more exposure than we planned. It means you're headed for more media appearances, possibly some travel. The inventory at *Surface Trend* will sell out quicker. They might even do a second run of dresses depending on how sales go the first week."

"What? That's incredible!" Shelby's hand landed on her forehead. She took a quick peek into the nearby cars' windshields to make sure no one saw her flipping out in the gym parking lot.

"We just got out of the editorial meeting. Legal is preparing an addendum to your contract and will email it to you. Gwen will send you the press release for a once-over when it's complete. Plan for the rest of the year to be unpredictable and extremely busy."

"Dennis . . . I'm in shock. Is this a normal thing? Do cover stories really get swapped at the last minute?" Shelby could hear the shake in her own voice.

"It's not the norm but not the first time. We just have to roll with it."

"Wow. I'm . . . wow. I just can't believe it. I'm so excited. And so . . . nervous."

"No need. Honestly, the reason you were chosen is because the feature turned out so well. The Christmas backdrop, the matching dresses, the wholesome family feel. It's the perfect image to anchor the holiday issue. Made it an easy decision for the editors."

Before saying another word, Shelby sat with the news. This was big. Cover story exposure as an up-and-coming designer could easily lock in her next contract at *Surface Trend*. As Paisley would put it, this was, quite possibly, the bestest thing ever.

"Dennis, I don't know what to say. Thank you, I suppose? Doesn't quite seem enough."

"You're very welcome," Dennis said. "Still a few details to knock out, so let's keep this under wraps until it goes to print. We'll announce it on socials after the press release hits. It's full speed ahead after that."

Full speed. That was the one thing Shelby held in short supply. She counted the weeks of the first trimester on her fingers. She'd be about eight weeks pregnant when the release went out. That was right smack at the beginning of when morning sickness mowed her over when she was pregnant with Paisley.

Given the timing, she considered telling Dennis about the pregnancy. But it was way too early. Nothing felt certain yet. She and Bryan agreed to keep the news quiet through the first trimester.

Come to think of it, in all their planning and preparing to become pregnant with a second child, she hadn't considered this timing glitch. She'd grown so used to not being pregnant each month, she never let herself think through how a first trimester might complicate a dress launch.

This news about the cover intensified absolutely everything. Their faces would appear on the front of 1.1 million magazines in mailboxes and grocery stores and nail salons across America. Online news and social media added another realm of exposure.

For the first time since the lines on the stick turned pink, Shelby felt a pinprick of regret—not about being pregnant or about growing their family, but about the timing. Getting pregnant with Paisley happened so quickly. But expecting a second baby had taken years. Why were they finally successful right when *Treasured Pockets* was launching in such a big way?

The most challenging month of pregnancy now aligned with the most defining month of her career. Like every woman she knew, she wanted all the things on her vision board to materialize— just not at the same time.

"Everything ok?" Dennis asked.

The pause drew on longer than Shelby meant. She blinked hard, refocusing her thoughts. "For sure. Just taking it all in. This is a pretty big deal."

"It's going to be great, Shelby. You've earned this. Time to enjoy the ride."

28 October 2012
Dear Shelby,

It was a joy to deliver the package to Runa at her school this afternoon. She was so excited to receive everything you sent. She asked my help to write this reply to Paisley, insisting I email it to you right away. She works very hard at school and is growing rather skilled in her English. I hope her words bring you as much joy as your family's gifts brought to her.

With thanks,
Ravi

Dear Paisley,

Thank you for the bear. She is very cute. It is great to meet you. I am 11 years old, and I love my school. I am learning English. I like to read books and learn new words. I like your drawing. I hope to play with you one day too.

We do not wear shoes in our house. My favorite princess is Rapunzel too! What foods do you like? What is the weather like where you live? Do you have brothers or sisters?

I thank your family for helping me go to school. Please write me back.

Love,
Runa

FOR IMMEDIATE RELEASE
Contact: Gwendolyn Rivera
303-BUZZNOW
(303-289-9669)

***Buzz Now Magazine* Introduces**
Award-Winning Label
***Treasured Pockets* for**
Surface Trend Market

Holiday issue features By Design contest winner Shelby Lawrence

Los Angeles – November 7, 2012 – *Buzz Now Magazine* is excited to announce the debut of a darling new clothing designer—for two. Shelby Lawrence is the founder of mommy-and-me dress label *Treasured Pockets*. She and her delightful daughter Paisley will star on the cover of *Buzz Now*'s holiday issue, which hits newsstands this week.

Treasured Pockets is a boutique dress label that specializes in producing matching mother-daughter dresses. "Mommy-and-me styles are becoming more popular, but *Treasured Pockets* holds the edge in fit," says *Buzz Now* Enterprises Director Dennis Chen. "Aside from pockets, the patterns look identical, but the dresses are designed to ensure the most flattering fit for both mothers and daughters."

Lawrence won *Buzz Now*'s 2012 By Design contest, taking home $25,000 cash and a once-in-a-lifetime design contract to mass-produce two holiday dresses for *Surface Trend* stores.

"A few months ago, I was a stay-at-home mom with a sewing boutique," Lawrence said. "Thanks to *Surface Trend* and *Buzz Now*, my designs will be worn by amazing mothers and daughters across the country. I still can't believe my dream is coming true."

Available in both missy (2-14) and girls (2T-14) sizes, *Treasured Pockets* coordinating dresses in two holiday party-ready styles are available in *Surface Trend Market* stores nationwide and online now through the end of the year, while supplies last.

Buzz Now Magazine is the nation's leading hybrid digital/print magazine that merges the online and offline worlds of fashion, lifestyle, and entertainment trends. Joining forces with New & Now *print subscribers in 2010,* Buzz Now *is transforming the role of print media in an increasingly out-of-print world for millions of global readers and followers. For more information, visit* buzznowmagazine.com.

The week following the press release was unlike any other in the Lawrence household. Shelby chatted away on Bryan's phone with a lifestyle reporter in L.A. Bryan took off from work to field calls and to pick up Paisley from school. Neither knew exactly how to handle this odd scenario, but they pretended their way through it.

"Oh, that's wonderful to hear. The pink or blue one?" Shelby asked the reporter.

Her phone rang, and Bryan answered it on the other side of the living room. Shelby watched him scribble notes onto a legal pad.

"Thank you so much, Angela. The pleasure was all mine, and I hope you love the dresses." Shelby hung up Bryan's phone. "Well, that was amazing. The lifestyle reporter has a little girl. She's buying the blue dresses to wear at their family Christmas party."

"That's awesome. I have more great news."

"Really? Who was that?"

"Dennis. Want to go to New York tomorrow?"

"No way! Are you serious?"

"The Weekend Style Blast wants to interview you and Paisley wearing the dresses on their holiday preview show. It films live on Saturday." Bryan looked up from his notes to catch Shelby's reaction.

"Seriously? New York? Tomorrow?" Her initial shock was followed by relief that her highlights were TV ready.

Bryan referenced his notes. "The travel desk will email your itinerary. He asked you to call him soon as you have a break from interviews."

"Bryan, this is unbelievable. I'm going to be on the Weekend Style Blast. *THE* Weekend Style Blast. LIVE. Whoa—live TV with a kid." Shelby's eyes widened.

"And you got a few more texts from people who saw you on the Bayou City Sunrise. I had no idea so many people watched local news."

"I put a teaser on socials last night. Sounds like I'll be putting New York on there next." Even with the first rounds of pregnancy nausea hitting this week, Shelby couldn't stop smiling. Nor did she try to.

"Here, call Dennis back. I've got to get Paisley." Bryan handed Shelby her phone.

"Good call. I totally lost track of time." Shelby pictured Bryan driving his oversized truck through the preschool pickup line. It wasn't Paisley's normal preschool day, but the school made an exception and squeezed her into another class. "Bry, do you think you can come with us—to New York?"

"I don't know. I'm guessing they won't pay for my ticket."

"Bryan, how many times do you think I'm going to fly to New York City to be on LIVE TV? You've got to come! Let's use some of my contest winnings. We can make a family vacation out of it . . . before everything changes again."

"I thought we agreed to put that money toward my student loans."

"We did. But not all of it."

"No, but quite a bit already disappeared with the first photoshoot."

"Yeah, which all led to this New York trip even happening. What's the problem?"

"Shel, you know taxes are taking a huge cut.

Once you add in last-minute airfare, extra hotel nights, all the meals out, and cab rides, there won't be much left."

Shelby felt a gust of outrage swirl up from the dark cave of her subconscious. How could $25,000 be so quickly made to feel like such a minuscule contribution? She felt a sudden urge to speak up. Instead, she swallowed her anger and stared at him, silent.

"I'm so excited for you. You know that." Bryan proceeded with caution. "I just don't think an expensive trip makes sense right now. And you know how I feel about flying together. I've got to go, or I'll be late to get Little P."

Shelby watched as Bryan grabbed his wallet and keys. Angry as she was, she knew where he was coming from.

In spring 2008, on the heels of Bryan's expensive graduate program, they had stretched every financial asset they had to pay top dollar for the two-story brick house in Acorn Heights. Shortly after the sale closed, markets plummeted, taking real estate values down with them. All the big architecture firms stopped hiring when Bryan was interviewing.

Unless *Surface Trend* invited her to design again, Shelby wasn't collecting any income from dress sales. A follow-up contract was the only way to get a hard cut of future sales, allowing them to pay down Bryan's loans, their expensive mortgage, and Paisley's tuition, relieving the financial pinch of a second child on the way.

"Let me talk to Dennis before we count you out," Shelby said. "I hear what you're saying, but this is once-in-a-lifetime stuff. I really want you with us."

"Of course, I want to go. But we need to think about what's best in the long run."

Bryan stepped out the door to the garage as Shelby's phone displayed an incoming call from a Los Angeles area code. She combed her fingers through her hair as if she were about to be on video. Closing her eyes and taking a yoga-inspired inhalation, she exhaled long and slow, visualizing what it would take to land the next design contract.

She opened her eyes and punched the call's green button with her thumb. "Hello? Yes, this is Shelby Lawrence."

Twenty-four hours later, the Lawrence ladies were in the air heading to New York City. As much as Shelby envisioned exploring the city with Paisley, she instead spent every spare minute Friday night and Saturday morning at the hotel updating, reposting, and engaging followers on social media while Paisley watched movies on her iPad.

Saturday afternoon, they took a taxi to the television studio. After hours of makeup, hair, and waiting for showtime, they were featured on the Weekend Style Blast, donning their sparkleberry holiday dresses and the thickest layers of makeup Shelby and Paisley had ever worn.

When filming began, Paisley the busybody completely froze, just as she had when the magazine photoshoot started. Much as it would have been nice to see her personality bubble over into the show, Shelby was relieved there were no surprises.

After the show, Paisley climbed into an umbrella stroller. As Shelby pushed her toward Seventh Avenue, Paisley squealed at the vision of thousands of people from all over the world meandering every direction across Times Square.

"Mama, look at that!" Paisley practically fell out of the seat, pointing at the enormous screens lining each skyscraper with ads for Broadway musicals, caffeinated beverages, and hit TV shows.

"Little P, check that out." Shelby pointed to someone in a giraffe costume dancing on a stage to loud, bass-heavy music.

A man wearing a superhero costume was selling solar-powered plastic cats that waved a paw back and forth.

"Mama, can I please have one of those?"

Shelby wasn't keen on buying tacky, overpriced junk, but Paisley had been a good sport all day. And she used her manners without being prompted.

"Okay. But this is the only thing we're going to buy."

"Can we please get one for Runa too?"

"Sure, why not?" Shelby pulled a $20 bill out of her purse. She swapped the cash for the cats and handed them to Paisley.

"Thanks, Mama. This is the bestest day ever!"

Shelby pushed the stroller around the corner toward the largest *Surface Trend Market* she'd ever seen.

"Mama, it's our dresses!" Paisley leaped out of the stroller toward the large window display, where pairs of mother-daughter mannequins wore both sets of *Treasured Pocket* dresses.

As they rounded the corner into the store, a young mom stopped her. "Hey, weren't you just on the Weekend Style Blast?"

Shelby blushed and shook the woman's hand.

She would have to agree with Paisley. This just might be the bestest day ever.

At home Sunday evening, Shelby finished her dinner in a still, silent kitchen while waiting for Dennis to call and confirm the week's media schedule. When nothing remained of her barbecue sandwich, she got up from the kitchen table and tossed her empty plate in the trash. If there were ever a week to skip dishes, this was it.

Bryan was upstairs putting Paisley to bed, an easy gig considering how little they'd slept that weekend. Shelby was ready to start the call so she could climb into bed herself. She texted Dennis.

Can you talk now?

Wrapping up. Will call soon.

Shelby used the free minutes to start packing Paisley's lunch for tomorrow. As she wrestled the turkey slices out of their packaging, her stomach felt heavy. For some reason, pulled pork didn't disturb her pregnancy preferences one bit, but deli meat repulsed her.

Also nonsensical was the fact that she'd been fighting off lingering nausea and fatigue for weeks, yet she was able to power through 36 mostly awake hours in New York City like she was back in college. Thankfully, for whatever reason, she wasn't getting sick every morning like she did with Paisley. The slump of the first trimester couldn't compete with the rush of fame.

Finally, her phone rang.

"Shelby Lawrence. Name of the hour. How are you?" The hint of victory in Dennis's voice provided a much-needed jolt of energy.

"Dennis—I'm exhausted. Y'all are wearing me out."

"Hah, I know. And we're just getting started."

"Tell me about it. The schedule this week looks insane. Y'all have me running all over the place."

"The PR team really crushed it. Gwen is about to email you the final schedule of *Surface Trend* appearances. We left it at one per day until Black Friday."

"And nothing on Thursday, right?"

"That's right. We can all enjoy Thanksgiving off. *The News Journal* piece should run on Sunday. Biggest Sunday edition of the year."

"That's amazing. When will the photographer be here?"

"Tuesday morning, before you head to The Woodlands."

"Ok perfect. We're ready with the Christmas tree."

Bryan hauling a blue spruce inside and hanging ornaments while watching the Texans game wasn't how any of them envisioned decorating the Christmas tree this year. The important thing was it was done. One less thing to scramble together before the *Houston News Journal* showed up.

"Perfect. Let me see here," Dennis said.

Shelby could hear his eyes scrolling through his task list.

"Social media has been explosive. Your numbers look great. The stores will be tagging you all week, so try to stay on top of shares and retweets as best you can."

"Will do. Everything has been nuts. I had 300 new followers in the half hour after The Blast. Definitely a record for me."

"That's great. Everything on my list is tracking well. The only thing we miscalculated was the dress numbers."

"What do you mean? They're not selling?" Shelby's heart began pounding.

"No, that's all great—a little too great. They're at risk of selling out in some stores before Black Friday."

"Really?"

"Just got out of the meeting with *Surface Trend*'s production team. They want to expedite a second order for online-only sales."

"A second run? Of the same dresses?"

"Almost. Same styles and patterns. Just different colors. The material for the berry dress is going to be a deep scarlet. The baby doll dress will be a winter white."

"That's amazing! But wait, the last run took six weeks. How can they turn it around so fast?"

"The designs and sizes are already finalized. The construction is rinse and repeat. They'll dye the scarlet material on site and start sewing the white dress immediately. Production begins as soon as contracts are in."

"Okay, wow. That's so fast," Shelby marveled. "I don't want to sound like I'm second-guessing you, but isn't this cutting it a little close for Christmas?"

"Assuming nothing gets held up in customs, the dresses should arrive at the distributor's warehouse the first week of December. They'll ship out directly to customers as soon as they're in. It's a tighter turnaround than we would usually do, but there are plenty of days left before holiday parties and Christmas pageants. They'll be on backorder for a week or two, but the important thing is we'll lock in the sales while the interest is there."

"Got it. That all sounds fine to me. But wait—is this all within my original contract?"

"No, this is additional. Legal will send over a new contract for you to sign. You get a cut of every extra dress that sells, very likely before the end of the year."

"Well, that's exciting. How many in this run?"

"We're looking at half the numbers—about 15,000 of each design. We know the demand is there, and both the red and white versions can roll into Valentine's. If nothing else, they'll sell out on clearance."

"Dennis, this feels like . . . like a fairy tale," Shelby said. A second run was in motion only a week after the first arrived in stores. That first chunk of earnings might be deposited in their checking account by Christmas. She couldn't wait to tell Bryan.

"Good things happen when you make something Americans want to buy at a price they're willing to pay."

"I guess so," Shelby said, her eyes blinking hard in disbelief. Moments ago, she was dozing off at the kitchen table. Now she wasn't sure she'd be able to fall asleep tonight.

They finished up the last few details and ended the call. Shelby studied the schedule of *Surface Trend* appearances. Monday evening in Sugarland. Tuesday in The Woodlands. Wednesday at Katy Mills. Finally, Black Friday at Houston's most popular locations: Memorial City Mall, Baybrook Mall, and the storied Galleria, just outside the loop. Shelby gritted her teeth, thinking through the nightmarish traffic and the late nights ahead of them.

Oh, but the second run.

Plus, the exposure from the week ahead could help her brand swing its momentum into *Surface Trend*'s 2013 line-up. A sweet smile floated across her face considering all this might mean.

Tucked away in a quiet corner of the week's agenda was an ultrasound appointment, scheduled for first thing Wednesday morning. Busy as this week would be, Shelby wasn't about to postpone it. Bryan rescheduled a meeting to attend with her, and Elise offered to take Paisley to school.

But more than that, having those pictures—the

blessed confirmation—in hand on Thanksgiving Day was too tantalizing to pass up. Five years ago, amid the sparkle of Christmas morning, revealing the news about Paisley brought a look of pure joy into her mother's eyes. There was something innately magical about the promise of new life.

This time, the new life would create a sibling—the piece of the puzzle that had always felt missing from Shelby's life. More than anything happening in the week ahead, Shelby couldn't wait to tell Paisley she was going to have a little brother or sister. A forever friend was on the way.

Hopefully.

Shelby's mind turned down the prickly path, wondering what she'd do if they found out something wasn't quite right. Her shoulders stiffened bearing the weight of uncertainty. How quickly hope could turn to doubt.

She closed her eyes tight and lowered her forehead to the mahogany kitchen table. She wasn't crying. Just processing.

A second run was huge. But the ultrasound would be even more life-changing. No matter what happened, the week ahead would weigh on their lives forever.

Chapter 6

Nothing about the ambiance of the medical complex was any shade of romantic, but that Wednesday morning Shelby and Bryan held hands as they walked through the parking lot toward the boxy brick building of her OBGYN.

Had she been the one to reach for his hand? Or perhaps he lured her hand into his. She couldn't remember. But his familiar palms aligning with hers felt strange and comfortable all at the same time. Ever since Paisley was born and her arms were always so full, there was no longer the same pull to walk holding hands.

But today, the pull was magnetic.

Trying for a baby for three whole years complicated so many aspects of their relationship. And it was so unexpected. She'd had no trouble getting pregnant with Paisley. Ever since, Shelby and Bryan hadn't always felt in step with each other. His climb up the ladder at the architecture firm had become more demanding than they would've ever imagined.

But on a day like today, they craved reassurance of their connection—no matter what. They continued holding hands as they walked up the stairs to the obstetrician's office.

At the top of the stairs, Bryan opened the door allowing Shelby to pass through like royalty. A perk of being pregnant were these extra caring gestures. Of course, she could still complete the same tasks on her own. But it felt luxurious not having to. Shelby signed in at the front desk, and they took their seats in the waiting room.

After what felt like an eternity, a tall woman in cornflower blue scrubs emerged. "Shelby Lawrence?" she called out.

They leaped up and followed the woman down a long hallway into the exam room, which happened to be the same sacred space where, five years earlier, they learned their baby was a little girl.

Shelby reclined on the padded exam chair and tugged up the tails of her flowy blouse to reveal her belly. Bryan sat in a chair beside her, facing the screen on the wall.

The ultrasound tech shuffled some papers on a clipboard, then washed her hands and sat down in a swivel chair next to Shelby. "Just a reminder—the gel will be a little chilly," she said. She squirted a golf ball–sized puddle of clear goop onto the skin below Shelby's bellybutton. Reaching into a tower of medical devices, she grasped a white stick resembling a microphone attached to a long cord. "Let's see what we can see."

She pressed the wand on Shelby's abdomen,

squishing into the puddle of goop. Moments later an image emerged overhead on a TV screen. Shelby squinted, trying to make sense of the grainy puzzle pieces. Then it all became crystal clear.

"There's your baby," the technician said cheerfully.

A feathery white bead floated effortlessly inside a dark balloon. Shelby leaned closer.

There it was. Their baby.

A tiny human, the essence of life, pin-balled from edge to edge in its cozy little world of liquid bliss. Shelby was fixated on the sight. Unexpected tears released one after the next, dripping silently down her temples into the pockets of her ears.

She didn't remember when, but she noticed Bryan slid his chair closer, right by her side. His fingers, once again, threaded into hers. For the seven heavenly minutes that followed, their hands fused tightly together while their eyes feasted upon the most transformative sight.

Life.

Their baby's life.

Their lives joining together.

Living. Moving. Breathing. Life.

Home and settled after their appearance at Katy Mills Mall, Shelby brought the photo roll to bed so she could stare at the eight images of the mystical, grainy bead into the final moments of the day. She tucked the proof away in the nightstand drawer and fell asleep before Bryan turned off the bedside lamp.

The next morning, the Lawrence household slept in. The stress from the week, from getting slathered with makeup and draped in accessories, from driving all over the massive expanse of Harris County, from greeting hundreds of new customers at *Surface Trend* stores, from constantly monitoring activity on socials, from hanging in the balance of pregnancy disappointment or celebration—all of it added up to complete and total exhaustion.

Perhaps more than any other Thanksgiving, Shelby was grateful for the day off. But more than that, her deepest thanks on this day of gratitude lay on the scroll of thin photo paper revealing the first glimpse of their family's next chapter. A whole new person to ponder.

When Shelby woke up that lazy morning, Bryan was still out hard. His head lay heavy on the pillow next to hers. She stared at the stillness of his face in the muted morning light. So endearing that a fully-grown man could resemble a helpless baby when he slept.

Feeling not that queasy, Shelby pushed the down comforter off her legs and swiveled her feet to the floor to find her slippers. Across the room, a sneaky eye peeked through the cracked door to their bedroom. A little mouse was investigating if the coast was clear.

Shelby smiled and nodded her head, signaling for Paisley to come in. Kicking her legs back under the covers, she welcomed Paisley into the feathery warmth. Bryan stirred, and they lay there all together, snuggled up with an unusual feeling that everything that truly mattered was present in the heap of blankets and sheets.

"Happy Thanksgiving, Little P." Shelby's arm wrapped tightly around Paisley's waist.

"Is today really Thanksgiving?"

"It sure is. We'll have a feast later."

"Can I have pumpkin pie and ice cream?"

Shelby grinned, amused by the sweet vision. "Sure."

"And deep-fried turkey and smoked brisket and mashed sweet potatoes and apple sausage stuffing and green bean casserole," Bryan added.

"You saw the order," Shelby said.

"Yep. Looks like a feast, alright."

Shelby squeezed her arms tighter around Paisley's little body. Then she looked at Bryan and spoke to him without saying a word, the way people who'd spent a decade of their lives together could do. She questioned with her eyes if this was the right time to tell Paisley.

He replied with a shrug and a scrunched brow that asked, *why not?* When *was* the right time to tell a child about the emergence of a new sibling?

No one, certainly not Bryan, knew the rules for this kind of thing. Shelby couldn't wait any longer.

"Sweetie, we have a surprise for you." Shelby sat up and propped the pillow against the quilted headboard.

"For me? Can I have it now?"

"Well, it's not really an it. It's a who. Here, look at this." From the drawer of the nightstand, Shelby pulled out the long, slinky roll of cryptic-looking black and white images. She didn't know why, but her heart was pounding like she was about to speak on stage.

"What is that?" Paisley reached for the pictures and looked closely into them.

"That," Shelby pointed to the round, white dot, "is a baby."

"That's a baby?"

"Yep."

"A person baby?"

"Yes." Shelby smiled at Bryan. "A person baby. Do you know where that baby is?"

Paisley inspected the full length of the photo roll. "Is it inside a film camera?"

Shelby and Bryan busted into an inside joke kind of laughter. Paisley had never seen a roll of film before, but she'd heard the outdated process explained in worn library books and when they looked through Shelby and Bryan's glossy old family photos.

"No, sweetie. But that's a great guess. That baby is . . . inside my belly." As if on cue, Paisley transformed into a firework of delight.

"There's a baby—in there?!" Paisley tossed the covers back wildly and pointed to the belly of Shelby's satin nightgown.

"Yes, sweetie. We're going to have a baby," Bryan said, rubbing his hand across Paisley's back. "You're going to be a big sister."

"I am?!" Paisley half asked, half exclaimed. "When? When does the baby come out?"

Shelby's eyes caught Bryan's in visual agreement. Far simpler answering *when* the baby comes out than *how*.

"Not until next summer, when you're all done with Pre-K."

"Next summer? But that's too far away."

"It might seem like a long time, but we wanted you to know now so we could all celebrate together." And because, realistically, there was no way to tell the rest of the family later without Paisley overhearing. Little ears tended to listen more closely than they ever let on.

Paisley stared again at the pictures of the dot. "Is it a girl baby or a boy baby?"

"We don't know yet, but we'll let you know as soon as we find out," Bryan said.

"If it's a girl baby, can we name her Rapunzel?"

Shelby snickered. "We'll think about it."

It was a paper plate Thanksgiving. Shelby's mom Irene, who Paisley called Mimi, arrived from Round Rock just as Santa Claus appeared on TV at the Macy's Day parade. Soon after the Texans kicked off against the Lions, the caterer showed up to deliver the decadent spread Shelby selected from the holiday menu. Bryan's parents, who usually hosted Thanksgiving at their lake house, were spending the week with Bryan's brother Todd, who was stationed in Hawaii.

Aunt Sharon and Uncle Charlie drove in from Port Arthur. They brought their Shih Tzu, Lullaby, along with a trunk full of packages.

In front of the Christmas tree, Paisley tore through the presents to find gingerbread cookie pajamas, monogrammed red and green smocked dresses, holiday activity books, and a chocolate-a-day Advent calendar. Ten seconds into the holiday season, and she was fully outfitted for the month of festivities ahead.

Shelby vowed to take the day off from social media to focus on family time, but when the food arrived looking and smelling so amazing, she couldn't resist the opportunity. The guys were engrossed with the football score, which stayed close well into the fourth quarter. Paisley was out back with Mimi, Aunt Sharon, and Lullaby.

Prepping the photo op, Shelby spread a white linen tablecloth across the long, formal table in the dining room. She arranged platters of decadent menu items, lit two slender burgundy candlesticks, and sprinkled dried cranberries across the table. Within minutes, she shared their spread with her now 44,000 followers across all platforms, tagging the caterer.

Soon as the game wrapped up, she called everyone over to the feast. Each family member piled sizzling meats and succulent sides onto fancy cardboard plates. When they were all seated, Paisley led the blessing.

"Dear Jesus, thank you for our food, our friends, and our family. Amen."

Bryan began the conversation to set up their big reveal. "I thought this year it might be nice to all say one thing we're thankful for."

"Well, that's a nice idea," Mimi said.

"I wanna go first," Paisley interjected.

"Sure. Go ahead, sweetheart." It wasn't how Bryan and Shelby had planned to announce their news, but it would make for just as priceless a moment if Paisley spilled the baby beans.

"I'm thankful for my new clothes and my new toys," Paisley said. Shelby beamed upon hearing her child's words of gratitude.

"How lovely," Aunt Sharon said. "You're so welcome, darling."

"I'm thankful I'm not like Runa. She doesn't have many toys." As Paisley said the words, Shelby cringed.

"Who is Runa?" Aunt Sharon asked.

"She's our friend who lives far away," Paisley replied. "The floor in her house is made of dirt."

"She's the little girl we're sponsoring," Shelby explained. "She lives in Bangladesh."

"We're pim pals!"

"*Pennn* pals," Shelby corrected.

"A pen pal? I'm glad to hear those still exist." Irene reached her arm around Paisley's shoulder, giving her a little squeeze. "Are you writing letters back and forth?"

"Yup!"

"Well, sort of," Shelby said. "Paisley tells me what to say, and I email it to this guy at the Caring Hope Organization. He prints what we send and takes the messages to Runa. We sent her a couple of packages, and she's written back a few times."

"Wanna see her picture, Aunt Sharon? It's on the fridge." Paisley popped up to retrieve the photo before her great aunt had time to respond.

"Yes, of course," Aunt Sharon said.

"Paisley is learning that not all children in our world are as fortunate as she is," Bryan added.

"Well, that's the truth," Aunt Sharon said as she scooped a lump of sweet potato mash onto her fork. "Not all children in this city, for that matter."

"What a nice thing to teach at such a young

age," Mimi said. "You and Bryan are doing such a wonderful job."

"Thanks, Mom." Shelby smiled and took a sip of sparkling water.

Paisley returned with the picture and walked around the table introducing everyone to Runa.

Bryan cleared his throat and reached for his glass. "Why don't you go next, Uncle Charlie?"

"Okay, sure. Well, I'm most thankful for the economy coming back. People are buying and selling homes fairly predictably again. So that's been good."

"It's been good for us too. Was a rough stretch there for a while," Bryan added. "Your turn, Aunt Sharon."

"I'm thankful Hurricane Sandy didn't hit the Gulf Coast. I certainly wouldn't wish that destruction on anyone else, but it feels like we've only just recovered from Ike and Rita." Aunt Sharon looked at Charlie. "I'm glad it wasn't already our turn again, you know?"

"Amen to that," Uncle Charlie said, shaking his head.

"Mimi, how about you?" Bryan prompted.

"I'm thankful I can see the light at the end of the tunnel. My TRS account has inched its way back up. I can't wait to retire so I can spend more time with you all, especially with Paisley." She stroked her hand down the length of her granddaughter's hair.

"We're ready for that too, Mom." Shelby met her mom's eyes with a sincere smile.

Mimi continued, "I'm having trouble finding the energy to make it through a full school year, especially with this whole standardized test nonsense. I'm ready for the working part of my life to be in the past."

"It would be really nice to see you more than just holidays," Shelby said.

"Hopefully this time next year, I'll be nearing the *R* word."

"That would be wonderful," Bryan said. "Your turn, Shel."

"For starters, I'm thankful I didn't cook any of this." Everyone laughed, and Shelby continued. "No, really. First off, I'm thankful for all of you. And, of course, for winning the contest. This time last year, I had no idea any of this was in store. It's been a wild ride, and I'm just really happy to be where I am."

"We're so proud of you, Shelby. Dear would be too," her mom said, the glow of candlelight reflecting in her eyes.

Shelby felt a pang of sadness hearing her grandmother's name around the Thanksgiving table. Every year growing up, Dear hosted the most memorable Thanksgiving dinners, from the menu to the decorations. In the weeks before, she'd ask each person attending to request a favorite side dish, which she'd prepare from scratch. Dear had a way of making every family member feel like the most special person at the table.

"Thanks, Mom," Shelby said. "Just wish she were here."

"So proud of you, Shel. Cheers to you." Bryan lifted his glass, and Shelby collected herself as everyone toasted.

Bryan stood up from his seat at the end of the table. "And last, but not least," he said, "I am thankful for next summer, when our family will grow by one."

"What?!" Shelby's mom and aunt gasped simultaneously. Hands flew across mouths and over hearts, as if attached by ripcords.

"I'm gonna be a big sister!" Paisley added, as if they'd rehearsed.

"Oh, how wonderful!" Mimi stood, reaching to hug Shelby.

"I'm so happy!" Aunt Sharon stood to join the huddle, her eyes sparkling with tears.

The room erupted with joyful squeals and clanking glasses and everyone abandoning plates to stand up and hug or shake hands with everyone else. They all gathered in front of the Christmas tree for a spontaneous group selfie before returning to the feast.

Excited as she'd been to share this news, Shelby was overcome by the merry rumble of the response. She didn't think this second announcement would garner near as much reaction as the first. Yet, having already welcomed a wondrous new branch on the family tree, everyone seemed even more thrilled at the prospect of another.

When the sauce-soaked plates and their unwanted crumbles of stuffing were piled in the trash, Shelby, Mimi, and Aunt Sharon mulled over how to distribute the mountain of leftovers. "They really outdid themselves with all of this," Mimi said.

"My fault for over-ordering," Shelby said. "Figured it would be better to have too much than not enough."

"No one's leaving hungry, that's for sure," said Aunt Sharon.

Shelby opened the fridge to stack away the leftovers. "Good thing I didn't get groceries. This fridge is about to be as full as Uncle Charlie."

"We still have pie and ice cream waiting in the garage fridge," Mimi added.

Paisley ran into the kitchen. "Can I have pie and ice cream now?" she asked.

"My, what a good listener we have," Aunt Sharon said.

Multiple flavors of pie and Blue Bell ice cream rotated as if on a carousel from the fridge in the garage to dessert plates on the table. As Shelby put away the pie buffet, she noticed the clock on the microwave. It was well past Paisley's normal bedtime, and another early alarm awaited them.

Shelby walked behind the sofa and squeezed

Bryan's shoulder. "Hey Bry—it's time for Paisley to go up." As Bryan pried Paisley away from drawn-out hugs and last rounds of fetch with Lullaby, Shelby went upstairs to the bedroom to prepare their wardrobe and makeup for the early morning. Something about Black Friday filled her with nerves, like the night before the first day of school. It felt like anything could happen.

Quite possibly, it was already happening. Many stores were opening now, the earliest they ever had on Thanksgiving night. Cable news channels showed hundreds of shoppers lining up outside a popular toy store. Others were already queuing up at an electronics store that didn't open until midnight.

Who are all these people?

Before heading downstairs to say goodbye to their dinner guests, she checked her social media accounts and posted one last reminder of tomorrow's schedule at *Surface Trend Market*. She sprinkled personal replies to followers' questions. Fifteen new people requested to follow her since she sat down for dinner, probably from the catering company's tagged post.

Finishing up on socials, she peeked at email. A flurry of new messages announced Black Friday discounts, online promo codes, early bird in-store deals, and Cyber Monday teasers.

Scanning subject lines, one email was worth opening. Ravi had written back.

Dear Bryan and Shelby,

Greetings of peace and thanksgiving. I pray this finds you and your family healthy and well.

This evening I went to Runa's school to deliver the box of items you sent. I have attached a photograph and the picture of a letter she wrote, which I translated below. She and her mother Nipa are most grateful for the dresses and for your abundance of gifts and blessings, most especially for helping defray the costs of Runa's school. It has always been Nipa's dream for her daughter to receive a good education.

Thank you again for your support. May God bless your family with good health and all your heart's desires.

Sincerely,
Ravi

Shelby clicked on the attachment to reveal the photograph. Staring back at her were Runa and her mother in front of a blue door and white wall. They stood side by side wearing the same bright sparkleberry dresses Shelby just pulled from the closet. A delicate purple shawl draped across Nipa's shoulders.

Compared to Shelby and Paisley's photo in the *Houston News Journal*, their smiles looked reserved. At first glance, the pair appeared timid and shy. But a closer look at their eyes revealed unspeakable joy.

It seemed like ages ago when Shelby mailed the dresses, well before the magazine hit stands. Now this mother-daughter pair halfway around the world looked back at her from a screen in her bedroom.

Seeing this girl and her mom wearing her dresses knocked Shelby over with pride. For the first time, this child, who had seemed more like an idea, an abstraction, seemed like someone she might know. She pictured Nipa and Runa meeting her and Paisley for lunch on the green at City Centre, arriving at the brick-lined front steps of a home in Acorn Heights, enjoying lemonade and fruit tarts at a backyard birthday party.

Shelby took a closer look at the picture. Cradled inside Runa's arm was Ballet Bear, the stuffed animal Paisley sent the day of the early pregnancy loss. Shelby's heart swelled with thanks thinking about the dream now growing inside her. Another little one on the way.

She scrolled down to read Ravi's translation of the accompanying letter from Runa.

Dear Bryan, Shelby, and Paisley,
My deepest thanks to you, my dear sponsors, for the kindness and blessings you have shared with me and my mother.

Thank you very much for supporting my school needs. Your help is very important to fulfill my dreams in life.

Thank you, kind sponsors, for the beautiful dresses. I am so happy to wear it, and my mother is too. She works very hard and takes good care of me. She wishes me to continue in school. I would like to become a doctor to help people who are injured. I hope to finish my studies, and one day, when I have a good job, I will help my mother to have a good life and also give back to Eternal Promise, my second home.

Once again, I thank you very much for the kindness in your heart. Your support means everything to me.

With love,
Runa Binu Zaman

Tears emerged in the corners of Shelby's eyes. Reaching for a tissue off the nightstand, she dabbed them away. This photo, these words, these smiles espoused the true purpose of her calling. There seemed endlessly more to her dresses' story than fabric and thread. Tucking that thought into her heart, she prepped their accessories for Black Friday.

Chapter 7

The day after Thanksgiving kicked off as every day did. With work to do.

Early that morning, darkness blanketed the neighborhood as Shelby assembled her hair, her face, and her mindset for the long hours ahead. Once sufficiently arranged, she crept into Paisley's room. The glow from a nightlight illuminated her baby girl's angelic face. Shelby hated to wake her.

"Little P. Good morning, Little P. Time for the big day." She stroked two fingers across the girl's forearm. Paisley's eyes darted open. A little hand grabbed the satin edge of the lavender fleece blanket. She flipped over, cinched her eyes closed, and tucked her knees in like a roly poly.

Shelby spent the next five minutes poking, prodding, and coaxing Paisley out of bed. Considering all the hours she and Bryan spent pleading their child to sleep, this struck as an unfamiliar challenge.

"But it's still night-night outside." Paisley sat up, rubbing her eyes with balled fists.

"Today's our big day. Remember?"

"But I want to stay in bed." The grouchy undertones didn't bode well for the long hours ahead. Who could blame her, though? It wouldn't have been Shelby's choice to trade sleeping for shopping.

Shelby helped Paisley maneuver the sparkle-berry dress over her head, threading arms through armholes. In the hallway bathroom, a curling wand waited hot and glowing. Shelby grabbed the hairbrush and set to work taming tangles.

"Ouch!" Paisley yelled, swatting the brush away. "Stop it, Mama!"

"Paisley, we don't have time for this. If we don't stay on schedule, we'll be late. Don't you want your curls to match Mommy's?"

"No, I don't." Paisley smooshed her elbows against her ears, holding her hair hostage.

Shelby set the brush down on the bathroom counter. If she could purchase cooperation at this moment, she would. She picked up her phone. Perhaps a screen would do the trick.

Then she remembered the email from Ravi.

"I have something exciting to show you if you let me brush your hair."

"What is it?" Paisley lowered her arms to reach for the phone.

"Check this out."

"Hey, it's Runa! Mama, she's wearin' my same dress!" Paisley laughed. "Mama, look!"

Shelby laughed, tugging the brush through Paisley's long strands. "Can you believe it? Runa and her mom are wearing *our* dresses. The same dresses you and I are wearing right now."

"We're all twins, Mama."

"Exactly like you wanted." Shelby wrapped a long strand of hair around the hot curling wand.

"Mama, she's holding Ballet Bear! And she's wearing the princess sticker I sent!"

"She is! And to think, she got that from you a month ago. She must really love it."

Paisley smiled, staring into the picture. "Did she write back?"

"Yes, she did. Here, hold it up and I'll read it."

After hearing Runa's message, Paisley scrolled down to study the picture again.

"Whatcha thinking about?" Shelby sprayed the mass of ringlets and affixed a bow atop her head.

"I wish I could play with Runa some time."

"I wish you could too. Why don't we send Runa the silly cat you got her in New York?"

"Oooo for her Christmas present?"

"Yes. Exactly."

"Can we send it today?"

"Not today, sweetie. Today's going to be very busy. But soon."

"Can we send them a picture of us in our dresses so they can see how we all match?"

"Absolutely. Let's take a selfie in front of the tree."

After their quick photoshoot, Shelby grabbed a couple of breakfast bars and a cup of coffee. When she started the car, Mariah Carey's "All I Want for Christmas" was playing. Belting out the chorus energized them both for the long, crowded day ahead.

By the time they exited toward Memorial City Mall, the sun was just starting to make an appearance in the eastern horizon. Barely onto the feeder road, they found their place in a lake of brake lights.

"Mama, are we in traffic?"

"Yes. Welcome to the Christmas shopping season."

After idling through three rotations of red lights, they crept through the intersection and turned into the great expanse of the mall parking lot, which was aglow in holiday splendor. Palm trees wrapped with colorful lights joined larger-than-life electric light displays illuminating the medians. A 50-foot-tall Christmas tree towered over the mall's main entrance.

"Mama, look at all the lights! It's just like Times Square."

"I think it's just as packed." They waited their turn as one car after the next pulled forward out of the feeder lanes.

"This is the mostest cars I've ever seen." Paisley unclipped the chest strap of her car seat, then leaned forward to investigate out the side windows. "Are these people all here to see the lights?"

"Not exactly. They're all here to go shopping."

"All at the same time?"

"I guess so. Today is a special kind of shopping day."

"Like a holiday?"

"Sort of. The stores mark their prices way down on the stuff they sell. Sometimes it's just for a few hours early in the morning."

"What happens after that?"

"Then the prices go back up. Everyone who wants to shop gets up early, so they don't miss the best deals."

"I'm glad we're not gonna miss it. There are so many people. And so many cars. And so many lights!"

Shelby watched the minutes flick away on the dashboard clock as they waited their turn to round the corner toward the lined spaces. It was half-past six, and the lot was nearly at capacity. The impatient consumer inside her felt a spark of annoyance until she remembered her role today. She wasn't attending any of this as a shopper. Today was her chance to meet customers in person. Plus, a successful day could invite that next *Surface Trend* contract she so desperately craved.

The fuller the lot, the better.

Shelby elbowed her silver SUV into a parking spot in the far back corner, the farthest away she'd ever parked.

Once out of the car, she loaded up Paisley's old stroller with a bag of supplies and a box of *Buzz*

Now holiday issues. The long walk in began.

They stopped outside the entrance so Shelby could change into heels. The automatic double doors parted enthusiastically to welcome them.

"That was sooo far, Mama," Paisley said. "I didn't think we were gonna make it."

Once inside, every set of eyes turned to face them. Chatter buzzed, and fingers pointed discreetly in their direction. Cashiers were busy checking out shoppers at every register. Each line backed up ten to twelve customers deep.

A hand tapped her on the shoulder. "Mrs. Lawrence? Is that you?"

"Yes, good morning. You must be Linda?"

"Yes, I was just about to call you. We're all so excited to have you with us today. And you must be Paisley?"

Paisley shrunk away, wrapping an arm around Shelby's left leg and pulling in close.

"We're excited to be here," Shelby asserted. "Sorry we're a few minutes late. The parking lot is truly unbelievable."

"It's just as packed inside. Here, let me help you with that."

Pushing the stroller load of supplies, Linda escorted Shelby and Paisley to the women's apparel section. A line of customers the length of the store formed in the aisle. It snaked around the corner, past the shoes, and into the housewares section. Shelby noticed dozens of mothers and little girls in line were wearing her matching dresses.

And that's when it struck Shelby why there were so many cars in the parking lot.

"They're all here to see *you*," Linda said. Then turning to address the crowd in line, she announced, "Good morning, *Surface Trend* guests. I would like to introduce Shelby and Paisley Lawrence of *Treasured Pockets*."

The line erupted into cheers and applause. Paisley curled in close to her mom, shuddering away from the unexpected noise. Phones and cameras pointed toward them.

"Smile, Little P." Shelby scraped Paisley's arms off from around her leg. "Can you believe they're all here to see you and me? Think you can give them a little wave?"

Relaxing her stance, Paisley smiled and waved back at the crowd. They stood in place for a minute, soaking in the applause. After everything she'd worked for, it felt so good for her effort to be not just recognized, but celebrated.

"Sweetie," Linda turned to Paisley, "are you ready to meet all these people?"

Paisley shook her head up and down like a bobble doll, and Linda walked them over toward the front of the line. Shelby and Paisley set to work shaking excited hands, doling out awkward hugs, taking endless selfies, and signing away issues of *Buzz Now*. It was a familiar feeling after a week of promotions, but today's crowd was monstrous compared to their other *Surface Trend* appearances.

After an hour or so, Linda returned, smiling. "Well, I've got some troubling news."

"What's wrong?" Shelby asked.

"All the dresses are completely gone from the floor and the back. We're going to have some very disappointed customers the rest of the weekend."

Shelby squeezed Paisley's hands, then let out a hysterical laugh.

"What's so funny, Mama?" Paisley asked.

The victory was so unexpected. Shelby hadn't the faintest idea how else to react. "We did it!" she said.

"Did what?"

"We sold all the dresses in the entire store."

"Why's that so funny?" Paisley asked.

"It's not really funny. Just exciting! It means everyone really likes our dresses."

"I know it's still early, but this looks like the best Black Friday we've had in ages," Linda said.

An hour later, Shelby pushed the stroller with one hand toward the doors of the *Surface Trend* at Baybrook Mall. Paisley clung to her mom's other arm, half walking, half hanging during the trek from the back of the parking lot.

Once inside, Shelby adjusted her eyes in disbelief, observing all the fans lining up in the central walkway and around the corner.

The receiving line continued through lunchtime. Shelby and Paisley took selfies, autographed magazines, and hugged eager fans. The store's inventory of *Treasured Pockets* dresses sold out around the time Bryan showed up with takeout. They all loaded into Shelby's car, and he drove them to their final stop while they wolfed down chicken strips and waffle fries.

At the Galleria, feeder roads were backed up at every parking garage entrance. Valet parking was no longer accepting cars. Their plan for Bryan to drop them off turned out to be a lifesaver.

"This place is nuts," Bryan said as they slowly approached a drop-off spot.

"On the plus side, no shortage of shoppers," Shelby said. "Little P, we'll get out of the car up here. Are you ready for one last shopping party?"

Paisley sat unmoving, her eyes drooping and head resting still against the high back of her car seat. "Mama, I wanna go home. Can we please go home?"

"Sweetie, this is our last appearance for the entire week. Then we can go home and watch a movie or do whatever you want."

When they finally made it to the curb, Shelby unloaded the stroller out the back gate of the SUV. Just one box of magazines and coloring books remained to give away. "Here, it's a bit of a walk. Why don't you ride in the stroller this time?"

"I don't wanna. I wanna go home." Paisley crossed her arms and stared out the side window.

They were so close to finishing the media sweep. And the Galleria was the most prestigious location of the whole week. "How about this? When Daddy gets to the store, he'll take you to go see Santa."

Paisley perked up at the favorable offer and slowly unbuckled her seat straps. Her body slid from the car into the stroller's bucket seat. Shelby rested the remaining magazines in Paisley's lap and began pushing the heavy load, when all of a sudden, her ankle snapped to the side.

"OUCH! You stupid!" Shelby yelled.

Bryan looked over from the driver's seat. "What happened?"

"My heel just broke! It got caught in this stupid crack. Just rolled my ankle."

"You okay?"

"I don't know." Shelby wiggled her right foot in a slow circle. "It's pretty sore." She massaged the muscles and tendons below the skin. It hurt, but she couldn't bail now. "I think I'm fine. Just go park, please, and come find us."

"Okay, will do."

Shelby chucked both shoes into the stroller pocket. She looked down at the back of Paisley's head. Paisley sat immobile, seemingly unfazed by her mom's injury—and her outburst. Hopefully she hadn't caught any of that.

"Why is this taking so long?" Paisley griped.

"Please hush," Shelby snipped. Shoppers whizzed past them left and right on their way through the heavy glass doors into the famous, multi-floor shopping venue with an ice skating rink in the middle. Shelby collected herself and began limping barefoot through the Galleria.

Shelby's ankle swelled up like a sock ball as she hobbled to the elevator and down the long corridor toward *Surface Trend*, where they arrived half an hour late. A line of customers stood packed and waiting in the aisle.

The store manager brought her a pair of flats in her size and introduced them to the crowd. Additional boxes of her *Buzz Now* issue were waiting there for her, courtesy of Gwen's amazing logistics. She stood at the front of the line resting all her weight on her good leg. As she began the ritual of greeting each person, she forced a smile across her face and extended a weary hand, hoping to still forge a connection with fans.

"We drove from Corpus Christi to meet you," said the mother of twin daughters wearing her blue dresses. "What you said on The Blast really spoke to me. That part about struggling to balance everything as a mom and wife. I feel the exact same way."

Another shopper said, "I've always wanted to match with my daughter, but I could never afford those kinds of dresses until now." Her daughter approached Paisley to reveal the trinkets in her pockets.

The upbeat comments and reviews blocked out the agony throbbing from Shelby's ankle. These words, these stories, these people. It all summed up exactly why she was here.

"And there's that darling little Paisley!" one mother exclaimed to her red-haired daughter. Paisley, still camped out in the stroller, folded her arms tightly and rolled toward one side.

"Little P, can you please say hi to these nice people?" Shelby prompted.

"You stupid!" Paisley blurted to the girl with red hair.

"Wait, what did she just say?" the girl's mother asked, wide-eyed, shielding her daughter behind her leg.

Shelby winced then shot Paisley the mom glare of death.

"*You* stupid!" the red-haired girl shouted from behind her mother's legs.

"Oh, my goodness, Ma'am. I am so sorry! We've had a very long day." Thinking quickly, Shelby added, "Here, would you like a coloring book?" She shoved a book into the girl's hands then turned to Paisley.

"Paisley, you cannot say that word!"

"Why not? *You* said it." Paisley snapped back.

"That's . . . that's because I got hurt. And I shouldn't have said it. And you shouldn't say it either." Her ankle throbbed with every syllable she spoke.

"Where is Daddy? I wanna go see Santa. NOW!"

As much as Shelby wanted to stay and greet fans, she could tell Paisley needed a quick escape, but she didn't think she could walk that far on her own. She needed Bryan to be there already. Thirty minutes, then an hour went by without a word from him.

Where is he?

Shelby was trying not to panic. In between conversations with shoppers, she texted him multiple times, but her messages went unanswered.

Ducking behind a rounder of dresses, she finally called him. "Where are you?"

"I got in a wreck," Bryan said.

"WHAT?!"

"Some jerk T-boned me in the parking lot. I was completely stopped. She was backing out of her spot and didn't even look."

"Unbelievable! Are you okay?"

"Yes, I'm okay. Your car's a mess. I don't think we can drive it home."

"Ugghh. Not what I want to hear right now. Why didn't you answer my texts?"

"Didn't get them. Was in the basement of the

parking garage. No signal. Just got to the first floor when you called."

"What do we do next?"

"Tow truck is on the way. We need to figure out how to get home."

"What about Paisley's car seat?"

"Not sure if I can get that out. I can take a cab to my truck and come get you."

"No!" Shelby blurted. She was not interested in being stranded with an overtired child in the city's most massive mall on its busiest day of the year. Worst of all, her ankle *really* hurt. She hoped it wasn't broken. "We have to go with you."

"Okay, I'm heading your way. Be there as soon as I can."

Shelby looked up from the call to see every pair of eyes watching her. The line of people waiting to see her looked just as long as when she arrived.

Much as she wanted to greet every customer, she needed to get Paisley home. Was there any way to escape without disappointing her fans?

She looked at Paisley in the stroller. Dark smudges encircled the girl's eye sockets. There was one sure way a parent could break plans and gain sympathy. It just might work now too. It would have to. She texted Bryan.

Let's meet where you dropped me off.
Pls hurry.

Shelby limped back to the receiving line and grabbed the microphone to address the crowd. "Hi everyone! Thank you all for coming. Unfortunately, Paisley isn't feeling well. I need to take her home. I am *so* sorry! I was looking forward to meeting every one of you. Thank you for supporting *Treasured Pockets* and for shopping at *Surface Trend*. I will announce any future appearances online. I hope to meet you again soon!"

She ignored the grumbling from line dwellers and packed up as quickly as she could, ditching the store's borrowed shoes. She apologized profusely to the store manager and asked them to distribute the remaining magazines and coloring books to the disappointed fans.

As Shelby limped away pushing the stroller, Paisley perked her head up. "Mom, do I get to see Santa now?"

"I'm sorry, sweetie, but we need to go home."

"But I want to see Santa! I WANT TO SEE SANTA!" Paisley screamed again and again, each time louder than before.

Every head in the vicinity twisted to stare at them. Shoppers in *Surface Trend* and three stories' worth of Galleria walkways gawked as Paisley melted down and Shelby limped barefoot and pregnant—in matching dresses—away from *Surface Trend*, away from Black Friday, toward Bryan and her useless wreck of a car.

Chapter 8

The next day, Shelby felt a new level of exhaustion, like after delivering a baby. At one end of the couch, a stack of pillows supported her back and shoulders. At the other end, a round throw pillow elevated her ankle, which was icing under a bag of frozen peas. Bryan's boss called him into the office to prepare for an unexpected client request for a redesign. So much for family time that weekend.

The only thing on her schedule today was a wrap-up call with Dennis. As soon as that was over, the rest of the Saturday was hers to relax.

As the call with Dennis began, Shelby let out a nervous laugh. "Two out of three ain't bad, right?"

"We'll call it six out of seven if you count tomorrow's *News Journal* feature. That's a pretty strong week overall," Dennis said.

"I knew a long day like that would push her limits. What a disaster."

"We all have days like that. Sounds like you handled it as best you could."

"I suppose. No one in the whole Galleria looked very happy with us."

"Well, if the numbers are any indication, there isn't anything to worry about."

"I'm anxious to hear. Where do we stand?"

"We're currently at 90% sold out nationwide. The next run is 60% pre-sold. Our production liaison tells me the order should ship any day. All in all, I'd say we're in great shape."

"Well, I guess that makes things better."

"Not for your car, though," Dennis laughed.

"Thankfully I'll only have a rental for a few weeks while it's in the shop." Shelby took a sip of coffee. "Glad it happened at the final stop. And that no one was hurt."

"True. You have a knack for finding the silver lining."

"Hah. Beats the alternative." Her right arm felt heavy, like thick rope. She switched her phone to the other hand. "Anything else for me this weekend?"

"Gwen will keep posting sale reminders all weekend. Please share as widely as you can. We want max exposure heading into Cyber Monday."

After the call, Shelby looked up post office hours. The main location a few miles away was on its regular Saturday schedule. After lunch, she and Paisley could mail Runa's Times Square cat and a Christmas card to Ravi's office. Paisley could use an outing to interrupt all the screen time.

But for now, it was time to rest.

Sunday morning, Shelby was pulling back the curtains to welcome the bright rays of dawn into the kitchen when another gushing text rolled in. The fifth this morning.

> Y'all look adorable. Congratulations!
> What a week!

Blakeley wrote.

Shelby pushed the button to start brewing coffee then tightened the tie of her bathrobe. Peering out the front door, she spotted the newspaper lying beside Maye's mailbox. Ignoring the ankle pain, she hurried toward the magnolia tree and crossed the street.

From Maye's front walk, she picked up the tight roll of newspaper and raced home. Inside she was greeted by the intoxicating aroma of stronger-than-average coffee. After pouring a cup, she sat down at the kitchen table. She propped her swollen ankle on a chair and sorted through the paper's numerous sections.

It must have been years since the last time she read an actual Sunday paper. Maye, who still had the news delivered daily, was her usual thoughtful self, insisting Shelby snag their copy so she wouldn't have to search for one.

World. Local. Sports. Ads. More ads. Finally, Lifestyle. Staring back at her on the front page was a picture of Paisley and her in matching dresses standing in front of the Christmas tree.

The headline read,

Mother of All Trends

In the age of smartphones and round-the-clock internet news cycles, there was something enchanting about laying eyes on their names and faces inked on newsprint.

The festive cover image evoked all the emotions she hoped it would. Paisley's smile looked a smidge fake, but Shelby suspected only a mother would notice. The evergreen backdrop offered a bold contrast to the bright berry dresses. Bryan deserved another round of thanks for all his behind-the-scenes work building the set.

In the silence of the morning, Shelby read through every glorious word of the article. When she stood from the kitchen table to get ready for church, a burst of stars dotted her vision. She dropped back into her chair, blinking the feeling away. Her body felt sluggish, as if hauling around a messenger bag full of books. Her ankle was still swollen and sore. Skipping church would be completely justified.

But church meant people. People meant hearing praise from the article with her own ears, not just reading it in texts and comments. Mother-daughter pairs may even appear wearing her matching dresses. Friends passing by in the hallways would stop to dote on the news coverage.

Shelby took a warm swig of coffee and posted

the article to her social media accounts. After a flurry of getting ready and grab-and-go cinnamon toast, their family left for church. Minutes later, Bryan pulled up to the drop-off area in front of the sanctuary just as the early service was letting out. Exiting his pickup truck, Shelby and Paisley were greeted by a familiar face.

"Good morning to my two favorite celebrities." Maye beamed.

"Good morning, Miss Maye." Paisley smiled, then bent down to poke around a flower bed full of pansies.

"Good morning, world's best neighbor." Shelby extended an arm for a hug. "Thanks again so much for letting me snag your paper. I'll bring it by soon as we get home."

"Thank you, darling, but it's all yours. I got my own copy."

"Wait, what? I could have gone out to get one."

"Yes, that's true. I couldn't wait a minute longer to see your article." Maye grinned.

A wide smile grew across Shelby's face as the sincerity of the gesture sank in. "Thank you, Maye. I really appreciate it. It was wonderful to read the paper copy for a change."

"Congratulations, love. I'm so incredibly proud of you and how far you've come."

Unexpected tears parked behind Shelby's eyes. Something about the way Maye spoke penetrated straight into her soul.

Shelby stuffed the emotions away, protecting her eye makeup. "Good heavens, Maye. It would only have been perfect if *you* had taken the pictures."

"Well, that's nonsense. But very sweet nonsense, nonetheless."

Bryan walked up from the parking lot and hugged Maye. After catching up, he dusted the garden soil from Paisley's hands and escorted her to Sunday School.

"Hey, listen," Maye began. "What are you hearing from Runa?" A wisp of concern floated on the top of her voice, causing Shelby to wonder if she heard it or not.

"Actually, I have something amazing to show you." Shelby pulled out her phone, unveiling their mother-daughter portrait like a trophy.

"Oh, my gracious." Maye's hand flew straight to her heart. "That. Is. Priceless."

"I know. I can't believe it. A mom and her daughter wearing our dresses halfway around the world. I start shaking every time I look at this. And the thank you letter she wrote is the sweetest thing ever. You have to read it."

"Shelby, this is too much," Maye said. "Look at their eyes. You can see how happy they are." Maye's voice was soft and light, as if descending from some other land. "Just look at how much joy you've brought them."

Shelby didn't know how to respond. Raking in

all that credit didn't feel right. But at the same time, Nipa and Runa's smiles stood at the heart of what led Shelby down this winding path. Her matching dresses stood for mutual admiration so magnetic, a mother and daughter were keen to display their connection to everyone.

"Oh, Maye. I feel like it's the opposite. They're the ones filling *our* lives with joy." Standing in front of the church doors, the words sounded canned. But she meant them like a vow.

"Can I ask, when did Ravi send this?" Maye's eyes were glued to the picture.

"I got the email Thanksgiving night. I wrote yesterday to tell him another box is on the way. Paisley wanted to mail Runa a souvenir from New York."

"And did Ravi write back?"

"No, not yet." Shelby detected the hint of concern again. "You know, there's such a huge time change. I'm sure he'll write back soon."

"Would you mind sending me a quick word when you hear from him?"

"Sure, of course." Shelby scrunched her forehead. "Is everything okay?"

"I'm sure it is, love." Maye allowed a smile to release the pull around her eyes.

"Of course. But—" Before Shelby could ask anything more, a boxy blue sedan pulled up.

"I'll check in with you later. Enjoy every minute of this morning. You deserve it."

Maye lowered into the passenger seat and shut the door. In the driver's seat was her daughter Junia. She may have been halfway through senior year, but petite and boyish, she hardly seemed old enough to drive.

Bryan walked up as Maye waved goodbye, and the car pulled away.

"Everything okay?" Bryan asked.

"I'm not sure," Shelby said, watching their neighbor's car exit the parking lot.

"Hi, Shelby."

Shelby turned to see Barbara from the church office standing beside her.

"Good morning, Barbara. How are you?"

"I'm great, thanks. Read your article this morning. You are so talented. I just love your whole story."

"Oh, well thank you." Shelby smiled.

"Pastor Mark was wondering if your family is available to light the Advent wreath on Christmas Eve. Will you be in town?"

"We sure will. Not planning to travel this year. What do you think, Bry?"

"We'll be here," Bryan replied.

"Okay, wonderful. Thanks so much. We'll send you the script. Y'all will be great." She walked into the sanctuary.

"Shelby Lawrence, is that you?" A woman in a sparkleberry dress walked over.

Seeing her design on another young mom, it felt

like a firework exploded inside Shelby's heart.

"Yes, that's me. Have we met?"

"No, but I've been looking out for you since your magazine landed in my mailbox. I'm Lindsay. We go to Faith Memorial too, but I haven't had the chance to meet you. Congratulations on everything, including your article today. My daughters and I absolutely love your dresses, as you can probably tell."

"It's so nice to meet you, Lindsay. I'm so thrilled to hear that. Thanks for saying hi." Shelby turned to see a meager but viable receiving line forming behind Lindsay, the tail of it drifting into the narthex. A pair of slate blue baby doll dresses caught her eye.

"Looks like worship is starting," Bryan said, eyebrows raised. "I'll go save us some seats."

Back at home, Shelby collapsed into a dining chair and began rubbing her thumb into her bulging ankle. Carousing the long hallways of the education wing in heels may have delayed her recovery, but every accolade was worth the setback.

Resting her ankle onto the adjacent chair, she picked up her phone to review the digital article. The pictures were so eye-pleasing, the Christmas tree behind them making the dresses look irresistibly festive. Refreshing the page loaded the most recent comments.

Super cute! I want this.
That is good stuff.
Don't bother. Sold out everywhere.

As she scrolled down the page, the word *Bangladesh* caught her eye. A few months ago, she wouldn't have given the place a second thought. Now she was mailing monthly packages there and clicking on recent headlines.

Except this wasn't the kind of headline anyone wanted to read.

More than 100 killed in garment factory fire in Bangladesh

On Saturday, a blazing fire broke out at a large garment factory outside Dhaka, killing 112 workers. As the eight stories of Tazreen Fashions Factory burned, hundreds of garment workers were trapped inside. The fire started on the first floor, blocking exits to the building's three staircases. Windows on lower floors were barred, further preventing workers from escaping. Some who escaped to the rooftop were rescued.

How unbelievably tragic, Shelby thought. The world and its 24-hour news cycle offered an avalanche of tragedies. The hair on her arms stood on end as she ingested more gruesome details of the fire.

Over 100 bodies were removed from the building by firefighters, 69 from the second floor alone. Another 12 died jumping from high windows onto the pavement. Hundreds more were treated at local hospitals for smoke and burn injuries.

Farther down the page, a mother was quoted wailing after losing her daughter-in-law and still awaiting news of her missing son. Many bodies were burned so badly they couldn't be identified.

Her heart pounding, Shelby scoured the paragraphs for an explanation of the blocked fire exits. None was given by the factory's owner. Officials from the exporting agency also fell silent.

Unthinkably, several behemoth Western clothing companies claimed to have no idea their garments were being sewn at this factory, which was just one of over 4,000 garment factories operating in Bangladesh. These familiar brands blamed a complex network of subcontracting between exporting agencies for subverting their quality control measures.

Looking up from the screen, Shelby's eyes turned toward Runa's picture on the fridge. It seemed unreal that in 2012, something as basic as a blocked fire exit still caused so much turmoil. It didn't seem possible that a vocation as humdrum as sewing could be so life-threatening. Her eyes returned to the article.

Accompanying the write-up was a startling image of firefighters extinguishing the blaze with water hoses. Shelby swiped right. The picture of fierce red and orange flames made her wince. She swiped right again. Bodies wrapped in white sheets were laid out one after the next.

Her phone chimed in her hand, startling her. It was a text from Whitney.

> The pics are so adorable.
> What an awesome week you've had!

Shelby replied quickly, then silenced her ringer and set her phone face down on the table. Paisley was nestled into the corner of the sofa, zoning out to a Barbie episode. A pig stuffy sat with her, choked in the crook of her elbow. Bryan was already out the door after church, meeting up with Jared to practice tomorrow morning's presentation.

Wanting to know more, Shelby sifted through the heap of newspaper sections stacked on the table beside her. The same disturbing images peered back at her on the bottom of the page.

Her thoughts pivoted to Maye's inquiries about Ravi. She'd been to Dhaka. News like this must seem so much more real to someone who has walked these streets, seen these buildings, shaken hands with these townspeople.

No question Maye would have read this article before church. Maybe this was why she asked about Ravi.

As Ravi came to mind, Shelby wondered if he might know anyone affected. She considered asking Maye if this factory, in a suburb called Ashulia, was anywhere near the children's home she and Roger visited.

Shelby looked again at the picture of Runa. The girl's face seemed to glow. Or maybe the cartoons across the room were reflecting off the photo. Standing up from the table, Shelby limped toward the fridge, allowing only gentle pressure on her ankle.

Removing the picture from beneath the butterfly magnet, she peered into the delicate, round face. Runa's eyes were mesmerizing, as if telling the most gripping of all stories.

She repositioned the butterfly and returned to the other magnet in the room . . . her phone. Turning the screen face up, she discovered a missed call from Dennis.

Strange. She hadn't planned to hear from him until their Tuesday catch-up.

Stranger still, he left a voicemail. His last voicemail weeks earlier had announced their spot on the cover of *Buzz Now*. Maybe he had exciting updates about the *Houston News Journal* article. Or perhaps the second order of dresses sold out.

Intrigued, she played the message. "Shelby— I've got some . . . some terrible news. There's been a . . . a glitch with the order. We lost everything. Call me soon as you get this."

The urgency in his voice froze her in place.

We lost everything.

Her heartbeat sped up as her mind hopscotched through possible explanations. Was there a misunderstanding with the timing? That wouldn't have been so shocking. The turnaround time for this order had always seemed fast.

But Dennis had assured her the timeline wasn't a problem. His voice sounded more urgent, more unexpected than a timing glitch.

As the possible explanations churned one after the next, her eyes landed on page A6. The red and orange fingers of the blaze sparked a horrifying possibility.

The fire.

A jagged blade of premonition gutted hard and raw through her. A burst of brilliant flames ignited across the screen of her mind. A hundred fragile screams shattered inside the hollows of her ears.

An unexpected gasp of air lurched into the room. Shelby froze, questioning whether she had really produced such a sound.

Paisley looked up from her show, her eyes wide with alarm. "Mama? What was that noise?"

"Nothing. It was nothing." Shelby set her hand on the countertop, bracing her body.

Oh, dear Lord, please let it be nothing.

Shelby tore through the living room while feigning calm. She skipped steps up the wooden staircase. Out of Paisley's sight, she raced down the hallway into the master suite, stepping lightly across the carpet to conceal her pressing pace. She pushed open the French doors leading into the bathroom.

The berry dress she wore to church lay flung across the back of the vanity chair. She reached for the tag, burying it deep inside the grip of her palm. Before allowing her mind to fall across its contents, she seared her eyes shut.

Made in China. Made in China. Please, God, let it be made in China.

She forced her eyelids to part.

Swirling across the tag was the familiar pink and green curly font of *Treasured Pockets*.

She flipped the tag up and scanned past the laundering instructions.

And there it was.

There, at the bottom of the tag.

Three haunting words stared back at her.

Made in Bangladesh

No. No. Please, No.

The air evacuated her lungs. Her vision blurred.

She checked again to confirm she was really seeing this.

The word *Bangladesh* leaped off the tag in her hand. Her knees buckled, sending her downward into the plush cushion of the vanity chair.

Beading with sweat, her head collapsed into the palms of her hands. She clenched her eyes, folding them away into darkness.

This couldn't possibly be lining up the way it appeared.

Over 100 bodies.

Hadn't the article said there were *four thousand* garment factories in the country? What were the chances the one that caught fire was the same one her dresses were sewn in?

The notion seemed . . . unreasonable. Unthinkable.

Dennis's voicemail pressed through her mind again.

There's been a glitch.

What on earth was happening? She wouldn't know the whole story until she talked to him. Now she questioned whether she wanted to.

Regardless of what he'd say, another concern needled at her. How had she not known where her dresses were made? This brand, this endeavor she poured her life's blood into for years.

Everything about this garment was so familiar. The names of the seams, the lay of the bias, the stitching around the neckline. Every feature of each dress was memorized, mother and child versions alike. Over *a hundred thousand* dresses sold out in two weeks. She and Paisley paraded around Manhattan and Houston, wearing them day after day, taking them off only to sleep.

Yet these words on the back of the tag went unnoticed. *How?*

Hadn't Dennis said they were being sewn somewhere in China? How could she have misunderstood such an important detail?

Raising her head out of the grip of her hands, Shelby peered past the open door of the walk-in closet adjacent to the bathroom. Her eyes skimmed rows and rows of neatly hung blouses and dresses and trousers. Come to think of it, she hadn't a clue where any of them were made. Nor had it ever dawned on her to wonder.

"Mamaaa!"

Shelby jumped as Paisley's voice interrupted the desperate internal rambling of questions. She walked out of the bathroom and yelled out the bedroom door, "What, Paisley?"

"I need a snack."

"Excuse me?" Shelby replied sharply. She walked toward the top of the stairs.

"I need a snack, *please.*"

Phone in hand, Shelby headed downstairs as another call from Dennis flashed across the screen. The tonnage of uncertainty filling her stomach indicated she better answer it.

"Just a minute," she told Paisley, then answered the call.

"Shelby—" The immediacy of his voice caused her throat to tighten.

"Dennis—What happened?" Shelby asked,

reaching for a bag of pretzels from the pantry.

"The reorder. The dresses . . . they're . . . they're gone." Dennis coughed the words out, as if trying to talk while swallowing crackers.

Gone.

"What happened?" Alarmed, Shelby abandoned the pretzels and slipped away to the downstairs guest room, closing the door.

"The factory . . . it's . . . it's closed. They weren't able to . . . to finish the order."

The lump in Shelby's throat relocated into her stomach. The lingering silence in the conversation made it feel like her turn to press for clarification just as Paisley would. *But how? But why?*

An honest part of her didn't want to know. Worse still, she feared she already did.

"There was a fire at the factory making the dresses."

"Dear God, please no!" Shelby collapsed like a load of books onto the soft cushion of the guest bed comforter.

"It sounds . . . really terrible," Dennis added.

Shelby swallowed hard, trying to mitigate the rising lump and the emerging truth. "I saw it. Saw it in the paper. I can't . . . I can't believe it."

"I can't either," he said.

A silence hung in the air as the disaster raked its way through her conscience. When Dennis didn't continue, she forced the next words out. "What do we do now?"

"We move on to damage control. The news coverage that's out so far hasn't connected the fire to us, but it's still really early. It might if someone leaks the tags from the order."

A fog rolled into Shelby's mind thinking about her brand emerging from the ashes of the tragedy and into the headlines.

"And what about the order?"

"It's gone. There's no way to recover. *Surface Trend* will offer refunds and a discount code toward the next purchase and hope for the best. Per the contract, you won't get a cut, but if things go okay, they should still include you in the spring line."

If that was supposed to offer Shelby relief, it didn't. There were so many things about this tragedy she still didn't understand. "Who absorbs the cost of the order?" she asked.

"We don't pay for an order until it's complete, so that's on the factory. But they have bigger problems right now."

Blocked fire exits.

"Dennis, how could this happen?"

"I don't know. *Surface Trend* was neither aware nor in any way has authorized the production of garments in the factory where this occurred. This factory is not on their matrix, and, other than your first run of dresses, they had never done business here before." The cadence of his response sounded like he was reciting talking points.

Shelby couldn't believe this was really happening. All the momentum she built during months of work evaporated in an instant. She suspected she had more questions than Dennis had answers. "What should I do? On socials? With media?"

"We're going to take a reactive but ready approach. Let's see if there's any backlash first. But be prepared to respond immediately if there is."

"But how? I have no idea what to say."

"The general rule is stick to the facts. Gwen is working on talking points and will distribute them during tomorrow's call. Hopefully we won't need them, but we'll be ready. Worst thing we can do is flounder while the news machine goes haywire."

"Okay, sounds good." As if any aspect of this ordeal could sound good.

Shelby eyed the unassuming stack of *News Journal* sections. Just 48 hours ago, she was selling out whole stores' inventories and taking selfies with fans. A week ago, she was just arriving home from New York. The speed of this dark shift was blindsiding. She tried desperately not to think about what it really meant. Or what everyone would think if they knew.

Bodies wrapped in white sheets.

"Mama, I need my snack!" Paisley hollered from the couch.

Shelby forced her shaking legs to rise and head toward the kitchen. As Dennis powered through more response tactics, she poured pretzel sticks into a bowl and dropped it into Paisley's lap.

When Shelby finished the call with Dennis, 14 texts, two missed calls, and 37 Instagram notifications about the *News Journal* article begged her attention. The last thing she felt she could stomach right now was praise from friends and customers.

Shelby sat down in the recliner, her eyes scanning the room. The built-in bookcases lining the flatscreen TV were embellished with Christmas decor, wedding day mementos, pottery from their travels. The familiar space felt somehow different on the other side of this ugly news.

Her eyes fell across each item and landed on a ceramic vase. *Someone made that.*

On a reindeer statuette. *Someone made that too.*

On the ornate walnut gallery frame surrounding their family portrait. *That too.*

"Mama!"

Shelby flinched. Paisley laid immobile on the sofa, her eyes dizzy from screen time.

"Can I have summore?"

"Please?" Shelby prompted on autopilot.

Manners felt especially frivolous in light of the news that just unfolded.

"Please."

Shelby stood up to walk to the kitchen. Nearing the fridge, her eyes returned to Runa.

A sick feeling emerged that she couldn't shake. A feeling like a monstrous storm was brewing, leaving no choice but to power through it.

Chapter 9

The next 24 hours proved even more intense than Shelby imagined. National media brought attention to two more major clothing retailers whose tags were discovered in the fire. It felt like a matter of days until *Treasured Pockets* or *Surface Trend* would join them in getting raked across network news and social media.

As Cyber Monday began, Bryan insisted on leaving work early to collect Paisley from preschool and take her to a movie. Shelby spent the extra hours memorizing talking points, researching lawyers, and obsessively checking global news sites.

None of the individual tasks were that taxing, but the sheer weight of the fire news made it impossible to focus on anything. It was like her brain had opened too many apps, all the needy programs bogging down her whole operating system.

While zigzagging from phone call to breaking news update, Shelby's mind was also racing ahead to coffee group on Wednesday. She didn't know how she would finally reveal her baby news while suppressing this huge debacle.

On top of all that, Maye kept checking in. For once, hearing from her well-meaning neighbor fueled Shelby's discomfort.

Maye texted Monday night. And Tuesday morning.

Anything from Ravi today?

Ravi's silence wouldn't have been so strange considering the time change, distance, and potential for connection issues. Except despite all of those factors, he'd always written back before.

Doing the time zone math from Texas to Bangladesh, Shelby figured out the fire began around 6 p.m., Dhaka time Saturday evening— early Saturday morning her time when she was recovering from Black Friday. By the time she emailed Ravi about the mailed package, the building must have been engulfed in flames.

Having heard nothing, it was hard to know how much to worry. Ravi didn't work at a garment factory, so it seemed unlikely he was impacted. And yet his silence added to all the reasons she'd slept so little last night.

Shelby replied.

Nothing still. Will let you know
soon as I hear from him.

She cleared the breakfast dishes off the table and hurried Paisley to suit up in ballet clothes so they could begin the day's run of errands and get to dance class on time.

Their first stop was meeting with a lawyer. She would never usually bring Paisley to a meeting as important as this one, but she had no alternative. The advice from *Buzz Now*'s legal team was to incorporate her business and add excess risk protection in case of a lawsuit.

The only time the lawyer, Bryan's referral from a high school friend, could meet with her on such short notice was right before ballet class. Unlike yesterday, Bryan had meetings and was unavailable to leave work to take Paisley.

On the ride over, Shelby laid out the game plan. "Sweetie, when we're in this meeting, you cannot interrupt me, okay? What mommy is talking about is very important, and every minute of this man's time is really expensive."

"Okay, Mama. Can I have your phone?"

"If you promise not to interrupt me. Deal?"

"Deal."

Inside the office, a woman wearing a white silk blouse and invisible rim glasses greeted them offering strong coffee, hazelnut creamer, and butterscotch candy. Soon after, a tall man with salt-and-pepper hair sporting a tidy dark suit and a blue striped tie introduced himself as Clayton.

"Great to meet you both. Here, come this way."

Following him into his office, Shelby sat down in front of a large oak desk lined with stacks of yellow pads and printed papers. Paisley collapsed on a black leather sofa, her mom's phone in hand and a hippo stuffy curled into her elbow.

As scatterbrained as she felt the last few days, Shelby lasered her full attention on this appointment. Not only did she not want to rack up an exorbitant bill, she also hoped to get Paisley to the studio on time so she could use the full hour of dance class to monitor social media.

When the meeting began, Clayton covered the legal basics of incorporating a small business. He was explaining risk protection when Paisley walked over from the couch.

"Hey, Mama?"

Shelby turned. "Sweetie, I thought we had an agreement that you wouldn't interrupt me?" Her eyes pierced into Paisley's.

"I think I did something. 'Cept for I don't know what."

"Please go back and sit down," Shelby said, eyes wide.

"But Mama, there's lots of messages."

"Sweetie, I always get lots of messages. Please don't interrupt me again or the phone goes away." Shelby plastered a fake, impatient smile across her face and turned her attention back to Clayton.

Paisley turned toward the couch, the layered tulle of her dance skirt swishing against her pink tights.

"I'm sorry. Where were we?" Shelby asked.

"Why don't you look this over and let me know if you have any questions." Clayton slid a thick packet of paperwork across the desk.

Shelby began scanning the intimidating stack of forms. As her eyes absorbed the legalese, her heartbeat escalated. *This is just a precaution,* she told herself. *Just one more safety measure. Just in case.*

"Mama?" Paisley's voice interrupted Shelby's focus.

"NOT NOW, sweetie."

"But Mama, I think you need to see this. I might have accidentally—"

"Give me the phone. You're so done. We had a deal." Shelby turned toward Paisley opening her palm to receive the phone.

Looking down with sheepish eyes, Paisley placed the phone into Shelby's waiting hand.

"I'm so sorry about this incredibly rude behavior." Shelby set the phone down on Clayton's desk. Eyeing the dashboard, she noticed 15 new texts since the meeting started. All from different senders.

Her cousin Amy wrote,

Congratulations!

Perhaps Aunt Sharon had mentioned their baby news to a few family members?

She scrolled down the list of texts. Most of

them were from friends. She clicked on the one from Blakeley.

Seriously, Shel?
Why am I finding out on FB?

Finding out what? Shelby wondered. She froze in horror.

The fire.

Did people know? Was her brand revealed in the news? Then why the congratulations?

"I'm sorry. I guess there's been some sort of . . . emergency. Can I get back to you on all of this?"

"Of course. As soon as you return the paperwork, we can finalize the process."

"I should have it back to you by the end of the day. Thanks so much for your help and for your time."

Shelby threaded her arm through the straps of her purse and grabbed Paisley's hand. She tore out through the reception area, towing Paisley toward the parking garage. Once inside the rental car, she opened Facebook.

154 notifications . . . in 20 minutes.

"WHAT?!"

And there it was, the source of the commotion.

Staring back at her from the virtual announcement board of her news feed was the sweet little oblivious bead of a baby.

Their unborn, unannounced baby—effortlessly floating through Facebook.

"Paisley! What have you done?"

"I tried to tell you, Mama. I was playing with photos, and then the baby's film picture came on there. I didn't know how to get it off."

A text rolled in from Maye.

> So happy for you Shelby!
> What a week of blessings!

"Paisley, I can't believe this!" Her closest friends were finding out her biggest news the same way her former coworkers were. "Of all the screwy things!"

Whitney was the next to text.

> Crazy news!
> Look forward to hearing details tomorrow.

And that's when it sunk in that tomorrow was ruined. Tomorrow, Shelby had planned to tell her dearest friends the three-year infertility struggle was finally over. Coffee group deserved to hear their celebratory news in person, but the weeks surrounding the launch had flown past without an opportunity.

There might have even been tears shed as she revealed the precious secret. Now she'd been robbed of one of the best gifts of pregnancy: sharing the hope of the pink line with those who linked arms awaiting it.

168

Still processing it all, Shelby rested her head on the unfamiliar steering wheel of the rental car. Her phone rang. She lifted her head and answered it.

"Shel, what's going on?" Bryan asked.

"Ughhh, Bryan. Everything's a mess."

"Jared just stopped by my desk to congratulate us. I thought we agreed to keep this offline until after the 20-week ultrasound?"

"We did. Paisley had my phone when I was with the lawyer. Somehow, she uploaded THAT picture to Facebook. Of all the thousands of pictures on my phone. I'm so upset my friends are finding out this way!"

"Can you take it down?" Bryan had never joined Facebook, so his understanding of its nuances remained limited.

"I could. But it's not going to make a difference. I have like 200 responses in 20 minutes. Taking it down won't make people unknow it."

"That's really unfortunate. I guess we'll have to hope nothing goes wrong."

It already felt like everything was going wrong. But Shelby knew what Bryan meant here. That nothing goes wrong *with the baby*.

He didn't say it, but he didn't have to. Having to retract the thrill of baby news for devastating opposite news was any expecting parent's worst fear.

"Mama, can we go?"

"Bry, I have to get Paisley to dance class. And Blakeley is clicking in. She's so angry. I can't blame her. I'm going to figure something out and will fill you in tonight."

"I'm sure it will be okay, Shel. I was just caught off guard, that's all."

"So was I."

Wednesday evening, Shelby put a bowl of mashed potatoes on the kitchen table and sat down in her chair closest to the kitchen. Nearly a week after Thanksgiving dinner and they were just finishing up the massive vat of leftovers. Not having to cook had been a huge timesaver, but their palates were all tiring of salty turkey and green bean casserole.

For all that had gone horribly wrong, some things were improving. The repair shop called. Her SUV wasn't totaled and would be good as new in a couple of weeks. Shelby signed and returned the paperwork to the lawyer. Most crucial of all, both *Treasured Pockets* and *Surface Trend Market* stayed out of the news.

Bryan walked in the house minutes before they took seats at the table. Paisley said the blessing.

As Shelby dipped a bite of turkey into mashed potatoes, her thoughts turned to Ravi. She still hadn't heard from him. Maye hadn't either. There wasn't any reason to think he was involved in the fire, and yet, the mere proximity of the tragedy to his office didn't mix well with his silence.

Hardest of all was hiding from absolutely everyone why her dress orders were canceled. Aside from Bryan and Clayton, Dennis instructed her not to tell anyone else for fear of it leaking online. The baby's unintended announcement was a bristly reminder of how quickly news could spread.

"So. How was your day?" Bryan asked, interrupting the oddly silent family dinner. Paisley's eyes were locked on the TV screen. They didn't usually allow shows during dinner, but tonight they welcomed that her attention was focused elsewhere.

"It was okay, I think. Less chaotic than yesterday."

"I would hope so."

"Dennis suggested I post about the pregnancy. So far, everyone thinks it's pretty funny." Then she reached over to rub Paisley's arm. "But we aren't ever going to mess with mommy's photos again, are we, Little P?"

"Nope." Paisley's eyes returned to her show.

"Glad that fire's out," Bryan said.

Shelby stared at him.

"Sorry, not the best choice of words."

"Nope." She stirred the mashed potatoes around in a circle on her plate, unable to force herself to take another bite.

"How was coffee group?"

"About the same. I got there first so I could apologize to everyone as they came in. It definitely hurt their feelings, but they all understood. By the end they were joking about it."

"Well, that's good."

"I also brought makeup samples I picked up at *Surface Trend* last week. That seemed to help. Oh, and Elise announced she's pregnant too, so that shifted the focus off me."

"Nice. That's exciting. Any more from Dennis on . . . the other?" Bryan was careful choosing his words so as not to pique Paisley's interest.

"So far, we've stayed out of it."

"Good. And any signs of shopper backlash?"

"No, nothing so far. Some disappointment over the online orders, but I think the discount code helped relieve the sting. *Surface Trend* doesn't usually offer coupon codes since their prices are already so low."

"And nothing impacting shopping overall?"

"The companies in the news are getting some flack. But total sales haven't wavered. No one has mentioned anything on my socials aside from the baby news."

"That's a relief," Bryan said, loading up a last forkful of stuffing.

"Can I have summore milk?" Paisley asked.

After clearing his plate, Bryan opened the fridge for the carton of milk. The butterfly magnet grazed his knee, and Runa's picture floated to the floor.

"Daddy, can you bring me that picture?"

"Please?" Bryan prompted.

"Please," Paisley said.

Bryan picked up the picture and brought it to the table. Holding it by the edges, Paisley danced Runa around her plate.

"Mama, did Runa get her wavy cat?"

"No, sweetie. Not yet. It takes a long time for mail to get there. It took almost three weeks last time." Surely she would hear from Ravi before then.

Ravi's silence gnawed at her. There was nothing normal about going this long—five days—without hearing from him. She sent a follow-up email on Monday. As of this afternoon, Maye still hadn't heard either.

Shelby tore off a thin strip of the paper napkin resting in her lap. She rolled the piece between her thumb and forefinger, then set down her fork. The unpleasant feeling growing in her stomach wasn't allowing space for dinner. Maybe it was too many days in a row eating the same rich foods. Or perhaps it was the sheer fullness of uncertainty.

She pulled the phone from the back pocket of her jeans and refreshed email one more time.

Still no word from Ravi.

Tap tap tap.

Thursday afternoon, Paisley stirred from her spot in the recliner. "Mama, who's here?"

Shelby looked up from scouring news sites at the kitchen table. Strange that Maye never replied to her text that morning. Perhaps she would stop by instead of replying, as she often did. Shelby peered through the window on the front door but saw only magnolia branches.

"Looks like no one."

"Then what's knocking?"

"Good question." She pressed her face to the kitchen window and looked along the side of the house. "There's a woodpecker on the gutter."

"Can I go shoo him down?"

"Sure. Here. Take the broom."

Shelby retrieved the broom from the utility closet, and Paisley hopped up from her perch on the sofa, abandoning the iPad. Shelby always found amusing any spectacle Paisley deemed more exciting than watching a show, which usually involved a surprise visit from some interesting critter. An earthworm family wriggling across the driveway. A toad trapped in the sandbox. A possum nosing for treasure in the trash.

Shelby grabbed her jacket and followed Paisley and the broom outside. They stood barefoot on the chilly driveway cement admiring the bird's stunning red helmet, the rhythmic drumming of his work, his determination at his task.

"Can I do it, Mama?"

At Shelby's nod, Paisley turned the broom upside down and whacked the metal gutter with the long wooden handle. *Bang.* The tapping stopped. The woodpecker darted up over the house.

"Where's he goin'?" Paisley craned her neck tracking his flight path.

"I don't know. Hopefully to an actual tree."

Bryan and Shelby always instructed Paisley not to disrupt nature, but relocating the woodpecker was justifiable—and not just for the noise or the holes he inflicted. This bird was hunting for food, for himself or perhaps for his family, and he was locked on a wayward path. Perhaps by intervening, the bird would find what he was searching for.

When the fascinating specimen was long gone, Paisley's eyes returned to the driveway. Broom in hand, she began sweeping stray needles and pinecones into playful piles. "Let's build a campfire," she decided.

The suggestion made Shelby bristle. There had been more than enough fires in her life this week. Surrendering to the much-needed break from social media, she walked toward the magnolia tree in the front yard, looking for downed sticks.

Not long into the search, the rumble of Maye's

garage door caught her attention. Fortunate timing. She could catch Maye in person instead of waiting for a text.

"Mama, look what I found," Paisley called out. "It's a pot leaf."

"Wait, what?!"

Paisley stood beside the pile of tree debris. Between her fingers, she squeezed the stem of a dried maple leaf. Its edges curled into the shape of a cup.

"A pot leaf. It's a leaf that looks like a pot." She held the leaf over the campfire, pretending to cook in it.

"You found a pot leaf alright," Shelby snickered. Too bad Bryan wasn't home. She pulled her phone out of her jacket pocket and snapped a picture of Paisley with the leaf to text him.

Replacing the phone in her pocket, she returned her attention across the street toward Maye's garage. As the blue sedan backed out of the driveway, Shelby walked toward the curb expecting the obligatory stop and visit. But Maye's car kept pulling forward, then accelerated.

Maye drove right past her, never turning to look.

An icy chill washed over Shelby. Her neighbor was never too rushed to return a wave. In fact, she always went out of her way to say hello, friendly banter bouncing from one curb to the next.

Surely Maye had seen them—and heard them. They were banging a gutter with a broomstick, for goodness' sake. Shelby didn't know what to make of it but didn't have a good feeling.

Perhaps the silence of not hearing from Ravi was getting to them both. Shelby couldn't endure the wait any longer. If Ravi wasn't emailing back and Maye wasn't even waving hello, she'd need to get more information any way she could.

Inside the house, Paisley returned to her perch on the couch and resumed her show. Shelby opened her laptop and emailed the only remaining contact she had, Caring Hope's sponsorship director.

After hitting send, she looked up at Runa's picture on the fridge. There was nothing to do now but wait.

Friday morning when Shelby returned home from preschool drop-off, she read the reply from Caring Hope, more confused than ever.

Dear Shelby,

Thank you for your concern about our dear friend Ravi. He is well, thankfully, and he continues the hard work of serving so many in need in Dhaka.

As per Runa Zaman, we are sorry to

inform you she will not be continuing in the sponsorship program. We are really saddened by this, and we hope for your understanding. If you wish to support another child, we will happily pair you with another student, in Bangladesh or elsewhere.

Again, thank you for partnering with us in this ministry. It is through the generosity and support of people like you that these precious children are closer to fulfilling their dreams. Wishing you all the best of blessings and love.

Sincerely,
Cedric Flores, Sponsorship Director
Caring Hope Organization

The email she'd sent to the sponsorship office had asked only about Ravi. She wasn't expecting to hear anything about Runa, especially not news like this.

She will not be continuing in the program.

But why not? And if Ravi was okay, why hadn't he emailed back all week?

Her frustrated reply thanked the director but insisted on more information about Runa. She reviewed the words in the email draft but didn't send it. If they were assigned another sponsor child, Paisley would be devastated. Her questions about Runa's disappearance would never end.

The longer it took to hear from Ravi, the more uneasy Shelby became. She wanted to talk to Maye, but Maye was completely unavailable.

She looked at Runa's picture on the fridge and said a quick prayer for her and Ravi before reviewing the week's remaining tasks. A follow-up call with Clayton to discuss next steps. Confirming with the babysitter for tomorrow's date night. Scheduling her 20-week ultrasound. Returning a long-overdue call with her mom.

Tap tap tap.

Shelby peered out the kitchen's side window to see if the handsome woodpecker was investigating the gutter again. She didn't see anything.

Tap tap tap.

Perhaps someone *was* knocking?

A blurry figure was visible through the frosted glass of the oval window in the front door. She pulled the door open and smiled at her neighbor, all bundled up in fleece.

"Great to see you, Maye. How are you?"

The downward pull of every muscle in Maye's face let on that something wasn't right. "Oh, Shelby. I'm afraid I don't have good news."

"What's wrong? Come in." Shelby opened the door wider, allowing Maye to step from the chilly outside to the warmth of her foyer. "Can I get you some coffee?"

"No, but thank you."

With all the small talk complete, Shelby stood silent, unsure what to say next.

"It's about Runa."

Shelby swallowed hard. "What happened?"

"Ravi wrote yesterday."

"Is he okay?"

"Yes, he is, thank the Lord. But I'm afraid I've been avoiding you since then. I didn't want you to hear what I'm about to say." Tears began streaming from the corners of her eyes.

Shelby's heartbeat started pounding at the sight of Maye's distressed face. A cloud of sweat rose up inside her, emerging like dew on her forehead.

Forcing her eyes to sync with Maye's, her fingers found their way to the phone in her back pocket, as if it could save her.

"It's Nipa," Maye said through tears. "Runa's mom."

"What about her?"

"She was there."

"Where?"

"In the fire."

"Please no . . ." Shelby's jaw slipped open, quivering.

Maye pressed her lips together, preparing to release the string of words that would unravel everything.

"She died, Shelby. She died in the fire."

Chapter 10

"Dear God, please no!" A flash of heat pulsed throughout Shelby's limbs. Teardrops tumbled down her face. Maye reached in her purse for a pack of tissues. She handed one to Shelby and took one for herself.

"I'm so sorry. It's so . . . it's so tragic," Maye continued as Shelby fell apart. "My heart is broken for them—especially for Runa."

Oh, Runa.

As Shelby dabbed her tears, she recalled the picture of Nipa and Runa in the matching berry dresses, their hands locking together. Their dreamy dark eyes, mirroring the other's. The glow of their joy eminent, half a world away.

Now that glow was extinguished forever.

"I can't. I can't believe it." Shelby willed her breaking voice to speak. "It was just a week ago when Ravi sent that picture."

Maye stood silently, wiping her eyes before continuing. "He asked me to tell you in person so you wouldn't be alone when you found out. He knows how deeply your family cares for Runa." Maye wrapped Shelby in a fleecy hug that should have felt comforting but didn't.

Captive inside Maye's arms, Shelby could think of nothing else besides Runa. Who would be there to embrace her? How was she feeling after learning such horrifying news about her own mother? What would her life look like after this?

"Caring Hope." Shelby tore away from Maye. "I wrote their headquarters. They said we couldn't sponsor Runa anymore. What's going to happen to her?"

"Ravi said a relative came to get her."

"Who?"

"I don't know," Maye said.

"Will she keep going to Eternal Promise?"

"Ravi didn't say. But if Caring Hope says she's no longer available to sponsor, it may mean she moved out of the area they serve."

Runa had said in her letter that her school was like a second home. Now the girl had been torn away from not just one home, but two.

And yet a third—the arms of the woman no one could ever replace.

"Do you know if she's safe? Will she stay in school?" Shelby sounded like Paisley, peppering off one unanswerable question after the next.

"I'm praying she is, but I honestly don't know. Ravi will be able to answer those questions better than I can."

"What else did he say? How is he doing?" Shelby asked, attempting to wipe her face back together with a soggy tissue. Maye handed her another.

"He's absolutely crushed. The factory is less than a kilometer from his office. He knew several seamstresses who were killed. Such a horrible way to die. Caring Hope assists first responders and family members. It's been a very difficult week for everyone."

Shelby's questions quieted, allowing the traffic in her mind to configure the heartbreaking pieces of this story. Runa lost her mother. A family evaporated right before her eyes.

Growing up without a father or a sibling, Shelby's mother was the anchor point of her life. They didn't always see eye to eye, but her mother was always there, putting food on the table and tucking her in every night.

"Ravi asked me to apologize for taking so long to reply," Maye added. "He hasn't been in his office all week, and knowing him, he probably didn't want to share the hard news."

Standing beneath the cathedral ceiling of the foyer, Shelby felt small. The innocent child on their fridge now navigated a world without parents, her life forever altered in the cruelest possible way. Shelby would never be able to ignore that her dresses were there, smoldering embers among the whole fiery scene.

She wanted so badly to admit to Maye what she knew, to reveal the gut-punching truth that just now came to light—her dresses and Nipa trapped in the same flames. The overlapping layers of devastation were just beginning to weave together in her mind. The words to explain it, if there were any, were choked away by sadness, if not by fear.

"Are you okay?" Maye asked.

Shelby avoided the question. "I didn't realize Nipa worked in a garment factory."

"She made clothes for a living. She did her best for Runa." Maye dabbed the tissue on her face. "What a terrible shame her life ended this way."

But for Shelby, the shame was just taking root.

That first December weekend, as Bryan disappeared to the office and Paisley flitted off to play at a neighbor's house, Shelby had every opportunity to knock pressing tasks off her list. But the quicksand of sadness, coupled with intensifying morning sickness, made it hard to even open the task app.

Everything on the list—social media updates, buying Christmas presents, coffee group plans, follow-up calls with Dennis—it all seemed so meaningless. Her thoughts were consumed by the fire. Not the lost dresses and the media scare— but Nipa, a woman Shelby knew only from a picture.

Tackling a heap of dishes piled on the counter, Shelby let her mind wander. Had it only been three months since Runa's name and photo arrived in their mailbox? Was Shelby overreacting to feel so distraught over the death of someone she didn't know?

Only in hindsight had it occurred to her that she and Nipa had anything in common besides having daughters. They both had mastered the ins and outs of sewing clothes. Of transforming basic pieces of fabric into something wearable, useful, so much greater than the sum of its parts.

But the skill of making clothes marked the end of their similarities in the sewing world. Every news article about the fire illustrated why. Barred windows. Blocked fire escapes. Managers who yelled at workers to keep sewing when smoke detectors sounded their alarms.

Such harsh working conditions were unlike any Shelby could imagine from her plush carpeted sewing nook in the front room off the foyer. She had certainly heard of sweatshops before. But they had always felt so hypothetical, so far away.

No doubt this perceived distance kept her from asking Dennis the hard questions about how her dresses would be constructed—not just the how, but the who.

Every seam of every garment ever sewn was administered by a person with a heartbeat, a fingerprint, and a once-in-forever face. Shelby saw this truth in the dresses she sewed herself and the awe of friends and family who praised her creativity. But until Nipa's death, the human element connecting every stitch of every piece of clothing had simply never occurred to her.

Scrubbing the soggy sponge over dried-up marinara sauce, her sadness over Nipa tunneled her back to another dark day. The day she lost a woman she dearly loved. Shortly after the stick turned pink with Paisley, Shelby's mom revealed the earth-shattering news. Her grandmother Dear was diagnosed with appendiceal cancer. The Stage IV prognosis was instantly dire. Three to six months.

As Shelby ingested the news, the whole of Dear's impact on her life crystallized. She remembered the long, hot summers she spent with her grandparents in Florida while her mom taught summer school. In the absence of a father, Dear stepped in as Shelby's devoted confidante and life teacher.

Dear was the person who taught Shelby how to sew. Beyond that, she championed sewing as a skill worth learning.

"There are only so many ways to be truly original in this cookie-cutter world," Dear had said, driving home from the fabric store. "Wearing your own creations is a way to define yourself instead of letting the world define you."

Her grandmother's many lessons extended beyond the sewing room. Dear was the neighbor who looked out for everyone on her street, dropping off homemade soup after surgeries, blankets for new babies, and anonymous envelopes full of cash when someone's finances were tight. She considered herself the neighborhood watch, not on the lookout for crime, but for opportunities to help neighbors when they needed it most.

"Take care of your people," she told Shelby. "Do not withhold good from those to whom it is due when it is in your power to act."

Hospice took over all too soon, when Shelby was entering her third trimester. Within the week, Shelby's mom called from Dear's bedside. She held the phone up to Dear's thinning, tired face, and they exchanged what they both knew would be their last earthly sounds to one another.

"I love you, Shelby," Dear half-whispered, half-creaked.

"I love you too," Shelby replied through sobs, refusing to believe this could be the end.

But the end came.

By the next sunrise, Dear was gone. She left the earth a few short weeks before her great-granddaughter, Paisley, was born. Shelby mourned that these two great loves would never set eyes on each other.

Nothing, not even fair warning, had prepared Shelby for the piercing finality of death. The never-again of it all. There were only so many sources of nurturing in a person's life that held on since the very beginning. Once they were gone, the sensation of being so completely known could never be replicated in the same way.

The phone in her back pocket rang. Her mom was calling. Timely that her thoughts about her grandmother would be interrupted by an unexpected call from her mother. Shelby set down the sponge, dried her hands, and answered it.

"Hi Mom, how are you?" Shelby tried to sound upbeat, but she knew how hard it was to hide emotions from a mother.

"I'm fine, thanks. Is everything okay? You sound tired," Irene said.

Thinking quickly, Shelby explained, "Just missing Dear some today. Must be everything with the launch. She would have loved to be part of it all."

"You know, sweetheart, in many ways, she is. Think of all she taught you."

It was true. Dear had taught her everything she knew about sewing. The long summers away from her mom had proven a bounty of time to learn the skill that had become essential for her business. Dear had taught her to install an invisible zipper, to iron-on interfacing, to reinforce a buttonhole.

Of all the sewing lessons, Shelby's favorite was learning to sew secret pockets into the side seams of her dresses. As a middle schooler, Shelby relished having a hidden place to tuck away money for the movies, a house key, the first heart-stopping note from a boy. Dear taught her how to align the pocket, pinning the fabric into the side seams, hidden from sight.

"She taught me everything." A tear slid down her cheek.

In the four years since Dear's death, Shelby accepted she would simply never stop missing her grandmother. This hard truth about grief intensified her understanding of what Runa must feel as the earth beneath her shifted forever.

"She would be so proud of you, sweetie."

Shelby blinked hard then fabricated a reason to end the call. Hiding the truth from her mother was more draining than doing dishes.

As Shelby said goodbye to her mom, she couldn't help but think about Runa's last goodbye with Nipa. This wasn't cancer in the later years. This wasn't a 78-year-old grandmother who had waltzed through decadent chapters of a long, fulfilled life. This was a young child's mother, her last breaths stifled by smoke.

Throughout that first weekend in December, Shelby found herself staring at the picture Ravi sent of Runa's hand gripping Nipa's. A couple of times Bryan asked if anything was wrong. But Shelby fended him off with explanations of morning sickness, exhaustion from the previous week, which were both true.

When the opportunity arose to speak, she couldn't bring herself to say the words out loud.

The thought of him—or anyone—knowing the full truth about Nipa's death and her dresses felt like too heavy a load to carry.

Maye, on the other hand, knew about Nipa but not about the dresses. Shelby couldn't bear the look of disapproval in her neighbor's eyes if she knew how everything played out. She was still sworn to secrecy, protecting her brand, *Buzz Now*, and *Surface Trend* from the media. That vow of silence offered a convenient excuse to hide the full truth. From Bryan. From Maye. From Dennis. From everyone.

Most of all, Shelby didn't want to tell Paisley their family could no longer sponsor Runa. She could already hear the dozens of questions Paisley would ask, trying to understand what happened. "But Mama, why did Runa have to go away?" There would simply never be a good answer.

She held out hope that Ravi could offer some solution. Perhaps their family could keep in touch with Runa and support her education.

The only foreseeable route forward was to wait and collect all the information she could. When the time came to tell everyone what happened, she'd recognize it. The question, when that moment emerged, was whether or not Shelby would be able to say aloud the unspeakable words that stitched together the dark truth.

Shelby's phone rang as she walked to her rental car after dropping Paisley off at preschool. Dennis was calling.

Winning the contest had made her feel visible, valuable, things she hadn't felt since becoming a mother. Calls from Dennis had been an exciting part of the journey. Now she felt ambivalent seeing his name on the screen.

"How was your weekend?" Dennis asked.

Shelby considered the heavy truth and opted for small talk. "It was fine, thanks. How about yours?"

"Eh, not great. Spent most of it working."

"Monitoring the news?"

"Some. And on the January issue. It's a headache every year when the printer closes for a week."

"Right. Any more updates on . . . anything in the news?"

"Thankfully, no. Gwen's been working closely with *Surface Trend*'s social media team. So far, they haven't seen anything outing you or them. The last time we heard from the exporters, your order was ready to ship. The boxes may have been sitting on the first floor where the fire started. It's possible none of your tags were recoverable, which explains why your brand hasn't leaked to the media."

A tightening sensation across her chest forced a

deep inhale. Perhaps Nipa and the others weren't actively sewing her order when the fire erupted. Still, her dresses fueling a fire that ruined all those lives didn't offer any comfort. She closed her eyes, picturing the blaze—and Nipa's eyes within it.

"Shelby, you there?"

She blinked away the fiery image. "Yes, I'm here. I suppose that's good?"

"It's great," Dennis replied. "If we can keep your brand out of the news, you'll be a lot more likely to lock in the next dress order."

The next dress order. That was still the goal, wasn't it?

"Dennis, what are you hearing about that?"

"Well, there's a post-fire investigation underway that should be released in the next week. Mitchell, the design lead at *Surface Trend*, says that if we stay out of the headlines until then, the whole ordeal should blow over. Then they'll regroup about the next order."

"So, you think there's a chance I'm still in?"

"Certainly. Your sales that first run were solid. They'd be lucky to work with you again."

"That's . . . very nice to hear." Shelby usually craved affirmations of her work. But today her voice wouldn't replicate its usual enthusiasm.

"It should be great. You don't sound convinced. Is everything okay?"

"Yeah." Shelby bit her lip. "I guess I just have some questions."

"Like what?"

"Well, for starters, I'm really confused about how the dress order made it to Bangladesh. Didn't you say it was coming from China?"

"Did I say that?"

"You said Guangzhou."

"Oh, well, that's probably because it's where they've placed orders before."

"So, how did it change?"

"*Surface Trend* uses an exporting agency to fulfill its orders. The agency sources the order from a list of approved factories based on the timeline, quantity, and a number of other factors."

"Okay, so that's what I don't get. How on earth could a factory with barred windows and blocked fire escapes make *Surface Trend*'s approved list?"

"It didn't."

"Wait . . . what?"

"Exactly. The factory where they sourced your dresses subcontracted out the order. You saw the official statements from the other retailers, right? They didn't know their clothes were being made there either. That's because their orders were subcontracted out as well."

"How is that possible?" Shelby squinted in disbelief.

"That's a question everyone in the industry

is asking. What we've gleaned is that some factories accept as many orders as they can, whether or not they can fulfill them. If they've reached capacity, they sell the order to another factory. That way, the original factory still makes a profit even if their workers don't construct the garments. Classic arbitrage, really."

"But that's so . . . conniving."

"Or opportunistic, depending on how you look at it."

Shelby found this response confusing. How could he sound so nonchalant?

"How are there no checks on any of this?"

"There are independent auditors, and each corporation has its own supply chain analysts. But sometimes when there are huge orders, fast orders, or large quantities of orders, things can slip through the cracks."

With every explanation offered, Shelby grew more frustrated, but over what, she didn't know. Her tone flung anger at Dennis, but none of this was really his fault. It technically wasn't *Surface Trend*'s fault either—was it?

Where did the blame lie? On the exporting agency? The subcontracting factory? The factory owners and managers? The whole tangled web of a system?

"I'm still so confused. Whose fault is it that this happened?"

"We don't know yet. That's what the investigation should clear up," Dennis said with an air of assurance. But to Shelby, nothing about this conversation felt reassuring.

"What do we do until then?" she asked.

"We stay the course. Keep growing your numbers on social media. Repost the holiday photoshoot pics as much as you want. Oh, and I thought you'd be interested to hear about a new opportunity to partner with some other companies."

"What's that?" Shelby welcomed the thought of something new to focus on.

"We've been contacted by a few small businesses that want to celebrate your pregnancy and piggyback on your recent success. They want to send you some products to promote. Is it okay if we provide your mailing address?"

"Maybe. What kinds of products?"

"It's mostly baby stuff and maternity items. This is in response to the Facebook announcement." Dennis coughed, testing the waters to see if Shelby found Paisley's phone mishap funny yet.

"What do I do with it?"

"Take pictures and promote it in your upcoming posts. Their company will pay you for the exposure."

"Like advertising?"

"Exactly, just by sharing with your followers. Could be a quick way to make some cash since the dress order didn't pan out."

No, it most certainly did not pan out, Shelby thought, anger bubbling beneath the surface of her skin. But Dennis wasn't the enemy here.

"Sure, tell them to send anything they want me to promote." Attracting such a large network of followers hadn't been easy. Shelby might as well squeeze something useful out of it. Any extra income would help as the month's expenses kept growing.

"Okay, great. Is there anything else you need from me?" Dennis asked.

Looking at her list, Shelby still had so many questions, but most of them had to do with Nipa. It might further complicate the situation if Dennis knew.

"I think that's all for now," she said. If she could just push through the week ahead and stay out of the news, maybe something would settle down, allowing her to accept another dress order.

But deep inside, where Dear's voice still nudged her with wisdom, Shelby knew that another dress order wouldn't fix what troubled her most.

Because none of it would help Runa.

By the end of the week, nearly two whole weeks after the fire, Ravi still hadn't written back. In this case, she had every reason to fear that no news meant bad news.

Shelby checked social media one more time before heading up the stairs with Paisley and a laundry basket of clean clothes. Paisley's bedroom greeted them with piles of stuff in every possible drawer and corner. Blankets spilled off the bed like a waterfall merging on the floor into a puddle of stuffed animals, clothes, toys, and books. The disorderly mountain bore a close resemblance to the campfire of sticks and pine needles in the driveway.

This child manufactured a mess wherever she went. They spent a few minutes clearing crayons, broken seashells, and hair accessories off the floor. Then Shelby pulled down an empty plastic bin from the top of her closet.

"Mama, what are you doing?" Paisley asked.

"I'm switching out your summer and winter clothes."

"But why?"

"So you have the right clothes for the colder weather." And so Shelby could close the drawers without fighting their contents.

Of all the mundane chores Shelby took on as a parent, she most loathed managing Paisley's wardrobe, figuring out what had holes and stains, what she'd outgrown, what might still fit when the weather turned again. The problem was there were just so many items to sort through. Paisley easily had two dozen dresses, all size 4T.

Eyeballing the stack in the bin, Shelby noticed

a few dresses she'd bought in the past year. All had been on sale or clearance. Each dress featured colorful patterns and kitschy prints she knew Paisley would love.

The other dresses were gifts from Paisley's grandmothers, aunts, and great aunts that arrived via mail for Valentine's Day, the start of summer, the first day of school. Christmas. Easter. Paisley owned three patriotic dresses for the Fourth of July. Another eight dresses Shelby had made for *Treasured Pockets* hung in the closet. Plus two from the most recent *Surface Trend* order and the Christmas dresses from Aunt Sharon and Uncle Charlie.

"This baby better be a little sister," Shelby said.

"Why's that, Mama?"

"Because what else will we do with all these dresses?"

The doorbell rang, causing Shelby to jump. The week's onslaught of surprises had made her skittish.

"I'll get it!" Paisley bounded through the hallway and down the stairs.

"Check who it is before you open the door," Shelby yelled. Her phone screen showed exactly two o'clock. Must be a package, which seemed strange. She wasn't expecting any.

Then she remembered her call with Dennis.

"Mama, it's for you. Can I open it?" Paisley yelled up the stairs.

"Bring it up here." Shelby welcomed any diversion from sorting clothes.

Paisley raced up the stairs and into her room with an orange bubble mailer in hand. Shelby tore open the envelope and pulled out a pink notecard.

Congratulations, Shelby Lawrence! We are excited to celebrate your wonderful news. Enclosed is a selection of our handmade bows. Should you find you enjoy them, please share with your followers and tag us @TangleMasters. Thanks, and wishing you all the best on your growing family. Your friends at Tangle Masters.

"Mom, what is it?"

From the envelope, Shelby pulled out a plastic bag containing a dozen hair bows in various colors, sizes, and patterns.

"New bows! For me!" Paisley grabbed the bag of bows and emptied its contents onto the floor. She picked up a pink-and-white pinstripe triple-looped satin bow, which immediately found its perch atop a patch of unbrushed blonde hair.

"I look beautiful!" she declared.

Shelby glared at the bows all over the floor— the same floor they just spent the last 15 minutes clearing. How, she wondered, did a project intended to streamline Paisley's stuff end up accumulating more of it?

"Sweetheart, you already have plenty of bows. This is more than you could possibly wear."

"I want them, Mama. I love them. Please don't take them."

The doorbell rang again.

"I'm getting it this time. If you want to keep those bows, they better be off the floor and put away."

At the front door, Shelby saw the letter carrier walking away from another five packages of varying sizes. Paisley helped Shelby carry the boxes into the sitting room where her sewing shop sat idle.

"Can we open them?" Paisley's eyes were wide with wonder.

Shelby stared at the unexpected tower. "Not now. Your room needs to be completely picked up before another new thing enters this house."

Later that evening, Shelby headed to bed before Bryan finished watching the Rockets game. Explaining to him why so much stuff showed up on their doorstep resulted in arguing about where to store it all and when to assemble the new baby's room. The last thing she wanted was to end the weekend fighting, especially when she still needed to tell him about Nipa.

Shelby sat in bed, replying to comments on

social media. She forced herself to post some-thing today to make her feed appear normal, then glanced one last time at her inbox. Staring back at her in dark, bold letters was Ravi's name. He had finally written back.

9 December 2012
Dear Shelby,

I am sorry it has taken me so long to respond. These past weeks have been utterly devastating for our community. I have spent little time in the office and am behind on many things.

I regret having to relay the sad news through your neighbor Maye. I have known Nipa many years. We helped her get her first job when her husband left so she could provide for herself and Runa. Over the years, she was very outspoken against injustices in her workplace, to her own detriment. She lost her job several times, voicing concerns too loudly or organizing protests.

More than once, she was physically beaten by factory managers. But despite her injuries, Nipa always rose again, always found another job to support Runa, even if it was not where she wanted to work. What happened to her and the others is so heartbreaking. I will always remember Nipa's resolve to pave a better path for her daughter.

I have watched Runa grow up from a toddler to an intelligent, thoughtful child. Sadly, I do not know much about what happened to her. Eternal Promise School informed me that Runa's uncle came for her the week after the fire. Where he lives is not in the area we serve, causing her removal from the sponsorship program. Schools here are approaching their end-of-year break. I regret I have no more information about whether Runa will attend school again.

I will keep you informed if I hear anything from Eternal Promise. I hope more information will turn up as the chaos settles.

I pray you and your family have a blessed Christmas. We thank you again for the love and support you provided to Runa while she was part of our program. She is a very special girl, and I will continue to pray for her every day. Know your family is a blessing from heaven, and she will always remember you kindly.

With highest regards,
Ravi

His words confirmed everything she feared. Runa was gone.

Their short season connecting with her through Caring Hope had reached a fast, tumultuous end. Paisley would never understand. How would they even explain? How would Shelby ever bring herself to reveal the whole story?

She read through the email one more time. This time Ravi's words struck not sadness, but fear.

Whether Runa will attend school again.

What were the prospects of a young girl in Bangladesh—or anywhere—who didn't attend school? As little as Shelby knew about that part of the world, she felt certain that not having an education was a dead end to many paths all at once. She had to know more about this uncle, about Runa's living situation, and most especially about whether or not the girl would continue her education.

She replied, thanking Ravi and pleading with him to find out anything else about Runa and her uncle. She asked if there were any way he could visit her and ensure Runa was okay. If costs were an issue, they would send money. Even if they could no longer sponsor her through Caring Hope, they could offer to help this uncle or support Runa's education in any way possible. Maybe this wouldn't really be the end.

Shelby knew too much about why Runa's life turned upside down. The question now was how long she could carry on pretending she didn't.

Chapter 11

The following week, Christmas spilled into every spare minute. Holiday gatherings dotted the calendar from every social direction. The preschool pageant, the office party downtown for Bryan's firm, and the neighborhood cookie decorating party all required various levels of preparation.

When Shelby wasn't scheduling babysitters, she was wrapping presents, baking cookies, and promoting products on social media. All of it served as a welcome distraction from telling Bryan about Nipa.

Camped out on the floor of the living room that Sunday evening, Bryan and Paisley assembled a train set that circled the Christmas tree. Across the room, Shelby stood in the kitchen preparing minestrone. Christmas carols streaming through surround sound speakers filled both rooms with the notion that everything was as it should be.

After the train made its second successful loop, Paisley announced, "I'm hungry. I want a snack."

As she scurried to the kitchen, Bryan leaned against the sofa and pulled his phone out of his jeans pocket, no doubt checking work email. The deadline of a shopping center proposal had consumed his attention all weekend.

At the cutting board, Shelby was in a daze,

her thoughts meandering every which way. She snapped out of it when Paisley's hand tugged open the refrigerator door.

"I don't think so, Little P. You know we're about to eat dinner."

"But Mama, I'm hungry."

"Then please set the table."

Paisley closed the fridge door, and Runa's face stared back into the kitchen. "Mama, did Runa ever write me back? It's been like forever."

A country rendition of *Jingle Bell Rock* blasted into the room with too much vigor. Shelby tapped her finger on the phone to halt the music.

"Not that I know of, sweetie."

"Well, what did Mr. Ravi say?"

Silence stretched as Shelby weighed what to share. "Sweetie, Runa might not be available to write back for a while."

Bryan looked up from the living room floor. "Really? What happened?"

Shelby hadn't realized he was listening. "I'm not exactly sure," she replied, half to Paisley at her side, half to Bryan in the living room. "Caring Hope emailed to say that Runa isn't available to sponsor anymore. I wrote back for more information, but they haven't replied."

"That's weird. We just started sponsoring her." Bryan joined them in the kitchen. "What about Ravi? Does he know anything?"

Her conscience tripped. This was her one

opportunity to connect the tragedies—her dresses and Runa's terrible news. If she didn't share now, every attempt to bring it up after this would reveal a lie.

Stirring the pot on the stove, her voice caught in a tight net of uncertainty. Bryan knew her dresses were destroyed in the fire. If he found out Nipa died in the same fire, he would join her in questioning whether this next dress order was worth the risk of another tragedy.

Shelby was already questioning that herself, but she didn't want to rule it out quite yet. She'd come too far and worked too hard building her brand to retreat now, especially considering how unlikely it was that a buyer as prominent as *Surface Trend* would ever seek her designs again.

"He's been busy dealing with the fire," she said, which was true. "I will email him and see what I can find out."

It wasn't a completely honest answer, but it bought her more time before confessing the miserable truth out loud.

"What fire, Mama?" Paisley asked.

Shelby's insides twisted. She was trying so hard not to let on to Bryan about Nipa that she forgot to camouflage her words in front of Paisley's curious ears.

"Oh, right. Well, a building caught on fire—very far away."

"Was it a big, scary fire?" Paisley asked.

"Yes, it was. A lot of people were . . . hurt."

"How did it happen?"

A wave of heat rose to Shelby's forehead, the implications burning within her.

"The news said some yarn and fabric were stored too close to an electrical generator." Shelby steadied her voice as she ladled steamy soup into dinner bowls.

"What happened?"

"Do you remember when you wrapped the gray cord of your lamp in pink blankets because you didn't like the color? And Daddy and I wouldn't let you?"

"Yes. Daddy yelled at me."

"That's because he was scared it would start a fire. Things running on electricity can spark. If a spark lands on something that burns easily, it can start a fire. Do you think if a spark landed on a furry blanket, it would catch on fire?"

"Uh-huh. Like the paper towel in the campfire."

"Exactly. And that's what happened in this fire. The generator that makes electricity for the building sparked. And that spark flew onto the fabric and started it on fire."

"Mama, they shouldn't put fabric so close to the cord, should they?"

"No, they shouldn't." Shelby's jaw tensed. A four-year-old understood, but factory managers ignored it.

"Did they use the fire 'stinguisher?"

"That would have been a good idea, but this fire got too big. The fire department came and washed away the flames with their big water hoses." Shelby delivered soup bowls from the counter to the kitchen table.

"But a lot of people got hurt?"

"Yes, unfortunately." Shelby stopped short of explaining all the deaths. She had learned during these child-led Q&A's to answer only the question asked.

"Where was it, Mama?"

"The fire?"

"Yeah."

"Bangladesh." Shelby couldn't let her eyes meet Paisley's as she delivered the last soup bowl to the table.

"Did Runa get hurt?"

"No, Runa wasn't hurt. She wasn't near the building."

Oh, but Nipa.

"Did she get her wavy cat? I want a picture."

Ready to finish walking the tightrope of questions, Shelby replied, "I promise I'll show you any pictures Mr. Ravi sends. Okay, sweetie? Hey Bry—dinner's ready."

Bryan tucked away his phone and joined them at the table.

Paisley sat at the table, her gaze locked on Runa's tattering photograph. "I just can't wait to see how happy it makes her."

"Let's say the blessing, please," Shelby said, folding her hands.

"Dear Jesus, thank you for our food, our family, and our friends, 'specially for Runa. Amen."

Despite Shelby's hesitations, coffee group planned a shopping trip at *Surface Trend* for the year's final gathering. If not for how badly she felt about the botched baby announcement, Shelby might have skipped. At least this location had a coffee counter.

Arriving at the store a few minutes late, Shelby received a text from Dennis.

> Sounds like the investigation report may be released soon. Will text as soon as I hear.

She tucked her phone in her purse and walked toward the entrance. Zipping past the bell ringers out front, she went inside and met up with Blakeley, who was wearing furry boots that looked brand new. Elise joined them after returning some items at customer service. Shelby waited in line to order a latte when Whitney showed up in dark skinny jeans, riding boots, and a gorgeous sage green cashmere sweater.

"Whitney, over here!" Blakeley said, waving with one hand, steaming latte perched in the other.

"Your outfit is soooo cute," Elise said, reaching in for a one-armed hug.

"Thanks, girl. Great choice for a meet-up. I'm ready for coffee and shopping. All this buying stuff for other people is wearing me out," Whitney said.

"I know. The sales are all so good right now. It's impossible not to shop for yourself," Elise said.

"I'm desperate for new shoes. Heard they have some really cute stuff," Blakeley said.

"Which is surprising," Elise said. "It's usually so crowded and picked over in December. They've really upped their game."

Shelby grabbed her latte from the bar and joined the group.

"Hey girl, any more news about the dresses?" Whitney asked.

"Nothing new." Shelby took a long sip of latte. She'd rehearsed this moment in her mind, but facing her friends brought on the jitters of walking on stage. *Buzz Now*'s response plan instructed her not to share anything about the fire. They knew what everyone on Instagram knew—some glitch, some unforeseen supply issues, messed up the second order, and, consequently, Shelby had a discount code to give away.

Technically, she could tell her friends about Nipa and Runa. But she still hadn't told Bryan. She simply couldn't bring herself to say the words. What would telling her friends even accomplish? There was nothing she or any of

210

them could do about the tragedy. Plus, mentioning a garment factory fire in the middle of a shopping trip was about as welcomed as highlighting the health risks of sugar at a bakery.

"I'm just waiting to hear if they want me to design for them again," she said.

"I really hope you get it. What else is going on?" Whitney asked.

"Just slammed getting ready for Christmas. What about y'all?" Shelby replied.

"Completely drowning," Blakeley said. Coffees in hand, the group walked toward the women's clothing department.

"We're doing Christmas with Jason's family in Atlanta," Elise said. "They're the kind of people who give presents to everybody, even cousins. We're buying and wrapping stuff for, no kidding, like twenty-three people."

"That's obnoxious," Whitney said, flipping hangers across a rounder of marked-down jeggings.

"I'm shipping everything there," Elise said. "Hoping my mother-in-law gets annoyed with all the boxes and wraps everything, so I don't have to."

"How do you even know what to get for that many people? Are you close with them?" Blakeley asked.

"Hardly. Some of them I met once at our

wedding. My mother-in-law basically told me what to get, or I just got gift cards. They can buy whatever they want," Elise said, inspecting a maxi dress against her petite frame in a full-length mirror.

"Does that mean you're carting stuff home *from* twenty-three people?" Shelby asked.

"Well, some of the total count are kids. It's like eight different families' worth of stuff, times our two kids."

"And one on the way," Whitney teased.

"That's why we decided to drive—I already feel sick enough, and air travel makes me sicker," Elise said. "But even more than that, we need a way to lug all the presents home."

"And then there's the worst part," Blakeley added. "Finding a place for all of it."

"We did the pre-holiday purge already," Elise said. "Hoping this year we'll be ready for the onslaught instead of buried in it."

"Hey, check this out," Whitney said to Elise. "This shirt is only $6.99. And it's maternity."

"Can't beat that." Elise reached for the blue racerback tank.

"What's everyone doing Christmas Eve?" Blakeley asked, combing through a stack of folded long sleeve shirts.

"We're going to the lake," Whitney said. "I am not even messing with church. It was such a disaster last year."

"Wait—what happened? I'm not remembering this," Blakeley said.

"Avery picked up a stomach bug in the nursery. We spent the week after Christmas puking. My parents were staying with us, and they got it too. It was sooo bad."

"That's the worst," Blakeley said. "Makes me queasy just thinking about it."

"I think I still have PTSD from it," Whitney said. "Shel, what are y'all doing?"

"The church asked us to light the Advent candles at the five o'clock service. My mom is coming in, and we're going out for Chinese food. It's our untraditional family tradition."

"I second all traditions that involve not having to cook," Blakeley said.

"I know, right?" Shelby said.

"Shel, this is cute. And oooo . . . it's cashmere! Could totally work over leggings. Here, try it." Whitney handed over a tunic-length sweater in a soft petal pink.

"Thanks. Bryan won't be impressed if I put one more thing on this credit card. Let me see." Shelby reached for the shirt. She gently circled the fabric between her fingertips. "Wow, that's really soft."

She checked the tag and was shocked to see it priced at $29.99. Not that long ago, cashmere sweaters were priced in the triple-digits. Astounding how much they'd come down.

Maybe it wasn't real. She checked the tag. It read 100 percent cashmere.

Also on the tag were the words *Made in Cambodia.* Like smoke, the image of an overcrowded garment factory stung her eyes. She blinked it away.

"Who wants to check out the boots?" Blakeley asked.

"I do," Elise said. "I've been wanting some of those over-the-knee boots."

"I like the way they look, but I can't imagine they're going to be trendy more than a season or two," Whitney said.

"That's why I buy that kind of stuff here," Elise said. "Not as much of a commitment. Can wear them while they're trendy and then pass them along."

One by one, they stopped turning hangers across clothing rounders and wandered into the walkway. As they traversed the store, electric pressure cookers, snowman-shaped waffle irons, and wireless speakers caught their attention.

Soon as Whitney turned away, Shelby slid the cashmere tunic back onto the rack. She followed her friends into the walkway and pulled out her phone.

"Everything okay, Shel?" Blakeley asked.

"Oh, yeah, sorry. All good. Just expecting something work-related."

Still nothing from Dennis. She returned her

phone to her purse. "Those are cute," she said, motioning toward Blakeley's furry boots. "Are they new?"

"Yep. I got them Black Friday online. They were 40 percent off, and I didn't have to set foot in the mall."

"Sounds like a win," Whitney said.

"I like them a lot. They're super comfy but too casual for a lot of places. I need something dressier."

"What about those cute riding boots from last year?" Shelby asked.

"Those are brown. I really need black ones to go with the dress I'm wearing Christmas Eve."

"You should get over-the-knee boots too," Whitney suggested.

"I might. Depends on the price," Blakeley said.

In the shoe section, each friend turned in to their respective-sized lanes. Shelby's phone vibrated. She slipped off into an empty aisle and pulled out her phone. Dennis texted a link to a news article.

Investigation is out. Talk soon.

The article was loading when she heard Whitney squeal from the row behind her. "Hey Blake, you have to see these."

Blakeley raced over to meet Whitney. "Super cute!"

Shelby peeked around the corner to see what the fuss was about. On the top rack sat a box the size of a kitchen drawer. Folded inside was a pair of matte black thigh-high boots. Whitney lowered the box to the floor, and Blakeley pulled the long boots over her leggings.

"How much are they?" Blakeley asked.

"$69.99," Whitney said. "They start around two hundred at the mall."

"That's a steal. I'm gonna see if they have them in my size," Elise said.

Shelby returned to the vacant aisle. Sitting on a mirrored bench, she started to read the article.

Gross Negligence Found
in Bangladesh Factory Fire

A foul taste emerged on Shelby's tongue as she ingested the headline.

"Unpardonable negligence," the verdict stated. *They knew.*

The thought knocked into her like a swift uppercut. Managers knew the corners they'd cut put the workers at risk. Investigators cited a track record of failed inspections to prove it.

The rest of the article explained the extensive, government-led report. Nine midlevel factory managers had stopped workers from leaving their sewing stations, even after the fire alarm sounded.

Reading those words, Shelby pictured the managers yelling over the smoke alarms for Nipa and her coworkers to stay at their sewing machines. Those workers were forced to stay put. If they didn't, it would have cost them their jobs.

Instead, it cost them their lives.

Once again, reps from several big outfitters were quoted denying any awareness that their clothes were contracted to this factory. Shelby's first inclination was outrage. How could companies *this* established, *this* mainstream, not know the basics of who was making hundreds of thousands of items for their stores?

But in hindsight, couldn't she claim the same unknowing? She had no idea her dresses were being made there either.

At that, Shelby felt another question needling her. Had she known her dresses were being sewn in a factory that failed its safety inspections, would that have changed anything? Would she have been concerned enough to speak up? To halt production while they researched safer options? Would she have risked a narrower profit margin and the chance to design a second time?

If the truth—the real truth—about that factory had been revealed up front, would she have been willing to trade her success for the factory workers' safety?

As much as she hoped the answer was yes, the brutal truth was probably not.

She wouldn't have connected the garments she was buying with the able hands, the warm smiles, the mothers and fathers and daughters and sons she was asking to produce them. That wasn't how a business worked. Transactions were made. Contracts were fulfilled. The workers might as well be invisible.

"Shel, what do you think?" Blakeley asked.

Shelby jumped. Her eyes unlocked from the screen to find Blakeley standing in front of her wearing the tall black boots.

"Shel—is everything okay?"

"Sorry. Yes, everything's fine."

"I don't mean to keep asking, but you just seem . . . distracted."

"It's okay. I'm just feeling bogged down by all this . . . holiday stuff."

"Totally get that. It's the worst. Well, what do you think?" Blakeley asked again, stepping each toe forward to showcase the boots.

"They look . . . they look . . ." Shelby stopped, considering what to say next. The boots created a smooth line up the length of her silhouette. Her friend looked taller, slimmer, trendy. Most of all, she looked confident. "They look . . . really cute on you."

"Think I should get them?" Blakeley asked.

Should her friend buy the cheap boots? Should any of them buy any of these items having no idea where they came from or who made them?

Shelby felt trapped, as if any answer she gave was the wrong one.

Stick to the facts, she reasoned. "They look great, Blake. And you can't beat the price."

The cost, though.

What was the cost?

Friday morning, a phone call from the body shop delivered welcomed news. Shelby's car repairs were complete. After preschool drop-off, Shelby returned the rental and picked up her car, strapping Paisley's car seat to its proper spot in the backseat.

Sliding into the familiar cushion of the driver's seat, Shelby felt a wave of calm wash over her as her car's engine rumbled to its start. The outside looked new, but the inside, with its worn carpet and favorite music presets, felt like a visit with an old friend. Finally, something in her life was settling back to normal.

Her seat and dashboard settings were messed up by repairmen driving it. After repositioning the seat and adjusting the rearview mirror, she turned on the radio.

She shifted to reverse and checked for cars in her rearview mirror. The voice from the radio spoke with such urgency, goosebumps broke out across Shelby's arms.

"BREAKING NEWS. If you're just joining us, a massacre has occurred and is still underway at Sandy Hook Elementary School in Newtown, Connecticut. An unidentified gunman has entered the school and has opened fire, killing at least 10, quite possibly many more, children, teachers, and school administrators.

"At this time, we have very few details as emergency officials are still responding. We don't know if the shooter is still active or has been apprehended. This story is still developing. Our station will share details and updates throughout the day."

Shelby shifted the car back into park. Her mind returned to Paisley, who, not an hour earlier, skipped off to her art-lined classroom for a day of learning and playing.

Her forehead dropped onto the steering wheel as she thought about the pure hell those parents, those children, those teachers must be going through. In the wake of Nipa's death, she felt her emotions hopscotching from one tragedy to the next.

Had the world always turned at such a pressing pace? Or did she just notice it now that she had a child's future to worry about?

Two children. Her hand rested on the curve of her abdomen.

And then there was Runa, a third child for whom she now carried a mother's weight of worry. Ravi hadn't replied with any more updates. It was so frustrating not being able to do anything but wait.

What was this girl doing right now? Was she safe? Would she return to school? Would Shelby's request to Ravi pan out, or would she have to piece together some other way to figure out if Runa was okay?

She turned off the radio and emailed Ravi one more time to ask for updates. Then she did the only thing she could think to do next. She put the car back in reverse and sped off to her next errand.

Chapter 12

Days of gut-wrenching interviews poured out of Newtown, but absolutely no news came from Dhaka. Shelby started the week with a jam-packed Monday morning, which happened to be Paisley's last full preschool day of the year. She had school on Wednesday too, but parents were invited early that day for the class Christmas party. Every kid-free task for the rest of the year needed to happen in the next four hours.

After dropping Paisley off, Shelby sat in the front seat of her car and listened to the news. Announcers and callers argued nonstop about the bloodbath at Sandy Hook Elementary. The shooting left 26 dead and two injured. As with all statistics, the numbers didn't illustrate the true horror.

Pictures of the mostly six- and seven-year-old victims flashed across screens large and small throughout the weekend. The nation sat with the story in expansive disbelief. The tears of family members, first responders, teachers, onlookers—their tears seemed to never stop falling.

Shelby turned off the radio as she pulled into the coffee shop drive-thru and ordered a half-caff peppermint latte. Waiting her turn to pull forward and retrieve her drink, she glanced at email. Still nothing from Ravi.

Next, she checked her bank statement. Already the credit card showed $2,000 more than usual. They hadn't bought any huge presents. But the extra hostess gifts, take-out dinners, custom Christmas cards—not to mention legal fees—all added up faster than she could track.

She pulled forward another car length, then stopped and checked her to-do list. Teacher gift cards to buy. A mountain of presents in the guest room to wrap. Social media updates growing past due. Boxes of promotional products lining the foyer to unpack, photograph, and store.

As she prioritized the list, her phone rang. "Dennis, what's going on?"

"Shelby—Good news."

"Really? I was starting to wonder if I'd ever hear you say that again."

"I know, right? What a terrible few weeks," he said.

"What's going on?"

"You're back in."

"What do you mean?"

"The media storm has died down. The fire investigation placed the blame squarely on the factory owners, not the retailers. Now the media and everyone else are focused on gun control. Sounds like this ordeal is finally blowing over."

It struck as the most disappointing good news Shelby could remember hearing. She pulled the car forward and exchanged her credit card for her steamy drink through the window. "How is that good—for me?" Exiting the drive-thru, she pulled into an empty parking spot.

"*Surface Trend* has requested you to design for the spring line. They want three designs this time—six dresses total. They're offering 40 percent of the profit. Sounds like another six-figure order, which could mean a huge payoff, depending on how they sell."

Shelby put the car in park. Over the past few weeks, she'd contemplated this moment over and over. What would she say if given another chance to design? Now the chance was here, and she felt unprepared. "This is, of course, everything I've been hoping to hear."

"Why am I sensing there's a 'but' coming?"

"Well, it's just—the fire really got to me."

"What do you mean?"

She cleared her throat and steadied her voice. "I feel terrible about what happened, and I'm worried it could happen again."

"I can assure you that *Surface Trend*'s suppliers are aware of these concerns and are taking every precaution to make sure nothing like this happens again. Trust me—everyone wants a smooth, uneventful outcome."

Shelby blinked hard. It bothered her how rehearsed his response sounded.

"Does that mean the dresses won't be made in Bangladesh?"

"Shelby," Dennis began. "I can't guarantee that."

"Why not?"

"The process is much more complex than that. They don't just pick a country and find a factory. *Surface Trend*'s supplier works with a buying agent to source each job. They receive bids for the entirety of the project and fulfill the order with the supplier that can meet the proposed price structure and timeline."

"Can't they do that somewhere else?"

"Maybe, maybe not. The country isn't what matters. Just a couple of months ago, there were two fires on the same day in Pakistan. Every factory is highly individualized as to how thoroughly it conforms to industry standards."

Shelby hadn't heard a thing about fires in Pakistan. "I don't understand. How do these factories not all conform to industry standards?"

"How about this? I'll put you in touch with *Surface Trend*'s quality assurance officer. You can ask all your questions. In fact, from this point forward, you'll be working directly with the design team at *Surface Trend*."

"Wait—not with *Buzz Now*?"

"That's correct. At this point, we've fulfilled all the agreements of the contest."

Shelby shut her eyes tight. She knew at some point Dennis would no longer be there holding her hand through the maze. But she hadn't expected to part ways today. She opened her eyes and continued. "I guess I have mixed feelings about that. About everything, actually."

"Let me just say I am beyond sorry that an unexpected tragedy tainted your experience. But I assure you events like this fire are an ugly exception, not the norm. I've been in this industry for decades, and I've never had to deal with a lost order."

When Shelby stayed silent, Dennis continued. "Consider this. There are millions of clothing items being made in thousands of factories around the world every single day. Honestly, they're like airline flights. Millions of safe landings a year that no one notices until a crash."

Nothing about that statistic was comforting. But Dennis had a point. There was every chance her dresses—and Nipa—came together at the wrong place at the wrong time. A truly tragic coincidence.

"I just want to know I'm doing the right thing," she said.

"Consider this. I grew up in China. When I was a baby, my mom and dad left me in the countryside with my grandparents. They moved to the city to work at a factory so they could support us. Eventually they earned enough to send me to a school that taught English. That's how I secured a good-paying job and was able to move here."

"That's . . . a really amazing story," Shelby said.

"These are good jobs, and the people there need them," Dennis said. "And hey, I don't want to pressure you, but it isn't very likely an opportunity this big will come around again."

Shelby's hand rested on the gearshift. Her finger traced its options. Forward. Neutral. Reverse. Her career as a professional designer was just beginning. She wasn't interested in going back to the way things were, to stitching every seam of every dress herself.

"When do they need to know?" she asked.

"Soon. Actually—" his voice trailed off. "If you're not going to accept, I need to know now so *Surface Trend* can contract someone else."

She could tell he didn't want this to sound like an ultimatum. Inhaling deeply, she hoped some of her pent-up anxiety would release in the long exhale to follow.

The task ahead—designing three mommy and daughter spring dresses—was doable. The order could yield a decent income to cover their growing expenses. The decision would be easy if she hadn't spent the last three weeks mourning the ashes of Ashulia.

"I know what you're thinking," Dennis began. "That fire was tragic, but it wasn't your fault or my fault or any of our fault. The factory owners and the managers are to blame for what happened. The fire happened because of *their* negligence."

Stowing the credit card in her wallet, Shelby let her mind picture what the check would look like. The tens of thousands of dollars written out to her name—the earnings, the reward for everything she'd built. The likes parading in from all ends of the social media stratosphere. The look on Bryan's face when the money posted to their account, their financial stress vanishing to zero.

Taking another sip of her drink, she let herself imagine the cushion that would prop them up at the start of a year with a baby on the way.

As for Runa—the Lawrence family would promise to help any way they could.

"When do they need the designs?" As the words left Shelby's tongue, she noticed her hands shaking, unsettled.

"They need everything Thursday."

"*This* Thursday?"

"Yes. By 5 p.m. Pacific time."

"Okay, so that's six designs in four days?" A churning inside Shelby's stomach alerted her suspicions. Something didn't feel right. But saying yes was the only open road that made any sense. To decline this offer would be equally reckless.

"I'll have them done Thursday by 5," she heard her voice say.

"Great. My colleague Mitchell will be your

contact at *Surface Trend*. He leads the design team. They'll be in touch with the contract."

"Okay, thanks." She wanted more time to think it all through, but there wasn't any.

"And Shelby? It's been a pleasure. You've been nothing but a dream to work with."

"Thank you, Dennis. I appreciate everything you've done for me. I would never have had this opportunity without you."

"You're very talented, Shelby. And you've got good instincts for what shoppers want. You'll do just fine."

The call ended. Shelby turned the ignition off and sat in silence, recapping what just happened. Her time working with Dennis was over. She just accepted a spot on *Surface Trend*'s design team. And her deadline was Thursday. *This* Thursday.

Christmas errands would have to wait. Now she needed every single kid-free minute to study the contract and design the dresses. Accepting this offer—along with its risks—meant these dresses needed to be perfect.

Inside the coffee shop, she sipped her drive-thru drink while sketching a dozen spring designs with varying necklines, hem lengths, and trims. But forcing herself to be creative on demand wasn't working.

The preschool hours evaporated before she had any semblance of a plan. Heading to pick up Paisley, she questioned how these designs could possibly be ready on time. She called Bryan to ask if he could take off work tomorrow, but his schedule wouldn't allow it.

So she called her mom, hoping to catch her teacher planning period. Shelby's heart started pounding, the combination of too much coffee and not enough time. Just maybe . . .

"Mom?"

"Hi, honey, what a nice surprise. How are you?"

"I'm slammed. I need help. Can you take off this week?"

Irene Simons hadn't missed a single day of school that semester, so she splurged her PTO and found a substitute for the last two teaching days before winter break. Having never requested her mom take off work before, Shelby felt justified asking the huge favor.

The plan was for her mom to head straight to Paisley's school. After the Christmas party, they'd go for lunch and a fun outing, allowing Shelby the full day to button up her designs.

As the sun lowered toward the treetops, Mimi's station wagon pulled into the driveway. Working all day without interruptions amounted to the best possible Christmas gift. Shelby had signed and returned the contract and already felt confident about four of the six dresses.

As she closed her laptop, Paisley raced inside,

panting like a puppy dog. "Mama! I got a Diggity Doll!"

"Wait, what?!"

"Mimi got me a Diggity Doll! Just like I wanted!"

Shelby's jaw dropped. Paisley was hugging the exact same doll Santa was planning to leave for her on Christmas morning—the same doll that had been hiding in a cardboard box atop Shelby's closet for two months.

"You've got to be kidding me," she said.

"I know! I've been wanting one like forever, and now she's finally mine!"

A wave of panic flashed through Shelby. Four days until Christmas. What on earth could Santa bring now?

"Where's Mimi?" Shelby asked, her voice frantic.

"At the car. She's bringin' in all the bags."

"What bags?"

"With the other stuff she got me."

"What other stuff?"

"The stuff she bought."

"Little P, why don't you go introduce your doll to her new friends," Shelby said.

Paisley rounded the banister and bounded up the stairs to her room.

Shelby stuck her head out the front door. Her eyes widened, seeing her mom balancing armloads of bags and a giant pink beanbag chair.

"Seriously, Mom? That's more stuff than we got her for Christmas."

"Why, hello! Great to see you too, honey. Not exactly the welcome I expected." Mimi set the beanbag chair and the bags beside the entryway table.

"That's not what I meant by doing something fun after school."

"Well, what do you expect? It's fun to take your only granddaughter shopping."

"Yes, except you got her . . ." Shelby glanced up the stairs then resumed in a searing whisper. "You got her big Santa gift."

"I did?"

"Yes. The Diggity Doll. I told you we got that *months* ago."

"Well, I must have forgotten."

Shelby's hand found its way to her forehead. "I can't believe this."

"You do know, I did all this for you. So you could have the afternoon to work. And I wanted to make her smile. That's my job as her grandmother."

"But she doesn't need any of this."

Paisley returned to the living room with the prized doll and a box full of baby clothes and accessories. She dumped it all into a colorful heap on the living room floor.

"Well, I hadn't planned to buy it. But her face lit up when she saw the doll. I just wanted to make her happy. Look how much she loves it."

Paisley sat in front of the Christmas tree, tugging a silver brush through the doll's realistic hair.

"I don't want to sound ungrateful, Mom. I appreciate you coming to help. It's just that—we have so much. We have too much. And we keep getting more. And Christmas hasn't even come yet."

Their eyes turned to the tower of cardboard boxes lining the foyer. Ever since the baby announcement, the packages hadn't stopped.

"Oh, so it's okay for perfect strangers to buy things for your daughter, but it's not okay for her own grandmother?"

"That's for my job," Shelby said.

"And *my* job is to be a good grandmother. I could never do this kind of thing for you growing up. Now is my chance to make up for all the times I had to tell you no."

Shelby could still remember feeling left out as the only girl at the second-grade sleepover without the trendy doll of the day. Her dad out of the picture, there was never enough money for a toy like that.

"Look!" Paisley darted into the foyer, hugging the doll against her chest. Her other hand gripped a picture book. "She looks just like on the cover."

Paisley and the doll twirled in circles throughout the living room. The same magazine cover smile from the photoshoot emerged across her face.

It was the Santa Claus smile. The smile of pure Christmas joy.

At the same time, a burst of delight bloomed in the worn lines around Mimi's sixty-year-old eyes. Until that moment, Shelby hadn't noticed how much her mother resembled Dear.

"Thanks, Mom," she forced herself to say. "Paisley, let's take all your new gifts upstairs."

When Christmas Eve arrived, things were looking up. Shelby met *Surface Trend*'s deadline with hours to spare. Santa was ready with a new light-up scooter that Bryan hunted down online. Her morning sickness waned.

Despite the rocky start, Christmas with her mom in town was shaping up to be sweet and memorable. But while getting ready for the Christmas Eve service, she made the mistake of checking email.

Dear Shelby,

I found out more information about Runa this week. I am sorry to say it is not good news. The administrators at Eternal Promise provided me with the number where they reached Runa's uncle. I spoke to him on the phone at his residence.

Unfortunately, there is not currently a

plan for Runa to attend school. Her uncle lives and works across town, making Eternal Promise inaccessible. He makes very little money as a janitor and cannot support the cost of housing, food, books, and uniforms on his own salary.

I regret the call ended quickly, and I did not get more information about where she stays while he works. He did not say whether she is working, though it is plausible. Many children begin working for the family around her age, and they could use the extra wages.

I know this is not the news we were hoping to hear. Having known Nipa for many years, she would not be pleased either. I believe this brother is her only relative in the district. Eternal Promise tells me they did everything they could to keep Runa.

When Nipa passed away, they were obligated to release the child to her next of kin.

I spoke with my director to see if he would grant special permission to track down Runa and offer the assistance you have pledged. Unfortunately, the request was denied, simply because there are so many in our service region who need our help since the fire.

Thank you for your vigilance in checking on sweet Runa. I regret I have no more answers, but I hope her life in her new home will be molded by the love and support of caring people like you. I wish you and your family a joyous Christmas, and all the fullness of love and hope in Christ.

Kindest regards,
Ravi

Shelby swallowed hard and set her phone face down on the bathroom counter. Stepping into her crimson and white Christmas dress, she stretched a hand behind her back and tugged the invisible zipper up the length of her spine. She smoothed the dress over her shapewear, which just barely still flattened her growing belly.

Four months had flown by at the speed of light since the last time she wore this dress. The photoshoot felt like a distant memory now. She remembered thinking then that when Christmas Day arrived, everything uncertain in her life would be settled. The launch would be complete. Her role as a designer would be formalized. Her career would feel concrete, steady.

Instead, everything felt shaky.

She bunched a pair of pantyhose into her fingertips, running one leg then the other through the sheer covering. Each foot slid into a matte black peep-toe heel. She positioned earrings and bracelets and hairpins. She smudged her eye shadow, blending the smoky effect. She pressed a thick layer of cranberry gloss between her lips.

One long look into her closet's full-length mirror revealed her final appearance, perfect from highlights to heels. How exciting Christmas Eve in their magazine cover dresses had once promised to be.

But now Christmas Eve was here, and her lips refused to curl into a smile. Her eyes blinked at her reflection in a blank stare, hiding away the misery rumbling beneath the façade.

Far away in a land Shelby couldn't accurately picture, a little girl, whose mother dreamed of a better life for her, no longer walked that hallowed path. Her eyes felt the edging of tears, but she fought them away.

In the driveway, Bryan rolled down the windows of her good-as-new SUV to let the unseasonable heat escape. Paisley was strapped in the car seat wearing her matching photoshoot Christmas dress. Mimi sat in the back next to her granddaughter. The Lawrence family rehearsed their lines one more time as they drove the short minutes to church, where Bryan's parents were saving them seats.

On the walk in, they mingled their way toward the large sanctuary, hugging friends and church acquaintances. Once inside, ushers handed out bulletins and candles. Bryan's parents waved to them from a pew at the front. A stunning Christmas tree and a garden of poinsettias brightened the altar.

Soon after they took their seats, a brass ensemble blared *Joy to the World* on trumpets and French horns. A prayer followed announcements, and then Pastor Mark called them forward. "And now the Lawrence family will lead us in lighting the Advent Wreath."

With Paisley at their side, Shelby and Bryan climbed up the altar steps as hundreds of eyes watched. Shelby took the microphone out of its stand and read her first line.

"While they were there, the time came for her to deliver her child. And she gave birth to her firstborn son and wrapped him in bands of cloth and laid him in a manger."

As she passed the microphone to Bryan, Shelby's eyes scanned the crowd. The time between speaking roles offered an opportunity to forge a connection with the audience, to leverage the immediacy of eye contact, the thrill of attentive smiles.

But the hundreds of faces seemed to disappear. Her eyes could see nothing but a room full of clothing, all stitched together by no one here tonight.

An older lady wore a red plaid dress. The crisscross pattern of gridlines didn't match up at the side seams, a shortcut employed by cost-cutting companies to use less material per garment and keep prices low.

At the side exit stood an usher whose sport coat swallowed him like an angry box. The suits Shelby's grandfather wore had all been smartly tailored to caress the curve of his back. He only had a few suits, yet their customized fit made the suits impossible to part with even though he never wore them in his wheelchair.

A young girl kicking her legs back and forth below the pew wore a large red bow and a new velvet dress. The dress couldn't be anything but new—the girl hadn't repeated an outfit at church the entire calendar year.

Shelby imagined her mother snipping the shopping tags off their plastic barb as they scurried out the door, forcing thick layers of unwilling velvet into the swampy Southern air. She pictured the girl's closet, overflowing with dresses and shoes and jewelry and hairbows. Just like Paisley's.

Bryan continued, "Tonight, angels far and near sing tender lullabies. Well-worn fabric full of years holds in the warmth of parental love. Animals and shepherds crowd in tight, glowing with adoration, while a muffled cry squeezes out to greet the world."

In a roar of unison, the congregation responded, "Tonight we give thanks for every child among us. Each new birth—regardless of circumstances—reminds us of the preciousness of life, the potential of tomorrow, the promise of God."

The Advent wreath, about the size of a car tire, perched on a tripod beside them, decorated with evergreen branches and bold red holly berries. Bryan passed the microphone back to Shelby.

"As we reflect on the Lord's fulfilled promises, we light the Joy candle," she said. Tonight, joy felt complicated.

Raising the acolyte wand, Bryan and Paisley lit the first candle.

Shelby's eyes scanned all the children bobbing about in parents' laps and on cushioned pews. She considered how many thousands of outfits grown-ups had bestowed upon the children in this room collectively.

"As we reflect on the Lord's perfect love for us, we light the Love candle," Shelby said, her voice ringing out earnestly over the crowd.

As Bryan and Paisley lit the next candle, Shelby's mind wandered. What did the future hold for a generation of children—including her own—who were taught to consume so furiously?

Shelby continued into the microphone. "As we reflect on the Lord's perfect provision, we light the Peace candle."

Bryan and Paisley positioned the flaming wand to light the Peace candle.

Peace, indeed. The children in this room faced more education options than they could possibly pursue. Highly ranked public schools. Merit-based college scholarships. Five-twenty-nines brimming with tuition payments, book fees, room, and board. The futures in this room twinkled as bright as the LED lights on the Christmas tree.

She continued, "As we reflect on the hope we share in welcoming the Christ child, we light the Hope candle."

Together Bryan and Paisley lit the final outer candle, its hopeful flame rising up, burning bright.

Shelby recited her final line. "On this Christmas Eve, we light the Christ candle for the lowly Lord, a babe wrapped in swaddling clothes."

Bryan raised the wand to light the oversized white candle in the center of the wreath. Shelby held the microphone in front of Paisley.

"And now we know Jesus is born." Just as they rehearsed, she delivered her line right on cue. "Nothing will ever be the same."

The woman in the plaid dress smiled, hearing Paisley's candy cane voice through the speaker. The usher with the boxy sport coat grinned from ear to ear.

As the brass band played the intro for "Away in a Manger," the Lawrence family returned to their pew. Familiar faces and strangers smiled at them. The girl in the red velvet dress threw her arms around her father's waist, nestling into the cushion of his belly.

Singing the words to the classic carol, her heart began to soften. Here she was standing in church on Christmas Eve, passing judgment on everyone in sight to mask her own guilt. That wasn't fair, and it wasn't at all in line with the purpose of this day.

As the service continued, Pastor Mark recited a Christmas homily, a story about a lamb searching for the right path. But Shelby couldn't focus.

The image from Ravi's email replayed through her mind on a constant loop. Runa, age 11, no longer attending school.

Her gaze turned back to the Advent wreath, with its supposed promises of peace, love, joy, and hope. Soon as her eyes settled upon the candlelit wreath, her breath caught in her throat. Her shoulders stiffened beneath her wrap. She grew tense all over.

The flame from the Hope candle had burned out. From its wick, a thin wisp of smoke rose up and up and up.

Chapter 13

For all its presumed magic, Christmas was one of the strangest days of the year. People did odd things they never usually did. Paisley took a nap. Shelby sat on the floor by the Christmas tree, doing absolutely nothing. Bryan rested in front of a dark TV screen, devouring a legal thriller. Mimi said goodbye after presents and brunch, on the road to visit Shelby's grandfather in Florida.

Late afternoon, Shelby started moving again. There was one last gift to exchange.

"Mama, can we go now?" Paisley asked.

"Soon as I'm done wrapping this. Bry, do you want to come to Maye's with us?"

Bryan in the recliner, still reading. "Think I'll stay put," he said, his eyes glued to the pages.

"Mama, can we please go?" Even after a morning overflowing with new toys and clothes, the lure of one more present fueled her impatience.

"Yes. Just about finished." Shelby assembled a gift bag containing dish towels. She hadn't expected to exchange gifts with Maye. Though completely impersonal, dish towels would have to do.

As they crossed the street, Paisley zipped figure eights around Shelby on her new scooter.

Maye opened the door. "Merry, Merry Christmas, Lawrence ladies!"

"Merry Christmas!" Paisley replied.

"Can you believe this heat?" Maye asked.

"It's so strange. Makes it hard to believe it's really Christmas," Shelby said.

"On the plus side, good weather for playing with new toys." Maye winked at Paisley, who was still wearing last night's Christmas dress.

"Miss Maye, look at what Santa brought me," Paisley said.

"He came? Oh goodness. You must have been a good girl to get such a fancy scooter."

"I was." Paisley beamed.

"Speaking of, I have a little something for you."

"Really?" Paisley's eyes widened.

"Follow me, ladies," Maye said, inviting them inside and up the staircase.

The noisy creak heard with each step up the cedar stairs confirmed that Shelby had never been up to the second floor of Maye's house. There had never been a reason to, which made her curious why they were going upstairs now.

Along the upstairs hallway, large photographs in thick wooden frames lined the walls. In them were younger pictures of Junia and Stephen, pictures of Maye and Roger on their wedding day, as well as stunning, though dated, portraits of their family of four.

They followed Maye to the end of the hallway into a library. Shelves packed with books and knickknacks lined the walls. A wicker rocking chair faced the window that looked out over the front yard.

Inspecting the space, Shelby understood why they had never seen it until now. This room was all about Roger. Shelby didn't know much about him, just that a sudden heart attack had ended his life not long before Shelby and Bryan moved in across the street.

The more they got to know Maye, the more Shelby wished she'd had a chance to meet Roger. As kind and hospitable a neighbor as she had been to them, Shelby sensed she was only experiencing half of something, only a portion of who Maye really was.

Hanging on the walls were a series of 8 x 10 photographs in bamboo frames from Maye and Roger's travels. Shelby knew they'd traveled extensively, but not to typical tourist destinations like New York or Paris. Their travels were largely off the beaten path.

Paisley spotted a framed photo full of children on the bookshelf. "Who are all these kids?"

"Those children are in El Salvador. Their neighborhood was destroyed by a mudslide after the big earthquake a dozen years ago. We went to build a house for this little girl's family." Maye pointed to a girl in a purple T-shirt dress who looked a few years older than Paisley. "We cooked a big dinner one night for the town and gave out clothing and food. These were all the kids that came to eat with us."

"What about these?" Paisley pointed to the next picture.

"That's a group of children at a school in South Sudan. We lived there for a few years when Stephen was little."

"You *lived* there?" Shelby interjected. "As a parent?"

"Yep. The people we met were so friendly and loving. Hated to leave, but I was pregnant with Junia, and our visas were expiring. I flew back eight months pregnant."

"You're not serious?" Shelby replied.

"There were some unusual circumstances, but it all worked out." Maye shrugged her shoulders.

"Isn't it super risky to fly that close to term?"

"I'm sure it is for some people," Maye said. "I didn't know of any medical concerns. I would have flown back nine months pregnant if I could have. We got so close to the families there, and I didn't know if I would ever see them again."

Maye continued her tour of photos on the bookshelves. A room full of children at an orphanage in Kenya. The collapsed roof of a church as hurricane relief began in Puerto Rico. Two wide-smiling teenage boys, selling iguanas and coconuts on the side of the road in Panama.

As Maye told colorful stories from her trips, Shelby scanned the souvenirs and artifacts on display throughout the library. Paisley reached out her arm toward a painted wooden flower on an end table beside the rocking chair.

"Little P, let's not touch anything," Shelby instructed.

"Oh, it's fine," Maye assured her. "Nothin' in here I can't part with if it breaks."

"What is it?" Paisley inspected the flower.

"That's a water lily."

"I really love it. Can I have it?"

"Paisley," Shelby snapped. "It's not polite to ask for something that isn't yours."

"Actually, that's why I brought y'all up here. This room is full of special trinkets from places we've explored as a family. I wanted Paisley to pick out one of our treasures as her Christmas present."

"May I please have this flower?" Paisley asked.

"Yes, you may. It's a fitting choice. The water lily is the national flower of Bangladesh. We bought it at a market not long after we met Runa."

A surge of heat pulsed through the underside of Shelby's skin. How was it that a place she'd never traveled to now haunted her? She knew she needed to share her connection to the fire with Maye. And she needed to tell Bryan about Nipa. She needed to tell someone before it burned a hole through her conscience. But she wanted Paisley out of earshot.

"They call the lily *shapla*," Maye explained. "Can you say that?"

"Shap-la," Paisley repeated. "Thank you, Miss Maye."

"You're very welcome. And this is for you, Shelby." Maye extended a snowflake-covered bag that was waiting beside the rocking chair. "Well, I suppose it's for your whole family."

Shelby reached beneath the tissue paper and pulled out what felt like a thin wooden box. It opened at its hinges, revealing two side-by-side photographs. Shelby found herself staring into the two faces that had imprinted on her mind for the past month.

Nipa and Runa. Together.

"Last week I sifted through a stack of trip pictures that didn't make it into the album. Found this one of Runa when she was a baby. Nipa came in to pick her up after work while we were there serving dinner. Roger must have taken this one of them together."

The picture on the right was from November, of Nipa and Runa wearing *Treasured Pockets* matching dresses.

Shelby sat silent, completely still, as her neighbor awaited her response. As far as Maye knew, this was a thoughtful Christmas gift to help them remember a special child who was now but a memory. This picture that once brought Shelby unspeakable joy now struck like a dagger to her soul. Maye had no idea why.

Steadying her emotions, Shelby showed the pictures to Paisley. "Look, Little P. See who it is?"

"Hey, it's Runa! Can we see that other picture of her?" Paisley asked.

Maye reached onto a bookshelf and pulled out the green album. She opened it to display the group picture.

"She was such a cute baby," Paisley said.

"She was. She's an adorable and very smart little girl," Maye said.

"My mom says Mr. Ravi will send a new picture of her very soon. Won't he, Mama?"

Shelby's eyes met Maye's, forging an understanding that this difficult conversation hadn't yet happened. She suddenly faced a tough choice. Either modify the truth and string her daughter along. Or come out with the truth and mop up the emotions to follow.

The empathetic creases around Maye's eyes suggested what needed to happen.

Taking a deep breath, Shelby made herself say the disappointing words. "Sweetie, I'm sorry to tell you this, but Mr. Ravi won't be sending any more pictures of Runa."

"But why not?" Paisley's eyes flooded with disbelief.

"Because, sweetie. Runa moved. She moved to a new town."

"Why'd she move?"

Shelby hoped Maye would step in to answer these questions. But Maye remained silent.

"You remember last year when your friend Joey from school moved to Austin?"

"Uh-huh. You said we could go visit him. Can we go visit Runa?"

"No, sweetie. We don't know where she is anymore. She moved too far away. That's why Mr. Ravi can't send us any more pictures."

"But we can still mail her letters. Right, Mama?"

"No, unfortunately we can't. They don't have her address to deliver the letters. But we can get a new friend to mail letters to."

"I don't want a new friend." The volume of Paisley's voice escalated. "I want Runa. She has Ballet Bear!"

Shelby's eyes begged Maye for help.

"Sweetheart," Maye began, "you were a special friend to Runa during a very important time in her life. I know she will treasure your bear for a long, long time."

A teak clock on the wall chimed. Paisley's head turned to investigate where the sound came from. Shelby saw a tear streaming down the girl's face.

Paisley ran her fingers over each wooden

petal of the water lily. She looked up at Shelby. "Mama, is Runa really gone forever?"

Shelby rubbed her hand in a circle across Paisley's back. With Maye's eyes staring into her, she forced the words to come out. "Yes, Little P. I'm afraid she's really gone."

Chapter 14

February 2013

The rain drizzled down onto the windshield. Shelby sat in a shopping center parking lot staring through tears at the coffee group text from Elise.

> Wanted you to know we lost the baby. Went in for the ultrasound, and there was no heartbeat. I'm so sorry to text this, but I didn't think I could get the words out in person. Found out she was a girl. I'm a mess. Cannot stop crying.

It was off routine for Jason to take their kids to school. Now Shelby understood why.

Wiping the tears from her cheeks, she spent a few minutes formulating a reply. It was beyond heartbreaking to lose a baby during any part of pregnancy, and extra tragic during the second trimester. There were no good words for a loss like this.

The drizzly, gray day matched the mood of this sad news. Shelby collected herself then pulled the trench coat hood over her hair. She stepped out of the car toward the morning's destination, a resale shop called *Second Spin*.

Whitney tipped her off that the girls planned a surprise baby sprinkle for a few close friends. Shelby figured she should at least attempt to depart from yoga pants for the occasion. Somehow, she'd made it nearly three months without buying any new clothes. Well, not counting the six figures' worth of Easter dresses *Surface Trend* ordered on her behalf.

For once, Shelby truly didn't have anything to wear. After the first two years of infertility, she gave away every maternity item she owned. The superstitious impulse left her without a pregnancy wardrobe.

Unwilling to participate in a supply chain she didn't understand, she couldn't bring herself to buy new clothes at the usual places. Their websites were all so vague about how they sourced their clothing. Research didn't yield any straight answers.

Sewing something was an option, but there wasn't enough time. The backup plan—borrowing from Elise—was now completely off limits. She wasn't about to remind her grieving friend that her maternity wardrobe would be sitting idle.

Shelby gripped her keys tightly as she walked toward the store. The inside of the retail space smelled like potpourri. Shoppers, mostly women, mulled through the aisles squeaking hanger after hanger across clothing racks. She joined them, starting at a rounder of sweaters, which she quickly realized were sorted not by size but color.

Realizing this, she went straight to her weakness—the pink section. She flipped through each garment, inspecting the tag. Most of the labels were brands she recognized.

Her first promising find was a loose-knit tunic sweater in her size that looked hardly ever worn. In a pinch, she could throw it over leggings. The price tag read $3.99. *Yes, please.* She flung it over her arm and continued sliding hangers left to right.

Three promising finds later, the store was growing on her. Shelby scanned the room for dresses. Against the store's back wall hung a row of silky dresses in every shade. A flowy maxi dress caught her eye but was six sizes too big. For $6.99, she could easily alter it to fit. She continued inspecting more dresses when her eyes spun ahead of her.

Her heart pounded its next pulse. The air caught in her throat.

The pink dress.

Hanging in a thrift shop two miles from her house was a sparkleberry *Treasured Pockets* dress, size 10. Shelby yanked the hanger off the rack, fumbling her collection of resale finds onto the floor.

She inspected the dress—*her* dress. It was brand new. The original sales tags were still attached. She let it sink in what this could mean. For *this* dress to be in *this* store, tags still on, it had to have been purchased, never worn, and discarded within a matter of months.

Shelby didn't think she could be any more shocked when an inquisitive voice interrupted her silent outrage.

"Hi, Miss Shelby. Nice to see you here."

Hearing her name, Shelby visibly jumped. "Junia! You . . . you startled me." Her young neighbor was pushing a shopping cart packed with clothes.

"I'm so sorry, Miss Shelby—I didn't mean to. Are you okay?" Maye's daughter was just as polite as her mother and had the same vivid blue eyes.

"Oh no, it's okay." Shelby laughed to lighten the moment. "I don't usually shop at thrift stores but figured I'd, you know, try something new." She waved a hand through the air casually, her enthusiasm masking her apprehension. "But wait, shouldn't you be in school?"

"It's my last semester, so I have some class periods off. I work here in my free time."

"You work here, at *Second Spin*?"

"Yup."

"Oh," Shelby said, surprised. "Well, maybe you can answer a question for me. Where do these clothes come from?"

"It's all from people who donated to the store."

The price tag on the berry dress stared back

at Shelby menacingly. "Do you ever get clothes from other businesses?"

"What do you mean?" Junia adjusted the thick black glasses resting on her nose.

"Like, does someone from, say, *Surface Trend* ever show up and drop off their clearance clothes that don't sell?"

"No, not that I know of. I believe everything here wasn't wanted anymore."

Shelby glared at the dress in her arms, its paisley label mocking her. She knew the next question seemed obvious, but she felt compelled to ask it anyway. "Junia, can you tell me, why would a dress like this still have tags on it?"

"Usually means someone bought it and didn't wear it."

"Why would someone buy something and not wear it?"

"That's a good question. Have you ever done that?"

"What, bought something brand new and not worn it?" Shelby thought for a minute. Sure, there were a handful of new items in her closet she hadn't had a chance to wear yet. But the season was wrong. Or the fit was off. Or she just hadn't come across the right occasion yet.

"I mean, don't you think most people would at least try to sell something new?"

"Miss Shelby, we see clothes with tags all the time. New clothes are so cheap, whether or not they've been worn doesn't seem to matter."

"What does matter then?"

"I don't know. Probably making more space in the closet. You know, for new stuff."

And there it was. Her *Treasured Pockets* dress design, sewn in a factory with blocked fire escapes, featured in *Buzz Now Magazine*, promoted and sold by *Surface Trend* stores nationwide, cast away, having never been worn, all to make room for the next trendy dress.

"Do you want to talk to my supervisor? She can probably answer your questions better than I can. She's worked here forever."

The churning inside Shelby's stomach indicated she wasn't ready to have this conversation. As she ran her fingertips over the sparkleberry seams, she wondered if the person who'd sewn this discarded dress had made it through the fire.

"Sure." Shelby found herself agreeing to the conversation before she could talk herself out of it. She stashed her shopping finds on a nearby clothing rounder. Junia led her to the store's back room, where a woman with a pixie cut and maroon cat-eye glasses sat in front of a computer screen.

"Hi, Pamela? My neighbor Miss Shelby is here. She has some questions about the store. Is now a good time for you?"

"Of course. Come on in." Pamela gestured at a padded orange swivel chair.

Junia waved goodbye, and Shelby took a seat.

"Nice to meet you, Pamela. How are you?"

"Very nice to meet you too. I'm well, thanks. What can I do for you?"

"Well, I'm . . . I guess I'm interested to learn more about the secondhand clothing market."

"On what account? Buying or selling?"

"Neither. Let's just say I've had some bad experiences with the fashion industry recently. I'm wondering what other options there are to shop for clothes without questioning what I'm buying."

"Questioning how?"

Shelby was thrown, not knowing how to answer. She wasn't sure who was interviewing whom.

"I don't know exactly. Like . . . questioning how the clothing is made. I'm just exploring alternatives."

"Well, what I can tell you is that what we do here represents a blade of grass in a football field. The clothing industry is enormous. We're talking trillions. Worldwide, about three out of every four pieces of clothing end up in the landfill."

"Wow. What about here, at your store?"

"Here at *Second Spin*, we make it our mission to keep some of that clothing cycling through longer, which provides jobs in our stores and warehouses. They aren't glamorous jobs, but some people just need that important first job to gain work experience. It's a decent steppingstone to whatever's next."

"Junia said you've worked here a long time?"

"I've been with the company 12 years at various locations. I'm a store director now, but sorting donations and running the register is how I started out. It was the only job I could get at the time."

"Twelve years—that's a long time."

"It is. A lot has changed."

"Really? Like what?" Unprepared as she was for this conversation, learning more information was strangely energizing.

"Well, I'd say the biggest change is the quality of the fabrics we see. Used to be, we'd have some fairly affluent buyers making the rounds, looking for solid pieces from top brands. And they'd find them too. But in the last dozen years, a lot of those companies have switched to high volume. So their fabric quality has changed, and long-lasting pieces are harder to find."

"What do you mean by high volume?"

"In the late '90s a few lead retailers started selling clothes in huge amounts—high volume. They order hundreds of thousands, sometimes even a million of each garment they sell. They pay only a tiny bit more per garment than it costs to make and ship, but they still make money 'cause they sell so many of them."

"And they use cheaper materials so they can

keep costs down?" Shelby fought against the lump in her throat.

"Exactly. And since shoppers don't want to pay too much for clothing anymore, these big chains own the markets because they keep the prices so low. They've forced a lot of mid-level retailers to either join high-volume, high-discount sales or go under."

"That's rough." Shelby recalled the years running her online store. She'd always wondered how clothing companies could get away with charging such rock-bottom prices when it cost her so much more to make a dress and a profit. A dollar of profit per tank top isn't much, until you multiply it times a million.

"The cheap fabric and all the extra trend cycles mean the garment doesn't last as long, sending shoppers back to the stores quicker," Pamela added.

"Does that mean thrift stores have done better since more people are getting rid of more clothes?"

"Not really. Overall inventory at our stores has increased, but a lot of the clothing can't be resold. It's too worn already or didn't wash well. In fact, only about half of all the clothing donated to a store like ours will be resold."

"What do you do with clothes you can't sell?" Shelby asked.

"That's starting to become a problem too."

"Why is that?"

"Well, we have a process in place. Rather than pay to landfill the unwanted clothes, we sell them by the pound to a company at a big warehouse by the port. They pack 500 pounds of used clothing into huge bales. Then an export company ships them off in pallets to places like Nigeria, Pakistan, and India. Businesses there buy the bales of clothes and either sell or use the fabric as raw material to make other things."

"Sounds like a huge global recycling process?"

"Not necessarily recycling."

"Why is that?" Shelby asked.

"More and more of the stuff that gets shipped over there ends up in landfills. The developing world is overloaded with our unwanted clothes. Now that billions of folks in China and India are starting to buy clothes like Americans do, we're competing with them to sell our unwanted stuff overseas."

Shelby fell silent. She thought back to how excited she was in November to launch her clothing line, to make a mark on mothers and daughters as they bought and wore her dresses at Christmastime. It never dawned on her to think of what would happen to the six figures' worth of *Treasured Pockets* dresses once Christmas ended. According to Pamela, most would end up in the landfill. The same would be true of the Easter line that was about to ship from Bangladesh.

"Do you have any other questions I can answer?"

Shelby fiddled with a silver tassel hanging off the zipper of her purse. "I guess I'm curious— from your perspective—what would you want people to know before they donate clothes to your store?"

"Great question. A couple of things. I wish everyone knew we rarely sell something unless it's ready to wear. So many people donate things with stains or wrinkles, things that could be easily fixed with one more wash and dry at home. That often makes the difference between resale in the store and exporting—or heading to the landfill at places without our recycling policies."

"So basically, wash and iron clothes before you donate them?"

"Exactly. We just don't have the labor to care for every item that comes in. If it's ready to wear, it's more likely to find a second life."

"Gotcha." Shelby's phone began vibrating in her purse. She glanced at the screen enough to see that Mitchell, the design lead at *Surface Trend*, was calling. She silenced the ringer. "What's the other thing?"

"This is my personal soapbox, so forgive me. I wish people would stop buying cheap, trendy stuff that's only going to last a season or two. It would serve all of us better here at the store to receive fewer high-quality items we can resell for bigger margins. And you know what else bothers me?"

"What's that?"

"There's no style to these clothes. It's the same basic shirts and hoodies with minor variations based on some trend some business thinks would sell. I much prefer to buy high-quality, timeless items I really love, and hang onto them as long as possible."

"That sounds . . . really sensible," Shelby said, tucking her hair behind her ear.

"If we all shopped like that, thrift stores would return to being a place where you could either stretch your dollar if you need to or find a true treasure if you're willing to hunt for it."

"Thank you for your time, Pamela. I really appreciate it."

"My pleasure, Shelby. And I'm sorry, I didn't catch your story. Are you a reporter?"

"No. I'm just a . . . a concerned shopper." Shelby forced the words out despite the truth they omitted.

"Well, we could sure use a few more of those."

Back at her car, Shelby tossed the bag containing two promising resale finds and the unexpected sparkleberry dress onto the passenger seat. After the months-long shopping hiatus, walking out of a store with new-to-her clothes made her want to post all over social media.

Which was actually something she needed to do. Her social media activity had dwindled ever since the fire. She knew it wasn't likely to happen to the same designer twice, but promoting the new dresses still felt risky. In response, she was posting much less frequently, attracting far fewer new followers.

Settling into the driver's seat, she pulled out her phone to call Mitchell back, drafting off her newfound energy.

"Shelby—How's my favorite Texan?"

"I'm great, thanks. Spent the morning shopping. How are you?"

"We are slammed, but otherwise doing well."

"That seems to be on trend."

"Hah, I suppose. Wanted to update you on the timeline for your dresses."

"Everything going okay?" Shelby held her breath, hoping nothing would ruin her boosted mood.

"Yes. We're right on track."

"That's a relief. Been trying not to bug you. I just want everything to go smoothly this time."

"Understandable. The order is scheduled to arrive in port the last week of February. The dresses will be distributed to *Surface Trend* stores in the weeks after. Soon as they hit the first stores, we'll start the online ad blitz."

"That all sounds great." Waiting for the order to ship, Shelby felt unsure about the whole process.

Knowing her dresses were off the factory floor boosted her confidence. "I'm curious, do you think there will be any media interest?"

"I wouldn't expect any. *Buzz Now* seeks out media attention. Our focus is customers."

"During the launch, I noticed a lot of traction after going on our local news show. I would love to keep that momentum going."

"That's fine. Any local coverage you want to arrange is up to you. Anything you can do to increase exposure should all help sales."

Written into Shelby's contract was a somewhat steep sales projection. If the 145,000 dresses sold well, she would make a decent profit. But she wouldn't make a dime until production costs were covered—no small feat considering the enormous size of the order. The Bayou City Sunrise charged a hefty sum to feature commercial guests. The expense would come out of her own pocket, but it could be worth the cost to boost her sales.

"I'm wondering, can *Surface Trend* provide any swag as a giveaway incentive for my followers?"

"Like what?" Mitchell asked.

"Like a discount code as an incentive for watching and sharing highlights from the show?"

"Hmm. We rarely offer discount codes since our prices are already so low, but I'll check with marketing. Maybe they can spare a gift card. I like the way you're thinking."

"Thanks." A smile grew across Shelby's face.

After months of doubting herself, she welcomed the affirmation. Maybe Dennis was right—perhaps she did have good instincts. And maybe, just maybe, she'd be able to turn her luck around and become part of the dream team at *Surface Trend*.

Chapter 15

Dress launch week was underway, and everything from distribution to marketing was moving forward seamlessly.

After a busy week, Shelby put the finishing touches on tomorrow's outfit for the Bayou City Sunrise. She plugged in her phone then collapsed into bed.

Bryan zipped up his suitcase, ready to fly to Nashville after Shelby returned from the show.

"Everything good to go?" he asked, getting into bed.

"Pretty sure. Been preparing for weeks. Think I've covered every possible hiccup. You set the DVR, right?"

"Yes. A week ago. And I double-checked it tonight. All good."

"Okay, thanks." Shelby pulled her phone from her nightstand and opened her calendar. "I got an email earlier from church about Easter services. How do you feel about hosting a brunch?"

"Sure. Sounds good," Bryan said. "Wait. What weekend is that?"

"March 31st," Shelby replied, her thumbs pecking away on her phone to create the calendar invite.

"Wait a sec. I think that's when I'm at Pebble Beach." Bryan checked his calendar.

"No, it can't be. That's Easter Sunday." Shelby looked up from the screen.

"Well, that's when we're going."

"Wait, what? You can't go. You have to be here. It's Easter."

"Well, I'm not going to be," he said, a little too matter-of-factly.

"Bryan, I need you here!" Shelby said in disbelief.

"I can't *not* go. Keith put this on our calendar months ago."

"How on earth could your boss have booked a golf weekend over Easter?"

"We're pitching our designs in San Francisco the week before. They tacked it on since everyone will already be there."

"Okay, but seriously, how can they make you miss a family holiday?"

"It's just . . . how it is."

"Well, I'm not okay with *how it is*. I feel like you're never here when I need you."

"Well, Shel, I don't have much choice. This project is what I've worked toward my entire career. And Pebble Beach is a big deal. They only invite associates on track for partner."

"This seems ridiculous, though. They're forcing you to choose your coworkers over your family."

"Sweetheart, it's one weekend. It just happened to fall on a holiday. Wasn't intentional. No one caught it."

Shelby shot him an annoyed glare. "So, what am I supposed to do on Easter? Haul a kid and our unborn child to church by myself while you're out golfing at a fancy resort?"

"Hey, I'm sorry. If it's that hard on you, you should go out of town or something. Go see your mom."

"I can't. That's the weekend people at church will be wearing my spring line. And we purposely did accessories for the guys to include the whole family. You're supposed to be there to complete the look. You can't *not* be there."

"Good to know you only need me here to complete the look. Makes me want to hang back, so we can all *match*."

"That's not what I mean, Bryan. Of course, I want you here. I want our family to be together. I want you here when Paisley opens her Easter basket. I want to sing next to you in church and have brunch with our friends after."

"I want to be here for that too. But I can't back out of the trip. It's too important."

Shelby took a deep breath, trying to calm her boiling anger. She'd married Bryan right out of college because of his extreme loyalty to her. And because of the stability he represented coming from a loving family with parents who remained devoted to their marriage. It was everything she dreamed her own family would look like one day. Now she was starting to question where Bryan's loyalty really rested.

Also bothering her was that the trip was even possible for him. As the mom, she could never skip such an important family weekend. Too many puzzle pieces wouldn't be assembled correctly if moms left town while dads stuffed Easter baskets and kept wiggly children quiet during church. The absurd inequality of expectations made her outrage boil hotter.

"I hope you have a great time, Bryan. I'll just be here, doing everything."

Laying on her side, Shelby pulled her knees into her chest. She wasn't sure how long she'd been awake and balled up like a pincushion. The clock said half-past one. Her argument with Bryan, combined with the angst of the early morning TV show, guaranteed she wouldn't sleep soundly that night.

Still, this didn't feel like a usual bout of pregnancy insomnia.

As the effort to draw each breath increased, a razor spiraled through her gut. A chill engulfed her. The hair on her forearms stood on end. The inside of her mouth dried up like a desert.

Her arm stretched toward the nightstand reaching for a plastic tumbler. She lifted her head

270

enough to sip a spoonful of stale water. A few missed drops dribbled along her cheek onto the pillowcase. Her mouth found relief, but in her stomach, the pain continued. She curled into a tighter ball. What was going on?

Was it nerves? Something she ate?

It didn't matter. Whatever was happening needed to move along so she could recover in time for the show.

Shivering, Shelby pulled the comforter up over her ears, but the chill remained. When the knives turning in her stomach became too intense, she untucked her legs and willed them to carry her to the bathroom.

Her toes caught a pair of shoes on the carpet, and she tumbled to the floor. Saliva pooled in her mouth. Her stomach began heaving. On hands and knees, she crawled toward the toilet just in time to release the unwanted tangle of fluids into the porcelain bowl.

And again. And again.

She flushed, her kneecaps pressing against the cold tile. She shifted her weight over her heels, feeling slightly less terrible. The only redeeming aspect of throwing up was the rush of relief that bounded in after. She rinsed with mouthwash and returned to the warm cave under the comforter. Snuggling in on her side, she felt the brush of fingertips on her back.

"You okay?" Bryan's midnight voice was sweet and gravelly.

"Not sure." Her words hung in the air as if gripping a clothesline of uncertainty. The day ahead was starting to feel like a disaster in need of recovery crews, and it hadn't even started.

Shelby lay still, clenching for hours, her stomach continuing to swirl as she rehearsed her interview responses over and over in her mind. Having never fallen back asleep, she eventually turned off the alarm clock.

She crept through the dark house to the guest room bathroom, where shreds of light and bits of noise were less likely to disturb Bryan and Paisley. Turning the light on, she double blinked at the sight of herself in the mirror. Her cheeks puffed like a soufflé. Her stinging red eyes sat atop the shadowy, dark patches, leaving her unsure if makeup could undo so much damage.

After washing her hair, she set to work painting over the evidence of her illness with thick, matte foundation, taking in little sips of sparkling water and tiny bits of rice cereal to quell her uneasy stomach. As she readied her look for the cameras, she continued to practice her talking points in a low mumble, smoothing over final wording.

As she tugged the long zipper up the back of a *Treasured Pockets* Easter dress, a distant sob interrupted her thoughts. She rushed to Paisley's room.

Entering the girl's room, Paisley sat up in bed, squeezing a stuffed pig between her chest and her knees. Glow from the nightlight revealed the glisten of tears on the girl's cheeks.

"Sweetie, what's wrong?"

"My tummy hurts," she said, her arms stretching out for her mom's.

"Okay, let's get you to the bath—."

Before she could pull her off the bed, Paisley threw up all over the pile of stuffed animals, across the comforter, into Shelby's guarding hands, and down the front of her TV-ready dress.

"No, no, no!" Shelby yelled. "You've *got* to be kidding me." Her eyes stung with disbelief.

Paisley began sobbing, wailing loudly.

"Bryan!" Shelby yelled. "We need you!" Surely, he'd heard the crying by now.

"Aah! What do I do?" Bryan's eyes widened, stunned by the scene.

"Grab some towels."

Once her hands were wiped, Bryan unzipped Shelby's dress. He wadded it up and dropped it onto the bed with the other mess.

"Get Paisley into the shower," Shelby instructed. "Pull out the braids and shampoo her twice." Shelby raced to their bathroom. She scrubbed her hands and leg, threw on one of Bryan's old T-shirts, then went back to Paisley's room to assess the damage in full light.

The mess was incalculable. Somehow there

were spots on the comforter, the sheets, across a dozen plush stuffies and dolls. It dribbled down into a puddle on the cream carpet. Her Easter dress for the show lay like a corpse in the middle of it all.

Shelby checked the time. The damage was going to take forever to undo. The Bayou City Sunrise started at 7 a.m., an hour from now and a good half hour drive away without traffic. Bryan was flying out to Pittsburgh later this afternoon. Cleaning this up amounted to a death sentence for contracting the virus and getting sick during his trip. He was already exposed, but she didn't want to risk upping his chances.

Maybe the show could push her spot to another day. Reserving the space had cost hundreds of dollars, which she didn't want to lose.

"Hi, Lionel. This is Shelby Lawrence. I'm supposed to be the first guest on the Sunrise this morning, but I've . . . I've run into a setback. Is there any way I can appear tomorrow or next week instead?"

"I'm sorry, but we're booked solid for the next three weeks," he said.

Shelby exhaled, feeling queasy. In three weeks, Easter would be done, and the prime window for selling dresses would be over. She'd been promoting this appearance for weeks. Her followers expected to watch her live this morning. Marketing came through with a $100

Surface Trend gift card. The giveaway hinged on a trivia question that could only be answered by watching the interview. "Are there any other options?"

"We can cancel and have our other guest do a double, but we can't offer a refund. Or if you can get here by 7:30, we can get you mic'd and fit you in last. That's about the best we can do."

Shelby started toward the hallway closet. "Okay, I'll be there by 7:30." She hung up and grabbed a bucket, paper towels, and a bottle of spray cleaner. She wanted to stop and sob at how this long-awaited day was unfolding. But there was no time and no use. Certain moments about motherhood just existed. Projecting emotions would do nothing to minimize the grueling work that needed to be done, the work it seemed no one else could do but a mom.

"What's next?" Bryan emerged, dark circles under his eyes. "Are you still going to the show?"

"I have to, or I lose the spot and the money."

"Let me do that. You get out of here." Bryan reached for the spray bottle.

"I don't want you to get this. I would feel even worse if you get sick on your trip."

"I don't want you to be late. What else can I do?"

"Make me some black tea, please. I don't think I can stomach coffee. And a piece of toast."

Shelby rechecked the time. Fifteen more

275

minutes to scrub, get cleaned up, find something else to wear, and hit the road. In just over an hour, the whole ordeal of a show would be over. She just needed to get through the next 75 minutes.

"Glad you made it," Lionel said. "Love your dress. Here, come with me, quick quick."

Somehow, Shelby made it there with five minutes to spare. Lionel slid a small wiry mic into her ear and planted the receiver on her back. They seated her in the room on deck beside the studio floor.

After her appearance on the show in November, she felt comfortable enough with the show's procedures to stay calm. She watched the screen as the news anchor, Carmen Simpson, introduced the next guest, a lady in a skirt suit from some nonprofit. Only fifteen minutes remained until Shelby's turn on stage.

She scanned the state of her appearance in the waiting room's full-length mirror. Not her best, but considering the morning she had, she didn't think she could look any better. A wave of ache passed through her, gnarling her stomach. She stuffed the feeling out of her mind and swiped pressed powder over the glisten forming on her forehead and cheeks.

Hearing the word "sex" in the current interview, she turned toward the small screen.

"So, help us understand, Lottie, who are

the children who are most at risk for being trafficked?" Carmen asked.

"The children most at risk are those who aren't supervised by a trustworthy caregiver, especially those being raised by someone other than a mother or father. Minors who are unsupervised for large amounts of time, who don't have a stable home life or adult mentor guiding them—these are the children who tend to be the most vulnerable to being trafficked."

"What kind of circumstances lead these children to become more vulnerable?"

"Often it's a sudden or dramatic change in family circumstance. This can come from substance abuse, divorce, maybe the death or incarceration of a parent, which leaves primary caregivers unequipped or unable to sustain a household. When the household falls apart, children are at risk for finding stability and care in places other than their original family unit.

"This is what a lot of our recovering victims have in common. Their family life fell apart. They experienced limited supervision. They were offered a meal and a place to sleep by someone who appeared trustworthy. Sometimes those offers come from the traffickers we're working to stop. These individuals and groups benefit financially from having control of a minor who has nowhere else to go and no one checking on their whereabouts."

The guest, Lottie McKnight, was the director of a nonprofit that worked to stop sex trafficking of minors. When Lionel emailed out the show's agenda, Lottie was originally listed as the final guest. Shelby's late arrival switched the order. She wasn't thrilled about having to follow such a heavy topic.

"What exactly is human trafficking?" Carmen asked.

"Human trafficking involves any kind of labor that someone is forced to do against their will. My work focuses specifically on minors in America, but of course, we know this is an issue globally. Sadly, Houston is considered to be a hub for human trafficking across the world."

"Lottie, this is such a serious and sickening issue, but it often feels like there's nothing the average person can do to stop human trafficking from happening. What are some things our viewers can do to identify or help a minor who's at risk of being trafficked?"

"The biggest thing any of us can do is pay attention. Pay attention to the children and teenagers who fall into your circle of influence in any capacity, whether in your neighborhood, at your child's school, at your place of worship. Especially if you work in a professional role that works with children like education, medical, legal, counseling. Pay attention to children who have a sudden change in family circumstances.

"Follow up and make sure they have a safe place to live, not just immediately following the change, but six months, nine months, a year later. If you're a teacher and a student drops out of school, go the extra steps to figure out why. You might be the only responsible adult in that child's life who notices or cares they are missing."

With that, Shelby's eyes stung with concern. Runa's tragedy seemed to follow her everywhere. She clenched her fists, fighting against her emotions. With only five minutes until her live interview, she didn't have time to wipe away and reapply the thick layers of eyeliner and mascara. Now wasn't the time to consider whether Runa, the girl they'd grown to love, might be living a life against her will, which was starting to sound recklessly plausible.

"Thanks for coming, Lottie, and thanks for the important work you're doing. For more information and resources on what you can do to stop the trafficking of minors, please reference the human trafficking hotline on your screen or visit our website."

"Thank you for having me, Carmen."

"Next up, a lighter topic for the end of our show. Our local fashion star and mommy-and-me dress designer Shelby Lawrence is back with this year's trends for spring fashion and Easter dresses. We'll see you right here after the break on the Bayou City Sunrise."

The whirlpool in Shelby's gut spun faster, forcing her to question why. Maybe it was her upset stomach. Or perhaps, the inferiority of walking into the spotlight peddling spring dresses on the heels of Lottie McKnight's lifesaving work. Most worrisome of all was her glaring inability to check on Runa. As soon as the show was over, she vowed to contact Ravi for another update. At this point, it was all she could do. About any of it.

Lionel's face peered through the curtain. "You ready?"

Ignoring her emotions and the churning in her stomach, Shelby replied, "Ready."

The set was styled to look like a trendy living room, with faux coffee service positioned on a pedestal end table. She walked onto the set with a friendly wave and took a seat in a curvy teal armchair.

"Hi, Carmen, great to see you. Thanks so much for having me."

"Shelby! Wonderful to have you back on the show. Glad you could make it."

"Me too. Thanks for shuffling everything around to accommodate my crazy morning."

"Oh, no problem. This'll be a fun way to close out the show."

"Ten seconds," the director cued.

Shelby smoothed her hair then folded her hands casually in her lap. Activating every muscle in her face, brightening her eyes, widening her smile, she ignored the warm rush of blood rising toward her head. Eight minutes remained until the top of the hour when it would all be over.

"In three, two, one."

"Welcome back to the Bayou City Sunrise. Our final guest this morning is Shelby Lawrence. Shelby won *Buzz Now Magazine*'s amateur design contest last year, landing her on the cover of the holiday issue. Her label *Treasured Pockets* sold out in *Surface Trend* stores last fall. The popularity of her mommy-and-me dress line has exploded. Now she's back to share with us the hottest fashion trends this spring—not just for mothers and daughters, but the whole family.

"We've prepared a fashion slideshow to share alongside our conversation. Shelby, great to have you back. What can we expect to see as we head into stores this spring?"

"Thanks so much for having me, Carmen. The key this spring is bursts of bold color. We're seeing a resurgence of stripes, with a nautical flair. Chevron patterns in bright spring shades are really popular."

"Oh, these are darling!" Carmen commented as a slideshow of dresses flashed across the screen.

"And best of all, they roll seamlessly into summer." Shelby swallowed hard. The room started to spin. Something wasn't right.

"So, it's like two for one. That's really smart. And speaking of, you specialize in mother-daughter matching dresses. Tell me, what's behind this trend?"

Shelby flashed a rehearsed smile and recited her well-worn talking point. "Whether or not we intend them to, our clothes send a message to the world about who we are and what's important to us. When my daughter Paisley and I started matching, I felt my whole identity shift in a huge way. That's when I really started to love my role as a mom."

"That's great," Carmen said. "I, for one, know that being a mom is no easy gig."

"It's not. Mothers do so much hidden work to keep a household running smoothly. I noticed when Paisley and I matched, the daily grind of cooking and cleaning didn't feel as much like a chore. Our matching dresses tell the world we belong together. That we admire each other. That's how our label *Treasured Pockets* emerged. This idea that in this big, confusing world, we have a simple little world together where she and I can enjoy just being us."

"That's such a special message. Can we get a peek at your Easter dresses?"

"Of course, Carmen." Shelby blinked hard, trying to focus her eyes as the room swirled. "*Surface Trend* is carrying three of our spring designs in women's and children's sizes. As you can see, what's unique about this line is that the dresses coordinate. So even if you don't want to match exactly, all the dresses worn together will look cohesive."

"Oh, I love these! And what a great strategy for a photo op."

A wave of heat surged into Shelby's forehead. She rested her head in her hand, as if it were too heavy to hold up on its own.

"And did I hear you're including the guys this time?" Carmen asked.

"Yes, *Surface Trend* has coordinating neckties for dads and kids and bowties for the littlest members of the family."

"These pictures are so adorable. And how wonderful that everyone gets to feel included."

Shelby wanted to speak the words she'd rehearsed for weeks. But the murky contents of her stomach rose into her throat.

"Are these available online as well?" Carmen asked.

Shelby couldn't answer the question. She bolted off stage and lunged at the wastebasket beside the studio door, throwing up the contents of her stomach into it.

"She's mic'd! Turn her off!" she heard someone yell.

Horrified, Shelby bolted out of the studio back to the waiting room.

"Oh dear, are you okay?" Lionel raced in to

check on her. He pulled the mic and receiver off her body.

"I can't believe this. I'm so sorry. What a disaster." Shelby dropped the weight of her head into her hands.

"Can I get you some water?"

"No. Thank you. I should never have come here." She didn't look up. Couldn't. She didn't want him to see her falling apart.

"Oh, honey, it's no trouble. We went to commercial. Carmen can wing it through the rest of the show. I'm gonna go finish out, then I'll be back."

Shelby's image in the full-length mirror stared back at her. Dark streaks of mascara dripped down from red eyes. Her nose looked like a toddler's, with an urgent need to be wiped. She reached for tissues to start putting herself back together, longing to escape to the respite of her car.

Appearing on the show had seemed like a great opportunity to connect with local customers. But now, she cringed thinking about what viewers would think—not to mention the team at *Surface Trend Market*. She could only imagine how the internet trolls would go wild with a misstep like this.

All of that was worrisome, but what made her feel like crying was her growing concern for Runa. The girl's disappearance was starting to feel like a terrifying mystery no one could help her solve.

As Shelby continued doctoring her makeup, Lottie McKnight walked into the room to retrieve her belongings. Seeing the emotions on Shelby's face, she asked, "Are you okay?"

Shelby considered pretending like everything was okay, but there was no point. Everything was a mess. She let the honest words spill out.

"I heard your interview. I know this girl who might be in trouble, but I don't know how to help her or if I even can."

"Well, it sounds like you're already doing something. You're concerned about her. That's where any kind of help begins," Lottie said.

"Yes, but it's complicated. She lives overseas and her mom was killed, and no one knows how to reach her now." Shelby wanted to stop the tears from sliding down her cheeks but couldn't.

"I can see how troubled you are by this. Something I suggest to adults in a position of influence is that there's often *one* more thing you can do. One more step you can take. Asking one more time about a child who could be in danger will never do more harm than good."

"Thank you, Lottie."

"Here's my card. Feel free to get in touch if you have more questions. I'm happy to help." Lottie left, leaving Shelby alone in the staging room.

Emailing Ravi. That was all she could do. But

she already knew what he'd say. And what if he replied again with no updates?

What then?

She had more questions than answers. But she had to try one more time to see what she could find out. At this point, she'd do anything to know for sure that Runa was safe.

Shelby gathered up her things, said her good-byes, and left the studio, on to the rest of her day and the brutal fallout of tossing her toast on live TV.

Chapter 16

"How are we looking?" Shelby braced, remembering the gory details of her downfall. Throwing up on live TV caused her to trend in the worst way—hashtag mockery. A series of memes swept across social media. "Going viral," the captions jeered beneath a looped image of her racing off set.

"To be honest, just okay," Mitchell said. "Sales aren't as high as we hoped, but the Easter promos could turn it around."

In the two weeks following the show, momentum and sales stalled. Worse still, competitors snuck into the market offering matching family outfits priced a dollar less per garment than at *Surface Trend*. Their dresses were instantly outselling hers.

"Stay the course. Your strong track record will pull you through," Mitchell assured her.

"I hope so." Shelby's thumb twitched, aching to start uploading the prewritten emails and tweets. "Everything's ready to send."

"I'll let you go. Let's talk Tuesday," Mitchell said.

Shelby hadn't worked with *Surface Trend* long, but she could decipher the undertones of a comment like that. Tuesday's call was monumental—the kind of conversation that would determine her future there. She was starting to wonder if she would ever be fully safe, fully established to not feel her career in jeopardy with every order.

"Talk to you then." As Shelby opened her laptop, she felt a nudge on the inside of her belly button. She looked down at the bump protruding toward the edge of the mahogany table. Rounding the corner from second to third trimester, the fertility sites likened the baby to the size of a pomegranate. This little life clinging to her every move was the only reason she wasn't completely alone in the house heading into the long Easter weekend.

She picked up her phone to check for messages from Bryan. Still nothing. He left for the Bay Area on Tuesday. Later today, he was driving straight to Monterey with his coworkers. Shelby hoped to catch him earlier that week, but the time change, his late dinners, and her early bedtimes to keep up with Paisley prevented them from connecting.

But Shelby sensed the disconnect was a symptom of a bigger problem. She and Bryan hadn't felt in step with each other for a long time. Trying for a baby strained their relationship in ways she could never have expected.

Beyond that, the sweet friendship that made

them inseparable during college seemed to have frayed among the nonstop demands of providing for a family. There weren't enough hours in a week to fill up all the reservoirs of family and career and marriage and friendship vying for their attention. Something had to give.

With Bryan out of town for Easter weekend, Shelby accepted her mom's offer to take Paisley to South Padre Island with Aunt Sharon and Uncle Charlie. Under the circumstances, Shelby welcomed the alone time. There were giveaways to monitor, sponsored products to promote, endless buzz to generate.

And she needed to be at church Sunday morning to catch photos with matching families. Since all the dresses coordinated, she could join any of her customers' photos, meshing seamlessly into every image. Wi-Fi permitting, her parents promised to send a video of Paisley opening her Easter basket.

Ding ding! Announce Easter promo, her phone blared. But Shelby needed no reminder. The last two weeks were a crescendo leading up to this exact hour. In the minutes that followed, she uploaded, posted, and emailed each pre-crafted message. *Easter Super Specials. Good Friday shopping means Black Friday deals. Deep Savings at Surface Trend.*

She shared the link with the secret Facebook

group of her brand's supporters and texted her close circle of friends.

It's go time!
Thanks for all the upbeat comments!

As she monitored her social media accounts, likes and favorable comments trickled in from Blakeley, Elise, Whitney, and others doing their part to lock in a steady stream of excitement for the rest of the afternoon.

Once the ads and posts were adrift in the virtual world, Shelby sat back in her chair and took a sip of green tea. She glanced at her personal email. Her eyes widened, seeing the bold letters. Ravi had written back.

29 March 2013
Dear Shelby,

I apologize for the delay. It took several days to hear back from headquarters about traveling outside the service area to check on Runa. Due to some policies, it was not approved, so I could not go until my day off.

I am sorry to report I did not locate Runa, but I have new information to share. I came to the building where I understood her uncle to live, but it was vacant. I spoke with a street vendor who tells me the building is owned by a nearby commercial center and is to be demolished.

Residents have been relocated to the outskirts of Dhaka, in a place called Savar. This is quite a distance from Caring Hope, and traffic is very heavy to get there. The director at Eternal Promise School had no additional information, except that because of the girl's age and the uncle's financial situation, she suspected Runa may be working to help make ends meet.

I am unsure how to proceed. I am traveling the next few weeks to our annual meeting in the UK and will be unable to find out more until I return at the end of April. I wish I could do more.

In addition, I want you to know my time in Dhaka is ending. This summer I will take on a director role at our headquarters in London. It is a big promotion I am obligated to accept. The transition will require much attention as I prepare to leave Dhaka after so many years.

I wish you and your family a blessed Easter Day. I continue to hope sweet Runa remains safe and healthy in the

Lord's loving care. You have my word I will keep doing what I can to find her when I return.

Kindest regards,
Ravi

Shelby pushed her laptop back on the kitchen table but continued staring at Ravi's words. With every update, Runa seemed to slip further from reach.

Runa, age 11, no longer a student, her whereabouts unknown. All hope of helping her seemed to evaporate.

As Shelby's followers liked and shared her posts, the load pressing on her shoulders felt heavier. This online community she created buzzed with excitement on her behalf. Yet sitting in the silence of an empty house, all she could hear was the lonely rumble of failure.

She looked at the picture still on the fridge. Were Runa's eyes smiling today?

Turning toward the screen, the tag on her cardigan scraped the back of her neck. *Made in Vietnam*, she knew it read. She'd begun to check every label of every garment she wore, as if acknowledging the maker would erase the tragic end of Nipa and Runa's days together.

As notifications clamored for her attention, Shelby stared at Ravi's email. What could she possibly reply? And what would she tell Maye? And Paisley?

Tap tap tap.

The knock at the door startled her. She blinked hard and manufactured a smile to suggest everything was okay. Hopefully it was the mail carrier or a little neighbor friend asking for Paisley. Someone she could rid of quickly and secure her solitude to process everything.

On the other side of the front door stood Maye. Through the peephole, Shelby could see her neighbor's car waiting in the driveway. She looked to be on her way out. The conversation shouldn't last long.

Shelby opened the front door. The lines across Maye's forehead deepened when her eyes met Shelby's.

"Hi, Shelby. How are you?"

"I'm all right, thanks. What's going on?"

"I just wanted to invite you over for brunch on Sunday."

"Thanks." Shelby hesitated. "I'm not sure. There's a lot going on. What time?"

"Whatever time you're free."

"When are your other guests coming?" Shelby asked.

"There are no other guests, dear. This invitation is just for you."

Shelby's rising emotions were on the verge of giving it all away. Something about this neighbor's unexpected, raw kindness bore light on the shaded places of her soul.

"Thanks. Can I think about it and let you know tomorrow?"

"Of course. Is everything okay?"

The question, so innocent, unmasked every upwelling of uncertainty. Shelby was starting to question how much longer she could hide the ugly truth.

"Is something the matter?" Maye asked.

"It's Runa." Shelby tried to hide her tears.

"Oh heavens, what have you heard?"

"Ravi found out she's not in school anymore. He thinks she's working." The tears broke free. "He's leaving Dhaka this summer. Any chance of helping Runa is about to vanish."

"Oh, how disappointing. I'm so sorry." Maye reached to hug her. "I'm so proud of you, Shelby. You've gone above and beyond trying to help her."

Shelby pulled back from the hug, the tears stopping. The dense, dark truth suspended in the air, like a fog begging to be lifted.

"Maye, I have something to tell you. Something I've kept hidden for too long." Shelby looked into the clarity of her neighbor's eyes then forced the ugly words to exist. "My dresses were there."

Confusion settled in across Maye's face, so Shelby closed her eyes and started again. "My dresses were there, in the fire."

"Oh heavens, Shelby." Maye's eyes widened. "When did you learn this?"

"The day of the fire. I knew it destroyed my dresses. That's why they canceled the second dress order. I was instructed not to tell anyone. Honestly, I didn't want anyone to know. Later that week when you shared about Nipa's death, I felt so blindsided. I didn't know she worked in a garment factory. I didn't even know my dresses were being made in Bangladesh."

"Oh heavens, dear child. That's such an unbelievable turn of events."

"Runa lost her mom. She's not in school anymore. No one knows if she's okay or not. And I'm part of the reason why."

"Shelby, you're being way too hard on yourself. You didn't know any of this."

"But that's just it. I didn't know. And it's not just me. *No one* knows. These clothes—we drape them on our bodies and stuff them in our drawers and flaunt them to our friends. We know nothing about these clothes. That's exactly why this happened to Nipa. *We didn't know.* And now Runa's life will never be the same."

A large round tear pelted down one cheek, then the other. Maye pushed her way into the foyer and closed the door. She wrapped her arms around her friend but said nothing.

"I'm so sorry, Shelby."

Shelby pulled away from the hug. "I am too."

"Well, now that you know all this, how can you make it better?"

"I don't know. I don't think there's anything I can do. If Ravi can't find her, I don't know anyone else who can. And he's moving to London."

"What about your dresses?"

"That's another problem. I have no faith in the process being used to source production. I tried researching the safety inspection records of the factory they used for this line, and I couldn't find out a thing. *Surface Trend* will tell me Tuesday if sales are strong enough for another contract. I don't think I can risk it one more time. I don't think I can turn it down either."

"Shelby, have you thought about going there yourself?"

"Where? To Bangladesh?"

"Yes."

"Um, did you forget I'm pregnant?" Shelby laughed. "And who would watch Paisley?"

"What if you went now?"

"Ravi is out of the country for the next few weeks." Shelby looked at Maye, confused. "At that point, I'll be in my third trimester. Pretty sure flying is prohibited that far along." Shelby realized she'd stopped crying. In the midst of sadness, there was something consoling about talking through a solution.

"Are you free for a bit?" Maye asked.

Shelby looked at her phone. Texts awaited her reply. Instagram notifications stacked one on top of the next. The locomotion of tasks whistled for her attention.

"Not really. Why?" And then she understood why Maye was asking. There wasn't anywhere else she would be heading the Friday afternoon of Easter weekend except the Good Friday service. The last thing Shelby felt up for was to show up at church all splotchy-faced and weighted with shame.

"I want to show you something."

"I'd need a few minutes to get ready."

"Actually, you'll be fine exactly as you are. We're just going across the street."

"But aren't you heading to the service?"

"I was. But there's somewhere more important I need to be right now."

Across the street, Shelby followed Maye up the cedar steps to the library. From the bottom shelf of a bookcase, Maye reached past the green scrapbook from Dhaka to retrieve a burnt orange photo album. She opened it to the middle and pointed to a vertical photograph. A younger, pregnant version of Maye stood next to a woman holding a baby who was also pregnant.

"This is from our time in South Sudan. We lived there for three years. Roger felt called to work at a hospital there. There was an extremely high infant and mother mortality rate. When we got there, I delivered babies and offered prenatal care to women. While we were there, I became dear friends with this woman, Kazima. I delivered her second baby, and shortly after, her third. During her third delivery, she almost bled out."

"That's terrifying," Shelby said.

"Yes, and it was also terrifying finding out she was pregnant with a fourth a few months later. I promised her I would stay for the delivery. But I found out soon after that I was pregnant too, with Junia. For various reasons I planned to deliver the baby in an American hospital, but that presented a tough situation. I needed to return to the States early enough to get settled with Stephen, but I wanted to keep my promise to Kazima too. Plus, I truly feared for her life."

"So, what did you do?" Shelby asked.

"I stayed. I waited and delivered Kazima's baby girl."

"How did it go?"

"It was scary. She lost a significant amount of blood delivering the placenta. But I knew what had worked during her previous delivery to stop it." Maye turned the page in the album. They both stared at Kazima, a baby bundled in her arms.

"So it was the right decision to stay."

"I suppose it was. Looking back now, I would say that." The sandy streaks in Maye's hair shimmered in the meager glow of the day's last sunlight.

"How far along were you when you flew back?"

"Thirty-five weeks."

"Seriously? I thought that wasn't allowed."

"Oh, it absolutely is."

"But aren't there rules about not flying in the third trimester?"

"The exact guidance is that so long as you have no complications, you shouldn't travel after 36 weeks."

"Wait, are you saying I should fly to Bangladesh . . . now?" Shelby noticed her heart was beating fast. Her skin beaded with sweat.

"Heavens, no. I would never say what anyone should or shouldn't do. I'm only sharing what's possible."

"But . . . isn't that super risky? What if something happened to me, or the baby?"

"Like what?"

"What if I get sick? Or go into labor early. Or don't have the right care. Or . . . or what if I have the baby on the airplane?"

"Did you have any complications with your pregnancy with Paisley?"

"No."

"And any complications with this pregnancy? Any reason to think you might deliver preterm?"

"Well, no." Shelby bit her lip. All the chemical

pregnancies caused her to lump herself in with the high-risk moms. But despite those early losses, every prenatal appointment, every blood draw and urine test, every ultrasound had been textbook since the stick stayed pink. Both times.

"There's always risk. Especially when it comes to children."

"But even if I went, what if I spend all that money and leave my family for a whole week and we never find Runa? What if I go all that way and . . . and fail?"

"That's also possible."

Shelby sat silent, her eyes drawing again to the image of the younger, expecting version of her neighbor in the album. Maye's face in the photo glowed. Her eyes were parcels of joy. Whimsical. Shelby hadn't felt that carefree in months.

"Perhaps you don't go now. Runa will still be there."

"True. But how would I ever find her?"

Shelby's eyes met Maye's. Maye continued to say nothing.

"This is my last chance, isn't it?"

"It might be. It might not be."

"It is, though. Because once Ravi leaves, we lose the only remaining link we have to her. There won't be any point in going. I would never find her without his help. And Runa knows him."

Shelby placed a hand on the bump of her belly,

as if the connecting touch would yield clarity of what to do. Maye remained silent.

"You're really not going to tell me what to do here, are you?"

"This is not my decision to make."

A large clock on the wall ticked rhythmically, interrupting the silence.

"Maye, how did you figure out you should stay?"

"It was tough. I took a few days. Collected as much information as I could. Prayed a lot. Ran through the hypothetical and worst-case scenarios for both of us and our babies. I figured out the part of me that wanted to leave early was scared. Scared of what I didn't know. Scared of staying, doing everything I could and still failing. Watching my friend or her baby die in my care would have been unbearable."

"Completely. How did you get past that?"

"I had a revelation that I was being guided more by fear than by love. In the end, I couldn't step on that plane knowing I'd let fear call the shots. After all I've experienced, that's just not how I feel called to live my life."

"So, you think by not going, I'm letting fear win? You think I should go."

"*Should,* my dear, is far too pointed a word. What do you want to do?"

"I just can't imagine Bryan will be okay with me going that far away this late in my pregnancy.

It feels too risky. And what would Paisley do for all that time I'd be gone? And what about the travel cost? And the jet lag? And the baby?"

"All important things to consider, but that's not what I asked. What do *you* feel called to do?"

"I honestly don't know. If I don't go, I'll never know what happened to Runa, and I have to be okay with having no idea what happens behind the scenes at the factories I source from. But if I decide to go, there are all these logistics to figure out."

"You know, I've found once I make a decision, the details tend to sort themselves out."

"So, I'm back to where I started. No idea what to do. And still sensing *you* think I should go."

"Is there anyone in your life who you turn to for wisdom in situations like this?"

"There used to be," Shelby said.

"Who?"

"My grandmother, Dear." Shelby could feel the tears rising behind her eyes as she said the name.

"What would Dear tell you to do?"

Shelby knew exactly. "She'd say, 'Take care of your people. Don't withhold good from those to whom it is due when it is in your power to act.'"

Maye smiled but stayed silent.

"I don't know, Maye. In some ways, this feels like the biggest decision I've ever had to make."

"The stakes are always higher when children are involved."

"That's never felt more true." Now more than ever, Shelby wished Dear were here to walk her through this hard decision.

"Then take some time. Talk to Bryan. Consult your doctor. And make the best choice you can with the information you have."

"You sound like a pharmaceutical commercial."

"Maybe." Maye laughed. "Or a nurse. I come by it honestly."

The phone rang in Shelby's back pocket, startling them both.

"It's Bryan." For days she hoped to connect with him. Now she stared at the green dot, her thumb unmoving.

"Does he know all this?" Maye asked.

Staring at the phone screen, the words weren't coming. The ringtone jingled on, threatening to go to voicemail with every turn of the melody.

"You know—" Maye's face brightened. Her eyes caught a smile. "—Sometimes if you lay it all out there, people will surprise you."

Shelby took one last look at the image of Maye, Kazima, and the newborn baby. Then she answered the call to start a conversation with Bryan that should have happened months ago.

Phone to her ear, Shelby waved goodbye to Maye and descended the cedar steps. As she crossed the yard, small talk with Bryan began. He was getting settled at the hotel in Monterey. Instead of going home, she walked down Oak Blossom Lane as the sun sank below the treetops.

"Sorry I kept missing you. It's been wall-to-wall meetings since I got here. How was your week?"

Shelby immediately felt deflated. Bryan always cited work as the reason why he was unavailable. She appreciated that he was a hard worker, but it seemed always at the expense of their relationship.

"It was busy. Had to get Paisley packed for the weekend and prep everything for promotions."

"How's that going?"

"Eh. Mitchell said numbers are just okay. I sent out the promos a little while ago. Now it's just a waiting game to see how everything sells."

"Sounds like you've done everything you can. Anything else going on this weekend?"

This was as good a segue as she was going to get. Approaching the cul-de-sac, she slowed her walking pace and steadied her breath. "Actually, there is. I have something to tell you. Something I should have told you a long time ago."

"That doesn't sound good."

"It's not. It's about Runa. Or her mom, actually." Shelby sat down on the curb at the end of the street.

"What about her? Have you heard something new?"

"Not exactly new. Back in November, the week of the fire, I found out something so terrible, I didn't want anyone to know."

"What?" Bryan asked.

"Runa's mom Nipa was there. She was in the factory making my dresses."

"Wait, Runa's mom was making your dresses?"

"Yes."

"And she was at the fire?"

"Yes."

"Is she okay?"

"No. She died, Bryan. She died in the fire."

The silence that followed seemed to never end. Shelby cleared her throat to fill the void. "Bryan? Are you there?"

"I'm here. That's terrible. Is that why Runa disappeared?"

"Yes. Her uncle came to get her. They moved to a different town. Ravi hasn't been able to track her down."

"So, wait, you've known this whole time? About Runa's mom?"

"Just about. I found out a week after the fire. Maye heard it from Ravi."

"Shel, why didn't you tell me?"

"I don't know. I—I tried to. I just couldn't get the words to come out. The holidays were so busy. You were hardly home. Paisley was so interested in Runa. I didn't want her to know the sad reason why she disappeared. And then I felt so responsible. I mean, how could I not? *My* dresses were there."

"This isn't your fault, Shelby. You had no idea any of that would happen."

"No, I didn't. But I had a feeling that second order was too fast. I didn't speak up or ask the right questions. I was so excited about the dresses and didn't want anything to get in the way of that."

"How is Runa? Does Ravi know any more?"

"Yes, unfortunately. He emailed today to say she's no longer in school and is probably working." As Shelby said the words, her eyes filled with tears.

Another long silence drew on before Bryan spoke. "Is there anything we can do?"

"That's what I'm trying to figure out." Shelby wiped her cheek with her sleeve. "Maye thinks I should go there myself."

"To Bangladesh?"

"Yeah."

"When? After the baby's born?"

"No, before."

"You're not serious," Bryan said. The disapproval parked in Shelby's ears.

"Ravi's leaving Dhaka. He's moving back to London this summer. By the time I have the baby, it will be too late to go."

"You're really thinking about going to Dhaka—now?"

Shelby bit her lip. "I'm considering it."

"Can't Ravi find Runa?"

"He's tried. He keeps hitting one dead end after the next. Looking for her isn't part of his job, so he's doing it in his free time, which he's running out of."

"What's your plan if you find her?"

"I don't know exactly. I just feel this incredible pull to make sure she's okay. And if she isn't in school, maybe we could find a way to change that."

"So, you'd fly all the way to Bangladesh attempting to locate a child that no one can track down?"

"There's more to it. If I'm going to continue to design for *Surface Trend*, I need more information about the factories we're sourcing from. I've scoured the internet and can't find out anything about these places."

It was a strange thing in 2013 to search the internet for *Golora Fashions Factory* and retrieve zero results. Not even a handful of unrelated items. Zero.

In the months following the fire, Shelby had read about questionable audits, rampant bribery, and underlying deception that plagued the garment industry, not just in Bangladesh, but throughout economically struggling nations. In the age of lightning-speed bandwidths and round-the-clock news cycles, there remained some information that could only be learned firsthand.

"I see where you're coming from," Bryan said. "It's just the timing with the baby I can't get past. Have you talked to your doctor?"

"I'm calling her next. And I agree the timing is rough. But it's probably my last chance. Once Ravi leaves, I'll never find Runa without him."

"What about Paisley—if you go?"

"I don't know. Maybe you two could spend some time together, without me there doing everything."

The words came out like a poisoned dart. Shelby immediately wished she could take them back. She hadn't intended to pick a fight.

His silence said everything his voice would not.

A shiny white rock caught Shelby's eye. She picked it up off the pavement, tracing its rough grooves and smooth curves with her fingertips. "Ever since Paisley was born, I feel like you haven't been around much, like all you ever do is work. I appreciate how devoted you are to your job and providing for our family, but sometimes I think you're more loyal to them than you are to us."

Shelby wasn't sure what his reaction would be. But this was a conversation they couldn't put off any longer.

"Shelby, that's not true," Bryan said.

"How is it not true? You're always working late and over the weekends. You're angling for a jobsite in California. We'll never see you if you take that."

"To be honest, you're right." The long exhale that followed came out like a confession. "It's not that I don't want to be home. It's just, I'm worried, Shel. I'm worried about getting off partner track and not being able to give you the life I promised."

Shelby thought back to the housing crash. Bryan had just graduated when architecture firms were making massive cuts. His promotion stalled, and student loan payments became due right as Paisley was born. The cash flow pinch was among the reasons Shelby turned her sewing hobby into a business. She wanted to lighten the financial burden however she could.

"Bryan, it's much more important to me that we're together as a family. I would rather we find a way to cut back than have you be absent from our lives over some prestigious building. We miss you. We need you here."

"I want to be around more. I really do."

"We want that too. Everything is better when you're home with us."

"Thanks, Shel."

Shelby could hear Bryan smiling. She slipped the shiny rock into her hoodie pocket and took the first steps toward home.

"What about Dhaka? Think you'll really go?"

"I don't know. I'm completely torn." She could

think of fewer decisions more complex than this one. The logistics felt insurmountable. Flying across 13 time zones all these months pregnant. Locating a single child in one of the most densely populated countries in the world—a country and culture she knew nothing about. Traveling solo all that way and back. Flipping her days and nights. The travel expenses.

Not to mention, Bangladesh wasn't exactly on her bucket list. "Any chance you'd come with me?"

"I would feel more comfortable staying with Paisley. In case anything happened." Bryan couldn't make a decision without heavily weighing the worst-case scenario. It was why they never flew anywhere together anymore. If something terrible happened, he didn't want Paisley navigating the rest of her life without parents.

"If I'm going, I need to decide soon." Shelby was still in disbelief at how this day was unfolding.

"Take the weekend to think it through," he said. "I'll support you, whatever you decide to do. Let me know how I can help."

Shelby was surprised to find herself tearing up, the way she did when Maye complimented her. Few things traveled as far into her heart as a personal vote of confidence.

"Thanks, Bryan. Can't wait for you to come home."

"Me too. Love you. Hugs to Paisley."

Back home, Shelby pulled the rock from her pocket and set it on Paisley's placemat for her to discover on Sunday. A call to her doctor's office was immediately answered by the weekend recording, which provided the after-hours emergency number. Notifications from the promo continued piling up. She swiped them away then texted Maye.

> Can't believe it, but it's a maybe.
> Now the hard part. Decision's all mine.

Shelby watched the screen anticipating the three dots that would indicate Maye was typing her reply. She hoped this neighbor, who seemed endlessly more equipped to make hard calls, would make the right choice obvious. The three dots appeared. Shelby's eyes locked onto them, awaiting the reply.

> You can do this. Mine the facts.
> Examine your heart.
> I'll be praying for you.

> Happy Easter, Shelby!
> I saw a light on over there.
> Everything okay?

> Morning, Maye. Can't sleep.
> What are you doing up?

311

Going to the sunrise service.
Want to come?

Don't think I'd be ready for that.

You've already done the hardest part,
being awake this early :)

Hah.

I'm leaving in 10.
Would love for you to come with me.
It's very casual.

Shelby looked out the window into the dark morning, then across the bedroom toward the lavender wrap dress flung over the back of the vanity chair. She needed to shower and begin the hour-long ordeal of photo-fixing her hair.

A look in the mirror revealed the damage from another sleepless night. She shouldn't have had coffee so late yesterday, but she was exhausted from not sleeping well the night before.

It all started when the obstetrician returned her call. She didn't have Shelby's chart in front of her but agreed the official guidance gave no restrictions on overseas travel for her current gestation period. The doctor recommended calling on Monday morning to receive more specific counsel, but that there was good reason to think international travel was okay considering her strong health history.

All Friday night, she tossed and turned, replaying the conversation with the doctor and with Bryan, weighing the pros and cons. One look at the dark shadows around her eyes revealed every lost minute of sleep. The shrill sight brought back sour memories from the Bayou City Sunrise. What a debacle, trying to be professional and productive on wrecked sleep. There was no reason to think today would be any different.

Honestly, she was just tired. Tired of it all. Tired of trying to look perfect. Tired of promoting. Tired of selling. Tired of weighing everyone else's opinions, especially *Surface Trend*'s.

She picked up a pair of jeans off the floor, threw on a long-sleeved T-shirt, and brushed her teeth. She glared at the waiting lineup of makeup, her hands drawing with magnetic force toward the bottle of foundation. She started untwisting its shiny silver cap but stopped.

Nothing inside that bottle would solve her problems or make the decision about Dhaka clearer. She'd spent so much effort covering up the blemishes of her life, showing the world what they wanted to see. Now she didn't much care for the person she pretended to be. If there were anywhere she would be welcomed as the least decorated version of herself, it was exactly the place Maye invited her.

Shelby put down the foundation, picked up her phone, and forced her reply.

Ready when you are.

Chapter 17

April 2013

Three weeks later, Shelby woke to the piercing jab of popping ears, the pressure abating as the plane descended back to the surface of the earth. Her eyes blinked open in confusion. The crisp glow out the window suggested dawn emerging, but the slow drag of her thoughts insisted a night of sleep should be underway.

Twenty-two hours of air travel lingered on, with less than an hour to go. The overzealous elastic of her compression hose pinched into her swollen calves.

The days-long trip had become increasingly more foreign with every step forward. The international terminal at Bush Intercontinental Airport felt normal enough, the intoxicating aromas of Tex Mex and spice-rubbed brisket elbowing at her cravings, the colorful makeup counters beckoning. Boarding the first flight to Dubai, the ratio of people who shared her look, her season of life, began to drop off like the seafloor.

Every hour on the hour, she abandoned her Dhaka guidebook to walk the length of the enormous economy cabin. The only words she spoke during the entire 15-hour trip were to the flight attendant, whose country of origin was concealed by her attractive oval eyes, dewy complexion, and hint of a British accent. Shelby admired the tailored princess lines on the woman's skirt suit, which perfectly matched her coworkers'.

Boarding the second flight from Dubai to Dhaka, Shelby stumbled into a new and extreme version of feeling out of place. Almost all the passengers were male. Female travelers stuck close to the men escorting them, their eyes suggesting pointed questions as to why a woman so far along with child was flying between continents unaccompanied. She craved an opportunity to answer them, to confirm aloud what in the world she was doing.

What *was* she doing? Writing in her notebook, she tried to make sense of how she got here— 35,000 feet above the earth with a baby bump she couldn't camouflage. But none of it made sense. The additional expenses on their overflowing credit card statements. Her sheer ignorance of the country where she was about to land. The ambitious, even prideful undertaking of locating and somehow helping a child she had no claim to. The husband and daughter she left behind.

Worst of all was the reaction when she told her coffee group. They said all the right things. Their verbal support might have convinced someone else they agreed. But Shelby could see the questions in their eyes that no one was asking. Questions like, would she still want to go shopping with them now that she was scrutinizing every supply chain?

Shelby could tell from Whitney's Instagram post that they went shopping without her. She couldn't remember the last time she cried as a grown-up from feeling left out.

All day on Easter Sunday, Shelby considered and reconsidered the decision to go to Dhaka. But that wasn't what ultimately helped her decide. The path became clear only when she considered the option not to go.

Six days from now, she might find herself again in the expansive cabin of a Boeing 777, having never laid eyes on Runa, tired and worn from the search. But taking that risk, leaving her comfort zone, meant she could resume routine life, certain she'd done everything she possibly could—for Runa and for the future of her company.

The wheels smacked into the ground, and the plane raced to a stop. The flight attendant's voice came on overhead, spouting off information in what must have been Arabic. Then, perhaps, Bengali.

A final voice relayed the same message in British-accented English. "Good morning, passengers. Welcome to Dhaka's Hazrat Shahjalal International Airport. Local time is 6:37 a.m., Saturday, the twentieth of April."

So strange flying the length of a day but arriving two calendar days later. Having never crossed the international dateline before, Shelby considered the parameters of time. What exactly happened to the lost day? The question drifted away unanswered as the shuffle of passengers and bags reached her row. Time to deboard the plane and leave the familiar space inside the cabin's walls.

Once inside the terminal, Shelby figured out the ATM. Fumbling with the foreign currency, she purchased the biggest bottle of water she could find. She waited in line after line—at immigration, baggage, customs. Then she found her way to the airport's exit, grateful so many signs were in English. Amid a sea of unmarked passenger vans and taxis began the final and most dreaded leg of the long journey: finding Ravi.

Shelby scanned the contents of each passenger window, her eyes tracking back and forth, left and right. She watched with envy as the men, women, and children from her flight boarded private cars, vans, taxis. But as the hour wore on, the comfort of recognized faces passed. She stood waiting, trying not to look as helpless as she felt.

A stalky man with thick eyebrows appeared from nowhere. "Need taxi? I can help!" His hands reached toward her backpack.

"No, thank you!" Shelby yelled, cinching her belongings to her body. Her heart pounded, the extra blood of gestation pulsing through her veins at record speed. The guidebook warned her that despite increased security, foreigners lingering outside the airport were often pestered, whether for bag services or out of sheer curiosity from seeing foreigners.

Standing there now, she felt like the perfect victim, her suitcase brimming with potential value items, her mind weary from days of travel. She found it hard to decipher who might be an overzealous businessman, assisting travelers with heavy bags, and who might be a common thief.

Shelby squeezed her backpack strap tight. Her phone was inside her waistband as a backup, but Bryan warned her of the extreme roaming charges for using it off Wi-Fi. Smartphones were still rare here. She didn't even know if it would work.

Another man approached her, his hands reaching toward her bag. She shook her head quickly, squeezing her belongings closer to her body. Her elbow pressed at the passport beneath her shirt, confirming its whereabouts beside the baby.

After that, it felt like she stood there for an eternity, until she heard the most wonderful word.

"Shelby!"

Her ears perked. She looked up to see a boxy black Toyota sedan approaching, and Ravi waving to her through the open passenger window, his generous smile exactly like his picture. Her heart skipped faster than her feet as she fled her lonely perch on the arrivals sideline, unloaded her bags in the trunk, and found refuge in the backseat.

"I must apologize for running late," Ravi said. "A motorcycle was struck by a Nasiman, and traffic was worse than usual."

"I'm sorry to hear that. What's a Nasiman?"

"One of those." He pointed across the arrival lanes to what looked like a pickup truck merged with a school bus. Dozens of people, who appeared to all be men, crammed inside and stood on the back bumper.

"Is he okay?"

"Sadly, no. But everyone on board is."

"That's terrible." Her hands finally free, she took a long sip from her water bottle, desperate to change the subject as thick traffic closed in. "Thank you so much for coming to get me."

"Our pleasure. The taxis here are not always so reliable. We did not want anything to happen to you."

"You're not making me feel like coming was a very good idea."

"Hah—I would not go that far. But it is different here, you will see."

"Oh, I'm already seeing."

"This is Tariq. He is an excellent driver and a good friend of mine. He knows Dhaka very well. We will be in good hands this week."

"Thank you, Tariq. I'm so glad to meet you."

Tariq lifted a hand off the steering wheel, sending a friendly wave to the backseat.

"He does not speak English." Ravi added, "I am happy to translate."

"Thank you. I'm afraid I'll need a lot of help with that. I've traveled overseas before, but never to this part of the world. Everything seems extra foreign."

"Yes, I understand. Very different from America. Where to now? Off to the hotel for a rest?"

"Yes, rest. That would be amazing. Thank you. Um . . . Donyabad?"

"Aaaah! That is very good. I can tell you have been studying."

"Some."

"We are so glad you came, Shelby. *Dhonnobad.*"

After a shower and a mind-jolting nap, Shelby stopped by the hotel's business center. When several attempts to load email were unsuccessful, she met Ravi at the café near the lobby.

Inside the newly renovated hotel with its contemporary furniture and modern decor, Shelby felt like she could be anywhere. Adjacent the café were enormous windows overlooking a dark, glassy pond. Impressive varieties of leafy tropical plants were scattered at the water's edges and throughout the hotel grounds. She didn't have to look far for reminders that she was no longer in Texas.

Ravi poured hot tea from a curvy silver pitcher. "So, you are here. Let's talk about what we do next."

"I'm here." Shelby took a sip of tea, letting the words sink in. "I just tried to email Bryan, but the internet is out."

"Email is easy. We can take care of that at my office."

"Okay, great. Beyond that, I'm not sure. Find Runa? Visit the factories on my list? That's all I've got."

"Visiting factories is not quite as easy. But I pulled some strings and set up appointments at your requested locations for Tuesday, and maybe for Monday. As for Runa, I am not sure what to do. I am just back from London and have no new leads."

"Has anyone been in contact with her uncle?"

"No one. I tried again to find him, but nothing. He relocated to the alternate housing, and I have no number to reach him."

"Can we go there?"

"Yes, we can, and we will. But it will be a needle in a haystack kind of search."

"I looked up that area on the map. It didn't look that far away. But now I see what you mean by traffic."

"Yes, our city has 16 million people. And they all seem to be on the same roads at the same time."

"Wow. And I thought Houston was big." Three million people had always seemed enormous compared to Round Rock. Sipping the rich tea, Shelby felt like she was coming back to life after the long journey. "Will we get to look for Runa today?"

"Today is not so good. By the time we get there, our daylight would be short. We will go early tomorrow and spend the whole day."

"Ok, great. Do you have any idea where to start?"

"Somewhat. I have a landmark."

"I guess that's better than nothing," Shelby said.

"Technically, yes. Is there anywhere else you want to go this afternoon?"

"Maybe. Can I see the site of the fire?"

"Sure," Ravi said. "Or at least what is left of it."

On the drive to Ashulia, Shelby noticed it looked like every building they passed was under construction. Rebar was sticking out from the tops of buildings. Scaffolding surrounded many entryways. Interesting that so many places were in progress.

After what felt like forever idling and honking on crowded roads, they drove up to a completely charred structure with black edges. About the length of a football field, the building was much larger than she imagined from reading the news articles. Debris lay abandoned on adjacent sidewalks. It looked like either the site of a fire or the remnants of a hard-fought war.

A young woman wearing a flowing red sari with a petal pattern walked past the car. Shelby did a double-take, noticing one of her arms was missing. The face beneath the scarf was rippled with scars.

"She was there," Ravi said. "Do you want to talk to her?"

Shelby hesitated. Ingesting the site of the fire was difficult enough. If she was honest, she didn't want to hear the woman's story. She didn't want to know how bad it was, for Nipa or for anybody. Yet she had come all this way.

"Sure." She opened the car door and stepped onto the dusty sidewalk. Standing in front of the burned-out building, a feeling of uneasiness stirred in the pit of her stomach, in a place deeper than where the baby lay.

"What should I ask her?" Ravi asked.

"I would like to know what that day was like."

"*Kemon achen*?" Ravi greeted the woman.

The scarred woman turned around, and Ravi began speaking quickly in Bengali. As she responded to his questions, he translated her responses into English.

"It was terrifying. One minute we were working. The next minute smoke was billowing up the stairwells. The alarms sounded. People were yelling 'Fire, fire, fire!' But our line manager told us it was a false alarm. He yelled at us to get back to work. We started to smell smoke, but he refused to let us stop working. When we finally did, we ran to each of the three stairwells, but they were already filled with flames. We went to the windows, but they were barred shut.

"Some people made it to the higher floors, only to die there. Some people passed out quickly from the smoke. They never made it to the stairs. We crawled around on the floors, the smoke burning off our eyelashes. I do not even remember when my cheek was singed. Remnants of the smoldering ceiling fell on my arm. I grabbed a piece of fabric and snuffed it out, but the damage was done."

As the woman spoke, her voice revealed little emotion compared to the devastation of the scene she described. Ravi continued relaying her story.

"Another worker called, 'Over here,' and we made it to a window where the glass was broken. We stuck our heads out the window for air, screaming for help, screaming from the pain. Some people were jumping out windows to a nearby rooftop. Others jumped to the pavement.

At the time, I remember thinking it made sense. They did not have any other choice."

"How did you get out?" Shelby asked, and Ravi translated.

"We could see people on a rooftop nearby, so we knew we needed to go up somehow. One of the stairwells was still open going to the next floor. I took a breath out a broken window and raced up the stairs. I remember tripping over someone, a woman I worked near. But the flames were chasing us. We could not stop to help."

"What was your recovery like? Did the owners compensate anyone?"

"No. The owners did nothing. The government gave each survivor 100,000 taka."

"That's about $1,200," Ravi broke from translation to explain.

"But that money was spent right away on doctors and medical bills. I was in the hospital two months after the fire. My wound became infected. They amputated my lower arm to save the rest of it. Now I am 17 years old, and for the rest of my life, I am missing a hand. I cannot sew. No one will hire me."

Shelby could detect the shame in her voice, even through translation.

"And I do not know if I could work right now. I wake up every night hearing screams, reliving the flames chasing us, the embers falling on top of me. I see women I've worked beside falling

326

from the second floor, their bodies smashing against the ground."

As Ravi translated her words, the woman's mouth quivered. Her eyes looked like they might cry, but that amid the weight of her struggles, no more tears would come. Her burns had skinned over into scars, but five months had done little to heal her countless wounds.

Shelby recognized it was her turn to speak but didn't want to cause this woman any more suffering. So she stayed silent.

"She says she's happy to share more," Ravi prompted.

"How many people survived?" Shelby listened as Ravi relayed the question and response.

"About a thousand. The newspapers do not report this. They report 200 injured and 112 dead. But we believe more than that died. And even those who made it out without needing to go to the hospital, they are still dealing with the pain from that night. They are scared to work in other factories. But if they do not work, they cannot provide for their families.

"My own parents are suffering because I am no longer able to send money back to my village. I came to the city for this job, to help my family. And now I cannot help anyone. Not even myself."

"What will happen next?" Shelby asked.

"Nothing will happen. Nothing ever happens. They talk of making changes, but this is not the first time this has happened. For my whole life I have heard about tragedies like this where good people die, working hard at their jobs. Nothing ever changes."

Ravi broke from translating to add, "There have been about a dozen garment factory fires in the last ten years."

"Wow." Shelby shook her head.

The woman continued speaking, Ravi translating her words. "We work so hard, yet we can barely afford to live. And then we die at the hands of our bosses who refuse to lose minutes of work on an order. Why are those minutes so important? Why are those clothes more important than our lives?"

Her questions landed like a punch. Shelby stopped breathing for an instant as their impact tore through her.

Ravi thanked the woman, and she continued on her path away from there.

Shelby wanted to race back and hand over all the taka in her wallet. But what would it do? Like the government assistance, it too would run out. And it might make a difference for this one woman and her parents for a few weeks, but what about all the others?

Oh, forget it. Going against every bit of safety advice, she pulled out the taka equivalent of $40 and asked Ravi to give it to her. It wasn't much, but it was something.

From down the sidewalk, Shelby could see the woman's scarred lips mouth, "*Dhonnobad.*"

Ravi walked back and turned his gaze toward the burned-out building. "Want to take a look?"

The lump in Shelby's stomach kept her from speaking. She nodded and turned toward the unsightly scene. Soot and ash hung thick in the air. So many workers—people with families—had taken their last breaths here.

Anyone passing by could sense that hell had rained through. Every window was shattered. Triangular pieces of glass jutted into the open air. The top half of the nine-story building looked like it had been pressure washed with liquid charcoal. The bottom floors revealed gray cinderblock streaked with black char.

A security guard sat on a folding metal chair out front but did nothing to stop them from approaching the building. Ravi stuck his head inside and motioned for Shelby to join him.

Peering inside the factory's first floor, her eyes stung. She blinked and blinked, fighting to absorb the images. Sunlight crept through holes in the walls, casting shadows across the ember-scourged workroom.

"This is where the fire started," Ravi said. "They think a generator short-circuited and the sparks caught hold of yarn and fabric that should not have been stored so close. Or possibly it was arson. No one knows for sure."

"Unbelievable," was all she could say. And it was. Staring at images of the building on news sites for so many months, she felt familiar with the aftermath. But absorbing the wreckage in person, inhaling the ash, running her finger across a charred workstation—all of it renewed the grief of this tragedy. Nipa's last moments, last breaths were in this same space. Tears began raining down her cheeks, whether from sadness or smoke.

Shelby wiped her face with the sleeve of her jacket. "So wait, you spent a week here?"

"Just about. My office is one kilometer away. Shall we go there, and you can email your family? Or would you like to see more?"

"I've seen enough. Let's get out of here."

A 10-minute walk later, they arrived at yet another unfinished building and climbed three flights of stairs to Caring Hope's office. Ravi logged in to his computer and opened a browser.

Taking a seat at his desk, Shelby realized this was the spot where Ravi had relayed the messages from Runa. Everything on the screen was in indecipherable Bengali characters, but navigation bars and keyboard buttons sat in predictable enough places that she could continue in Gmail without assistance.

Bryan,

I made it. Travel was smooth but long. I'm feeling good, just tired. Traffic here is next-level ridiculous. Seems like every building is under construction. It would drive you crazy.

I'm writing you from Ravi's office computer. The internet was down at the hotel business center, which sounds like a regular occurrence. If you need me, please copy Ravi's email or call the hotel. My room number is 206. I will check in whenever I can, but I'm not sure how often that will be.

Just went to the site of the fire. It was awful. We start searching for Runa tomorrow. Glad I'm here. Please give Little P a hug for me. I miss you so much.

Love,
Shel

Hitting send, her eyes pooled with tears. She'd only been gone a few days, but the ache of missing her family was intensifying. Aside from the web browser, everything familiar felt oceans away.

Just then, a budding knee or an elbow rubbed into the tight skin of her belly. She pressed her fingertips into the sensation. Risky as it was making this trip so far along, it was strangely comforting having a member of her family with her. Their first big adventure was underway.

After sending the email, she stared at the computer screen, blinking back her emotions. It wouldn't do any good to spend the rest of the visit longing for home, second-guessing her decision to come. There were a thousand reasons why she shouldn't be here. And yet, here she was.

Here and exhausted. Which made sense considering it was 4 a.m. in Houston.

"I think I'm ready to call it a day."

"Very well. Tariq will take you back to the hotel. Tomorrow we will start searching for Runa."

Chapter 18

Thanks to jet lag, Shelby woke for the day several hours before hotel breakfast began. She devoured a power bar and got ready to spend the day searching for Runa.

As recommended, she dressed in neutrals, wearing wide-leg dark cotton pants and a long tan duster over a plain white shirt. Ravi had suggested a headscarf, but she had forgotten to add it to her pack list. Anticipating lots of walking, she wore sandals with a sturdy athletic sole.

Once presentable, she went straight to the business center and was relieved to see her email load. Ignoring everything else in her inbox, she went straight to Bryan's reply.

Shel,

Great to hear from you, and glad every-thing's going ok. I tried calling the hotel, but the guy at the front desk wasn't too helpful. I will try to call later, but I suspect we'll have better luck with you calling us. It's hard to tell when you might be awake or asleep.

Everything's good here. Went to the

Astros game yesterday. We lost 6 to 19. One of the worst games I've ever seen. Glad I can work from home this week. Excited to spend more time with Paisley.

Good luck with the search for Runa. Hope you find her quickly. Paisley asked for you to send pictures whenever you can.

Please don't push yourself too hard. I miss you so much. Home isn't the same without you.

Love,
Bryan

Ten failed Skype attempts later, Shelby gave up on chatting live with Bryan and Paisley while they were all awake. She went back to her room to wait for breakfast to start.

By the time Ravi and Tariq picked her up, she was already dragging.

As the Toyota sped off to find more traffic, Ravi greeted her. "How are you this fine morning?"

"Feeling like I should be going to bed soon. It's going to take a few days to adjust to being here."

"Yes, and by the time you do, you will be already on the plane home."

"Classic."

"At least you've done the hard part. Always

easier to fly west than east. I am still recovering from my return last week."

"Well I'm glad to know I have the easy part to look forward to."

"Is there an easy part? I have found traversing the world is always challenging."

"Even for you, doing this as much as you have?"

"Oh yes. I have tried every jet lag trick and sleep medicine out there. There is no avoiding just being very tired for a while."

"Sounds like having a newborn."

"Hah. I suppose it would." Ravi motioned directions to Tariq. The car merged over three lanes and made a quick right turn, narrowly avoiding slamming into an unyielding taxi.

"*Oi! Dekhe cholte paro na*?" Tariq yelled.

Shelby had no idea what he said but knew exactly what he meant. Bad driving was universal. Between the possible bag-grabbing incident at the airport and a couple near misses on the roads, Shelby scratched tally marks in her journal, noting the number of times she had feared for her life just 24 hours into a world of different norms.

"So where are we off to first?" Shelby asked. The car appeared to be on some kind of freeway now. No intersections or streetlights were slowing them down. Just thick, honk-happy traffic.

"We are heading to the best lead I have so

far. On Friday, I contacted a site manager at the commercial center that is going up at her uncle's old residence. It took a while to track someone down, but I finally did. He told me an intersection near where he believes residents were moved. Savar is south and west of here, farther from the city center. Lots of big factories in that area."

"Garment factories?"

"Yes. Many businesses here are connected to garments. Banks, exporting agencies, and legal firms also work with RMG in some capacity."

Shelby knew from her research that RMG, short for ready-made goods, became the country's golden egg. Just two years earlier, Bangladesh had moved to become the second-largest exporter of RMG in the world. Projections indicated that in five years, the country could surpass China as the biggest producer of ready-made apparel.

"So then, are you connected to the garment industry?" Shelby asked.

"Indirectly. Caring Hope brought me here to support families who work in this region. Many people work in the factories. I run the education sponsorships and work with other community organizations in the area to identify emergent needs of workers."

"What kind of needs? Like meals?" Shelby asked.

"Not typically. If you supply food, a few hours later, everyone is hungry again. Instead, we support workers to learn a new skill, like how to sew a zipper or dye synthetics. Then they can get a job and provide for their families for the long term."

"I'm curious, how well do these jobs pay?"

"Well, it depends. Some factories pay living wages, and workers are able to live comfortably. They have a set work schedule. They live in a home with their family. Some offer on-site childcare and even schools. Some workers send extra money to their families in rural villages. But jobs like these are hard to get. Once workers have these very good jobs, they do not leave."

"Why aren't there more jobs like that?" Shelby asked.

"Big retailers often squeeze so much out of the production process, factories have very little margin for accepting the contracts and meeting their expenses. So much blame is often placed at the factory level, but the retailers are a big part of the problem. They are the ones making the money—often enormous profits that never get passed back to workers."

"What was it like for workers at Tazreen?" Shelby asked.

"From what I heard, managers forced workers to stay long hours for low pay. Runa was nearly released from Eternal Promise because Nipa was always late picking her up. She was able to stay because their sister school provides orphan care, where childcare workers are present around the clock."

"That's fortunate."

"It was Runa who begged to stay. She loved spending time there. She offered to wash dishes and bathe babies on the days she stayed late, and on Fridays and Saturdays when Nipa worked weekends. Fridays here are part of the weekend. It is the holy day of worship, and workers are supposed to have off."

"Was it not possible for Nipa to get another job?"

"It was technically possible, but it would have been very difficult. If she did not go to work just one day, she could have been fired. Even for what we would consider undesirable jobs, there is an impressive line of people who would take it. Nipa was out of work several times, having been fired for speaking up for workers' rights. She was committed to keeping Runa in school, so she stopped taking risks that might jeopardize their family's stability."

As Shelby jotted notes in her journal, a question formed. "Could Caring Hope have helped Nipa find a better job?" Soon as she asked it, she wished she could lasso the sharp words from the car air back into her mouth.

Ravi cleared his throat. "Shelby, you have to understand, every year we help hundreds of women like Nipa. Her situation was tough, but she had a safe place for her and her daughter to live. She held a stable job. And, thanks to your family, Runa had sponsorship to help with her educational expenses. That $39 a month you paid was a whole month's worth of wages."

"Wait, what? $39?" Shelby's jaw dropped.

"The minimum wage for garment workers is $37 a month."

Shelby was quiet. Forty dollars was less than she usually spent at one dinner out with friends. To her, the amount was forgettable. But to someone like Nipa, it was more than a month's worth of day-in, day-out labor. She thought back to the $40 she handed the woman at Tazreen, wishing she'd given more.

Ravi continued, "Nipa was finally able to pay off debts and start saving small bits each month. Many of the men and women we support are unable to find a job. They sleep on the streets or make very meager earnings doing laundry or washing dishes. Often they cannot afford to feed their families."

"I'm sorry, Ravi. I didn't mean to sound critical. I'm just trying to understand."

"Of course. That is why you came."

A silence hung in the air. Shelby looked out the car window at the endless line of garages and storefronts adjacent the busy street. No amount of reading or interviewing could lead her to understand this foreign place or any other in the span of a week.

The car turned off the busy thoroughfare and onto a narrow road full of brake lights. "Are we close?" Shelby asked.

"Yes, just a short drive more. But now the hard part begins."

Out her window, Shelby could see a street vendor searing strips of meat over an open fire. A young boy washed windshields of stopped cars. A grown man peed on a light post.

"Quite a sight, isn't it?" Ravi asked.

"So disgusting."

"You can imagine with this large a population there are insufficient public restrooms. And many people live on the streets."

"Ravi, how long have you lived here?"

"Almost ten years. I cannot believe it has been that long."

"Where did you live before?"

"I lived in the UK and attended university in London. But I grew up in India."

"Had you planned to come here?"

"Never. When I started working for Caring Hope, I thought I would stay in London or go back to India. But I speak Bengali, so it was easy for them to send me here. Until recently, I have felt called to stay."

"So, wait, how did you get from India to London?" Shelby knew so little about Ravi's background. In all these months emailing with him, she'd never thought to ask.

"When I was young, I moved with my family to a small town in West Bengal. My father grew very sick. He could not walk. It did not seem to matter how many doctors he saw or how many cures he tried, nothing made him better. One day he traveled to receive care from a remote hospital. At the time, a group of volunteer doctors was visiting from the UK."

"Offering free medical care?"

"Yes, exactly. This doctor gave my dad some medicine. He put his hands on his abdomen and prayed. I have no idea what the doctor did, but my father stood up and walked out. Over the next few days, he was completely healed."

"That's amazing."

"My father is Hindu, but he began to study the stories of Jesus of Nazareth and the way he cared for the hurting and poor. He instilled these lessons in my brothers and sisters and me."

"So, how did you end up in London?" Shelby felt nosy asking all the questions, but Ravi's background was so intriguing.

"The doctor checked up on my father periodically. They kept in touch for years after his illness. When I wanted to go to university, his family invited me to live with them. London is oppressively expensive. They allowed me to live with them free of housing costs while I completed my studies."

"What an incredible gift."

"It was. And living there, I continued to learn from him and his wife about how to care for those in need."

"What an amazing influence to have on your life."

"What about you, Shelby? Is there anyone who helped shape what is important to you?"

This was a question she immediately knew how to answer. "My grandmother, Dear. She taught me how to sew and also to look out for people who are hurting. But honestly, I don't think I've done a very good job following her lead. I've been so focused on growing my business and raising our family."

"Probably why you ended up across the street from Maye."

"What do you mean?" Shelby asked.

"I believe certain people show up in our lives at the precise moment we need them to, to nurture our path. Maye's emails to me have revealed so much love for you and your family. I can tell you are in wonderful hands."

For the zillionth time on this journey, Shelby felt herself tearing up. Their family had moved into the house on Oak Blossom Lane a few months before Paisley was born. Maye introduced herself to Shelby and Bryan just weeks before

Dear passed away. Now this helpful neighbor guided and showed up for her, much like her grandmother used to.

"You're right. I am really fortunate to have Maye in my life." Shelby smiled, recalling all the ways Maye had boosted her confidence in the uncertain years as a new mom, always ready with her camera or an understanding ear.

"We are getting close." Ravi directed Tariq to turn onto a side street.

Shelby's nerves twisted with excitement. Finally, the moment arrived to look for Runa.

But seeing the thousands of people traversing the streets by foot, by car, by cart hinted at the insurmountable challenge of finding this girl.

Tariq pulled the car into a narrow alley next to a tall cinderblock apartment building covered in scaffolding. Shelby collected her backpack and exited the car.

"Watch your step," Ravi said as Shelby placed a foot on the sidewalk. Dog droppings littered the pavement everywhere.

"I'm sensing that will be a theme for the day," Shelby said.

She got out of the car, and suddenly a group of men rushed up to her. Hands rubbed against her body. She yelled and pushed them back.

Ravi shouted loudly and fought the men away. A few more terse words, and the mob dispersed.

"What was that?" Shelby asked.

"Not many foreigners come to this part of town. They think you look like a movie star. They just want a picture."

"So much for my attempts to blend in. Is this going to keep happening?"

"Probably. They don't mean to scare you. They are just very curious. To be safe, please keep your pocketbook on you at all times. And first chance you get, buy a headscarf."

Ravi exchanged words with Tariq. "After he parks, he will come help us look for Runa and fend off any troublemakers."

"I'll take all the help I can get." Shelby wished Bryan were here. Another American in the group might draw even more attention, but she knew she would feel safer by his side.

"This is the neighborhood I was told Runa's uncle relocated to," Ravi said.

"So now what? We just . . . look?"

"Yes. Now we look. But first, a plan. If we get separated, let's meet at the last place we were together."

"Got it." Shelby gave Ravi a duplicate of Runa's photo.

As they walked the length of the street, they stopped each person who passed by.

"*Apni ei meye-ke dekhechen*?" Ravi asked.

Shelby continued to get pestered for photos until they passed a bazaar. In one of the stalls, a vendor was selling headscarves in every color and pattern. Shelby picked out a gray scarf for herself, a pink one for Paisley, and a silky white one for the baby. Covered in the scarf, the search for Runa resumed, with less extra attention.

"*Apni ei meye-ke dekhechen?*" After hearing Ravi ask "have you seen this girl" a hundred times, Shelby grew comfortable reciting the Bengali words herself. She knew her pronunciation was correct when heads began shaking no. Tariq joined in, which allowed Shelby and Ravi to split up, walking on opposite sides of the street. Among the people they stopped and the stores they entered, the answer was the same.

"*Na.*"

They crossed block after block. The smell of garbage and sewage lingered in the air, heightening Shelby's nausea. Three hours of walking and asking left her exhausted and famished. They found a place to sit down for lunch. Ravi recommended the biryani, a flavorful mixture of curry and rice.

Their search for Runa continued, with another dozen "*na*" responses. After another hour, Shelby said, "I'm starting to think this isn't going to work."

"All we can do is to keep looking," Ravi assured her. "It's our only chance to find her."

They looked for another hour, showing the photo, asking everyone in sight. No one had seen her.

"Are there any parks or playgrounds where we could look?"

"Probably not. There are not many green spaces in the area."

Ravi asked for directions to the nearest park. Shelby could tell from the na-shaking head that there was no park. But there was a school.

They walked the kilometer to the school, asking everyone they passed along the way. "*Na.*" No, no one had seen Runa.

Finally, someone responded with something other than "*Na.*"

"*Ami okey chini.*" A man in a pale blue collared shirt lifted his sunglasses to look closer at the photo.

Shelby's heart pounded with hope, until Ravi translated his reply. "He thinks she grew up down the street."

Shelby shook her head. "No, that's not her."

With each inconclusive conversation, the day dragged on. Shelby's ankles swelled. An ache grew in the hinge of her hip from so much walking and standing.

"We aren't any further along than when we started," Shelby said. "Is there some way we can narrow down the search? Are there any other people who knew Nipa who might know how to contact her brother?"

"I am not sure. The director at Eternal Promise

did not have any more information beyond that first phone number."

"Is there anyone else? A teacher or some other caregiver we could ask?"

"Maybe. Nipa's roommate is the only other person I can think of, but I do not have her contact info. Eternal Promise would know."

As they waited for Tariq to drive up, they continued showing the picture to everyone who passed the school entrance. *Na, na,* and more *na.*

In the backseat of Tariq's sedan, Shelby gulped her bottled water and kicked off her dusty sandals. She wanted to rub her aching arches, but they were filthy. Her ankles were as swollen as after the flights. It was impossible to stay hydrated.

As her body stilled, she felt the baby kick and wiggle. Was that a tiny elbow? A heel? She pressed her fingertips into the nudges.

"Are you okay to keep going?" Ravi asked.

The afternoon had just begun, and Shelby felt ready to go back to the hotel and pass out. But she wanted to take advantage of every opportunity to find Runa.

"Yes," Shelby said. "Let's keep going."

After an hour-long drive across town, Tariq dropped them off at Eternal Promise. As they walked up the steps, Shelby noticed something remarkable. The blue door—the same blue door from the pictures of Nipa and Runa wearing her sparkleberry dresses. An unexpected calm washed over her. Finally, something looked familiar.

They walked through the bright blue doors of Eternal Promise School, and a cheerful woman in an orange patterned sari and headscarf greeted them.

"*Assalamu alaikum*," Ravi replied, nodding. As they exchanged conversation, Shelby stood by, awaiting translation.

After hearing why they came, the woman turned down the hallway, disappearing into another room. "That is one of the teachers. She is going to find Sarah Chowdhury, the director for 20 years. Sarah knows everything about the students at Eternal Promise."

A thin lady with kind eyes and a tidy bun walked toward them and extended her hand to greet Ravi. Seeing Shelby, she switched to English. "So wonderful to see you, Ravi. We've missed you around here."

"Wonderful to see you, my friend," Ravi continued. "Yes, I have been traveling and have not had any packages to deliver for some time." Shelby realized he was referencing the gifts Paisley had insisted they send to Runa. "I want you to meet my friend, Shelby Lawrence. She was Runa Zaman's educational sponsor through Caring Hope."

"Welcome, Shelby. So wonderful to meet you."

"It's a pleasure to meet you, Mrs. Chowdhury. I'm glad to be here. I've heard so many wonderful things about Eternal Promise."

Ravi continued. "You may remember, Shelby is the sponsor who sent the packages I delivered here in the fall."

"Oh, yes, the dresses. I could never forget that day. Runa was so pleased to show her mom. They put on the dresses, and we took pictures in the courtyard. Runa didn't want to stop. I think we filled a whole memory card."

"So, wait, you took the picture? The one Ravi emailed in November?"

"Yes, and a couple hundred others," Sarah laughed.

"That picture meant so much to me." Shelby realized she was clenching her fists, her jaw, her forehead, trying to hold in the emotions. This mother, who had been so alive, had worn Shelby's label in this very place. Now she was gone.

Of all the people Shelby would meet on this trip, the person she most wished to speak to was Nipa. The finality of this woman's fate pained her in a new way. Death was so unspeakably permanent.

"And to us too, dear Shelby. After the fire, it was such a blessing having those pictures of Runa and her mother. We wouldn't have those pictures if the dresses hadn't come. We have you to thank."

Shelby was silent, unable to accept any semblance of a compliment about Nipa's final days.

"Come with me," Mrs. Chowdhury said. They followed her down a long, bare hallway into an office, which filled the space of a small bedroom and was shared by three others. From atop her wooden desk, Sarah picked up a small picture frame.

"The days after the fire were so chaotic. By the time I was able to print the picture, Runa's uncle had already come to take her. I hoped we would see her again, so I framed it. But we haven't heard anything since she left."

The conversation stopped as Shelby stared into the picture of Nipa and Runa standing together. *Together.* Something the mother-daughter pair would never again be.

"Now I have a question for you," Sarah resumed. "Our children have had educational sponsors for decades, but none has ever come to visit. What brings you here? Why have you come all this way?"

Shelby returned the picture frame to the desk, knowing the words she needed to say. "Mrs. Chowdhury—"

"Please, call me Sarah."

"Sarah, please understand what I'm about to

tell you is very hard for me to say. I am a clothing designer, which is why I sent the dresses. It turns out my dresses were being sewn at the site of the fire. Nipa and her coworkers died while working on an order placed there on my behalf. When I found out about Nipa, I was devastated."

"I see." Sarah lowered her eyes.

"On some level, I feel responsible for what happened to Runa. I came to look for her. Ravi has tried, but no one seems to know what happened since she left your care. I want to make sure she's okay and see how we can help. I owe her that, if nothing else."

"Please understand, the death toll would have been high no matter whose clothes were there. That factory was repeatedly cited by safety auditors for poor wiring and lack of evacuation plan, but their leadership made no improvements. Emergency escapes were locked. There was no outside staircase. They had added multiple extra floors without approval. It is all so sad."

"That's all true. But at the very least, I was part of the problem."

"Perhaps," she said, her eyes smiling. "But now, my dear, you are very much a part of the solution."

Shelby nodded then continued. "So far, we have made no headway finding Runa by searching the streets. Do you know anything else about her uncle that could help us find them?"

"I'm afraid I don't know any more than what I've shared with Ravi. Nipa's brother is Golam Kibria. For years he worked in the shipyards in Chittagong, dismantling junked ships, but he was injured by a rusty propeller several years ago. Almost lost an arm. When we called him, he was living in Dhaka, cleaning offices as a janitor, which pays very poorly. But in his case, he could do no other labor because of his injury.

"As far as I know, he was not involved in Nipa or Runa's lives. I believe they had a fight over sending money to their parents in late ages. After her parents passed, Nipa never talked about him. He was the only family Nipa had and was listed as her next of kin."

"How did you get in touch with him the day of the fire?"

"That was tricky. The number provided was not Golam's own. It was to the property manager of the room where he stayed. He shared a bunkroom with five other men. You can imagine our concern sending Runa to live with him. But he assured us he would find a more suitable place once Runa was in his care. He seemed determined to carry out his sister's wishes."

"How would he do that, though? With such a limited income?" Shelby asked, wondering if she was wording these questions correctly.

"Most likely by Runa working alongside him, at least for a short time," Sarah said. "School was about to let out for winter holidays when the fire happened. He said Runa would return to school in January, but it is not uncommon for people to say what they think you want to hear. In fact, it is very unlikely he could afford the food, rent, and a child's educational costs without a second income."

Shelby swallowed hard before continuing with questions. "What about Nipa's friends. Would they have kept in touch with Runa or know where to find her?"

"Rehana was her closest friend and roommate. Nipa lived with her after her husband abandoned them. Her children are not at Eternal Promise, so I do not have contact with her, but I can tell you where to find her."

"Ravi, can we go speak to her now?"

"Yes, Tariq can take us."

"Sarah, how did Runa and Nipa get home most days?"

"They walked. They walked everywhere," she said.

"Then let's walk," Shelby said.

Sarah accompanied them out of the office, outside into the courtyard. "I hope we will see you again."

"Thank you, Sarah. So wonderful to meet you."

"Please—take this with you and give it to Runa. Tell her Sarah Aunty misses her." She held out the framed picture.

"I would love to, but I can't guarantee we will find her. I'm only here until Friday, and we have so few leads," Shelby said.

"Well, if you don't find her, please take the picture home and remember the joy you brought them both during their final days together."

Pressing her lips together, Shelby forced a smile.

The glow of the lowering sun reflected back in Sarah's eyes. "Something tells me you will find her."

Sarah walked them to the exit of the schoolyard, where girls of all ages were huddled together over books and sidewalk chalk drawings. A young girl, maybe six, chased after a faded red ball.

"I hope your search is successful. Ravi, don't stay away so long next time."

"I won't, dear friend," Ravi said. "Thank you for the good work you are doing to raise up these little ones."

In the heat of the sunbaked afternoon, Ravi and Shelby walked to Runa and Nipa's old house, Shelby feeling the figurative weight of the framed photo in her backpack. Retracing the steps of Nipa and Runa's former commute wasn't easy. But more than ever, she believed the journey was worth taking.

"This sounds strange, but I feel better just having talked to Sarah."

"She is an amazing woman. Doing this work, she has seen many miracles happen. She has also seen many tragic things happen too."

"I can't even imagine," Shelby said.

"Did you notice the girl playing with the red ball?"

"Yes, I did."

"This girl was found barely alive in a dumpster just hours after her birth."

"That's . . . that's so horrible. I've actually seen headlines like that in Houston. It's beyond tragic."

"It is. The miracle is that the girl was found in time, and after years of care, she is healthy and happy. She is even learning English by watching American movies."

"That's amazing."

"Have you ever witnessed a miracle?" Ravi asked.

"Honestly, besides our children, I can't think of any." The miracle Shelby always hoped for as a child never came true. More than anything, she'd wanted her dad to walk back into her life. She wanted to feel like part of a family again.

"I believe sometimes, when we are right where we are supposed to be, the miracles find us," Ravi said the words with such certainty.

But Shelby wasn't so sure.

They walked another 15 minutes without exchanging words, Shelby's thoughts drifting to possible miracles. She thought about the emotional morning in September when she found out her pregnancy had ended. Without even asking, Paisley showed up at her bedside to snuggle and comfort her. Then there was Maye's unexpected connection to Runa, and to Ravi. Maye said from the beginning that wasn't a coincidence.

Perhaps Shelby had, indeed, experienced miracles and just hadn't realized it. In both cases, those miracles had found her. It made her wonder if she was approaching the search for Runa all wrong, trying to force a breakthrough. But with so few days to work with, what other options did they have?

Sweat dripped down her back as Shelby navigated dirt path, pavement, and potholes. Her swollen feet rubbed against the heel of her sandals, igniting a blister on her swollen ankles. "They did this walk every day?"

"Yes. Every day."

"After a full day of work?"

"It did not cost them anything to walk. And with traffic, not much time is saved by rickshaw."

"It's a decent commute."

"Yes. You doing okay?" Ravi asked.

"I'm starting to fade. It's four in the morning back home."

"We will take you back to the hotel after this."

After 45 minutes of walking, they arrived at

a mud house with a tin roof, just as depicted in the introductory letter from Caring Hope. Behind the home's wooden door, Shelby heard the kissy voices of children. Ravi knocked, and the noises dropped away.

A voice spoke near the door. Ravi responded.

A woman wearing a long faded blue sari opened the door. Standing only as tall as Shelby's shoulders, she balanced a doe-eyed toddler on her hip.

Speaking Bengali, Ravi introduced them and explained why they came. Rehana invited them inside.

They spoke in Bengali for several minutes. Eventually Ravi resumed in English. "I asked if she has any other information about Runa. She said when the uncle came, he seemed very impatient. He yelled at Runa while she collected a few things. Rehana said it was hard to hear because the girl had just lost her mother, but he was in a hurry because he was missing work. He would not let her bring any books and only a few clothes. He said they had no place for any of it."

"Did he say anything about where they were going?"

Ravi spoke to Rehana, then to Shelby. "He did not say."

"What other questions do you have?" Ravi asked Shelby.

"Can I see where they stayed?" Ravi translated,

and Rehana walked them to a small room, steps away from the entrance. Bed mats wrapped in mosquito nets were spread out across the floor.

"Another mother and her three children rent the other side of the room," Ravi explained.

Stepping into the room, Rehana lifted a corner of one sleeping pad, exposing a painfully familiar color—sparkleberry.

"*Runa-r jonno.*" Rehana held out the well-traveled dress.

"For Runa," Ravi translated.

Shelby accepted the dress, draping it over her arm. Something in the pocket pushed against her skin. Curious, she reached her hand inside, her fingertips returning the most unexpected sight: a folded page of unicorn stationery. Runa had stored Paisley's very first note in the pocket of her dress.

Unfolding the note revealed the stick figures of Paisley and Runa holding hands beneath a marker-drawn rainbow. In Shelby's handwriting, the note read, "Runa, I hope I get to play with you one day." Shelby ran her fingers along the rounded edges, remembering the quiet moment in the kitchen when Paisley trimmed each corner.

As Rehana spoke, Ravi translated. "Runa loved the dress. Nipa sewed this order at work. Until you sent the dresses, she had never owned anything her mother had made. Rehana is asking if you will take it to her?"

The words to answer her wouldn't come. This whole heartbreaking mess had started with this dress. And now, a new thread connected everything. Nipa had sewn the first order. The chances still seemed so unbelievable. And yet, here she was in a mud hut in the slums of Dhaka holding a pretty dress with an ugly story.

"Please tell Rehana we will do everything we can to find Runa." Shelby nodded, tucking the note and dress into her backpack with the picture.

"Anything else?" Ravi asked.

Shelby hesitated, not knowing if the heaviness of her next question was appropriate. But in two days, she would return halfway around the world, never to see this woman again. If there were ever a time to force conversation over the fences of small talk, this was it.

"I would like to know, how is she doing?" Shelby asked.

"Who, Runa?"

"No, Rehana." Shelby watched Rehana's face as Ravi translated the question.

Rehana stood close-lipped. Big honest tear-drops fell from her silent eyes. Before speaking, she pressed her cheek against the carried child's wispy hair.

With a tender tone, Ravi relayed her response to Shelby. "She is devastated to lose her dear friends. She is glad you have come and wants to know if we find Runa."

They said goodbye to Rehana then walked toward the busy bazaar where they planned to meet Tariq. Ravi seemed extra quiet ever since they left Rehana's.

"Everything okay?" Shelby asked.

"I'm starting to wonder how we can find Runa," Ravi said.

Shelby felt her shoulders tense. "Why do you say that?"

"Remember what Sarah said? That Runa's uncle was a janitor."

"Yes?"

"And the comment from Rehana that he didn't want to bring Runa's books?"

"Yes. What are you thinking?"

"That Runa is also working, probably with her uncle or perhaps as a domestic helper."

"What does that mean for our search?"

"If she is working inside, there is very little chance we will see her coming or going, which is the only strategy we have. She could be working in any of these buildings, in a private residence or office. She likely would not come outside except to walk home. And if she has not been enrolled in school, probably no one we ask will know who she is."

Shelby tried not to think about stepping on the airplane, having not found Runa. She took a deep breath and focused her thoughts. Tariq's Toyota waited for them across the street. "What do you think is the best strategy for tomorrow?"

"We need to be in Savar very early to catch her walking to work. Then we can tour *Golora Fashions*, which is on your list."

"I emailed them several times, but their owner never answered my request to visit."

"Well, it is not far from where we will be. We'll go anyway and see if we get lucky. Maybe they will let you in as a potential customer. Anyway, I planned lunch nearby there with a friend who works for an advocacy organization. She will accompany us to tour another factory on your list. In the evening, we may try again to find Runa walking home."

Shelby's hand found its way to her belly as she processed the long day ahead. Searching for Runa and visiting factories were the reasons she was here. But the throb pulsing through her ankles and calves made her question her stamina for another long and winding day.

As they walked toward Tariq's car, Shelby asked, "What time do I need to be ready?"

Tariq sat in the driver's seat, listening to music. Ravi exchanged a few words with him, then replied, "We will pick you up at half-past five."

"I know I'll be up then, but that sounds awfully early for you two."

"It is early. I join you in hoping that we find Runa," Ravi said, the sincerity in his eyes matching his voice.

"Thank you, Ravi. I really appreciate your help. All of it." After worrying about Runa solo for so long, it was nice to feel part of a team.

"Let's get you back. We need to rest up for whatever tomorrow holds."

Chapter 19

The sun wasn't yet up, but Shelby woke easily. She threw on a gray T-shirt over loose cotton pants and put a bandage over her blister. After packing her bag with a protein bar and scarf, she headed to the lobby.

Internet was out again, so she helped herself to simmering black tea in her travel mug. Moments later, Tariq and Ravi pulled up. The three of them hurried off into the web of traffic toward Savar, some 25 kilometers southwest.

Streets and sidewalks buzzed with a different urgency during the early morning than they had during yesterday's midday search. Young children dressed in school uniforms were herded through the streets by older children. Street vendors sold tea in Styrofoam cups. Bicycles whizzed past. Car horns beeped with urgency.

Along the drive, Ravi was generous to answer Shelby's two hundred questions about everyday life in Dhaka. Shelby recorded the helpful tidbits in her notebook to study during the long idle spells stopped in traffic.

As Shelby watched Ravi point directions for Tariq, uneasiness grew as the moment approached to exit the protective bubble of the car. Every nuance of this trip had pushed Shelby out of her comfort zone, but hardest of all was pacing the sidewalks asking if anyone had seen Runa. The likelihood of finding the girl was starting to feel completely improbable, but they were left with no other options.

When the car stopped and Ravi opened his door, Shelby forced herself to exit the car. She tossed the gray scarf over her head and planted her feet on the sidewalk. By now the sun was up, but its beams of light weren't yet visible over the tops of the never-ending buildings. The break in passing clouds hinted at a blue-sky day.

"Ready for round two?" Ravi asked.

"I guess so. Wish we had a little more hope."

"I like to think there is always hope." Ravi stopped a woman wearing a bright pink head-scarf. "Have you seen this girl?"

And so began the flood of *na* responses. *Na, na, na.*

Identifying the first passerby to ask, Shelby had a sinking feeling about how the next few hours would unfold. And they did. No after no after no. No Runa. No leads. No hints at finding her.

"Well, at least we worked up an appetite," Ravi said. "Ready to get some good food?"

"You are one of the most positive people I've ever met. And yes, I'm famished, and I really need a restroom."

"Hmm . . . food is easy. Restroom, not so much. Let me think."

Shelby now regretted drinking the tea. "Any chance of finding a public restroom?"

"Very little. And if we found one, I would not let you use it."

"So, wait, what do women do if they're out and about and need to use the restroom?"

"Hmmm. Far as I know, they plan not to need one."

"They don't drink anything before they leave the house?"

"I suppose not."

"But it's so hot and humid. How could you go for hours in traffic or long walks to and from home without drinking water?"

"If you can wait until we are at *Golora Fashions*, there should be one you may use."

Shelby noticed he avoided answering the question, which she took to mean there simply wasn't a good answer.

"Sounds like I'll have to."

They passed a street vendor standing over a cart full of round green fruit that looked like the cross between a lime and a Granny Smith apple.

"You're in for a treat."

"What is it?"

"*Masala Amra*."

"And that is . . . ?"

"Ambarella fruit mixed with citrus juice and spices. It is delicious."

Ravi spoke a few quick words in Bengali then

Shelby watched the street vendor manipulate a small knife, peeling the skin off and slicing the ambarella fruit in the palm of his other hand. He tossed the slices into a large plastic jug and sprinkled a spoonful of spices on top, then closed the lid and shook it. He dumped the contents into a small plastic bag, then poked a toothpick into the flesh of one slice, handing it to Shelby.

"*Dhonnobad*," she said, but the vendor was already peeling and slicing the next order.

"Give it a try," Ravi prompted.

Shelby stabbed a toothpick into an ambarella slice. It tasted like mango, lime, and chili seasoning. The mixture of salt and citrus atop the sweet juicy fruit was addicting.

"Wow, that's amazing." She pulled out her phone and took a selfie with Ravi and her morning snack to share with Paisley.

They snacked on the rest while walking to meet Tariq. Back in the car, they resumed their spot in the day's traffic, heading toward the factory where her Easter dresses were made.

Soon after, they pulled up to a large compound with chain link fences around it. A uniformed security officer guarded the entrance.

"Doesn't look very welcoming," Shelby said from the backseat. For once she was thrilled to get out of the car, anxious to relieve herself, and excited to meet the actual workers who constructed her latest dresses. She grabbed her backpack and joined Ravi on the sidewalk, expecting the guard to turn and open the gate. But Ravi's conversation kept going, and the guard wasn't moving.

"What's going on?" Shelby asked.

"He said they do not allow visitors."

"Did you tell him I'm a buyer from the U.S., and I want to talk to the manager about placing an order?" Shelby asked.

"Yes, I told him. He said you need to call the manager."

"I did call the manager. We have an appointment," Shelby insisted, though it wasn't the truth. She had tried to contact the manager, but he never replied to her emails or phone calls. She hated the thought of coming this close and being turned away.

Ravi relayed her comments, but the answer was a firm "*na.*" Ravi returned to the car and motioned for Shelby to do the same.

"Didn't realize that would be such a difficult ask." Shelby resumed her spot in the backseat. "I thought they would want to talk to a customer."

"They are probably more on guard about auditors since the fire. There was a lot of extra news coverage on garment factories. Much of it hurt businesses, which is a shame because that ultimately hurts garment workers."

"What are the chances they'd let me use the restroom?"

"Not a chance." Ravi shook his head.

"Well, that was a bust. What now?" Shelby asked.

"Let's head to the café. We are a little early, but I will see if my friend can meet us there earlier than we planned."

"Please tell me there's a restroom?"

"Yes, of course," Ravi said.

"Oh, thank goodness."

The aroma of curry hovered like an intoxicating cloud outside the café. Once inside, Shelby immediately excused herself to the ladies' room.

The seating area was nearly full. Ravi chose a small table in the corner. Shelby was asking questions about the food when a petite woman with prism-bright eyes, short dark hair, and a celebrity smile appeared in the doorway wearing a soft pink headscarf and matching textured blouse.

As the woman walked closer, Shelby noticed a spark of light in Ravi's eyes, as if he'd been jolted by electricity. He stood to greet her, never allowing his gaze to budge.

"*Salaam alaikum*," Ravi said matter-of-factly, reining in his usually generous smile.

"*Wa alaikum as-salam*," the woman replied, just as reserved.

"Shelby, I would like for you to meet my colleague Priti Rahm. She is a garment rights activist with the STARA Foundation, a very active and highly respected organization based in Dhaka."

"It's so wonderful to meet you, Priti." Shelby extended her right hand, her left over her heart as the guidebook suggested.

"I am pleased to meet you too." Priti smiled and returned the gesture.

During every introduction, Shelby felt awkward and out of place. There were so many nuances to greeting a person in a different culture. She suspected she was messing up every line of this script. Thankfully, every friendly Bangladeshi she met sheltered her under an umbrella of social grace.

Priti took a seat at the table across from Ravi, who seemed to be watching her every move. Blind as Shelby was to so many cultural nuances, attraction this magnetic was as universal as a smile. A strong connection existed between these two that Ravi hadn't mentioned.

"Shelby, how has your trip been so far?" Priti asked, her voice friendly and warm.

"Busy, but smooth overall thanks to Ravi and Tariq. The food is delicious, and I'm loving all the gorgeous flowers and trees. The people we've met have been lovely. So gracious and kind." Shelby looked at Ravi. "Except at *Golora Fashions*."

"Is that where you came from?" Priti asked.

"Yes. Security would not let us in," Ravi said.

"Ah, yes. That doesn't surprise me. The factory has a terrible reputation."

"I'm sorry to hear that." Shelby was genuinely disappointed to confirm another dark dungeon in *Surface Trend*'s supply chain.

"If a factory is taking care of its workers, they will be very proud and will want to show off their facility."

"That's what I figured," Shelby said.

"Ravi tells me you are here because of the fire?" Priti asked.

"Yes. Unfortunately, the dresses I designed were being sewn there. When I heard about the fire and all the workers who died, I thought there was going to be major backlash from American shoppers. But there was very little. Then I had such a difficult time researching the factories we work with. It seemed like the only solution was to come and learn what I could in person."

"The garment industry is very complex. You are not imagining this," Priti said. "Makes it hard to fix what isn't working."

"I'm curious, how frequently do tragedies like this fire happen?" Shelby tucked a strand of hair behind her ear.

"Tragedies like the fire attract the most media attention. But considering the millions in the

370

garment industry, these events impact a relatively small number of people. Far more labor injustices are hidden. Someone works more hours than they get paid for or works overtime without being compensated. Sometimes factories accept orders too large or deadlines too fast, so they force workers to work 16-hour days without any days off."

"That's brutal," Shelby said, eyebrows raised.

"If workers complain, they are told to keep working or lose their jobs. Some women have told me they were threatened with their lives if they reported these disparities or tried to organize a protest. In addition, some facilities are not sanitary, and workers do not have good options for nutrition or health services. Toughest of all is the extremely low wages these workers receive."

"Why *are* wages so low?" Shelby asked, suspecting she should already know the answer.

"So Bangladesh can compete with other countries," Priti answered. "Every order has unavoidable fixed costs: machinery, materials, notions, packaging, and shipping. One of the only variable costs is labor."

"Bangladesh's economy has grown quickly by attracting huge retail contracts," Ravi added. "If those contracts went somewhere else, much of our labor force would be out of work completely. Then everyone, including garment workers, would suffer."

371

"I read that's why the boycotts in the '90s were really harmful," Shelby said.

"Yes, boycotting is probably the worst strategy. It puts garment workers out of a job," Ravi confirmed.

"A better approach is to support the brands that encourage factory workers to speak up for their own rights." Priti's voice was smooth, almost melodious. "Each factory has different policies, and some prevent workers from organizing. Garment workers who complain could lose their jobs. This often makes them powerless to change anything."

Shelby's discomfort grew the more she learned. "That's so unfair. And all for clothes. Is there anything someone like me can do to change the system?"

"That's a good question, but it has a difficult answer. The STARA Foundation tries to amplify the voices of workers in the apparel industry, hoping to gain safer working conditions, living wages, and professional growth opportunities, especially for women. We seek a more ethical fashion industry."

"What would an ethical fashion industry even look like?" Shelby once again felt like Paisley asking so many questions, thankful Priti and Ravi were gracious to oblige.

"This is another complex question," Priti said. "Ethical fashion is more than just fair wages and safe working conditions. It means making value-based decisions at every level of the supply chain, including fashion design, production, purchasing, and retail. Everything from sourcing of raw materials, water waste, climate impact, and even treatment of animals must be considered."

"The vast majority of this gets sorted out in parts of the world that are hidden from consumers," Ravi added. "Makes it easy for shortcuts to continue unchecked."

The server arrived, shuffling bowls of rice and curry from tray to table.

"This looks incredible." Shelby was listening so intently, she forgot they were here to eat.

"And it tastes even better." Ravi picked up his spoon.

They took the first tasty bites.

Shelby was eager to continue the discussion. "The more I research fashion supply chains, the more shocked I am by the number of people it takes to produce one item of clothing. Something as simple as a T-shirt involves so many processes and countries."

"This is very true," Ravi said. "And if you take a single element like cotton and follow it from seed to drawer, you can learn a lot about the true costs. Much of the world's cotton is grown in India. It is bought at such shamefully low prices that many farmers have committed suicide over their debt. It is some outrageous statistic, like 200,000 suicides since the mid-90s."

"Wait, what? Seriously?" Shelby stopped loading her spoon with curry and froze.

"The cost of fertilizers and pesticides to yield a cotton crop are greater than the income they receive," Ravi said, matter-of-factly. "All it takes is one season of bad weather to wipe out a whole harvest. And that says nothing of the long-term impact of fertilizers and pesticides."

Shelby's eyes lowered toward her curry, where her gray cotton T-shirt crowded her peripheral vision. She knew the shirt's tag read, *Made in the USA of imported materials.* It never occurred to her to question where and how the cotton was grown.

"An Indian farmer commits suicide every 30 minutes. You can imagine how destitute this leaves their families," Ravi said.

"I can't imagine." For every number in that overwhelming statistic, a family was demolished. "If that were happening in the United States, I feel like the media would be all over it."

Priti set down her spoon. "In the United States, cotton farms are subsidized by the government. And the media is only so effective in highlighting injustice. People in power often prevent the system from changing because it benefits them."

Her voice wasn't accusatory. Still, Shelby couldn't help but feel like Priti was talking about her. As a buyer and a shopper, she had benefitted from every shortcut. Like so many players in the fashion industry, she'd made decisions about clothes based primarily on price. It had been easy to do, so far removed from the injustices. So far removed, in fact, she didn't know about any of this.

"So then, why does the world need so much cotton?" Shelby asked.

"Why does the world need so many clothes?" Ravi countered.

"That is a question I wish more people were asking." Priti's prism-bright eyes looked straight at Shelby.

Shelby took a sip of water and a deep breath. "So, what can we do? What can someone like me do differently to change any of this?"

"Dear Shelby, don't you see, you have already answered your own question?" Priti asked, her gaze gentle but focused.

Shelby sat silent and still, staring into this woman's poised eyes awaiting the solution—any solution—to this impossible puzzle.

"Do something different." Priti's words were soft but sincere. "If what you have always done isn't working, do something different."

Chapter 20

After lunch, Priti accompanied Shelby and Ravi to the next factory. Leaving the café, Tariq drove them all a short distance in nonstop traffic. Shelby extra appreciated the breezy A/C sheltering them from the oppressive mid-day heat.

Talking to Priti in the backseat made the drive, even in traffic, feel not long enough. Shelby asked more questions, and Priti's responses were informative and reassuring.

As they drove through crowded streets and jam-packed neighborhoods, she pointed out every garment-related business. In addition to factories, there were yarn producers, fiber weavers, dyers, and export agencies.

Tariq pulled up in front of *VenTextile RMG*, a garment factory *Surface Trend* identified to source her fall line. This time, Ravi had emailed the manager confirming their visit. Still, Shelby waited nervously as Ravi approached the security guard.

After a short exchange, the guard called some-one on a flip phone then escorted their group of three into the multi-story concrete building. Five days after Shelby left home, it finally felt like she was making progress on one of her goals.

As they walked up a dark stairwell, Shelby

noticed every detail. Her excitement mixed with nerves as they walked into an office on the first floor. A man wearing a maroon button-down, collared shirt greeted them.

"Good afternoon. My name is Anwar. It is great to meet you all."

"Great to meet you too," Shelby said. "Thank you for having us."

"What questions can I answer?" Anwar flashed a friendly smile.

"I'm researching factories to source our next order. I'd like to learn about your facilities and see your workers in action."

"Excellent," he said. "Please, come with me."

Anwar walked the group down the hallway past a small daycare. Shelby wished more companies in America offered on-site childcare. It seemed like a perfect solution for parents—especially mothers nursing babies—to share geography during the workday instead of being separated by distance and traffic.

Inside the daycare was a small shelf of toys and surprisingly few children. A woman in a long blue tunic carried a toddler boy while overseeing three playful toddlers. Shelby wanted to ask the childcare worker what her days were like, but their group was hurried along to the next stop.

Walking toward the stairs, Anwar highlighted every safety feature, including smoke detectors, fire extinguishers, and an outdoor stairwell that served as an emergency exit. "As you can see, our generator is housed in a separate room from fabric storage," he pointed out.

"How often does the generator come on?" Shelby asked.

"Unfortunately, fairly often," Anwar said. "Power outages are not uncommon in Dhaka when the grid is overtaxed. They usually only last 15 minutes or so. Generators allow us to ensure we meet our production targets."

Going up the stairs, Shelby noticed the windows were clear of bars. On the second floor, endless rows of women were busy working at sewing tables. A stack of fabric sat on each table. Garment workers fed each piece of fabric expeditiously through a sewing machine bolted to the table.

At the top of the stairwell, Anwar opened a door to reveal a restroom with a single commode. Shelby stepped forward to take a closer look, but Anwar shut the door and directed their attention to the busy factory floor.

"This is where our clothing is produced. As you can see, our workers wear protective equipment, including face masks and hair coverings. As we walk through, I ask you not to disturb the seamstresses. They do not like to be interrupted while they are working."

As they walked through the floor, Shelby noticed every woman's headscarf was a uniformed bright pink. Managers inspecting rows of garment workers wore pink button-down, collared shirts over their street clothes. Few of the workers sewing were men. None of the line managers were women.

"Can we walk through the floor?" Priti asked.

"Yes, of course." Anwar led them into the heart of the factory. Leading them through the row of seamstresses, he walked backward facing them, his eyes never leaving their group.

Shelby wished she had a decibel reader to measure the noise of a hundred-plus sewing machines buzzing at once. Recalling the long sewing sprints during her start-up days, she marveled at how quickly each seamstress stitched one garment, then another.

As they reached the end of a row, Ravi directed Anwar's attention to the far corner of the floor where a sewing station sat idle. "What can you tell me about that empty workspace?" he asked.

"That machine broke a few days ago. We are awaiting a new part to fix it. It should be operating by the end of the week," Anwar explained.

As Ravi continued the sidebar conversation with Anwar, Priti slipped a small piece of paper into the lap of a young seamstress. Shelby's heart skipped a beat, feeling the anxiety of a middle schooler passing notes during class, careful not to be caught.

Their group toured three more floors full of women cutting and stitching fabric. As they reached the stairwell on the fifth and final floor, Shelby realized how relieved her eardrums felt escaping the battering of an army of sewing machines.

Sensing the tour was ending, she asked if she could use the ladies' room.

"Of course. Come with me." Their group descended flight after flight of stairs back to the first floor where they began. The owner led Shelby to a simple but clean restroom.

Upon rejoining the group, Shelby had more questions, but next thing she knew, Anwar was walking them toward the exit. Their goodbyes and thanks felt abrupt. Ravi called Tariq.

"Am I imagining it, or did that feel rushed?" Shelby asked. She checked her watch. Only 35 minutes had passed since they stood at this same spot by the security guard.

"You are not imagining it," Priti said.

Once Anwar was out of earshot, Shelby asked, "So tell me, what was on the note?"

"It was a request to meet us at a café down the street after work," Priti said. "I have no idea if she can read it, but it's worth a shot."

"Do you think she'll come?" Shelby asked, impressed by the bold move.

"I suspect she will come if she feels the need to voice concern," Priti said.

"What should we do until then?"

Ravi raised his eyebrows. "Let's keep looking for Runa."

The search for Runa proved as unsuccessful as ever. *Na, na,* and more *na.* Considering their early morning and so much walking, Shelby was exhausted. Her ankles were the most swollen yet. Her belly bump felt heavy and achy.

As the afternoon sun lowered toward the treetops, she was more than happy to sip tea in the café and wait for the seamstress. The three took their seats in the simple café chairs, and Shelby guzzled bottled water, one of the lone remedies to ease symptoms when pregnant.

"I see her. She's coming," Priti said, watching through the front window.

Priti walked to the door to meet her. The two women returned to the table, and Ravi and Shelby stood to greet her.

Through Priti's translation, Shelby learned the woman, named Fatima, had worked at the factory for seven years. She was 23 now and couldn't stay long, needing to get home to her husband and young daughter. Ravi ordered her tea.

"What questions do you have, Shelby?" Priti asked.

"For starters, I'm curious about the daycare. Are workers happy with the care their children received?"

"The daycare room is used to store fabrics. Those children were brought in from nearby neighborhoods to demonstrate compliance. Their parents were paid to loan them out. The teacher is a garment worker who was pulled from the line for the tour."

The answer shocked her. "So, who takes care of your daughter while you are working?"

Fatima spoke her reply quickly, and Priti translated. "My husband works as a rickshaw driver, so he is gone during the day. His mother lives with us and cares for her. But when she is sick, I cannot work. Or if the baby is sick, my mother-in-law cannot care for her. I have to bring the baby to the factory to show them how sick she is so they will excuse my workday. Otherwise, I risk losing my job."

Shelby shook her head and continued. "Does she feel her basic needs are being met at work?"

"No, the toilet on my floor was removed weeks ago but has not been replaced. We are required to relieve ourselves in a bucket. Workers take turns emptying the bucket at the end of the day. It is repulsive."

"But wait. Didn't we see a toilet?" Shelby said.

"They placed a nonworking commode there to give the appearance of sanitation," Fatima explained.

Ravi appeared visibly upset by this. The

anguish from the fire's aftermath was once again perceptible on his exterior.

"What do they pay you?" Shelby asked, via Priti.

"I make minimum wage, 1700BDT per month, paid at the end of the month."

"That's about $37 a month, which means her pay hasn't increased in seven years working at the same factory," Ravi said, agitation in his voice growing.

"Is this sufficient to pay for your housing and food?" Shelby asked.

"No. I returned to work six weeks after delivery, which meant I could not breastfeed my baby. I must buy canned powder milk, which is very expensive and not as healthy as breastmilk. I used to make more money with overtime, but they have not been giving us overtime."

"Did you receive your maternity benefit?" Priti asked.

"I was given maternity benefit for four weeks, but they owed me for sixteen. I had to ask and beg the managers just to get this amount. They told me the factory was not getting many orders, so they could not pay more. We believe they are subcontracting orders to other factories instead of giving us more work, so they do not have to pay us overtime."

Subcontracting. The same miserable way the fire had entered Shelby's life.

"What happens if workers strike over lost benefits?"

"Anyone caught organizing workers will lose their job. The last time there was a strike, they fired the leaders first. The workers who stayed had no voice."

As more words were exchanged in Bengali, Shelby listened eagerly.

Priti turned to Shelby. "Fatima needs to get home. Do you have one last question?"

Shelby thought, then spoke. "If she could change one thing, what would make the biggest difference to her family?"

Fatima replied quickly, definitively. "Higher wages. Even 600 taka a month would make a big difference. We could buy milk for the baby and food for our family. Right now, we can barely afford rent and my mother-in-law's medication, even though we are both working full-time."

"Please relay my sincere thanks for her coming to speak to us." Shelby placed a wad of taka into Fatima's hand. Fatima thanked them and stepped out onto the sidewalk, disappearing into the city.

"Well, that was eye-opening." Shelby shook her head.

"That was very brave of her to come," Priti said. "She could lose her job if they find out she spoke to me."

"When we were on the tour, did you know the

factory was cutting so many corners?" Shelby asked.

"I had a feeling." Priti's voice was soft, but certain. "The fact that he did not want us speaking to the workers was the biggest give-away. If a factory is treating its workers well, they have nothing to hide. Their workers will be forthcoming."

"I just feel so bad for her and everyone else who works there," Shelby said.

"Yes, but it is important to understand that often factory owners' hands cannot spare the funds to make improvements because retailers negotiate the contracts so low. Some factories must choose between accepting low-paying contracts and staying in business."

"I don't understand. How do brands pay so little for what they buy?"

"Because there is no accountability on retailers. The amount of competition allows brands to lowball unit prices. Low prices make consumers and shareholders happy. I wish more pressure were put on big retailers to pass profits back to the workers."

Shelby felt every one of Priti's words in the pit of her stomach and found it astonishing how few consequences the brands in the fire had suffered—including her own. It was becoming clearer where the suffering was happening.

"It seems like the workers are taking hits at

every turn. And am I just imagining it, or are women at an even greater disadvantage?"

"They absolutely are." Priti nodded. "Women like Fatima are not receiving the basic benefits they are owed, which requires eight weeks' pay before and eight weeks' pay after a worker has a baby. Some pregnant women are let go, so factories don't have to pay the maternity benefit."

"That's terrible."

"Yes, but often the factories operate on such low margins, they have to make hard decisions to stay in business." Priti took a sip of tea.

"Aren't most garment workers women?" Shelby asked.

"Yes, about two-thirds of garment workers in our country are women. Maternity rights offer an essential safety net, but many women do not have access to those benefits because the companies they work for simply refuse to pay them."

"How do the factories get away with not paying the benefit?"

"Many workers do not know what their benefits are. Some are told they have to work at a company eighteen months to receive maternity pay, when the law states only six. Some are illiterate and rely on others to stay informed. Misinformation is a key tool used by those in power to coerce those who have none."

"Sounds like a vicious cycle," Shelby said. "And it sounds like childcare is also problematic."

"Childcare is very difficult for women garment workers. Many women leave their babies to be raised by grandparents in remote villages. Some factories have on-site childcare, but many see it as a compliance requirement, not as a mechanism for increasing worker productivity.

"I talked to one woman who was not allowed to breastfeed her baby in the on-site daycare because it was deemed too time-consuming. Her baby was in the same building, but she still had to purchase powdered milk."

"Unbelievable." Shelby's jaw tensed. "But what other choice do these mothers have?"

"That's exactly it, Shelby. Often there is no choice."

"The more I learn about this whole situation, the worse I feel for these workers."

"Shelby, they do not want your pity. What they need is your help."

"But how?"

"They need their voices to be heard," Priti said, her gaze locking onto Shelby's. "They need people like you outside the system insisting their lives are worth more than the clothing they make."

As the sun set on Monday evening, Tariq drove through the maze of traffic to the hotel. Priti went home in a taxi. Shelby nearly dozed off in the backseat, but the rumble in her stomach from all the foreign fare kept her awake.

Thinking through the day, every part of it discouraged her. Their fruitless search for Runa. Two disappointing factory visits. The frustrating report from Fatima about the never-ending challenges for working mothers in the garment industry.

Coupled with her physical aches and exhaustion, Shelby arrived at the hotel, feeling completely depleted. She wanted to go pass out in her room, but it had been far too long since she checked in with Bryan. It was the middle of the night in Texas, so email would have to do.

As she sat in front of the hotel's computer, it struck her that only three days remained of this trip. In terms of finding Runa, the time seemed too short. But considering her current energy level, she wondered how she would sustain this pace. The veins in her legs throbbed, angry from dehydration and lack of rest. This wild goose chase was wearing her out, tanking her health along with her spirit. Nothing positive had yet to materialize.

Opening her email, she unpacked everything weighing on her heart.

Hi Bryan,

Another day of searching led to nothing. Our chances of finding Runa are starting to feel hopeless. If she's working as a domestic helper, that means she's inside all day. We don't know where she's walking to or from, which makes it impossible to know where and when to look for her.

On top of that, I'm worn out. My legs are aching and swelling from all the walking. Even compared to Houston, it's viciously hot and humid. I can't seem to drink enough water. There's nowhere to use the bathroom. And now my stomach is messed up. I'm starting to question the decision to come. I can't wait to be home, but I'm also dreading the long trip back.

We tried to visit the factory that made my Easter dresses, but they wouldn't let us inside. The factory that did let us in rushed us through five stories in half an hour.

One of their seamstresses met us at a café after work. The stories she told about working there are so disheartening. I asked what could make a difference in her life. She said an extra 600 taka a month. That's only seven dollars. $7.00! And yet, I'm trying to wrap my mind around what it would take to get Surface Trend to raise prices by ten cents a dress.

Knowing all this, I can't continue

designing for them. At this point, I am set to return home without finding Runa, without a career, and without any solutions. I hate to dump all this on you, but it's been a pretty heavy few days. We are supposed to tour a more promising factory in the morning, but my expectations are pretty low based on what I've seen.

I love you and hope everything is going well. Counting down the long days until I'm home. I miss you so much. Wish you were here. Give Little P a hug and a kiss for me.

Love you,
Shelby

Chapter 21

Exhausted from the long Monday, Shelby slept until the last possible minute. When she arrived in the hotel lobby, Tariq and Ravi were already waiting for her, leaving no time to check for Bryan's reply.

An hour of traffic later, they picked Priti up from her office. Together they drove another hour outside the city, passing endless acres of rain-soaked rice fields.

After the long drive, they finally arrived at the garment factory. The building looked newer and more modern than any in Dhaka.

"Shelby, I want you to see what is possible in garment production," Priti said with enviable confidence as they exited Tariq's car.

A tall man in khaki pants and a blue collared shirt welcomed them at the building's entrance. "Welcome to *Soubhagyo Enterprises!* My name is Nurul, and I am the owner. I am excited to show you our facility and introduce you to our amazing team."

"It's very nice to meet you," Shelby said. As they were escorted inside, she welcomed the chill of air conditioning against the morning's rising heat. With its floor-to-ceiling windows, the lobby was so well lit, Shelby considered leaving her sunglasses on.

"We want to show you the very best of what we have to offer at *Soubhagyo*. In case you did not know, our name means *good luck* in Bangla. We wish good luck for everyone in our company, from our newest helpers to our customers across the world. We are very proud of the work we do here to create quality clothing."

Nurul's welcome message sounded rehearsed but sincere. He pointed their attention to a wall full of framed certificates. "These certifications show our commitment to reducing our energy and water usage, as well as our compliance with national and international laws."

Across the expansive lobby, women in every color sari and headscarf lined up to face a screen. "Upon entering and exiting the factory, workers scan their faces, so we have an accurate recording of their work," Nurul explained.

The group followed Nurul inside the massive work floor, which was about the size of a football field.

"Our workday begins with basic exercises and stretching to warm up the body. Sewing can be physically taxing, especially when workers assume the same position for long periods. For this reason, our workers take scheduled breaks throughout the day."

After a few minutes of arm circles and leg stretches, workers began moving piles of clothing from tables to machines one stack at a time.

Movement filled the enormous room, but there remained a distinct sense of order.

"Next, I want to show you our training center." Nurul led them through wide hallways and up a staircase to another room. "This is where we teach our new employees the skills they need to work in our production line. Some of our workers have never worked in a factory before. We train them to use the machines and to work efficiently as a team."

"What can you share about their wages?" Priti asked.

"Upon graduation, our workers start with a good salary, above minimum wage. The longer they work with us, the higher their pay rises."

Next they went to the warehouse on the ground floor where raw materials were stored. Forklifts buzzed throughout rows of supplies delivering enormous tubes of raw fabric that looked like rolled-up area rugs. Additional warehouse shelves were stacked neatly from floor to ceiling with boxes of accessories, trim, and notions.

Upstairs, they toured computer-filled work-rooms where patterns were being constructed using software. Shelby was most impressed with the cutting room. Large bolts of fabric were unrolled across a table, and a huge machine sliced through 50 layers of denim at a time. The mightiest of all sewing scissors could never compare to that kind of efficiency.

Nurul invited them to the cafeteria, which served a savory curry with vegetables. "Please, stay and eat with our workers," he said.

Their group took a seat at a table and began to eat.

"Wow, this is delicious," Shelby said upon first taste. "Pretty amazing place. How are they able to operate so differently here?"

Priti swallowed a spoonful of curry and responded. "The clothing companies that source from this factory are willing to wait longer and pay more for orders. Rather than negotiate for super-low contracts, they pass higher costs of clothing production on to their customers."

"And people are really willing to pay higher prices?" Shelby asked.

"Yes, because the brand they built attracts a customer base that is willing to pay more for socially conscious fashion."

"What a difference," Shelby said.

"It is not perfect. The life of a garment worker is still hard work, even somewhere like here. But it is a step in the right direction," Priti said.

Shelby let her mind wander, imagining what it might be like to work with Nurul and his team. She pictured her dresses being cut by the hundreds by workers who were surely more valued and better protected than at the factories she visited yesterday.

"Priti, what would happen if every company

placed orders only at factories like this one?"

"That would be very good because it would allow owners to build more factories like this and hire more workers with fair wages and benefits."

Shelby smiled, hearing the first hint of a solution since she arrived in Dhaka. If nothing else, it was a start.

After lunch, they returned to Savar on the out-skirts of Dhaka to look for Runa. Tariq pulled his car into an alley, and the three exited.

Once again, treading from street to street sharing Runa's picture produced absolutely no results. The picture frame was starting to feel heavy in Shelby's backpack.

As they walked toward the central part of town, thousands of people were gathered outside a large shopping center, which was, like so many others, covered in scaffolding.

"What's going on there?" Shelby asked.

"I am not sure," Ravi said. "Could be a workers strike."

"I don't see any signs. And everyone is standing," Priti said.

"Perhaps they evacuated?" Ravi looked up at the building, squinting.

They walked toward the jam-packed plaza. While Ravi asked the men in the crowd for more information, Priti spoke to the women.

"The building has cracks in it," Ravi said, his

voice sharp and urgent. He pointed up at the place where the concrete structure had split apart. "They evacuated mid-morning. Workers were told to come back at two o'clock."

Shelby looked at her watch. Quarter to two. "They're not going back in, are they?"

"That's what everyone is waiting to find out," Priti said.

As they waited, Priti and Ravi collected more information from workers.

"I am scared to return to the work floor," a seamstress told Priti. "They need to fix the building before I will feel safe."

"The building has been under construction for years," another seamstress said. "If they do not finish it, they do not have to pay the completion tax."

It finally made sense why so many buildings were unfinished. Shelby made a note in her journal to tell Bryan. He wouldn't believe it.

After a long wait in the hot afternoon, a man emerged from the building and blasted a message over a bullhorn. The crowd grumbled and began shuffling away from the building in every direction.

"They are saying go home and come back tomorrow morning," Ravi said, his agitation growing.

"I cannot believe they are considering opening," Priti said. "The building is falling apart."

"We should return tomorrow and see how we can help." Ravi locked eyes with Priti.

She looked away, checking the time. "I am going back to my office to make some calls. Let's meet here in the morning."

"Is it okay if we head back to the hotel now?" Ravi asked Shelby.

With her return flight scheduled for two days away, Shelby felt a growing sense of urgency to look for Runa. Her time was running out. But she was starting to sense Ravi didn't believe they were going to find her—at least, not by scouring the streets of Savar.

"That's fine. I'm pretty beat," Shelby said.

The group finalized their plans for the morning then split up. Priti left in a taxi, and Tariq drove on with Ravi and Shelby.

With Priti out of earshot, Shelby could no longer contain her curiosity. "Ravi, I know I've asked way too many questions this trip. Please forgive me if this is too personal, but what's the story with you and Priti?"

The silence hung on so long, Shelby thought Ravi might decline to answer.

When he finally spoke, his voice was low and wavering. "It is complicated. We were seeing each other for the past two years. But she wants to stay in Dhaka, and I am called to London. We agreed it simply would not work to be together. So, we ended it."

"That sounds so hard," Shelby said. "She seems like a beautiful person, in every possible way."

"She is. I wish it were as simple as that." He looked out the passenger window.

"What are your plans for London?"

"Everything is set. I never thought I would be here this long, so I own very few things. I will sell what I can and travel light. The doctor and his wife have invited me to stay with them until I settle in."

"Sounds like you have everything figured out."

Ravi let a laugh escape. "I am not sure about that. I cannot say my life in Dhaka has unfolded as I hoped. I thought I would be in a different place by now. Thought I would have a family. But not every dream comes true."

"Perhaps it will in London," Shelby said, trying to end the conversation on a positive note. Her heart ached for this kind man who had given so much of himself to improving others' lives. She wrote down Ravi's name in her journal, adding his longing for a family to her growing prayer list.

It was almost dinnertime when Shelby returned to the hotel. Disappointed as she was not to look for Runa, she was grateful for some downtime. The trip had been nonstop since she hit the ground. Every part of her body ached from the pace of the day.

Her first priority was to email Bryan the update

about the promising factory. But once again, email refused to load. After half an hour of refreshing the page, she asked the front desk staff for help.

"I am very sorry for the trouble," the front desk worker said. "Perhaps the connection is poor this time of day with many people using it. We will send someone to see what is wrong."

Frustrated, Shelby went to the café. She ordered a bowl of broth and rice to calm her stomach. Back in the room, she showered and wrote in her journal. Three more frustrating trips to the lobby and the internet still refused to connect.

"It will be fixed by morning," the lady at the front desk assured her.

Shelby thought about asking Ravi to check her email. She considered calling and waking Bryan in the middle of the night. Instead, she set her alarm extra early to allow time in the morning. She curled up in bed, laying on her side with a pillow supporting her achy belly.

As she drifted off to sleep, she couldn't stop thinking about Runa, wherever she was. Shelby could feel the girl—and Nipa's dream—slipping away.

Chapter 22

Early Wednesday morning when Tariq dropped them off at the commercial center in Savar, a large crowd of workers had already gathered outside. Meeting up with Priti near the corner market, they walked toward the building's main entrance. In the morning sun, the mirrored panels of the ground floor's modern exterior reflected the streetlights and treetops at their backs.

Atop the stairs at the building's main entrance, a man with oil-slicked hair and jagged teeth stood between thick, square columns blasting sharp words to the crowd through a bullhorn. The large glass doors behind him were propped open.

"What is he saying?" Shelby asked.

"He's saying if any workers refuse to come in, they will withhold a month of wages," Priti translated.

"He is telling them it is safe to go inside." Ravi shook his head.

"But the engineers who inspected it yesterday said the opposite," Priti said.

Ravi and Priti continued speaking to workers and translating to Shelby. "We do not want to go in," one woman said. "The inspectors said a thorough investigation must be done. But managers tell us to go to our workstations."

400

For the better part of the hour, no one entered the building. Eventually, the urgent instructions over the bullhorn won out. Workers filed through the entrance, four at a time, ascending the stairs to their respective work floors. For half an hour, Shelby watched face after face pass by her.

"How many people work here?"

"Thousands," Priti said. "There may be four or five different factories inside. They take up the top floors. The bottom floors contain hundreds of shops and a bank, but those stores all closed."

"What can we do?" Shelby asked. With the hours of her trip trickling away, she hoped they would resume the search for Runa.

"I will be back," Ravi said.

"Where are you going?" Priti asked.

Ravi's eyes narrowed. "I am going to talk to them."

"Please don't." Priti gripped hold of his arm. Their conversation switched at once from English to Bangla.

The words may have been foreign to Shelby, but their intensity was clear as day. The lines on Ravi's forehead matched the urgency of Priti's terse replies.

When they finished speaking, Ravi turned to Shelby. "I will meet you here shortly." He filed into the crowd of workers walking toward the entrance and disappeared into the cavity of the cracked building.

"What is he thinking?" Shelby asked, the hairs on her forearms standing on end.

"He thinks he can get the managers to evacuate the work floors." Priti stared at the doorway where Ravi vanished.

"But didn't they already decide not to?"

"Exactly. Ravi thinks he can convince them. But he knows nothing about how factories run. His work is with people. He doesn't understand that the bottom line rules. He doesn't know how to persuade from this angle, and he will not listen to me."

"Why not?" Shelby began on impulse.

"Because." Priti hesitated but continued. "Because I broke his heart."

"What happened?" The question spiraled into the air with both curiosity and regret. But Shelby was leaving the country in two days. Any harm from prying would follow her out.

Priti stopped, catching her breath. "We were together off and on the last few years. He's a wonderful man with a big heart. He is so good at his job and cares so much for the people he serves."

"No question about that."

"But he wants me to go to London. That is something I cannot do."

"Why not?" Shelby was past the point of feeling nosy. She wanted to understand what forces were keeping these two apart.

"I cannot leave my country. There is too much work to do here. Here I can make a real difference in the lives of women and children and families." Her gaze turned toward the building. "This very moment confirms we have a long way to go toward putting people over profit."

"Why is Ravi so intent on going then?" Shelby asked.

"He gave his word years ago that if this position ever opened up, he would return to fill it. He never goes back on his word."

They stared at the entrance in tense silence, hoping to see Ravi appear. But minute after long minute passed, and he never did. Priti tried incessantly to contact him, but every call and text went unanswered.

They waited. They watched more workers enter the building. But none came out.

Half an hour had passed since Ravi left when abrupt yells descended from windows above. Suddenly lights went off throughout the building.

"What happened?" Shelby asked.

"The power probably went out," Priti said. "Let's go find Tariq. Soon as Ravi comes back, we will go look for Runa."

Shelby nodded, grateful for the hope of one more search for the girl. They walked away from the building crossing the side street toward Tariq's car. A large city bus jam-packed with riders pulled away from its stop. Passengers

403

leaped on and off even as the bus pulled away.

Somewhere in the background, a generator rumbled to a start. Moments later, the ground shook beneath their feet. A blast like a bomb exploded in their ears. Shelby and Priti turned around to watch the top floor of Rana Plaza collapse onto the floor below.

Another floor collapsed.

Then the next.

And the next.

And the next.

Floor after floor after floor fell down and down and down.

The towering heights of Rana Plaza—eight full floors of factories and shops and garment workers—crashed against the earth.

Passersby fled in horror. Screams meshed together with the crushing blow of concrete crashing onto concrete. Rocks spewed like fireworks. A plume of dust and smoke billowed toward them, clouding their eyes from the sun, from each other, from the demise of everything and everyone housed inside.

"Ravi!" Priti cried.

They took steps toward the building, toward Ravi. Terrified, they withdrew, stepping back. Shrill yells for help filled the air. People ran past them away from the crumpled remnants of structure. Thousands of others from neighboring markets and shops ran toward the scene.

Traffic halted to a standstill on nearby roads.

"Cover your face!" Priti yelled. She pulled her scarf over her nose, mouth, and eyes, and Shelby did too. "Are you okay?"

"Yes, I think so. Are you?"

"Yes!" Priti yelled.

"Where is Ravi?" Shelby half asked, half yelled, her horror growing.

The scene before her revealed complete and total devastation. It reminded her of the shock of watching the collapse of the World Trade Center tower on TV. Except now, the dust burned into her throat and eyes. The face of every man and woman who just marched into the building seared into her memory.

And Ravi.

Oh God, please no. Not Ravi.

Crouching amid the chaos, she wanted to cry or scream. But doing so wouldn't help a single one of them. She considered the fate of this moment, of coming here to redeem Nipa's death, only to lead Ravi to his.

No. No. Nooooooo.

People continued flooding in from nearby streets. Rescuers mounted the structure while others ran from it. Survivors spilled out from the wreckage, exasperated and traumatized. Others were trapped and screaming. Most remained unseen, hidden within a city block's worth of rubble.

Priti held the phone to her ear, hoping Ravi would finally answer. "Nothing's going through."

"What do we do?" Shelby asked.

"We have to find him." A tear painted a wet streak into the dust covering Priti's cheek.

Shelby nodded in firm agreement. But given the complete disarray, people running everywhere, debris covering the entire block, smoke and dust consuming the air, neither of them knew which direction of pavement to step a foot toward next.

"We have to believe he's okay." Shelby closed her eyes and prayed for mercy on this horrific scene, for Ravi's life, and for the thousands of men and women cradled in the unknown space between life and death.

As she prayed, a tiny voice inside projected through the noise. Ravi's words during the search for Runa replayed in her mind.

"If we get separated, let's meet at the last place we were together," she heard him say.

"Let's go back to where we last saw him," Shelby yelled over the noise. She grabbed Priti's hand, and they zigzagged through the dusty sea of people toward the place where they said goodbye to Ravi. But like everything else, it was covered in rubble. Had Ravi been waiting for them there, he would have been crushed.

Shelby couldn't speak. There were no words for this moment.

"If Ravi is safe, I don't think he will be looking for us," Priti said. "He will be rescuing others."

The two women raced through the cloudy air, their hands still clenching one another's. They tunneled through the chaos of people and rubble until they reached a group of rescuers. Dozens of men had climbed on top of the debris. Together they formed a human chain to carry survivors from the wreckage.

The scene was gruesome, like nothing Shelby had ever witnessed. Emergency vehicles swarmed the area, their sirens blaring. Women and men carried out on stretchers were bleeding, wailing, screaming in pain. It looked like the aftermath of a bloody war.

"Do you see him?" Shelby asked.

"No. Not yet," Priti said, her voice wavering. "We might as well help however we can. If he's okay, we'll find him."

Shelby tried not to let her mind venture to the other side of that if. So many people needed help. She agreed they should do whatever they could. They joined the line of rescue workers on the ground leading survivors to a triage area where they would await hospital transport. As Shelby helped, she kept her eyes out for Ravi, hoping and praying for the best.

Time passed at a pace different from normal. Whether too fast or too slow, she wasn't sure. Was it minutes or hours? When cases of water finally arrived, Shelby and Priti passed out bottles to survivors awaiting care. They poured water into thirsty mouths, over dusty hands and faces.

A while later, Shelby was helping a young woman with a crushed foot when she heard Priti's voice yell.

"Ravi! RAVI!"

Atop a tall tower of rubble, Shelby could see the dusty, blood-streaked face of sweet Ravi.

He's okay. Oh, thank you, Lord. He's okay. Tears of relief stung her dusty eyes and rained down her face.

Shelby and Priti watched as Ravi, two stories up, carried an injured woman out from the rubble toward rescuers. Priti ran to him as he passed the woman gently to the next person in the rescue chain. Hearing his name, Ravi climbed down toward Priti.

From the distance, Shelby could see his forehead was brushed with blood. Whether it was his or someone else's, she couldn't tell, but he appeared to be okay. Shelby kept her distance from the rubble and watched their reunion through tear-filled eyes.

Ravi reached for Priti's shoulders, wrapping his arms around her, pulling her in close. They held onto each other, then gripped hands and exchanged words. Ravi turned away to climb back inside the wreckage.

When Priti returned, tears streamed down her face.

"What a relief!" Shelby said. "Is he okay?"

"Miraculously, yes. The floor he was on collapsed all around him. But the spot where he stood was protected, like a cave." Her voice shook as she spoke.

"Thank God, he's okay."

"He said workers are trapped throughout the rubble. Some alive. Some not." Priti scanned the wreckage. Silent. Still. "This is so bad. No one deserves to die this way."

Shelby's lip quivered. Oh, what she would give to undo the events of the last hours. She wished there was a way to rewind it all, to prevent the bloodshed and suffering.

Priti clenched her teeth. "They should never have forced anyone to go in."

Another long hour passed with no signs of Ravi. Shelby and Priti would periodically look up to locate him delivering more survivors to the rescue chain. Thousands of people had come to the scene doing anything they could to help.

Piercing screams rose and fell in the background as survivors confronted their injuries. Workers from nearby businesses brought water, food, and first aid supplies. Ambulances arrived on a running loop transporting severely injured patients to hospitals. Surrounding roads were completely blocked, making it difficult for emergency vehicles to approach.

When Ravi finally reappeared at triage, his face and clothes were covered in more dust and blood, but he remained unharmed.

"Why were you gone so long?" Priti asked. She poured gulps of water into Ravi's mouth. He swallowed it, panting.

"They carved a tunnel inside the wreckage. Those of us who are small enough are crawling inside to pull others out." He gasped for breath. "They just cut off a woman's arm to free her."

Shelby's hand flew over her mouth. Everyone had heard the screams. Now they knew why. Her stomach churned.

A reporter and crew from a local TV station came over to speak to Ravi. He tried to push them away, but the photographer turned on his video camera and began recording. The reporter shoved a microphone in front of Ravi and asked the first question.

"What's he saying?" Shelby asked.

Priti relayed Ravi's responses. "He's saying he has never seen human tragedy like this. There are body parts everywhere. There are people screaming for their lives. Countless workers have already died. He said there must be a call to end the unjust treatment of garment workers."

More hours passed as Shelby and Priti helped injured workers in triage. They were all exhausted and covered in dust, but the stream of survivors needing extensive medical attention seemed to never end. News crews reported a few hundred deaths. But everyone on the ground knew that number would climb much higher.

Ravi came by again, covered in dust, his clothing splattered with more blood.

"I think it is time for you both to get out of here," he said sharply.

"But there are still so many people who need help," Shelby said.

"The army is here now. More medical crews have arrived. They are more equipped to help, and it is simply not safe here."

"How do we find Tariq?" Shelby asked.

"The roads are impassable for several blocks in every direction," Priti said.

"I will see if I can reach him." Ravi called Tariq, but the call wouldn't go through. He sent a text and hoped for the best.

They started formulating their plan for the next day. As they spoke, a small voice called out through the dust, "Ravi Uncle!"

Running through the crowd, the face of an angel appeared. A thin girl in a muted blue dress came racing toward them. One look at her eyes.

Those eyes.

"Runa!" Ravi yelled.

"No. No way." Shelby blinked in disbelief seeing the face from the picture standing before them now. Her eyes, parched from dust, swelled up with tears.

Ravi knelt down to greet the girl. Runa threw her arms around his neck. As the two exchanged words, Priti listened in. A man in black pants and a dark blue long-sleeve shirt stood behind Runa, waiting for a chance to speak.

"This is unbelievable," Shelby said to Priti. "I don't understand. How on earth did Runa find him?"

Priti exchanged words with the man in the blue shirt, who Shelby assumed was Runa's uncle.

"The news!" Priti said. "The collapse was on TV in the building where she was cleaning. It is not far from here. She recognized Ravi in his interview and begged her uncle to bring her. They requested off work and ran straight here."

"But there are thousands of people. How did she find him?"

"They saw the news truck. The reporter directed them to look here at triage."

Shelby couldn't believe it. All those hours, searching the streets for Runa.

And yet, Runa found them. In the unlikeliest place on a disaster of a day, a single glimmer of hope appeared through the dust.

Ravi guided the girl out of his arms and wiped the tears from his face and hers. He stood to greet her uncle. Then he spoke to Runa, switching to English.

"Runa Angel, I want you to meet your sponsor, Shelby Aunty. She came here all the way from Texas to look for you."

"Shelby Aunty!" Runa flung her arms around Shelby's waist, nestling her head next to the baby.

Shelby knelt to embrace the girl, this mirage of a child who had come to life in her arms. "Sweet Runa, it is such a joy to meet you," Shelby said. "We have been so worried about you. Paisley asks about you all the time. How are you?"

In a blink, Runa's face turned from joy to sorrow. "I miss my mother. I miss everyone at my school."

"They miss you too." Shelby brushed a strand of dark hair from Runa's eyes. "Sarah Aunty said to tell you hello."

She smiled, hearing the familiar name.

"Runa, would you like it if we found a way for you to go to school?" Shelby asked.

"Yes, Shelby Aunty, I would like that very much!" Runa's eyes sparkled.

"We need to get her away from here," Priti said. "Let's go meet Tariq. We can sort everything out on the way."

Shelby nodded. The frame and dress were waiting in the car. It wouldn't be long until she could give them to Runa.

"I'm staying here," Ravi said. "They need people who can fit through the tunnels."

413

Priti stepped toward him, drawing his hand into hers. "Please be careful. I can't ever lose you again."

"I can't lose you either." He wrapped his arms around her one more time, the dust settling around them.

While Priti and Ravi said goodbye, Shelby reached out her phone and took a selfie with Runa. This child was why she came.

As Shelby, Priti, Runa, and her uncle walked away from the endless wreckage of the Rana Plaza collapse, Shelby turned around to capture the devastating scene. No one there that day would ever be the same. The image of so much destruction would burn in her mind forever.

So would the memory of a miracle girl, emerging through the dust.

A few blocks away, when the sights and sounds of chaos faded, Shelby felt a gentle touch on her hand.

Sweet Runa smiled, her eyes telling a thousand stories within a glance.

Shelby folded Runa's hand into hers and smiled back.

They walked on, not knowing what the future might bring. But gripping hold of the hope that Nipa's dream was coming true.

After waving goodbye to Tariq, Shelby entered the hotel lobby, questioning how it could be the same Wednesday. Her backpack was lighter after giving Runa the dress and the wooden frame. But everything else felt heavier.

Televisions overhead looped news of the collapse with subtitles in English. Already the station reported dozens of deaths and hundreds of injuries, though everyone knew those preliminary numbers would climb much higher.

A few hotel guests stood motionless, watching interviews and video footage recapping the horrific scene. When Shelby walked by, they turned to stare. Her clothes were completely covered in dust, her pant legs torn, her headscarf streaked with dirt.

As she walked past the café, her eyes glanced at the empty table where only days before she and Ravi had discussed a plan to find Runa. No one could have ever predicted how the week would unfold.

And then, across the lobby, her eyes met the most unexpected gaze imaginable.

"Bryan?" Shelby froze.

"Shelby!" Bryan arose from the sofa and raced to meet her, folding himself around her shaky frame.

She fell into his arms, surrendering into the familiar comfort of his embrace. Bryan held her tight, like he might never let go.

Before long, she pulled back to look him in the eyes, still in disbelief it was really him.

"What on earth are you doing here?" she asked.

"I came to accompany you home. I was worried about you."

"I had no idea you were coming. Why didn't you tell me? Or Ravi?"

"I emailed you both. I also called the hotel and left several messages at the front desk."

"I didn't get any of that," Shelby said.

"Clearly," Bryan laughed.

"The internet has been down. And Ravi hasn't been in his office since Monday evening. He must have missed your messages."

"Well, then. This must be a bit of a surprise."

"Yes, more than a bit. I would never have expected you to come all this way."

"Me neither. Almost couldn't find my passport. Paisley had it in her bed. She was playing airport."

Shelby wanted to laugh, but her body ached too much, the long, horrendous day settling into her joints. The tendons supporting her belly bump felt stretched to their limits. She wanted to collapse onto the nearest sofa, but she was worried about the residue her filthy clothes would leave behind.

"What happened to you? Are you okay?" Bryan asked.

"Yes. Technically I am." Shelby nodded toward the TV. "I was there."

"Wait, you were *there?* At Rana Plaza?"

"Yes. I can't even." Shelby shook her head, her

emotions so wrecked, she couldn't find the words to say more. "Who has Paisley?"

"Maye stayed with her Monday night until your mom could get there."

"My mom took off from teaching? Again?"

"Yes. And she said we can get used to it. She's retiring at the end of the year. Wants to spend more time with her grandchildren."

"That's amazing."

"You're amazing. I missed you." Bryan's forest-green eyes locked onto hers.

"I missed you too. What made you come?"

"Your email. Reading it Monday morning, I couldn't stand the thought of you flying back alone."

"But didn't you have all those meetings?"

"I took the week off. Told them my family needed me. They didn't question it."

"What about the airfare? It must have cost a fortune." Shelby realized she was commenting about the expense on autopilot. The cost of him being here seemed inconsequential during a day of incalculable human loss.

"Maye put us on the prayer list, and her Sunday School class pitched in miles. When the logistics came together so easily, I couldn't say no." He reached for Shelby's hand. "I just had this feeling like I needed to be here with you."

"I'm really glad you're here." Shelby teared up.

"I am too. I was having a great time with

Paisley. But it was so different being home without you there. Made me realize how hard that must be for you when I'm away."

"We miss you so much when you're gone."

"I asked Keith to reassign me from San Francisco. He's making me the lead on the new building downtown."

"Downtown Houston?"

"Yes. I shouldn't have a reason to travel for a long time. Well, you know, besides coming here."

"That's such a relief!" Shelby said. But the opportunity to celebrate was fleeting. A yelling voice arose from the television, redirecting their eyes to the chaos of rubble and debris. Interviews with injured women and wailing men filled the lobby.

"Bryan, words cannot describe how horrific it is." She searched for a way to explain how the day unfolded. Floors crumbling on top of floors. All the people trapped inside. Searching for Ravi. The relief of finding him, alive and miraculously okay. The endless stream of injured workers. The hundreds of lives already lost.

"And you'll never believe this." Shelby pulled out her phone and showed Bryan the selfie with Runa.

"Wait, what? You found her?"

"No, she found us." Shelby told the story, more tears forming in her eyes. "She's okay, Bryan. She's safe. Her uncle agreed to let us sponsor her to go to school while he's working. Priti's getting him set up with a nonprofit in Savar. We'll work with their office to make sure they have the support they need."

"That's incredible."

"It is. But Bryan, I could never fully describe how horrible today was. I'm glad you're here, but in some ways, it feels wrong that I'm safe at a hotel while so many people—living, breathing people—are trapped beneath concrete beams. They were told they had to work—to sew orders that couldn't wait. It's all so . . . so senseless."

"It's terrible, Shel. But it's not your fault. It's clear the structure wasn't built to code."

"People keep saying, 'It's not your fault.' But it doesn't really matter whose fault it is, does it? This cannot continue happening," she said.

"I completely agree," Bryan said. "Something has to change. Someone has to do something."

"We all have to do something," Shelby said.

Bryan nodded. "Can I meet Ravi?"

"Yes, we're meeting up in the morning before he returns to Rana Plaza. And you can meet Runa. Priti and I are going to spend the day with her. And now with you too."

"Paisley will be so jealous," Bryan said.

"She sure will. Hopefully one day they'll meet each other." The very thought of Paisley meeting Runa made Shelby smile.

"I'm sure you're exhausted." Bryan took

Shelby's hand. "Let's go settle in. I'll find us something to eat."

They started toward her room. On the heels of a day filled with devastation, Shelby found so much comfort in the simple gesture of his hand holding hers. She couldn't believe he was here by her side, on the heels of a harrowing tragedy. The good fortune of her day—of her life—didn't make sense against the backdrop of so many suffering.

And yet here she was, together with Bryan, her search for Runa gloriously conclusive amid a world of soul-crushing despair. So many lives were lost, injured, forever changed on this day. This day full of lies tumbling out into the open.

All because a global pattern of greed and shortcuts toppled Rana Plaza in the unsuspecting hours of a Wednesday morning in April.

What would the future hold? For Runa? For these workers and their families? For this striving nation and others like it?

Shelby didn't know.

But one thing was certain.

She had to emerge as part of the solution. No matter how small.

Chapter 23

May 2013

"I love that you had us meet at a resale shop," Whitney said. "I haven't been thrifting in years."

"Well, you wanted to go shopping, and this is my new obsession," Shelby said.

"Doesn't it amount to a lot of searching?" Elise asked.

"Sometimes. But you won't believe the cute stuff people get rid of," Shelby said. "I found a gorgeous leather jacket last week for $8. And I didn't have to do a thing to make it look worn in."

"Some of it's cute, but none of it's in my size," Whitney said, sliding hanger after hanger across the long metal bar.

"This shopping trip comes with one free offer to alter, tailor, or hem any item you love that doesn't fit," Shelby announced.

"Interesting," Blakeley said. "In that case, I vote we head to the dresses."

"Sounds good to me. That's all I plan to wear the rest of the summer." Elise was nine weeks along, and so far, everything was going well. The group meandered to the back wall of the store, where a long row of dresses hung at eye level.

"Shelby, I want to hear more about your trip," Blakeley said, turning hanger after hanger. "I feel like we got the Cliff Notes version."

"I want to know what was the look on your face when you saw Bryan at the hotel?" Whitney asked. "Please tell me there's a video."

"That was wild. Completely wild. I mean, that whole day—Rana Plaza collapsing—it was something out of a horror film. Then Runa raced in, and it was like the resolution of an epic mystery. After all that, to see the whites of Bryan's eyes in a hotel lobby turned it into this unexpected romance, but against the backdrop of such tragedy. My emotions were all over the place. They pretty much still are."

In the days and weeks since Shelby and Bryan returned to Houston, the death toll and injury count continued to rise. All told 1,135 men and women were killed when Rana Plaza tumbled to the ground. More than 2,500 experienced physical injuries.

Countless other workers would never escape the emotional trauma of that day. One young seamstress survived 17 days in the rubble, the last to be found alive.

"I still can't believe how you met up with Runa," Blakeley said. "The things that had to align are pretty unbelievable."

"Sounds like you were in the right place at the right time," Elise said.

"I suppose. I've really struggled with that," Shelby said. "For so long, I felt responsible for her mom's death and for her life changing so suddenly. I mean, y'all certainly know how long I hid that. But I decided I can't keep beating myself up for past mistakes. All I can do is forgive myself and change what I do next."

"So, what does that look like?" Blakeley asked. "Not making dresses for *Surface Trend*?"

"Yep. And not shopping for them either." Shelby's eyes drifting toward the dresses.

"Does that mean you're destined for homemade and secondhand clothes the rest of your life?" Whitney asked.

"Absolutely not. Lots of clothing brands are more transparent in how they source materials and labor. Some even show on their website which factory makes each item. More companies are taking a stand as the fashion industry gets linked to the climate crisis. These are the companies I want to support when I buy new clothes."

"Goodness. You're starting to sound like a liberal," Whitney said, elbowing Shelby in the side, but well away from the basketball of a baby bump.

"Hah," Shelby smirked. "This isn't a political thing. It's a human thing. It's a moral thing too. I believe there's a basic way we're called to treat our world and the people in it. I wasn't aware how much harm I was causing before—and not even meaning to. I was operating on autopilot, participating in a system I've always been part of. But the system clearly isn't working for all the people in it."

"So, what actually works? Is there some right way to shop?" Blakeley asked.

Shelby detected the earnest curiosity in her friend's voice. "I think of it this way. When you're sewing one kind of dress, and you want to make a different kind of dress, you have to change the pattern. You can use the exact same fabric and equipment. But if you change the pattern, you change the outcome entirely."

"Makes total sense," Blakeley said.

"I think we can all reevaluate our shopping patterns. Might mean changing where we shop or being willing to pay more—a lot more—for something we love that will last. Because chances are if you think you're getting a good deal on clothes, someone in the supply chain is getting short-changed."

"Whoa! Twelve dollars for a *Kassie LaMond*?" Whitney squealed.

"That's gorgeous," Blakeley said. An embroidered print of delicate rosy flowers framed the neckline of a flowy, plum-color tea-length dress.

"Totally not my size. Can this be my pick for the mending pile?" Whitney asked.

"Of course." Shelby smiled, so pleased her friends were on board.

"Great find, Whitney. But not as good as this one. It's by *Treasured Pockets*!" Elise held up one of Shelby's sparkleberry dresses, no store tags this time.

The sight of the dress brought Shelby back to her big decision the night of the photoshoot, to her initial choice to mass-produce the design she believed would sell the most. It was a good strategy with the information she had at the time. But it wasn't sustainable.

She thought of the threads connecting that moment to this one now. Of Nipa's able hands sewing the final hidden seams. Twirling around the guest room with Paisley the day the samples arrived on their doorstep. The shy smile on Runa's face as she held hands in the dress with her matching mother.

How she wished the story of this dress had ended there.

"Mind if I buy that one?" Shelby asked.

"Of course not. I mean, it's your dress," Elise said.

"I suppose it is. Might as well own it. Because what matters most isn't in the past. It's what happens next."

An hour of Paisley's school day remained when Shelby drove into the preschool parking lot.

Anxious about the upcoming conversation, she wanted to be ready for pickup in case the call ran long.

"Shelby Lawrence. Great to hear from you. How are you?"

The familiar urgency of Dennis's voice brought Shelby back to the early days of the launch. For all that had changed since they last spoke, she still preferred to take important calls from the driver's seat. Her belly now rested just inches away from the steering wheel.

"I'm doing well, thanks. Great to talk to you too."

"Catch me up. What's new?" Dennis asked.

So much had happened, Shelby didn't know where to start, so she cut to the chase.

"I have something important to run by you. I'm starting a new dress line, and in order to do this well, I can no longer hide what happened. I feel like I need to come clean to my customers. Unfortunately, I can't do that without bringing *Buzz Now* and *Surface Trend* into the conversation."

"Interesting," Dennis said slowly. "I'm wondering why you'd want to do that now?"

Shelby explained her trip to Dhaka and her connection to Nipa.

Dennis listened intently. He'd seen Rana Plaza in the news, but he hadn't known anyone personally impacted.

"Makes more sense why you didn't jump at the spring contract," Dennis said.

"I wasn't ready to give up on my dream with *Surface Trend*. Thought it was easier if no one knew what I knew, so I never told anyone."

"To be honest, Shelby, I don't think the editors will want to drag our name into the aftermath of the fire. It took a lot of effort to stay out of it."

Shelby feared this roadblock. But given everything that happened, she wasn't ready to let anyone take the easy way out. "What if the editors decide to reveal the truth in order to create change? As humans, as citizens, they have to agree that what happened in Dhaka is unacceptable. We've passed the point of hoping a tragedy like this doesn't happen again. Workers shouldn't be killed trying to give their families a better life."

Dennis was silent.

Shelby took a deep breath and continued. "Plus, taking a strong stand could position *Buzz Now* as an advocate and a leader."

"You have a point," Dennis said. "I'll talk to the editors and see what they think. But even if they say yes, you'll have a much harder time getting *Surface Trend* to agree to this."

"I'm working on it. It will help if *Buzz Now* is already on board."

"I'll let you know what they say."

"I appreciate it, Dennis. Just like I've

appreciated all your help since the very start."

"It was great working with you, Shelby. I wish you all the best with your new line. Once you're up and running, hit me up for a feature."

"Thank you, Dennis. I'd love to team up again." Shelby couldn't help but smile.

Ending the call on a hopeful note, Shelby looked at her reflection in the rearview mirror. With plenty of time still left in the preschool day, she put her phone on silent and slipped into the Pre-K classroom to join Paisley for story time.

May 24, 2013
Dear friends and customers,

Six months ago, I learned something about Treasured Pockets I never wanted to know. I learned our dresses were being sewn in a factory overseas that didn't follow basic worker safety guidelines. I found this out when an order was canceled because the factory sewing my dresses caught on fire.

That night, thousands of workers lost their livelihoods. Hundreds more were injured or killed. Hearing this news, I was ashamed to learn the brand I created was involved in a complex revenue stream built on cutting corners and taking advantage of laborers who have incalculable skills but no collective voice.

There are wonderful, human-rights-conscious garment factories in Bangladesh and elsewhere. A big part of the problem was I had no idea my dresses were being made at a factory that didn't adhere to basic safety standards. Sadly, it never dawned on me to ask. I was so excited to see my designs worn by you and your daughters. I never considered how the dresses were being made or who was making them.

I can vouch that my counterparts at Buzz Now and Surface Trend were also not aware where their order had been sourced. Turns out, the unregulated practice of subcontracting makes it possible to manufacture products without directly working with the factory that makes them.

Isn't that messed up?

But not asking, not knowing—that's not a good excuse, is it? It's not an excuse any of us can claim anymore, especially after the horrors of this past month.

Last month I traveled to Dhaka, Bangladesh, to visit garment factories in person. While there, I met with victims and witnesses whose lives changed forever that tragic day. Their stories convinced me that we as consumers cannot continue under the status quo, leaving every purchasing decision up to the brands who profit from clothing they don't actually make.

And then it got worse. So much worse. A month ago today, Rana Plaza, an eight-story building, overstuffed with extra floors and heavy machinery, collapsed, trapping thousands of workers in the rubble. The death toll is over a thousand people. Thousands more endured debilitating injuries that will limit their ability to provide for their families for the rest of their lives.

Friends, as a mother, a business owner, and a shopper, I am shaken to the core. I have lived my consumer life valuing the price tag of my finds over the worth of the hands who made them. I cannot go another day without speaking up for the hardworking, skilled men and women trapped in a system that pays a dollar a day to sew our clothes.

Please don't hear this as a call to avoid one geographic zone in favor of another. This problem isn't unique to Bangladesh. Exploitation of garment workers happens in nearly every country where clothing is produced, including the United States.

Boycotting a specific country actually hurts the same workers who rely on income from these jobs. We need a more thoughtful, comprehensive solution. Otherwise, we'll end up outsourcing the next Rana Plaza somewhere else.

So, what, then, is the solution? Unfortunately, it's as complex as the network of subcontracting that opened my eyes to the problem. Every player, from designer to shopper, has a role. And any solution must incorporate the fundamental value that's missing across the fashion industry: Transparency.

What if our favorite clothing companies told us exactly which factories each garment was sewn in? What if brands openly shared the wages their workers were paid? What if corporations showcased the farms and mills their fabrics were sourced from? What if our favorite labels listed precise shipping and energy costs?

In other words, what if we knew exactly what we were buying, how it was constructed, and by whom? How would that change the way we buy clothes? How would it change the lives of garment workers? How would it impact the health of our planet?

Partnering with the Caring Hope Organization, my fashion focus is heading in a hopeful new direction. Together, with worker's rights groups and top-of-the-line garment factories, we aim to design a clothing company that provides a living wage, offers opportunities for career advancement, and produces quality, earth-friendly clothing that you'll be proud to wear.

So, after five amazing years of sewing and growing with Treasured Pockets, today I am announcing my new label Treasured Seams. I am grateful for all the hard lessons, and to all of you for sharing our vision of mothers and daughters aligning together.

Perhaps we can grip hold of that common thread—unity—and join together on behalf of the mothers and daughters and fathers and sons the world over who make our clothes. This time let us match, not in our outward appearance, but in our resolve, in our intentions, and in our values.

With love and transparency,
Shelby
Shelby Lawrence
Principal Designer
Treasured Seams LLC

Chapter 24

June 2013

Shelby's eyelids peeked open to discover slivers of sunrise invading the bedroom. She tucked in her legs and shifted onto her back, wincing at the ropes of pain throbbing around her abdomen.

Lifting the loose edge of her nightshirt, her fingertips traced the railroad track of stitching across her belly. It was, perhaps, the finest of all seams—the one that pieced her back together.

Beside her lay the most glorious sight, a vision that could override all the aches. A tiny petal of a human wrapped in heavenly sleep. An untested life to dream and gush over. A built-in best friend for their first little love to adore and pester and shepherd along.

Shelby lifted their baby girl from the mattress and laid her gently in the adjacent bassinet. She hadn't meant to fall asleep nursing the baby in bed. But the forces of weariness in the dark hours of the early morning were somehow stronger than the persistent SIDS warnings from the nurses in the recovery ward.

The patter of footsteps turned Shelby's gaze toward the bedroom entrance. Her eyes met Paisley's in the crack of the door. Curling her finger, Shelby invited the anxious new sibling into the cave of whooshing white noise and lavish warmth.

"Can I please hold her, Mama?" Paisley raced to the bedside, her eager eyes glued to the sleeping bundle of baby.

"Sure. Soon as she wakes up. And great job using your manners." Shelby patted the empty side of the bed. "Hop up."

Paisley climbed into bed, coddling a white stuffed bunny. She burrowed deep down into the blankets. Shelby patted her hand across the wiggling lump of child.

Bryan walked into the room carrying a tray of scrambled eggs, scones, and coffee.

"Wow, the royal treatment," Shelby said.

"If there were ever a time for it. Maye baked the scones. I'm sensing she can't wait to hold the baby."

"Oh, sweet Maye. This looks delicious."

"You should see the casserole she made. How are you feeling?"

"Tired. And sore. But overall, pretty great." Her eyes glanced left and right at the two breathtaking girls in their midst.

"Can you please help me sit up?" Shelby asked.

"Yes. After a proper good morning." Bryan set the tray on the dresser. He reached over the baby to plant a kiss on Shelby's lips.

"Good morning, indeed," Shelby said.

Bryan braced Shelby's hips as she scooted against the headboard. An emergency C-section wasn't in her birth plan, but the baby's tanking heart rate at her 39-week check-up decided otherwise.

The baby was delivered 48 minutes later. If Bryan hadn't come with her to the appointment, he would have missed his second daughter's grand entrance, not to mention the live gender reveal. Thankfully, he was exactly where Shelby needed him to be—right by her side.

"Thanks, Bry. Coffee, please?"

"Of course." He placed a slender white mug into her waiting hands, the magical potion steaming its nutty aroma into the air. Then he climbed into bed next to Paisley, tickling her through the covers. Her shouts and giggles filled the air.

"Is it just me, or does Little P suddenly look enormous?" Shelby asked.

"I think everyone looks bigger after spending four days with a tiny newborn," Bryan said.

The pediatrician recommended the baby stay a few extra days in the NICU to monitor heart rhythms. After the third day of breathing steadily, nursing well, and gaining a few ounces a day, the doctor felt comfortable discharging her.

"So glad we're home." Shelby drew in a mouthful of coffee.

Paisley popped her head up from beneath the

comforter. Her hair stood on end, frazzled and static-charged. "Mama, can we wake her up now?"

"We can't, my dear."

"Aww. But why not?"

"There's one sacred rule you need to learn now that you're a big sister."

"What's that?"

"Never wake a sleeping baby," Shelby said in a whisper.

"Ugh. It's so hard to wait, Mama."

"But you can stare at her all you want."

Paisley peered past her mom at the nest of blankets cocooning her sister.

"What do you think of her so far?" Shelby asked.

"She's good," Paisley assessed. "But she needs a baby. Can I give her my Nibbles?"

"Sure." Shelby set down her coffee on the nightstand as Paisley placed the fluffy bunny from her Easter basket next to the baby's tiny head.

"Here you go, Lacey," she said. Then she snuggled up under Shelby's arm. "Mama, do we really get to keep her?"

"Yes, Little P. She's all ours."

Across the bed, Bryan was thumbing away on his phone. "Daddy, can I look at pictures?"

"Sure. I'm just texting Mimi back. She's asking how our first night home went."

"About what you'd expect with a newborn," Shelby said, an eyebrow raised. "But I've had worse nights."

Paisley shifted into Bryan's lap. They scrolled through the latest photos from the hospital.

"What's she doing in that Tupperware?" Paisley asked.

Shelby and Bryan snickered.

"That's the hospital's bassinet," Shelby explained. "The plastic cover keeps the babies safe and warm. And the nurses can still see them while they're sleeping."

"She sleeps a lot," Paisley said.

"And yet, not nearly enough, right?" Bryan said.

"We'll get there," Shelby replied, rubbing an eye with her palm. She glanced at her phone on the nightstand. An email notification caught her eye. She reached to check it. Ravi had replied to their birth announcement.

"Oh, my word, Bryan!"

"What?"

Shelby handed him her phone, tears forming in the pockets of her eyes. "Read this."

Dear Shelby,

Greetings of joy and peace from Dhaka. Priti and I are overjoyed to join you in welcoming baby Lacey to your family and to the world. She is a precious gift from God. We could not be happier for you.

Priti and I also have news to share. She has accepted my proposal. We are getting married in August! Due to the devastation that unfolded at Rana Plaza, Caring Hope is promoting me to a regional director role focused on helping families of garment industry workers in Cambodia and Sri Lanka as well. I will remain based out of Dhaka. Priti and I will make our home here together.

And now for the part I cannot wait to share. Runa's uncle has approached us about taking her in. He says she is not happy at her new school. She misses her friends and teachers. It was Runa's idea to ask us, and we said yes!

As soon as our marriage is final, we will go fetch her and bring her to live at our home for as long as she wants. She will start back at Eternal Promise immediately. We could not be more overjoyed by this news. And we have you to thank.

Shelby, I am so grateful you came into our lives. I am confident that meeting you was not a coincidence. For years I have prayed for a family, and now my prayers have been answered.

Our hearts are so full. Dear Runa has suffered so much. From now on, we will walk through our struggles together. We promise to hold her hand and lead her to a good life, where Lord willing, all her dreams may come true.

Truly, our cup runneth over. I pray yours as well.

With love,
Ravi

P.S. As soon as we are able to get passports and visas, we hope to come visit you in Texas!

"Wow. How wonderful for Runa. For all of them." Bryan thumbed the corner of his eye, then reached for a tissue off the nightstand. He passed it to Shelby along with her phone.

"I still can't believe all of this." Shelby wiped her cheeks.

"Pretty amazing," Bryan said.

"Except for Nipa. I know it's strange since we never met, but thinking about what happened to her will always make me sad." Shelby knew it wasn't just postpartum hormones fueling the rush of emotions.

As she learned from Dear, the grief of loss was something that settled and stayed—a tapestry of tears accessible for a lifetime. Once a loved one was gone, their presence could never be replaced. The lesson, the mission ahead, was to transfer the love from that grief. Transfer it to others, in hopes of making their lives somehow fuller and better for it.

"Mama, did something happen to Runa?" Paisley asked.

"Yes, sweetheart. Mr. Ravi and Ms. Priti are getting married. Runa's going to live with them. And it might take a while to get everything in order, but as soon as they can, they want to come visit."

"Visit us? In Acorn Heights?"

"Yes," Shelby said.

"Yipeeee! That means I'll finally get to meet Runa!"

As Paisley's delight overflowed into the room, a creaky grunt floated up from the bassinet. The baby's eyelids fluttered. A tiny thimble of a nose scrunched at the air. Lacey began to wiggle.

Shelby and Bryan had a boy name picked out from last time, but struggled with naming a second girl. On the flight back from Dhaka, they settled on Lacey, which evoked the delicacy and fragility of life. Lace was a cherished fabric adorned on the most celebrated occasions, handled with great care. Precisely what Shelby and Bryan wished for their long-awaited daughter.

"Mama, she's wakin' up. Can I please hold

her?" Paisley abandoned Bryan's phone and began reaching toward the baby.

"Loving these manners. Yes, you may." Shelby made a mental note to add "embracing a new sibling" to the list of spectacles more enticing than a screen.

Bryan walked around the bed and slid his hand under Lacey's warm square of a back, lifting her tenderly from the bassinet. Her ocean eyes fluttered open, bursting forth into the room, mesmerizing them all.

Paisley sat up tall and proud against the headboard. Bryan placed the snug package of baby and blanket into her waiting arms.

"Hi, Lacey. It's me, Paisley. I'm your big sister."

"Be sure to hold her head up," Shelby said. "Bryan, can you please prop a pillow under her elbow?"

"Sure. Hold her up like this," Bryan instructed. "There you go, Little P. Great job."

Paisley stuffed her nose toward Lacey's silky wisps of hair. "Ooo, she smells yummy."

"You like her new baby perfume?"

"Yeah, I do."

"Must be what heaven smells like." Shelby's smile synced with Bryan's. Their eyes locked together.

"Mama, this really is the bestest day ever."

"I think you're right, Little P." Shelby's eyes

pooled with the immensity of joy—a whole new person full of it. "Bry, can you please take a picture of our daughters?"

"I'd love to." After retrieving his phone from below the covers, Bryan framed the photo to capture their two darling girls sharing their first-ever morning snuggle. "How about one of the family?"

Shelby hadn't seen a mirror, but she knew exactly how she must look. Exhausted and unkempt. Blubbery and disheveled. Splotchy and wrinkled. Precisely how any woman should look after facilitating an unprecedented act of creation.

"That would be wonderful," Shelby said.

Bryan climbed back in bed. He and Shelby leaned into the mirroring screen beside the glowing faces of their two bright-eyed treasures. Smiles turned into giggles as they each absorbed the unfamiliar new normal of their bigger-by-one family. All four together, forever stitched to one another.

"Here we go, everyone. One, two, three . . ."

Author's Note

When I read researched-based novels, I'm always curious what's true and what's fabricated. The details about the Tazreen Fashions Factory fire and Rana Plaza collapse are based on videos of first-person interviews, on-the-ground footage, and local and international news sources.

The information about garment workers' rights is based largely on reports from the AWAJ Foundation and my interview with their incredible leader Nazma Aktar, a child garment worker turned fashion industry activist. Unfortunately, the research trip I planned to take to Bangladesh in April 2020 was canceled due to COVID-19 restrictions. I look forward to traveling there in the future.

For the plot timeline to be realistic, I took some liberties with clothing production schedules. That said, in my research, I learned that some brands manufacture clothing from design to store in as few as four weeks, making the November reorder timeline unlikely but plausible.

As for Shelby's decision to travel during her third trimester, I'm not advocating anyone, pregnant or otherwise, take risks beyond their doctor's recommendation. The idea came from friends in Guam deciding if or when to travel back to the States for their labor and delivery.

My ultimate hope for writing *Beneath the Seams* is to inspire others to shop with conviction and to change the broken system for garment workers. Fueling my passion was Proverbs 3:27, "Do not withhold good from those to whom it is due when it is in your power to act."

Some encouraging news is that physical safety conditions in Bangladesh factories did improve and the minimum wage for garment workers did rise following the Rana Plaza collapse. However, wages are still not a living wage, and many garment workers' livelihoods were decimated as a result of the COVID-19 pandemic.

I realize the suggestions presented within this story are incomplete and inconclusive—but for garment workers, they aren't inconsequential. If we change our shopping habits, adjust our price point, and raise our voices, meaningful change will follow.

It's up to each and every one of us to abandon autopilot, pressure irresponsible brands, and choose clothing that acknowledges the workers who make them. For these hardworking women, men, and children trapped in a broken system, the actions we take from here may make all the difference.

For a list of my top conscious fashion tips, please visit www.peyton-roberts.com/book-clubs.

Resource List

The following works greatly informed this story and are recommended for more information:

Overdressed (Penguin, 2013) and *The Conscious Closet* (2019) by Elizabeth Cline

Where Am I Wearing by Kelsey Timmerman (John Wiley & Sons, 2012)

Made in Bangladesh, Sri Lanka & Cambodia: The Labor Behind the Global Garments and Textiles Industries by Dr. Sanchita Saxena (Cambria Press, 2014)

Secondhand: Travels in the New Global Garage Sale by Adam Minter (Bloomsbury, 2019)

The Daily Good – Daily sustainable fashion newsletter at www.TheGoodTrade.com

The Book of Dhaka: A City in Short Fiction Ed. by Pushpita Alam & Arunava Sinha (Comma Press, 2016)

Made in the U.S.A.: The Sex Trafficking of America's Children by Alisa Jordheim

"112 killed in Bangladesh factory fire." Julhas Alam. The Associated Press. Nov. 24, 2012.

"Horrific Fire Revealed a Gap in Safety for Global Brands." Jim Yardley. *The New York Times*, Dec. 6, 2012.

Additionally, I am grateful to the following individuals for their input:

Nazma Aktar, Executive Director of the AWAJ Foundation (Garment workers' rights organization), Dhaka, Bangladesh

Dr. Sanchita Saxena, Director of the Center for Bangladesh Studies, UC Berkeley

David Halder, Director of Good Samaritan Children's Home, Savar, Bangladesh

Kelsey Timmerman, author of *Where Am I Wearing* (John Wiley & Sons, 2012)

Jenna Kape, International Promise Foundation

Christmas Eve liturgy was written by Pastor Amy C. Wake and used with permission.

Discussion Questions

1. As the story begins, what are some of the hurdles Shelby has already overcome to start her mother-daughter dress company? What are some of the obstacles she faces in scaling her business so quickly?
2. At the start of the story, Shelby and Bryan's marriage is not as strong as it used to be. What are some factors of young parenthood that can strain a relationship? What are some things young parents can do to alleviate this tension?
3. Much of Shelby's journey unfolds during the minutia of motherhood. Washing dishes, sorting laundry, making dinner, school drop-offs, running errands. How does the ever-present reality of housework and family routines shape a woman's story and a family's culture?
4. How does giving and receiving gifts play a role in the story? Under what conditions do gifts demonstrate love? Under what circumstances are they just extra items? What are some other ways to show love?
5. Many aspects of the story expose the polarizing conflict between what's visible on the surface and what lies beneath it. How

do social media, photography, religious services, and even book publishing fit this description? In what other aspects of the story or your life have you witnessed this duality of seen and unseen? How does what is seen impact what is not seen?

6. Shelby struggles with guilt related to her company's role in the fire. Throughout the story, different characters place fault on different players in the supply chain. To what extent does the blame rest on Treasured Pockets, *Surface Trend Market*, the export agency, the outsourcing factory, and/or the production factory. To what extent does it rest on consumers?

7. During the story, Shelby has to make several crucial decisions. What are some of these decisions, and what criteria does she use to make them? Do you agree with the decisions she made? What do you think she should have done differently, and why? How do you make pivotal decisions in your life?

8. Conscious fashion advocacy organizations make it clear that fast fashion, in which clothing trends are replicated and produced quickly and sold cheaply at high volume, is harmful to the environment and to workers in the supply chain. How does slowing down the production process improve conditions for workers and the earth?

9. It is estimated that in the United States only 10% of clothing that is donated is resold. The rest ends up in the landfill, where synthetic clothing can take up to 200 years to decompose. What changes could be made by retailers and consumers to keep clothing from being disposable?
10. Tragedies like Tazreen and Rana Plaza amass a lot of media attention. What struggles do minimum-wage-earning garment workers face every day? Even though both of these tragedies happened in the same country, why is it not advised to boycott clothing based on where it's produced?
11. There's no perfect clothing company, but many brands strive toward an ethical, sustainable, and transparent supply chain. Which brands are making a clear effort to do more good? Which brands need to be called out for harmful practices or greed? How can consumers pressure retailers to pass along more pay and resources to garment workers?
12. The next time you shop for clothes, what might you do differently?

Additional discussion questions and creative ideas for book clubs are available at www.peyton -roberts.com/book-clubs.

Acknowledgments

Writing a novel has felt like I suspect it might to summit Mt. Everest. Technically, I was the one stepping one foot in front of the other to reach the top, yet I couldn't have succeeded without the support of so many who equipped me and walked alongside me.

The first heap of gratitude goes to the power-house team at Scrivenings Press for believing in this story. Thank you to Shannon Vannatter for the surprise phone call that took me from folding laundry to making my publishing dreams come true. Thank you to Linda Fulkerson for championing this book to excellence. The opportunity to learn from you both continues to be a gift.

Labor rights activist Nazma Akter at the AWAJ Foundation and fashion industry expert Dr. Sanchita Saxena of Berkeley's Institute of Bangladeshi Studies were so generous to share their time, research, and expertise. Thanks to the nonprofit Remake for mentoring me as a sustainable fashion ambassador and for reviewing the list of conscious fashion tips on my website.

Speaking with missionary David Halder in Savar about the amazing work of Good Samaritan Children's Home helped create the fictional Eternal Promise School for Girls. Good Samaritan is a privately funded school that provides housing and education for some 700+ orphans and street children in Savar, Bangladesh.

When COVID prevented me from visiting Dhaka, International Promise Foundation's (IPF) director Jenna Kape was so generous to share her years of travel memories from serving at Good Samaritan Children's Home. To sponsor a student in Bangladesh through IPF, visit www.internationalpromisefoundation.com.

I owe a debt of gratitude to Nandita Hore for sharing so much personal insight about life in Dhaka and the fashion industry in Bangladesh. Your input and ideas were the connecting threads that tied the story together.

I would like to thank the angel workers at Concordia Children's Services Orphanage in the Philippines, where our family has sponsored children for nearly a decade. Correspondence with staff and thank-you notes from students helped shape the story. Ravi's position was based on my interactions with missionary Sean Harlow, who orchestrated the logistics of our trips to serve at CCS.

Conversations with several notable authors impacted my writing process. Alisa Jordheim's book *Made in the USA: The Sex Trafficking of America's Children* informed the character Lottie McKnight. Authors Kelsey Timmerman and

Corban Addison were generous to share their experiences writing about the dark side of the fashion industry. Bangladeshi writer and activist Shazia Omar was generous to introduce me to her incredible network of garment industry contacts.

My all-time favorite author, Jane Holston, served as my alpha reader. Thank you, Mom! Your devotion to my revision process pushed this story out of stuck. Thanks for teaching me to sew and for showing me it's possible to be a devoted mother and writer at the same time.

I owe endless, infinite thanks to early readers Mallory, Hollie, Kelly, Kate, Reagan, Pat, Tracy, Ann, Amber, Beth, Annie, Diane, Nikki, and Jenn. Your feedback and encouragement spurred the story forward every time. Extra special thanks to Tulika for advising on characters from India.

So many friends from book club, Bible studies, church, writing groups, and military communities helped launch this book into the world, and I am so thankful! Courtney and Krissy went above and beyond leading me through the maze.

Heartfelt gratitude goes to dear friend and fellow writer Kate Lewis who convinced me I could write this story long before I believed I could. Her enthusiasm for this idea and her memorable assertion, *"You can do this,"* are the reasons I both started and finished writing this story.

Two books were especially motivating when

I was in the writing cave: *Still Writing* by Dani Shapiro and *Fearless Writing* by William Kenower. I recommend both books to everyone, whether writer or not. The wisdom inside relates as much to life as it does to writing.

Therein lies the identity shift that served as my telltale: Life and writing are intertwined. One does not exist apart from the other. I am most grateful to my husband Nick for understanding this about me and for supporting me to carve time out of motherhood to write. Thanks to Sadie and Nate for inspiring Paisley's character, verbatim at times. Y'all are my dream team.

My final thanks is to you, dear reader. It's a strange feeling to come to an end of a project that has filled the space in my heart for so many years. It turns out the ending is a beginning in disguise. The movement to create a more equitable fashion industry is underway and needs more willing hands and voices. My hope is that you will join me putting Proverbs 3:27 into action.

About the Author

Peyton H. Roberts grew up writing poems and sewing dresses on the sunny Gulf Coast. At the University of Florida, she studied global business but stacked her course load with creative writing electives. She earned a Master's in Communication from San Diego State University and went on to teach church youth and college students.

As a military spouse, Peyton lives and writes wherever the Navy sends her family. In the DC Metro area, she was assistant editor of AMVETS' *American Veteran* magazine. In San Diego, she managed communication for the American Red Cross. Two years on tropical Guam offered unforgettable opportunities to travel and blog across Asia, from diving with sharks in Palau to leading her church's youth group to serve at an orphanage in the Philippines.

Living and serving overseas forged a passion for social impact causes, especially shining light on the dark side of the global fashion industry. Peyton enjoys hiking and going to the beach with her husband and two children in the San Francisco Bay Area where they currently call home. Connect with Peyton and read more of her work at www.peyton-roberts.com.

| Books are produced in the United States using U.S.-based materials | Books are printed using a revolutionary new process called THINKtech™ that lowers energy usage by 70% and increases overall quality | Books are durable and flexible because of Smyth-sewing | Paper is sourced using environmentally responsible foresting methods and the paper is acid-free |

Center Point Large Print
600 Brooks Road / PO Box 1
Thorndike, ME 04986-0001 USA

(207) 568-3717

US & Canada:
1 800 929-9108
www.centerpointlargeprint.com